1919: Over the veto of President Woodrow Wilson Congress passes the Volstead Act, which provides for strict enforcement of the 18th Amendment to the Constitution. Across the nation federal agents begin to actively ban the manufacture, sale, and import or export of liquor. Prohibition has begun. (*The Detroit News*)

1920: The publication of *This Side of Paradise* catapults young F. Scott Fitzgerald to national fame as the foremost chronicler of the Jazz Age. That same year the author—enriched by the novel's success—marries Zelda Sayre, who had earlier broken their engagement due to Fitzgerald's dim financial prospects. (Brown Brothers)

1921: In a highly publicized trial Nicola Sacco and Bartolomeo Vanzetti are found guilty of the murders of a factory paymaster and a guard committed during a robbery in South Braintree, Massachusetts. Many protest that the judge and jury were prejudiced against Sacco and Vanzetti—who are Italian immigrants and political anarchists—but the verdict remains. Six years later the two men are executed. (Culver Pictures, Inc.)

1923: Bessie Smith makes her first recording for Columbia Records. The "Empress of the Blues" had begun her career in the gin mills and small theaters of the rural South and went on to record well over 150 songs and to establish herself as the premier blues singer of her day. (Culver Pictures, Inc.)

1924: A dance called the Charleston has Americans flocking to ballrooms and dance halls everywhere. Originally an African-American folk dance, the Charleston was adopted by professional dancers at the beginning of the decade and became fashionable after being featured in the musical revue *Runnin' Wild* in 1923. (The Missouri Historical Society)

1925: Charlie Chaplin writes, directs, and stars in *The Gold Rush.* Originally signed for slapstick one-reelers by the Keystone Company, Chaplin emerged as one of the leading silent film stars with the development of a character called the Little Tramp. (The Museum of Modern Art/ Film Stills Archive)

THE AMERICAN CHRONICLES

VOLUME THREE

THE LOST GENERATION

ROBERT VAUGHAN

BANTAM BOOKS

NEW YORK · TORONTO · LONDON · SYDNEY · AUCKLAND

THE LOST GENERATION

A Bantam Domain Book / September 1992

DOMAIN and the portrayal of a boxed "d" are trademarks of
Bantam Books, a division of Bantam Doubleday Dell Publishing
Group, Inc.

ISBN 0-553-29680-9

Published simultaneously in the United States and Canada

Bantam Books are published by Bantam Books, a division of Bantam
Doubleday Dell Publishing Group, Inc. Its trademark, consisting of
the words "Bantam Books" and the portrayal of a rooster, is
Registered in U.S. Patent and Trademark Office and in other
countries. Marca Registrada. Bantam Books, 666 Fifth Avenue, New
York, New York 10103.

PRINTED IN THE UNITED STATES OF AMERICA

OPM   0 9 8 7 6 5 4 3 2 1

CHAPTER ONE

SPRING 1921, PARIS

"Oh, do come along, Tanner, won't you? We want to get to the— What is it called, Lucy?" the young man in the Harvard sweater asked.

"A *bal musette*, darling," the young woman named Lucy answered. She fitted a cigarette into a long holder, stuck it in the crimson gash of her lips, then leaned forward in her chair, waiting. The young man who responded and lit it for her was wearing a University of Pennsylvania blazer. "It means a dance hall," she added.

"Yes, yes, that's it, a *bal musette*," Harvard continued. "Well, I'm intrigued by the whole idea. I'm told there will be apaches there."

"Apaches? Look here, old boy, do you mean wild Indians?" Penn demanded.

"No, these apaches are much wilder," Harvard replied, grinning.

1

The young Americans laughed gleefully, drawing the stares of the other patrons in the hotel lobby.

"And there will be harlots there, too," the third young man in the group—this one wearing a Princeton school tie—added. "You must come, Tanner. Wouldn't you like to see an actual harlot? I'm going to dance with one."

"Now, why would she want to see a harlot?" Harvard queried. "Pay no attention to him, Tanner. That's exactly the type of thing you might expect from a Princeton man."

"Well, why wouldn't she want to see a harlot? I know I'd like to see what one looks like," Lucy said, making a production of flicking the ash off the end of her cigarette. "You must come with us, Tanner. I certainly have no wish to be the only female in this motley group."

"I can't go," Tanner replied, waving the small leather case that contained her letter-writing pad. "I simply have to write some letters to my family. After all, they're the ones who paid for my grand tour of the Continent."

"Well, we *all* have someone to whom we're obligated for this adventure. So don't you think we owe it to our benefactors to get out and *have* an adventure? Otherwise, what is there to write about?" Harvard asked.

"Well . . ."

"She's weakening, Harold. Keep up the attack!" Penn gloated.

"What do you say?" Harold from Harvard urged.

Tanner laughed. "All right. I'll go with you. As long as I don't have to dance with one of the harlots," she quipped.

"Oh, you won't have to, darling. We all heard Lester offer to give up his body for the cause," Harold replied, and again all laughed.

They rose from their chairs and smiled at each other in a way that suggested that they were all members of the same club—which in a way they were. Tanner had attended Jefferson University in St. Louis, while Lucy was a product of the University of Chicago. Harold had gone to Harvard, Bill to Penn, and Lester to Princeton. All had graduated within the last year and were now taking the "grand tour" of Europe. Far from being old friends, they had only known each other less than two weeks, having met on the ship coming over from America. Initially drawn together by the similarity of their situations, they had been together ever since—though already Tanner was beginning to wish that she was alone. It wasn't that she didn't like her new friends. On the contrary, she found them all very amusing. But the necessity of always doing things as a group had caused her to miss out on some of the experiences she had planned for herself.

Tanner's real name was Brunhilde Tannenhower. Her father, Ludwig, and her uncle, Rudolph, owned Tannenhower Brewery in St. Louis, the largest brewery in America. Because of Prohibition, however, the brewery was now turning out soda pop, near beer, and such things as barley malt syrup—which was advertised as a health supplement, but everyone knew that it was actually used by its purchasers to make their own beer.

The name "Tanner" came from her own mispronunciation of Tannenhower when she was a very young girl. It had stuck with her, and now few people knew her given name. That suited her fine, for she had no love for the Teutonic name her parents had bestowed on her.

Tanner was a very pretty girl with hair the color of ripened wheat. Her large green eyes so sparkled with reflected light and a verve for life, they seemed to glow from within. Her nose was somewhat snub, and her mouth full and sensual. Tall and as slender as a reed, her form was almost boyish, though rounded rather than angular, and she had small, well-formed breasts.

"Well, if we're going to go, let's go," Tanner finally said, closing the leather case.

"Whoop, whoop, whoop! Tanner, Tanner, Tanner!" the three boys shouted, led in their cheer by Lucy, who used her long black cigarette holder as a baton.

Oblivious to the disapproving stares of the hotel's

other patrons, the five young Americans marched across
the lobby, and a half hour later they piled out of a cab in
front of the Cardinal Club Danse on rue du Cardinal
Lemoine.

It was hot and crowded inside. The music was supplied by a five-piece band, and the floor was so con-
gested with sweating, swirling dancers that the young
Americans found it difficult to pick their way through to
one of the few empty tables.

"I say, chaps," Harold said, pointing to the bar, "do
you suppose those three girls over there are actual
harlots?"

"I don't know," Lester replied. "Do you think they'd
dance with us?"

"We'll never know until we ask," Bill said.

"Do you mind, girls?" Harold asked Lucy and
Tanner.

"Oh, no, you go right ahead and leave us to our
fate," Lucy replied dramatically. "But you had better get
a good look at us so that tomorrow morning when the
gendarmes ask you to come down to the station to
identify our bodies, you'll be able to do so."

"Well, now, Lucy, that's the whole trouble, you
see," Harold responded. "How could we identify your
bodies? We've never seen either of them naked. Perhaps, just as a safety precaution, you understand, we
should take care of that later tonight."

Bill laughed appreciatively. "I say, Harold, that was
a good one."

"Go away," Lucy said, laughing with them as she
pushed them toward the bar.

"Aperitif?" the waiter asked, coming to the girls'
table after the young men had left.

"Pernod," Lucy said. Tanner ordered beer.

By now all three boys had persuaded some of the
French girls who'd been standing at the bar to dance,
and they were doing the tango in a greatly exaggerated
fashion, holding their partners' arms out stiffly and
staring with expressionless faces as they high-stepped
across the room, then, with great sweeping motions,

reversed the process to come back in the opposite direction. The boys were getting several laughs, as was their clear intention, but they were also occupying so much of the dance floor that other patrons, less interested in the antics of the young Americans, were finding it difficult to dance.

"Look at them," Lucy said, laughing. "Aren't they the silliest things you ever saw?"

"Yes," Tanner said, "they are silly." She wasn't assigning the same meaning to the term that Lucy was.

"I've been thinking about it, but I don't know which one it will be," Lucy said a moment later.

"I beg your pardon?"

"Harold, Bill, or Lester. I just don't know which one."

"Which one what?"

"Which one will take my virginity," Lucy said as she raised the glass to her lips.

"Lucy!" Tanner gasped.

"My dear, don't tell me you haven't wondered the same thing?"

"I most certainly have not!"

"Really, now. You expect me to believe that you planned to come to Europe and return to the States with your virginity safely intact?"

"That's not something I considered, one way or the other," Tanner insisted.

"Well, my dear, it's about time you considered it," Lucy said. "You *have* read F. Scott Fitzgerald, haven't you? Aren't you interested in being a modern girl?"

"Well, yes, but I don't think I have to hop in bed with someone just to prove that I'm a modern girl," Tanner said.

"It's not that you *have* to," Lucy countered. "It's that you *can*—and no one will think the worse of you. And I, for one, intend to. Of course, there is a drawback to losing my virginity to one of those three," she went on. "For one thing, he might talk. And for another, he may not take it in the lighthearted way I intend it. If he were to fall in love with me and then return to the States and follow me around like a moonstruck calf, it could well turn into a bit of a sticky wicket, as our English friends say. Perhaps it would be better to give myself to a Frenchman. After all, they do have the reputation of being great lovers. And some of them are absolutely divine. Like that fellow there."

Lucy smiled broadly at a man who was standing at the bar. He wore a wide-striped blue-and-white shirt and a beret. Seeing Lucy smile, he started toward the table.

"Oh, my, he's coming over here," Lucy said.

"*Americaine?*" the man asked.

"*Oui,*" Lucy answered.

"*Danse?*"

"*Oui,*" Lucy said again, getting up from the table to join him.

"That's just great," Tanner muttered to herself. "Here I am, the odd man out in America's European Seduction Force."

Tanner sat at the table alone for another five minutes, turning down numerous invitations to dance. Finally she left a franc under her empty beer glass and got up to leave. There was nothing to keep her here. After all, she wasn't enjoying the evening, and the others were obviously having too much fun to miss her.

Making her way through the club, she stepped outside, and it was as if she had suddenly stepped into another world. Since their arrival no more than a half hour before, a thick fog had rolled in off the Seine, reaching out with long, gray tentacles to wrap everything securely in its grasp. Tanner walked a dozen steps into the wet, warm blanket, and the club behind her disappeared as totally as if it had been taken into the bowels of the earth.

There was a dreamlike quality to the night, and it became difficult to distinguish fantasy from reality. No cars were on the cobblestoned street, but Tanner could hear the hollow clomping of horses' hooves and the iron ringing of a steel-tired carriage being pulled along. She strained to see it, but unlike automobiles the carriage was without lights, so she couldn't even make out its shadow. The few pedestrians she encountered seemed no more than apparitions, appearing then disappearing as if summoned and dismissed by some sorcerer.

Tanner walked about half a block, then began to feel that she had made a terrible mistake in leaving the club. The casual quip Lucy had made, suggesting that the boys might have to come down to the station to identify their bodies, came back to haunt her. Suppose she *did* wind up on a slab in the police morgue? She could be accosted by someone stepping out of an alley or climbing up from the sewers. She had read about the Paris sewers, about how they formed a network that ran beneath the entire city and how some parts of it had been officially closed for over a hundred years. But Tanner didn't need alleys or sewers to be apprehensive tonight. On a night like tonight someone could materialize from the very ether.

Tanner turned around, intending to go back to the club, but the fog was so thick that she was completely disoriented. How could she go back? She didn't even know where back was.

"*Bon soir, mademoiselle,*" a deep voice said.

"Oh!" Tanner gasped.

As if he had been created by her own fears, the man who had spoken appeared suddenly and from nowhere—and he was standing right in front of her. He was smiling at her, but there was something sinister and frightening about his smile.

"Where did you come from?" Tanner asked. Her throat was so tight with fear that the words sounded choked.

"Forgive me, *mademoiselle,* if I frightened you. You are American?" The accent was thick but understandable.

"Yes," Tanner replied. She started to step around him, but he stepped in front of her.

"An American *prostituée,* looking for business?"

"A *prostituée?*" For the moment, Tanner was more shocked than frightened. Did he mean what she thought he meant? Before she could stop herself, she voiced the question. "Do you mean a prostitute?"

"*Oui*. Prostitute." The man smiled again. "Name your price. Whatever you ask, I will pay."

"No! I am not a prostitute!"

"That is no matter. We can have a, how do you say, good time, anyway."

"No," Tanner said firmly. She tried again to step around the unwelcome night visitor, but again he stepped in front of her, blocking her way. "Please," she said, her voice nearly breaking now. "Please let me go."

"Do not be in such a hurry, ma *chérie*. I think we will have a very good time together, no?"

"The lady asked you to let her go," another male voice abruptly said. The voice was deep and resonant and steely. The accent was definitely American, but it was not the voice of any of the three young men Tanner had been traveling with. In fact, it was not a voice Tanner recognized at all.

"Who is there?" the Frenchman asked, staring into the fog.

The man who stepped out of the fog was a big man, almost a head taller than the Frenchman and very broad-shouldered. He was square-jawed, sandy-haired, and wore a mustache.

"I am a friend of the young lady's," the man said.

"No, I do not think you are," the Frenchman replied. He squinted at the American, then grinned. "I know who you are. I have seen you before. You are the American *journaliste*. I think you just want her for yourself."

"If you think that, why not let the young lady choose between us?"

"No, I do not wish to do that," the Frenchman said. "I prefer to keep what is mine."

Suddenly a knife materialized in the Frenchman's hand. He assumed a fighter's stance—leaning forward a little, his knees slightly bent, his arms low, and the knife lying flat in the palm of the right hand—and moved his hand back and forth so that the point of his knife took on the appearance of the weaving head of a cobra, hypnotizing its prey. "If you want her, *monsieur journaliste,* you must fight for her."

"I'm sorry, I don't carry a knife."

The Frenchman smiled evilly. "That is too bad. Then it is my advantage, yes?"

"Your advantage, no. I don't have a knife, but I *do* have a gun," the American said, pulling a short-barreled revolver from his pocket and pointing it at the Frenchman.

The Frenchman's eyes grew wide in fear, and a line of perspiration beads popped out on his upper lip. He took a step backward and held up his hands as if warding off an evil spirit.

"No, no, monsieur," he said. "I was only making the joke. I meant nothing by it . . . nothing." He turned and began to run, disappearing into the fog bank within just a few steps. A moment later even the sound of his footfalls was gone, muffled by the thick fog. Tanner and her rescuer were alone, perhaps the only two people on the street . . . in Paris . . . on the face of the Earth.

"He's gone," Tanner said, breathing a sigh of relief. For just a moment she wondered if she had been rescued from one danger merely to face another. But as she looked at the face and into the large, expressive brown eyes of her benefactor, she knew that she had nothing to fear. "I'm Tanner Tannenhower," she said, extending her hand. "You have my undying gratitude."

"Eric Twainbough," the American replied, reaching out his hand to hers. He squinted at her. "Did you say Tannenhower? There's a large brewery by that name. Are you related?"

"My father," Tanner said. "That is, it's run by my father and my uncle. It was started by my grandfather."

"Which one is your father? Ludwig or Rudolph?"

"Ludwig. Do you know of my father and my uncle?"

"Know *of* them? I *know* them," Eric said. "And I knew your grandfather as well. I met all of them when I was writing sports stories for *The St. Louis Chronicle.* They used to own the St. Louis Grays baseball team."

"They still own the St. Louis Grays."

Eric chuckled. "And is it still as bad a team as it always was?"

"Wait a minute, Mr. Twainbough. You may have saved my life, but that doesn't give you the right to pick on my Graybies," Tanner replied, laughing.

"I'm sorry," Eric said. "I'll be gentle with them. Lord knows they can't take too rough a handling." He paused, then asked, "Where were you headed? I'll walk you there."

"I was going back to my hotel."

"The Crillon?"

"Yes, how did you know?"

"Lucky guess. You're an American college student seeing Paris," Eric said. "The Crillon is where American college students stay when they're seeing Paris."

"Am I that transparent?"

Eric laughed again, an easy, rich laugh. "Well, you don't exactly come across as a French shop girl," he said, taking her by the elbow and leading her protectively along the street.

"I guess it was a lucky thing for me that you came along when you did," Tanner said, enjoying the touch of his hand.

"Tanner, that was no more luck than my carrying this gun was. I was in the *bal musette* when you and your friends came in. I saw you leave, and I saw him follow you, so I borrowed this pistol from Jacques, the owner of the club, and came after you."

"How did you know I might be in danger?"

"Oh, I know our knife-wielding friend. Not socially, of course, but by reputation. He's a procurer who specializes in young American and English girls. First he gets them to work for him; then, once he has them working for him, he beats them and takes most of their money, leaving them barely enough to live on."

"How awful! But I don't understand. Why would anyone let him do that to them?"

"He gets the girls addicted to heroin, then becomes their supplier. Do you know anything about heroin?"

"I've heard of it. I know that it's something very bad, something that no nice person would ever do."

Eric shook his head. "*Anyone* will do it if they're hooked on it," he explained. "And once they're hooked, they'll do anything to keep a steady supply, including working as a prostitute for someone like the disagreeable gentleman you just met."

"How awful!" Tanner said, shivering involuntarily. "Well, luck or not, I am very glad you came along. So, you used to do sports stories for *The Chronicle*. Do you still write for *The Chronicle*?"

"Sometimes. Right now, however, I'm trying to write a book. A novel."

"A novel? Oh, how wonderful! I bet you're a very good writer."

"I like to think that I am. But what makes you say so?"

"I studied English lit in college, so I know what makes a good writer. 'A good writer uses words to create ripples of emotional response in the minds of his readers, like casting marbles into a garden pool.'"

Eric smiled. "That's good. Who's that a quote from?"

"From me," Tanner said. "That was from my thesis." She grinned. "I got an A."

"You should've. That's a pretty good observation."

"It's also my observation that only a very sensitive person can do something like that. You have sensitive eyes, so you must be a sensitive person, ergo, you must be a good writer."

Eric laughed. "Maybe I should send a photograph of my 'sensitive eyes' to the publishers. That would save a lot of work for both of us."

"You're making fun of me."

"Yes, I am. I'm sorry." Eric sighed. "I guess I'm just a little frustrated right now. I do think I'm a good writer, Tanner. I couldn't do what I do if I didn't think so. And the responses I've received from some of the articles I've written make me believe that I'm not the only one who thinks so. But the book I'm working on now . . ." He paused and ground his right fist into his left palm. "This book is getting away from me. I'm losing it, and I don't know why."

"Is it about the war?"

"Yes, it is." He looked surprised. "How did you know?"

"You look as if you were in the war."

"I was."

"Maybe you're too close to the war to write about it."

"But that's just it. I *have* written about it, many times," Eric said. "Before I was a soldier *fighting* the war, I was a journalist *covering* it, from the Russian front."

"Yes, but what you wrote before was factual," Tanner said. "You lived with it, and you saw your friends dying in it. Now you're trying to turn it into fiction, but you have too much of an emotional investment in it to do that. I think you see doing that as a form of trivialization, which is something you're not yet ready to accept."

Eric abruptly stopped walking and stared at her.

"I'm sorry," Tanner said. "Did I speak out of turn?"

"No, no, don't apologize. My God, I think you may be right. I've never considered that, but it does make sense to me. You may have put your finger squarely on the problem. I wish you could read it, Tanner. I would really value your opinion."

"I'd like to sometime. You know, for all my big talk of being an English lit major, I've never even seen a novel in its working stage," Tanner said.

"Would you really like to read it?"

"Of course."

"How about now?"

"Now?"

"Sure. You could come with me," Eric invited. "My apartment is only a couple of blocks from here. And I have a coffeepot . . . I could ply you with coffee while you read."

"Well, I don't know," Tanner said.

"Why not? What else do you have to do? Your

friends aren't going to be worrying about you. They've found their own diversions."

"I'd better not," Tanner said, though part of her mind protested her caution.

"Oh, of course, I understand," Eric replied. "You have every reason to be afraid of me, a stranger coming up to you from out of nowhere. Listen, forget I even asked. I'll walk you straight to your hotel."

"No, no, I'm not afraid," Tanner said quickly.

"You aren't?"

"Not a bit."

"Then you will come?"

Tanner ran her hand through her bobbed hair and studied the face of her rescuer. It was an interesting face . . . handsome enough, but interesting, nevertheless. It wasn't a young face; it was a face that had seen a great deal of living, and yet it wasn't terribly old, either. Tanner guessed that Eric Twainbough must be in his thirties. She had to admit that there was something appealing about the idea of going with him. After all, he had appeared in the middle of a dark and foggy night to come to her rescue. If she went with him now it would be like an adventure . . . a romantic adventure.

Romance overcame reason.

"All right," Tanner finally said, smiling at him. "I'll go with you."

"Great!"

Eric took her by the elbow again, guiding her the short distance to his building. His flat was on the fifth floor; more accurately, it was in the attic over the fourth floor of an apartment building. The elevator stopped at the fourth floor.

"It's slightly inconvenient, but on the other hand I'm the only one who lives up here," he explained as they walked up the final flight of steps. "So if I hear someone coming up these stairs, I know they're coming to see me."

The door didn't lock the way an apartment door normally did. It was more like the door on a tool shed, held closed with a hasp and secured by a padlock.

However, the key to the padlock was hanging on a string on the wall, right next to the lock itself. Tanner laughed when she saw it.

"What's wrong?"

"What's the purpose of locking your door if you're going to keep a key hanging right beside it?"

Eric shrugged. "If someone's going to break in, I'd just as soon they unlock the door and go right on in. It would cost me more to fix the door than it would to replace anything they might steal from inside."

He pushed the door open, then reached around and turned a switch. The room was filled with a soft, golden light. "My palatial estate," he said, taking in the room with a sweep of his hand. "Have a seat. I'll get you the manuscript and start the coffee."

The one-room studio was much larger than Tanner had anticipated, taking up a sizable portion of the attic without competing with other apartments for floor space. The side walls were formed by the sloping mansard roof, which meant that Eric could stand erect only in the very center of the room. Tanner could walk farther toward the side than Eric, but even she had to bend over before she reached the sofa.

"I have over three hundred pages written," Eric said, handing her a sheaf of papers.

"Oh, it's typed?"

"Yes. I write first in pencil," he explained, "and then I pay a typist to transcribe it for me. I had this done at the American Express office. You read, I'll make the coffee."

Tanner was already into the story when Eric handed her the first cup of coffee. Within a short time he had handed her another and then another, and she was only vaguely aware of his being in the room with her. She was totally absorbed in the writing . . . not the story, but the writing.

Eric had been correct when he said the story itself wasn't working. From a purely objective point of view, Tanner could see that there was too little plot and no direction. On the other hand, the characterization was richer than anything she had ever read.

One scene that Tanner found particularly moving had Eric's hero, Justin Barclay, an American journalist, and the heroine, Katya, a member of Russia's nobility, together:

They lay side by side in the dark room without touching and without speaking. Outside the open balcony door it was still raining, and the rain made music. Justin found the music perfectly orchestrated, from the rhythmic, harmonic bass notes of the large drops falling on the balcony floor to the melodious trills and tinkling of the water running off the roof and cascading over the eaves and banisters just outside the window.

They didn't speak, as if by mutual design they wanted to preserve this moment, lock it forever in their hearts as a time when cold, hard reality had been set aside so that pure, unrestrained truth could surface. And the pure truth was that despite all reason and common sense, Justin and Katya were in love.

The rain suddenly stopped, and the room was invaded by noises from Petrograd's streets—the rattle of steel-wheeled carts and the songs of the soup vendors, the whir of motorized lorries and the impatient whistles and curses of the teamsters and their wagons. They had lost their moment.

Katya slid her hand across the bed and took her lover's. She held it for several seconds and then squeezed it tightly. "It hurts," she whispered.

"I know," he answered, knowing that Katya, too, had just said good-bye to their moment.

When Tanner finally put down the last page hours after starting, she realized that Eric was sitting on the sofa beside her. She had no idea how long he had been there. He was looking at her, clearly anxious for her reaction, and she could tell by his eyes that, for some reason, what she thought of the book was very important to him.

Eric was Justin. That was obvious. And because Tanner knew that, she had the unusual sensation that even though she had just met him, she already knew more about him than she knew about any other person.

They looked into each other's eyes for a long, silent moment. Then, though Tanner wasn't aware of how they got that way, she suddenly found that their lips were just a breath apart.

The kiss started innocently enough, no more than the sharing of an instant with a man whose soul she had just examined. Then, before she realized what was going on, the kiss robbed her of consciousness of time and place and circumstance, and she found herself kissing him with an ardor she didn't know she possessed. She began to test its limits, to see how far it would take her. She gave herself up to it, then felt her self-control completely desert her. Her head spun faster and faster with dizzying excitement, and for one frightening moment she was afraid she was going to pass out.

It was going to happen! She was going to give herself to this man or be taken by him! How odd that she and Lucy had talked about this very thing earlier tonight . . . or was it yesterday . . . or a hundred years ago? Eons seemed to have passed since that innocent conversation. Worlds had been born, destinies rearranged, and lives changed forever.

"It . . . it isn't possible," Tanner murmured. "This can't be happening."

When Tanner opened her eyes the next morning, she found herself looking up through a skylight. Pigeons were on the other side of the glass, and she lay in bed watching them, feeling deliciously comfortable and wondering why she had not noticed this skylight in her hotel room before.

Suddenly she realized that she wasn't *in* her hotel

room. She sat bolt upright, gasping aloud as she did so, and the bedcovers slipped down, exposing her bare breasts. She was nude! With another gasp, she pulled the bed sheet up to cover herself.

Then images of the night before came flooding back to her. She remembered an angular yet well-muscled torso, a sharp and momentary pain, then sensations of pleasure unlike anything she had ever experienced before. And even as she recalled the events of last night she felt her skin becoming sensitized and her blood turning hot. A small smile played across her face, and she looked around the room for Eric.

He wasn't there!

Had he used her and discarded her?

But, no, he couldn't have. This was his apartment. There had to be some explanation as to where he was.

Then, even as she was thinking that, the door opened, and Eric backed in. He kicked the door shut and turned around with a big smile on his face.

"Hungry?" he asked her. He was carrying a paper bag in one hand and a bouquet of flowers in the other. "I have hot croissants and coffee."

"And flowers," Tanner said.

"Yes, and flowers." Eric took his bundles over to the counter, then opened the armoire, where he found an empty vase. He held the vase under the single water tap in the sink, put the flowers in the water, then put the vase and the croissants and coffee on a wicker tray. "There are a number of flower vendors down on the street," he explained, carrying the tray over to the table. "Occasionally I'll buy flowers just for them." He smiled broadly. "Today I bought them just for you."

"I'm glad you did. They're beautiful!" Tanner exclaimed. "Oh, my, what time is it?"

"A little after ten."

Tanner threw the bedcovers aside and got out of bed, naked and without shame. She started getting dressed, pulling on her panties first, then her camisole, then her stockings.

"As soon as we eat I must go," she said.

"Go? Go where?"

"To the railroad station. I leave for Germany today. I'm going to Hamburg to visit my cousin."

"Write a letter instead."

Tanner laughed, pausing in her dressing to walk over to kiss Eric. The nipple of her breast brushed against his arm as she leaned into him, and she felt a tiny jolt of pleasure course through her body.

"I can't. My visit with him is the whole justification for my trip to Europe, you see. But not to worry, we'll see each other again. I'll come back through Paris, I promise."

"Tanner, when you do come back, I want you to stay with me," Eric said.

"Instead of the Crillon? I must say, that would be deliciously wicked. Wouldn't Lucy just die if she knew about this or that I was going to stay with you when I came back through?"

"When I say stay with me, I don't mean just when you come through Paris again."

"Well, what do you mean?"

"I mean for the rest of your life," Eric replied.

CHICAGO, ILLINOIS

It was Saturday night, and uptown Chicago was at play. In the speakeasies and nightclubs muted trumpets blared jazz music to cover the sounds of laughter and the tinkling of ice in the glasses of "bootleg hootch" and "bathtub gin." Flappers and their sheiks danced the Charleston, the Blackbottom, and other dances that had been created for this, the "Jazz Age."

On dozens of movie screens across the city Alphonso Delavente, Pola Negri, Gloria Swanson, Douglas Fairbanks, Greta Gaynor, Dolores Costello, and Ronald Coleman held sway over their adoring fans. A half-million Chicagoans a week watched the flickering light-and-shadow performances of their favorite stars in theaters that were silent except for the organ or piano music heightening the drama. There were many, however, who found their entertainment in the home, listening to the radio, playing records on the Victrola, or reading the latest novel by F. Scott Fitzgerald, whose chronicles of "flaming youth" scandalized the older generation.

"Our century has come of age," one newspaper editorialist raved. *"More homes have telephones than do not, radio has ceased to be a novelty, autos are a necessity, and the airplane has become so commonplace that one scarcely looks aloft to note its passing overhead. Life today is wonderful and full of gold and bright, shining promises of this the third decade in the marvelous twentieth century."*

One of Chicago's residents, Kerry O'Braugh, was standing under a huge, wall-mounted billboard on East Eighteenth Street. The billboard, intended for observation by the passing "El" passengers, showed a smiling, tow-headed youngster sitting at a table, holding a spoon in one hand and a cereal bowl in the other. On the table was a box of Canfield-Puritex Corn Toasties, its blue-and-white diagonally striped logo prominently displayed. THE BREAKFAST OF WINNERS! the copy read.

From his vantage point under the billboard Kerry could see a glare of bright lights from the center of the city and hear the grinding gears, racing engines, and impatient horns of automobile traffic over on State Street. Despite all the activity going on in uptown Chicago, it was quiet on this street at this time of night.

Though it was within hearing distance of all that was beautiful about Chicago, this area right under the El was one of the city's worst. Had the advertising company that bought the billboard done a bit more research, they would have realized that this was not a good place to project their message from since few of the commuters training by actually noticed the sign. Most passengers read their newspapers or examined their fingernails to keep from looking outside, not wanting to see the tired, rundown buildings or the even more tired and rundown people of the area. Residents here had not yet caught up with the bright and shining promises of the third decade

of the marvelous twentieth century. Nothing was bright
or shining in this neighborhood. Even on the clearest
day a blanket of dirty, brown air hung over everything.
It marked the boundaries of despair, beyond which no
inhabitant could escape and into which no outsider
dared venture.

Kerry wasn't a permanent inhabitant of the area,
but the young man wasn't exactly an outsider, either. He
belonged to that twilight world of criminals who moved
freely across all the economic boundaries of the city.
Kerry's boss was Johnny Torrio. Johnny Torrio and his
second-in-command, Alphonso Caponi, who now preferred to be called Al Capone, were the real bosses of
Chicago. Torrio and Capone controlled every vice and
illegal activity that went on in the city. As a result of the
enormous amount of money these nefarious activities
generated, the two men were able to buy off judges,
policemen, and city officials, thus assuring that their
criminal operations ran smoothly.

In a very real sense it was they and not the police
who were the enforcers of the law. Within their zone of
control they wouldn't tolerate burglary, armed robbery,
murder, or any other such violation. When such a
violation did occur they'd locate the lawbreaker, assess
the sentence, and carry out the punishment. Of course,
that enforcement only extended to those lawbreakers
working independently. Such activities could be, and
were, carried on by those criminals operating under a
franchise granted them by Torrio and Capone.

Enforcement was why Kerry O'Braugh was in this
part of the city on this particular night. Johnny Torrio
had learned that an independent operator named Tony
Fusco was using the back room of his automobile repair
garage as a storehouse for bootleg whiskey, and Torrio
asked Kerry to take care of it. It was a very responsible
job, but Torrio knew that Kerry was up to the task.

Though only twenty-two, Kerry enjoyed a position
of great power and authority within Torrio's organization. He was very much at home with Torrio, Capone,
Frank Netti, and all the other Italians involved with the

Syndicate because despite the Irish surname, Kerry was half-Sicilian, having been born in Sicily to an Italian mother and an Irish father.

In order to accomplish the task given him tonight, Kerry had brought two carloads of Syndicate men with him, directing the cars to park in the middle of the block, away from the corner streetlamps and out of sight from any curious passerby. However, even if someone had tried to look into the touring cars, they wouldn't have been able to see much, for the windows were almost completely fogged over from the heat of six men inside each auto.

Leaving his car, Kerry had gone out alone to check out Fusco's Garage. Then he had heard the hum of an approaching elevated train and felt the track platform above him begin to rattle and shake. Taking no chance that someone might glance out a train window and see him, Kerry had stayed back in the shadows, looking up at the Canfield-Puritex billboard as the train drew closer. The hum had swelled into a loud roar as the train hurtled by, bound toward its destination somewhere in the center of the city.

When the train was past, Kerry continued his walk toward the garage. The garage cornered on an alley, and Kerry slipped down it, hugging the brick wall. He found a garbage can and climbed on top of it to look in through the window.

The first thing he saw was a wheelless yellow Maxwell roadster sitting on blocks. A blue Jewett touring car sat beneath an A-frame, its engine hanging from a chain attached to a pulley. In the corner was a tan-colored Chandler coupe with a raised hood. Scattered about the floor were numerous engine parts and two or three tool chests. A big sign on the wall read: CLEAN YOUR TOOLS BEFORE PUTTING THEM AWAY.

The place gave every illusion of being a working garage because it was one—but the cars didn't fool anyone. Kerry was certain that the police knew about the bootlegging operation and just as certain that the cops on the beat were collecting a payoff for protecting the place. And it would have been impossible for the closest neighbors not to know about the illegal operation, for there was just too much activity going on. Kerry had to hand it to Tony Fusco. The man had guts, trying to pull off something like this without getting Johnny Torrio's okay.

"I mean, if he had just come to ask me," Torrio had told Kerry that afternoon when he was setting up the job, "we could've worked somethin' out, I'm sure we could've. This is America, for Chrissake," he had added with an expansive spread of his hands. "Free enterprise; good, honest competition. That's what built this country. That and cooperation between friends. What hurts me," he had gone on, tapping his chest expressively, "what hurts me, Kerry, is that Tony Fusco is Italian, just like us. I mean, if he was a Jew or a mick or a goddamn nigger, I could understand." He had looked at Kerry and held out his hand. "I don't mean nothin' by the mick remark, you understand. You can't help it your ol' man had an Irish name. You know what I mean when I say to be double-crossed by our own kind." He had sighed.

"Yeah, I know what you mean," Kerry had said.

Torrio had reached out to rub the young man's hair. "You're like a kid brother to me, Kerry. Closer than that, even. I couldn't get along without you."

"I am honored, *Padrone*."

"Yeah, well, that's why I'm givin' you this job. It's got to be done by another Italian, you know what I mean? It's bad enough one of our own has to be rubbed out. It just wouldn't do unless we took care of it ourselves."

"I'll take care of it," Kerry had promised.

"Tonight," Torrio had said, sighing again, "they've got a shipment coming in tonight. Fusco'll be there and so will his top two or three men. Take care of all of 'em, and then move the shipment to one of our own warehouses."

"I'll get there early," Kerry had said, smiling. "That way the hootch'll still be on the truck, and we won't have to work gettin' it loaded."

Torrio had laughed. "Yeah. That's smart thinkin'."

Now, Kerry stood looking through the window of the garage, waiting for the right moment. Suddenly a door slid open at the back of the repair bay, exposing the large room at the rear of the garage. Through that open door Kerry could see a Reo truck, its bed covered with a tarpaulin, and he knew that the whiskey shipment had already arrived. He hopped off the trash can and ran back down the street to his men. They were going to have to move fast . . . otherwise the whiskey would be half unloaded by the time they got there.

"Let's go!" Kerry shouted to the driver as he opened the right front door and slid into the seat.

"Did you see 'em?" one of his men asked.

"Yeah, they're already there," Kerry replied as the car started up. He reached down between his legs and picked up a sawed-off double-barreled shotgun. Breaking open the barrels, he shoved in two shells, then snapped the barrels shut. He had prepared the shells himself, replacing the normal load of buckshot with cut-off nail heads.

"How're we goin' to get in?"

"All we have to do is stop outside the big rear door and honk the horn," Kerry replied. "We got somebody on the inside who's goin' to open the door. Once it's open, we go in blastin'."

"Any of Fusco's men packin' heat?"

"Some of them probably are," Kerry said, nodding. "But they'll all be busy off-loadin' the booze. We open up right away, they won't have time to get to their guns."

"What about the *paesano* openin' the door for us? Shouldn't we look out for him?"

"Don't worry about him. He'll get out of our way." Kerry shrugged. "If he don't, it's his problem, not ours. When we leave I want everything in there down . . . every man, dog, cat, and bug. You got me?"

One of the men in the back seat chuckled. "Yeah, boss, we got you," he said.

"Carmine, douse the lights," Kerry ordered, and the driver turned off the car lights. Twisting around in his seat to look at the car behind, Kerry saw that it, too, had turned off its lights. He turned back and gripped the shotgun as he stared through the window at the dark street ahead. He could feel a fluttering in his stomach and a tingling in his arms and legs. He didn't recall ever being this excited about anything before.

The two cars turned onto the garage's street, then stopped outside the double-wide door. Kerry and the others got out, and he put his finger to his lips in a signal to be quiet. The car doors were closed softly, and the men stood in a loose semicircle around the outside of the garage door.

"Honk the horn," Kerry instructed.

Carmine reached in through the open window and honked the Klaxon. The jarring *ah-oo-ga* pierced the night.

Kerry heard the sound of a bolt being thrown, then the rattle of a chain being pulled. As the door started up, a widening bar of light spilled out from beneath it into the dark street.

"Get ready!" Kerry hissed. He looked up and down his line of men, all of them holding guns pointed at the door.

Kerry didn't wait for the door to be opened all the way. As soon as it was waist high, he signaled the others, then hunched over and rushed inside. His men immediately followed him.

Tony Fusco was halfway between the truck and the open door when the mobsters stormed in. A curious expression was in Fusco's eyes, as if he'd been wondering who had opened the door and why. He was wearing a pistol, but it was in a shoulder holster; when the twelve armed men came barging in, he took several steps backward and made a desperate claw for his gun.

"Jesus! Who the hell are you?" Fusco shouted.

"This is from Johnny Torrio!" Kerry yelled back. He pointed his shotgun at Fusco and pulled the trigger. The gun roared and bucked in his hands, and for a split second Kerry was blinded by the two-foot-wide flame pattern that erupted from the end of the barrel. When the flame receded, he saw Fusco going down, his face and chest turned into raw hamburger by the blast of nail heads.

"Son of a bitch!" someone shouted.

Immediately after Kerry's opening shot the other men began firing.

Kerry's nostrils burned with the acrid smell of gun smoke, and through the billowing clouds he could see the muzzle flashes of over a dozen other guns—his own men's plus those of a few of Fusco's men who managed to shoot back. Bullets swarmed by Kerry's head like angry bees, frying the air with deadly pops as they snapped by.

"Kerry, over there!" one of his men shouted, pointing to the other side of the tan Chandler coupe. Two men were trying to use the car as cover as they popped away at Kerry with their pistols. Kerry, who by now had his shotgun reloaded, loosed another double-barreled blast toward the car. The windshield of the Chandler disappeared in a shower of glass, and the wing-shaped raised hood was torn from its hinges. One of the gunmen fell forward across the front of the auto; the other was tossed back against a tool cabinet, knocking it over with a clanging scattering of wrenches.

The shooting was furious, sustained, and accurate, and it was over in less than a minute. Tony Fusco and every one of his men in the garage with him—his torpedoes, the men unloading the truck, even the driver—lay dead, dying, or badly wounded. The bodies were draped over cars, spread across a tool cabinet, and crumpled on a concrete floor that was now covered with blood. When the last echo of gunfire rolled away, Kerry became aware of the sound of something gurgling. He quickly realized that several of the barrels of whiskey had been hit, and what he was hearing was the liquid pouring through the holes in the barrels. The strong smell of alcohol mingled with the acrid smell of expended gunpowder.

He stepped over the dead and wounded and looked into the back of the truck. Since only a few barrels of liquor had been taken off, the truck was still nearly full.

He pulled the canvas flap back down to cover the tailgate, then looked over at one of his men.

"Vinnie, you get the truck out of here," he ordered. Then to the rest of them, "Let's go."

He and his men spilled out of the garage and raced back to their cars. As they drove away, Kerry's adrenaline was still pumping so fiercely that he couldn't stop his leg from jerking. The whole thing—the raid, the gunfight, even the carnage—was the most exciting thing he had ever done. He could feel the blood pounding in his temples, and it was all he could do to keep from whooping with sheer exhilaration.

They had driven nearly a mile before they saw the first police car, its siren wailing, heading in the direction of the garage.

"Look at 'em! Look at the dumb bastard cops!" Kerry shouted. "They're so goddamned confused, they don't know whether to scratch their ass or wind their watch! We got away clean, boys! We got away clean!"

CHAPTER TWO

MAY 1921, HAMBURG, GERMANY

"Karl, you didn't tell me your American cousin was so beautiful," Uta Tannenhower said, brushing back a lock of blond hair and smiling at her husband.

"I didn't know she was," Karl Tannenhower replied, his blue eyes twinkling. "You must remember, the last time I saw her, she was hardly the grown women she is today."

"Papa, was she ugly?" three-year-old Max Tannenhower asked.

Karl sputtered while everyone else around the dinner table laughed.

"No, she was quite pretty, but she wasn't beautiful. I mean, she was beautiful, but she wasn't yet . . . uh . . ." Karl's explanation stuttered to a halt while the others laughed again.

"Perhaps you'd best quit while you are ahead," Uta suggested.

"Perhaps I'd better," Karl agreed.

"More sauerbraten, Brunhilde?"

"No, thank you," Tanner replied. She laughed and patted her stomach. "It was very delicious, but if I eat too many more meals like this, I will *look* like Brunhilde."

"I beg your pardon?" Uta asked, obviously confused by the remark.

"Brunhilde," Tanner said. "In the States we have—" She couldn't think of how to say the word "caricature" in German, so she asked Karl in English.

"*Karikatur*," Karl answered. He smiled. "Almost the same, you see."

"Karikatur," Tanner repeated. Then, returning to German, she continued her thought. "In the States we have a caricature of the German opera singer. Always she is an enormously fat woman with metal breastplates, a horned helmet, a shield, and a spear. And always her name is Brunhilde." Tanner laughed, and though Uta and Karl laughed with her, she perceived that they didn't really find the illusion all that funny, especially Uta.

Karl indicated his muscular torso, very much a wrestler's build, and said, "I suppose if I am not careful, I will become the male equivalent of this Brunhilde."

"Actually, I've always thought Brunhilde was a beautiful name," Uta put in. "My grandmother was named Brunhilde."

"Oh, I quite agree, it *is* a lovely name," Tanner said quickly. "It's just that it's not a name that's very common in America. It would be like naming a German boy Dick."

"Dick? That means fat," Uta said. "Who would name a child so?"

"In America it's quite common for boys named Richard to be called Dick."

Uta laughed. "Now, *that* is funny," she said. "Karl,

when you were in America, did you know anyone with a funny name?"

"Not that I recall," Karl replied.

"Do you ever miss America?" Tanner asked her cousin.

"Yes, of course. I especially miss some of the friends I made there—in particular, my fellow football players at Jefferson University."

"Maybe you should come back for a visit."

"Now is not a good time," Karl said. He got a faraway look in his eyes. "Besides, my best friend was killed during the war."

"Yes," Uta put in, "the war was awful, causing friend to fight against friend and family to fight against family."

"I remember when you left St. Louis," Tanner said to Karl. "Papa told us that you were going to war, but I wasn't sure what war was then."

"That was the whole problem," Karl said, shaking his head slowly. "None of us knew what war was. Not really. I think we all had visions of glory and medals."

"Papa got a medal," Max said proudly. "The Blue Max. That's for the bravest soldiers, and it's named after me."

Uta laughed. "Maybe it's the other way around, Max," she said. Then she told Tanner in a soft voice, "The war was especially terrible for Karl. Did you know that his best American friend, a pilot, was shot down and killed while attacking the very Kasserne where Karl was? I'm sure Billy had no way of knowing that his bombs were falling on Karl, any more than Karl knew that his bullets were killing Billy."

"Uta, please," Karl said gruffly. "Let's not bring up unpleasant memories."

"You're talking about William Canfield, aren't you?" Tanner asked.

"Yes. Did you know him?" Uta asked. "Karl often speaks of him."

"No, I didn't know him," Tanner replied. "But I do know his brother, Robert. Mr. Canfield built a library on the campus of Jefferson University in honor of his brother." Inexplicably, she laughed. "It's officially named the William Canfield Library, but the students call it Billy Books." She said the words in English, but it was close enough to German that everyone understood.

"That's disrespectful, is it not?" Karl asked.

"No, I don't think so," Tanner replied. "I mean, I suppose on the surface it may seem disrespectful, but it isn't meant to be. The students use the term in a rather proprietary and even affectionate way."

Karl smiled. "I remember many good things about America and about college life at Jefferson. How we used to get together and drink beer while we studied, for instance." He chuckled. "Sometimes we did more beer drinking than studying."

"Tell me, is it true that you can't drink beer in America now?" Uta asked.

"Yes, it's against the law to sell beer or to drink it."

"If you can't sell beer, how is it that your father and your uncle can still make a living?" Karl asked.

"Oh, we do other things besides make beer," Tanner replied. "For example, my father and my uncle own a professional baseball team."

"Yes, I remember. The St. Louis Cardinals, isn't it?" Karl asked.

"Shame, shame on you!" Tanner teased. "The Cardinals play in the National League. Papa's team plays in the *American* League. Surely you remember that."

Karl laughed. "Please forgive me. I don't know if you remember, but I knew much more about football than baseball. Tell me, the baseball team, does it make money?"

"Yes, though it made a lot more when we could sell beer at the ballpark," Tanner said. "But, everyone says that Prohibition won't go on forever. In the meantime, I'm certain there's enough money to last."

"Yes, that's what we thought as well, but events proved differently," Uta said.

"Uta!" Karl said sharply.

Tanner was surprised by Uta's comment. This was a beautiful house, and the furnishings and table settings were equally lovely. Tanner would not have thought that her cousin Karl had a money problem—yet Uta's comment seemed to indicate otherwise.

"Is something wrong?" Tanner asked.

"No, nothing," Karl said quickly—too quickly to be convincing.

"Cousin Karl, we are family," Tanner said. "If there's something wrong, I'd like to help. My father would like to help. Before I left America he told me the story of my grandfather and your father. I know that it was your father's money that sent my grandfather to America and started him in his business. Everything our family has, we owe to you."

"That is true, Karl," Uta said.

"No, it is not true," Karl replied. "Perhaps Uncle Adolphus owed something to my father, but Cousin Ludwig and Cousin Rudolph owe nothing to me."

"Nevertheless, if there is something we could do for you, I'm certain my father would want to do it," Tanner persisted.

"There is nothing your father can do," Karl said sharply. Then, apparently realizing that Tanner was only trying to help and his response had been a bit harsh, he softened. "I appreciate it, Cousin Tanner, really I do, but there is nothing anyone can do. You see, the problem isn't just mine, and it isn't just the Tannenhower family. The inflation affects us all."

"Yes," Tanner said, "I've heard that Germany is suffering from terrible inflation right now. I suppose it's going to be very difficult for everyone until it passes."

"Difficult?" Uta asked. "Until it passes? Excuse me, Cousin Tanner, but you don't know what you are talking about."

"Uta, please," Karl said. "She doesn't understand."

Uta started to speak again, but then she closed her mouth. Tears welled in her eyes and began to slide down her face.

"Uta, I'm sorry," Tanner said, reaching over to touch her hand. "Whatever I've done, whatever I've said to offend you . . . please forgive me."

"Oh, no, *liebchen*, it isn't you," Uta said. She lifted Tanner's hand and kissed it. "Please forgive *me*. I meant nothing against you. It is this . . . this terrible thing done to us by our enemies that has caused this situation."

"Tell me about the inflation," Tanner said.

Uta looked at Karl, but Karl got up from the table and walked over to the sideboard to begin preparing his pipe. "I don't think I can," he replied. "It is of such a magnitude that it defies description."

"I can tell it so that she understands," Uta offered, and she turned back to Tanner. "Suppose an American family had twenty-five thousand dollars in the bank. Would you say that is a lot of money?"

"Twenty-five thousand dollars? Yes, of course," Tanner said. "I wouldn't call it an *enormous* sum, but it's quite a tidy amount."

"When the war ended, the rate of exchange was about four Reichmarks for one American dollar," Uta said. "When Karl came home from doing his duty for the Fatherland, we had in the bank a little over one hundred thousand marks—the equivalent of twenty-five thousand American dollars. We thought that would be enough for us to live comfortably until Karl decided what he would do next."

"Yes, I would think so," Tanner agreed.

"Then the inflation came, and the accumulated savings of several generations was wiped out in a matter of a few days. I will give you an example. For the meal we had tonight, the bread alone cost one hundred marks," Uta explained.

"One hundred marks?" Tanner gasped.

"Inflation continues to go up and up, more and more every day," Karl added, returning to the table, his pipe lit. "There is a joke, a cruel joke, making the rounds here. Like most cruel jokes, the cruelest part of this one is that it's true. Before the war, the joke goes, one would take a pocketful of money to the market and return with a basketful of food. Now, one takes a *basketful* of money to the market and returns with a *pocketful* of food."

"My God," Tanner said. "What can be done about it?"

"By the government we have in Berlin?" Karl answered. "I'm afraid nothing. They simply don't have the answers or the confidence of the German people. But I know this: If something isn't done soon, Germany will cease to exist as a country, and a thousand years of civilization will have been for naught."

"I had no idea things were in such a state over here," Tanner said. "Someone should be told . . . something should be done."

Karl laughed out loud.

"What is it, Karl?" Uta asked.

"I had almost forgotten the childlike innocence of the Americans to believe that all wrongs can be righted if the cause is just and the heart is true. America is a nation of Don Quixotes."

"Well, what's wrong with that?" Tanner asked, smiling, as she raised her beer glass. "Otherwise, to quote my father"—she switched to English—"we'd be up to our asses in windmills."

JUNE 1921, ST. LOUIS, MISSOURI

It was a beautiful afternoon, and Sportsman's Park was filled to its 30,000-seat capacity for today's baseball game. The sky was such a bright blue that it almost hurt the eyes, and the foul lines, 365 feet down to the left field wall and 295 feet to the right field wall, were illuminated crisp and white against the dark-green grass. Pennants fluttered from poles atop the large wooden pavilion, with the most prominent positions given to the pennants of the St. Louis Grays and the New York Yankees, the two teams playing today.

The outfield fence was plastered with colorful advertising billboards, including one for Tannenhower Brewery proclaiming, MAKERS OF SOFT DRINKS, BARLEY MALT SYRUP, AND OTHER HEALTHFUL, NON-ALCOHOLIC PRODUCTS; one for Willys-Knight automobiles, asserting, MEMORABLE DAYS

IN A KNIGHT; one for Royal Baking Powder that was ABSO-
LUTELY PURE; and one for Canfield-Puritex Corn Toasties,
THE BREAKFAST OF WINNERS!

Just above the blue-and-white diagonally striped
logo on the Canfield-Puritex Corn Toasties sign was a
huge scoreboard that told the story of today's game. The
Grays had picked up one run in the bottom of the eighth;
the Yankees had eight zeros showing. The Grays had just
been retired and were now taking the field for the top of
the ninth.

"Here you are, Mr. Tannenhower," one of the
vendors said, coming down to the owner's box and
handing a hot dog across the gate to Ludwig.

"Thank you, Jimmy," Ludwig answered, handing
the vendor a coin.

"Ludwig, you shouldn't eat so many of those,"
Hulda Tannenhower scolded. "They are bad for you."

"I *have* to eat them," Ludwig said, justifying his
rather prodigious appetite. "If the fans don't see me
eating them, they may think something is wrong with
the food we sell, and that would be bad for business."

"But must you eat so many?"

"I want to *sell* many," Ludwig said. His physique
gave evidence to his public relations effort, because he
was a very large man, weighing over three hundred
pounds. He had already eaten six hot dogs today, plus
several schooners of near beer. He didn't really like near
beer, but he drank it as if he did, hoping by his example
to convince others that it was a suitable substitute for the
beer his brewery could no longer produce.

Bob Canfield, whose personal box was right next to
the owner's box, leaned over to talk to Ludwig.

"Our boys have played pretty well today. Just three
more outs and we've got them," he said.

"Yes," Ludwig replied. "But don't forget, Babe Ruth
may come up this inning."

"Maybe not. He's the fourth batter. If Hogan can
get them down in order, we won't have to face him. And
anyway, even if we do, we've been lucky with Ruth so far
today," Bob said. "Two walks and a strikeout."

"That just means he's due," Ludwig groaned.

"Come on, Ludwig, all you need is a little faith," Bob prompted.

"No. What I need is one more good pitcher. As it stands now, it's 'Robbins and Cain and pray for rain.'"

Bob laughed, for that had been the refrain on the sports pages of *The St. Louis Chronicle* last week, when the sportswriter suggested that the St. Louis Grays had only two quality pitchers. Emil Cain had lost a close one in the first game, but Robbie Robbins had managed to pull out a win yesterday. Kip Hogan was handling the chore today in this, the third game of the series against the Yankees. Hogan had been a good pitcher in his time, but he was thirty-eight years old, and his best days were behind him.

Bob's wife, Connie, and their two teenaged sons, John and Willie, were in the box with him. Connie leaned over to speak to Hulda Tannenhower.

"Hulda, what have you heard from Tanner? Is she enjoying her trip to Europe?"

"Oh, yes, very much," Hulda answered. "She spent some time in Germany, but I think by now she's back in Paris. I believe she intends to spend a little more time there before she returns home."

"You'd better watch her in Paris," Bob bantered. "She may meet some handsome Frenchman and not come home at all."

"Oh, don't tell me that," Hulda said, half laughing and half moaning.

"Hey, Pop, Whitey Witt is up," fourteen-year-old John Canfield piped up, calling Bob's attention back to the game.

"What do you think, Ludwig? Does Hogan have three outs left in him?" Bob asked.

"I don't know," Ludgwig said. "He's done a good job so far, but he's pitched the whole game. He has to be tired."

Ludwig chewed his hot dog nervously as he watched his pitcher work, then groaned when Whitey got on base on four straight balls.

Evert Scott, the Yankee shortstop, swung on the first pitch, popping it straight up in the air. The Grays' catcher whipped off his mask, then stood on the plate waiting for it. When the ball came back down he caught it, then glanced over at first to make sure Whitey stayed where he was.

Bob Meusel, the Yankees' third hitter, sent a long, lazy fly deep to left, advancing Whitey Witt to second base. Then, almost as one, the thirty thousand fans in the huge wooden stadium leaned forward in their seats as a large, ambling man with a doughy face sauntered out to the plate.

"And now . . ." the field announcer said, his voice echoing from speakers all around the field, "batting for the New York Yankees . . . Babe . . . Ruth!"

Ludwig looked at his pitcher. He could tell that Hogan was nervous—and Hogan had a right to be. Ruth had tagged Hogan for three home runs last year and four the year before that.

Hogan's hands went up, then dropped to his chest. He turned his head to study the runner on second, then sent his first pitch smoking toward the plate, dead through the center. Ruth watched it go by.

"Stee-rike!" The umpire's voice could be heard clearly through most of the stadium.

Ludwig saw a small smile break out on Ruth's face, and Ruth nodded at Hogan, as if congratulating the pitcher for slipping one by him.

Hogan took more time with the second pitch than he had with the first, and Ludwig had the feeling that his pitcher hadn't intended to split the plate with the first pitch. This time Hogan threw a curve and Ruth watched it hook away, low and outside. The count evened up.

Ruth swung on the third pitch and caught a piece of the ball. It sliced up from the bat, over the catcher's head, and back into the stands, rattling into the seats some thirty-five rows above Ludwig's box. Ludwig turned around just long enough to see the fans scrambling for the ball, and then he looked back down at Ruth. Ruth had stepped out of the batter's box to tap the bat against his spikes. Now he stepped back in and looked toward the pitcher.

Hogan had two strikes on Ruth. He had struck him out the last time he faced him, and now he was one pitch away from another victory. Hogan waved off the catcher's first signal, then nodded at the second. He raised his hands over his head, brought them down to his chest, looked toward the runner at second, then fired the ball toward the plate.

Ludwig felt his heart drop, for he knew what was going to happen a split second before it did. Hogan had thrown a blazer, right over the middle of the plate, just as he had for the first pitch. This time, however, Ruth wasn't going to watch it go by. Before the ball was a third of the way to the plate, Ruth whipped the bat around off his shoulder, making contact with the ball in the exact middle of his swing. Ludwig was certain that people across the river in Illinois could hear the crack of the bat hitting the ball. The ball took off like a bullet toward center field, climbing up and hurtling out with incredible power. Ruth stood there for just a minute, still in his patented, funny-looking twisted-pretzel position as he watched the ball sail up and away, disappearing as a small white dot over the back wall of the center-field bleachers. It was a home run of monumental proportions, and even though it was against his own team, Ludwig couldn't help but feel a momentary thrill over watching such a blow.

Finally, after the ball was undoubtedly already rolling down Grand Avenue, Babe Ruth dropped his bat and began sauntering around the bases.

"My God," Bob Canfield said. "Have you ever seen such a hit?"

"No wonder Ruppert built a new stadium," Ludwig replied, referring to Yankee Stadium, which Jake Ruppert, owner of Ruppert Brewery, had just opened this season. "If I had someone like Babe Ruth to draw the crowds, I could bring sixty-five thousand people to a game as well."

• • •

"We lost, two to one," Ludwig Tannenhower told his butler, arriving home with Hulda after the game. "We were just one strike away from winning."

"Yes, sir. I listened to the game on the radio. That must have been some home run by Babe Ruth. The announcer said it was the hardest hit ball he ever saw."

"It was, Napoleon, it truly was," Ludwig said. He saw a pile of mail sitting on the hall table. "Is this today's mail?"

"Yes, sir," Napoleon replied. "There's a letter from Miss Tanner. I put it on top for you."

"Good, good. Thank you, Napoleon."

"Oh, a letter from Tanner?" Hulda asked. "What does she have to say?"

"Here, you can read it while I look through the rest of the mail," Ludwig offered.

Hulda tore open the envelope, read for a moment or two, then gasped aloud. "Oh, my God! I've got to sit down."

"Hulda! What is it?"

"She's married," Hulda said in a voice so weak it was barely audible. "Our little girl is married."

NINE MONTHS LATER, PARIS

"Eric?" a small, pained voice said. "Eric, are you awake?"

Eric opened his eyes and found himself looking directly at the skylight over the bed. The early-morning sky was a leaden gray, and raindrops were splattering against the glass. Eric rubbed his eyes and ran a hand through his hair.

"Are you awake?" Tanner Twainbough asked again.

"Yes," Eric replied. He put his hand out to stroke his wife's hair and was surprised to feel sweat on her forehead. He raised up on one elbow. "Tanner, what's wrong? You're drenched with sweat."

"Yes, I am, and it's your fault."

"*My* fault?"

"Yes. You *are* the father of this baby, after all. I'm having some pains."

"Do you want me to rub your back?"

"Some pains, darling," Tanner said in an exasperated voice. "You know, like *labor* pains?"

"Oh. Oh!" he repeated when he realized what she meant. He was fully awake now. "Do you think we should go to the hospital?"

"Unless you want to finish the job in the same place you started it in," Tanner quipped.

Eric scurried out of bed. "We'd better get dressed. I'll get your clothes for you. What do you want to wear?"

Tanner laughed. "Anything, dear. I'm not exactly going to a cotillion. Oh!" she suddenly gasped, and her face contorted with pain. A moment or two passed, and she breathed, "Ooh. That was a pretty good one."

Eric brought her a bathrobe and a coat. "Maybe you had better just put the robe on, then put a coat over it. Paris in the spring is glorious, but Paris in March is cold and miserable."

Tanner sat heavily on the edge of the bed and began putting on the thick chenille robe over her flannel nightgown.

"I can't believe we're having a baby already," she said. "We've only been married nine months."

"Nine months is all it takes," Eric reminded her as he slipped into his trousers.

"Yes, but most people are married for several years before they have children."

Eric looked at her and smiled. "Do you want me to call the doctor and tell him we've changed our minds?"

Tanner laughed goodnaturedly and put her hands over her enormous stomach. "No. We've come this far with it. I think we should go on, don't you?"

"Well, only if you're sure," Eric replied, continuing the banter while he finished dressing. He came over and kissed her forehead. "I'll go down to the concierge's apartment and phone for a taxi."

He raced down the stairs and woke the concierge without too much trouble. Because it was so early, there was no competition for a taxi when Eric called, and when he explained that his wife was about to have a baby, a cab was immediately dispatched. The driver responded so quickly that in the time it took for Eric to go upstairs for Tanner and bring her back down, the taxi was sitting by the curb in front of the apartment building. Eric took off his own coat and held it over Tanner's head, shielding her from the rain, as they walked across the sidewalk to the car.

In a matter of moments they arrived at the hospital, and the nurse at the admitting desk saw at once that Tanner was in labor. She barked a quick order, which brought two white-coated orderlies out of a room just off the hall. One of the men had been smoking, and he pinched off the end of his cigarette and stuck it in his jacket pocket as he hurried toward Tanner. He and his companion helped her onto a gurney, then wheeled her off while Eric stayed to answer the admitting nurse's questions about Tanner's name, age, and health.

When the admitting form was completed, the nurse instructed Eric, "Maternity is on the third floor."

Too impatient to wait for the elevator, which seemed to him preternaturally slow, Eric took the stairs two at a time up to the third floor. There he learned that Tanner had been taken directly into the delivery room.

"Are fathers allowed in the delivery room?" he asked the nurse on duty.

She gave an expressive shrug. "It depends on the doctor. Some will allow it, others won't. The room is at the end of the hall, if you wish to try your luck."

Nodding, Eric hurried to the end of the hall and bowled through the swinging doors. He found himself inside the delivery room facing a set of raised knees draped with a sheet. He assumed the legs were Tanner's, though her face was obscured by the back of the doctor who was standing at the foot of the operating table. The doctor was so intent at doing his job that he didn't even notice the intruder. The assisting nurse did notice him, however, and she started toward Eric.

"Nurse, come here," the doctor snapped, calling her back. "I need you."

She turned around, and Eric stayed where he was.

It seemed to take forever, and Eric felt a sense of uselessness as he stood watching and—worse—listening. He started to experience some difficulty in breathing and began sweating profusely; then his knees grew weak, and he had to lean against a wall to stay upright.

The doctor and Tanner were talking. The doctor's voice was low and confident; Tanner's was high-pitched and weak.

"I'll try," Eric heard her say, and his feeling of uselessness doubled as he realized that whatever it was that Tanner was trying to do, he was unable to help.

"Oh!" Tanner abruptly shrieked. "Oh, Doctor, it hurts! Oh, dear God, it hurts so bad!"

It seemed to Eric that he could almost experience the pain that Tanner was feeling, and though there was nothing he could do, he automatically pushed away from the wall and took a step toward the table. The room began to spin.

The horrible, foul smell of ammonia wafted up through his nostrils to his brain, and Eric opened his eyes, spitting and coughing and fighting for breath. He realized then that he was lying on the floor, and when he tried to sit up, the doctor stuck out his hand to steady him.

"Take it easy, Monsieur Twainbough," the doctor said. "You had a fainting spell."

"I *what*?" Eric batted aside the doctor's hand and sat up. Then he remembered where he was and what was happening. "My wife!" he demanded. "How is my wife?"

"She is fine. And so is your son."

Eric felt his heart beat faster. "My son? I h
son?"

The doctor smiled. "A fine, big boy."

"Where is Tanner?"

"She is in her room. With the baby. You can go see her now, if you wish. I'm sorry I didn't attend to you when you first fainted, but, as I'm sure you can appreciate, I had my hands full." The doctor chuckled. "I always like to say that I haven't lost a father yet, but I was afraid for a moment that you might spoil my record."

Eric let the doctor assist him to his feet and out of the delivery room. Then he walked quickly down the hall to Tanner's room.

"Are you all right, darling?" Tanner asked anxiously when Eric stepped into the room.

Eric laughed. "Am *I* all right? I'm supposed to be asking *you* that."

"Oh, I'm fine. And so is our son."

It was at that moment that Eric first looked at the tiny, drawn-up little creature with a wrinkled red face, tightly closed eyes, scowling mouth, and a tuft of downy black hair.

"Look at that!" Eric said in an awestruck voice.

Tanner grinned. "Isn't he beautiful?"

"The most beautiful baby I've ever seen," Eric agreed.

"Eric, can we name him Ludwig, after my father?"

"Sure. As long as we don't have to *call* him that."

"You can pick the name we'll call him by."

Eric was silent for a moment, then said, "Hamilton. We can call him Ham."

"Hamilton? Why Hamilton? I don't remember you ever—" Tanner broke off and smiled. "Oh, wait a minute. Isn't Sam Hamilton the name of the editor at that publisher you hope to sell your novel to? Pendarrow House?"

"Right on the first guess." Eric reached down to touch his son's hair. "Maybe naming this little fellow Hamilton will bring me luck."

CHAPTER

THREE

GANG WAR CONTINUES, the headline in *The Chicago Tribune* read.

But Rex "Rocky" Rockwell wasn't reading the headline or even the front page. He was absorbed in a story on the sports page, though it was abundantly obvious that the story wasn't to his liking, for he groaned in disgust and lay the paper down.

"What's wrong, Rocky? Is there a story about something that'll affect your flying the mail?" Wally Peterson asked without turning around. The young meteorologist was standing in front of a large wall map, marking the known weather patterns with pins.

Rocky was a veteran of the Great War and had flown both for the Lafayette Escadrille and the American Air Service. Now he was a mail pilot, flying the route between St. Louis and Chicago. He shook his head, even though Peterson had his back to him and couldn't see the gesture. "No, nothing like that. I was just reading about the St. Louis Grays," he replied. "They blew a lead in the ninth inning yesterday. Babe Ruth hit a homer with a man on."

"I'm afraid I don't follow baseball," Peterson said.

"What do you mean, you don't follow baseball? It's your patriotic duty to follow baseball."

"I used to, but the White Sox scandal soured me on the game."

"Yeah," Rocky said. "Well, all those guys throwing the '19 series like that, it was pretty bad. I don't know, maybe I ought to follow the Cardinals." He snorted. "No, I couldn't do that. I hate the damned Cardinals." Folding the paper, he put it aside. The leather of his flying jacket squeaked as he leaned over the counter to take a closer look at the map. "Okay, Peterson, you've been working on that damned map for a half hour now. What have you got for me?"

"It looks like there's a front moving in," Peterson answered without turning around. "There's quite a good chance you'll encounter it between here and St. Louis."

"Come on. Is that the best you can do for me?" Rocky grumbled.

"I'm afraid it is."

"How about three hours? Can you give me three hours?"

"I can't guarantee it," Peterson said. He turned to face Rocky and pushed his glasses up his nose. "I only chart the weather, you know, I don't make it."

"Yeah, bullshit. That's what you all say," Rocky teased.

They heard the sound of a motorcycle stopping out front. A moment later the door opened, and a uniformed mail clerk came in, carrying a canvas bag.

"Forty-six pounds of mail," the mail clerk said. "Who's going to sign for it?"

"I will," Rocky answered, taking the receipt from the clerk. "Forty-six pounds, let's see, that's . . ."

"One hundred thirty-eight dollars," the clerk said.

"We have the check already made out." He handed the check to Rocky, who put it in his inside jacket pocket.

"Hardly enough to risk your life for, what with the front coming in," Peterson suggested.

"Well, I can't very well sit around on the ground like a fat turkey just because there's likely to be a raindrop or two in the sky," Rocky countered.

"What does that mean, a front is coming in?" the mail clerk asked.

"It means I'm going to get wet," Rocky replied. He patted the canvas bag. "But tell your boss not to worry, the mail bag will be high and dry."

"Listen, if you want, give the mail back to me, and I can take it down to the depot and put it on the train," the mail clerk suggested. "'Course, I'd have to take back the check, too."

"No, no," Rocky said. "The good citizens who mailed those letters paid extra to have them carried by air. I can get them to St. Louis tonight, and they'll be in the hands of the addressees before ten o'clock tomorrow morning."

"The reason I asked, some of the other pilots won't fly when the weather's bad," the mail clerk said.

Rocky smiled. "Well, then, that's all the more reason you should use only Rockwell-McPheeters Aviation, isn't it?"

"You're sure you want to fly it? It'd be no trouble for me to take it down to the station."

"I'm sure."

"All right, I'll be getting back, then," the mail clerk said, waving as he left. A few seconds later came the sound of a motorcycle being started, and then it drove off.

Rocky picked up the mailbag. "I can't earn any money standing around here. I guess I'd better get started."

"Rocky?" Peterson called.

Rocky stopped and looked back.

"Don't forget this." The weatherman was holding out a shoulder holster with a .38-caliber pistol.

"That's five pounds of weight I don't need," Rocky grumbled.

"I know, but it *is* U.S. postal regulations, and I can't clear you unless you have it. If you're going to carry the mail, you must be armed."

"You know something? That is a dumb regulation," Rocky growled, walking back to strap on the revolver. He grinned broadly. "But, then, so is Prohibition. See you on my next run," he said, and again he started to leave. He got as far as the front door and was stopped by a young woman stepping through.

She glanced back and forth at the two men, then asked, "Would one of you gentlemen be Mr. Rockwell?"

Rocky looked at her. She was slightly shorter than average, thin, brown-haired, and had blue eyes made larger by the wire-rim glasses she wore. With the proper makeup and clothes she might have been pretty, though she gave the appearance of someone who didn't care much whether men considered her pretty or not. There was, however, an innocence to her that was appealing.

"Yes, I'm Rockwell. What can I do for you?"

"My name is Kendra Mills, Mr. Rockwell. I was told by the man out by the airplane that you are the one who is going to drive it to St. Louis."

"I am," Rocky said, not bothering to correct her terminology.

"I want to go with you."

Rocky frowned and shook his head. "I'm sorry, Miss Mills, I'm afraid I can't take any passengers tonight. Maybe next time."

"No, I have to go to St. Louis with you tonight," she insisted.

"I'm sorry. I wish I could help you, I really do. But it's out of the question." Rocky looked back toward Peterson. "When you hear me pass over the building, get my 'off' time through to St. Louis, will you?"

"You've got it, Rocky."

"Excuse me, Miss Mills," Rocky said, starting by the woman. "I have some mail to deliver."

"Mr. Rockwell, please?" Kendra called, and there

was such an urgency to her voice that Rocky stopped and looked back toward her. "I have to get to St. Louis before ten o'clock tonight. I simply *have* to. And you are the only chance I have of doing that."

"What's so important that you have to be in St. Louis before ten o'clock?"

"I'm a student at Jefferson University. I'm a senior, due to graduate this month. But if I miss bed check tonight, I'll be expelled."

Rocky smiled. "Well, maybe you should have found a party closer to home."

The girl's eyes misted over. "Please," she said again, "don't you understand? If I don't graduate, all of it will have been for nothing."

Rocky was quiet for a long moment; then he sighed. "Do you have the fare?" he asked. "It's eighty-four dollars."

"Yes," she replied, brightening now. "I have it." She opened her purse, counted out the money, then held it out toward Rocky.

"All right. If it's that important to you, I'll take you," Rocky said, accepting her money.

"Thank you," she breathed.

"Listen," Rocky said. "Before we go I think there's something I should tell you. A front's moving in, and that means we're likely to get some bad weather. And even if we don't, St. Louis is right on the river, and every front raises a thick fog. This trip isn't going to be like a drive through the park, honey, it's going to be rough. Tell her, Peterson. You're the weatherman."

"He's quite right, Miss Mills. There is apt to be some danger to this flight."

"You're going, aren't you?"

"Yeah, sure," Rocky said. "But I have to go. It's my job."

"I have to go, too," Kendra said. "And the way I see it, you're going to make every effort to get yourself there in one piece, so if you make it, that means I will, too."

Rocky looked at her for a moment, then laughed. "Can't argue with that logic," he said. "Okay, let's get you ready and get out of here. The longer we delay our takeoff, the more likely we are to run into bad weather."

"Ready? What do you mean, ready?"

"Miss, you're going to be riding in an open cockpit at one hundred miles per hour and perhaps flying as high as ten thousand feet," Rocky informed her. "At that altitude the temperature is going to be below freezing."

"Oh. I see what you mean."

"Go into that room over there and you'll see a bunch of leather flying jackets hanging from hooks. They're all fleece lined, so they'll keep you good and warm. Find one that fits." He glanced over toward the wall clock. "And find it in about thirty seconds. We really must be going."

"I'll be right back," Kendra promised as she headed for the room.

"Do you have any luggage?" Rocky called after her. "I'll put it on the plane."

"Just one piece," she answered. "A train case. It's right outside the door."

Rocky opened the door and looked outside at the girl's luggage. "Oh, Jesus," he breathed. "A train case, she says. A damned steamer trunk would be closer to the truth. It's a good thing my load is light."

The airplane Rocky was flying was an RM-3, a big biplane designed and built especially for carrying mail by Rocky's partner, Bryan McPheeters. Though right now the primary source of income of Rockwell-McPheeters Aviation was carrying mail, their ultimate goal was to design and build airplanes.

The mechanic helped Rocky strap the large suitcase down in the cargo bay of the RM-3.

"Did some girl find you?" the mechanic asked.

"Yeah. She's going to St. Louis with me."

"I thought maybe that was what she wanted, but I didn't know if you'd do it."

Rocky looked around and saw Kendra approaching the airplane. She was wearing a jacket that was much too large for her.

"Will this do?" she asked, as she approached the

wing of the airplane. "It was the smallest one I could find."

"Yeah, it'll do. Come on, if you're ready. You'll be riding up here."

Rocky helped Kendra into the front cockpit of the airplane. His "airline" didn't carry passengers too often because the U.S. government paid three dollars a pound to have the mail carried, whereas the fare for a one-way passage between St. Louis and Chicago was only eighty-four dollars. Pound for pound, passengers were not a very lucrative source of revenue.

Settling into his own seat, Rocky instructed the mechanic, "Okay, Arnie, crank her up and let's go."

Arnie stuck a crank into a small hole on the side of the engine cowling and began turning it, which spun a flywheel on the inertia starter. When the whine of the spinning flywheel was at its highest pitch, he pulled the crank out and signaled Rocky. Rocky nodded and flipped the "engage" toggle. The spinning flywheel transferred its energy to the engine crankshaft, and the whine wound down sharply. The engine coughed and caught, and the propeller became a spinning blur.

The big biplane trundled out to the end of the runway, and then Rocky turned it into the wind and opened up the throttle. A moment later the plane was climbing out over the administration building, the engine making a deep-throated roar. This was the signal to Peterson to put in his long-distance telephone call to St. Louis, informing the postal service there that the Rockwell-McPheeters plane had just departed Chicago.

Rocky leveled out at 5,000 feet on a magnetic heading of 195 degrees. Far to the southwest he could see the rapid buildup of clouds as the front worked its way east. If the front closed in on him, it could shut him off from the ground below, and Rocky would have only the instruments on his panel to see him through.

There was enough fuel in the airplane's tanks to provide him with four hours of flying time, which included one hour of reserve. Since the estimated flying time between Chicago and St. Louis was three hours, he should be able to make his destination with an hour's flying time remaining.

He throttled back the engine so that the roar was temporarily subdued. When Kendra turned around, as Rocky knew she would, he held up a speaking tube and showed her how to use it by alternately speaking into it or holding it to her ear. She smiled and put it to her right ear.

"How are you doing?" he asked. He put the tube to his ear for her answer.

"Fine," she called back. "This is my first time ever in an airplane. It's great fun."

"Yes, it is, isn't it?" Rocky remarked.

"Look at those clouds over there, at the sun shining on them like that. Aren't they beautiful?" Kendra asked.

"As long as they stay over there, they're beautiful," Rocky agreed.

They didn't stay. As the front moved east, the plane began bouncing in the rough air. Rocky climbed to ten thousand feet where he found the air a little smoother, but the clouds began drifting in under him. Fortunately, the cloud mass wasn't completely solid, and here and there were ragged holes that allowed peeks at the ground below. It was mostly farmland, though Rocky sometimes got a glimpse of a barn or a railroad or some other feature that he recognized, giving him bearings and reassuring him that he hadn't entirely severed his bonds with humankind. Ahead of him the clouds were built up much higher, far too high to go over, so he braced himself to go through them.

It was dark in the clouds and raining and rough. The vapor was so thick that Rocky couldn't even see his wing tips. He wasn't too concerned, however. There was very little likelihood of another airplane being out here at this precise altitude and location—and in this weather.

Without ground references he had no way of knowing exactly where he was, but when he had flown for two hours he began to gradually lower his altitude. He broke through the bottom of the clouds at just over twenty-five hundred feet. It had stopped raining, and the air was clear at this altitude. Directly below him he picked up the town of Edwardsville and he smiled, pleased with himself over the accuracy of his navigation. But when he looked toward St. Louis, he groaned. A solid bank of fog ran north and south along the Mississippi River and east and west along the Missouri. In addition, coal smoke from the chimneys of the city's factories and homes mixed with the river fog to make it even more impenetrable. Local newspapers had created a word for this phenomenon that was unique to St. Louis—smog—and that encircled and marked the city like a gloomy halo.

"Damn," Rocky swore. "How the hell am I going to find the airport?"

He put the airplane into a long, banking turn while he studied the situation. Below him a train headed for the city, and Rocky wished there were some way he could land on top of the train before it disappeared under the fog bank and ride on in with it into St. Louis.

The front of the train started through the fog bank, and when it did, Rocky noticed that the wind of its passage stirred up the vapor, forming a long furrow—easily seen from above—just like a furrow in a plowed field. All Rocky had to do was follow that furrow into the middle of the city. From there he knew he could estimate the direction and distance to the airport. He knew, too, that there was a very high water tower near the airport, with a blinking light to warn aviators away. If Rocky could find that water tower, he could use it to line up with the runway. Then he'd only have to let himself down slowly, using his instruments to keep his wings level and his altimeter to tell him how high he was above the ground.

Rocky turned, aligning himself with the railroad and then following it, using the channel created by the train as his beacon. He throttled back and descended until he was just a few feet above the fog bank. Skimming along that close to the mist gave an illusion of great speed, and wisps of vapor worked up to be caught in the whirling propeller or snagged on the wing tips and struts and braces for a second before being whipped back at seventy miles per hour.

The furrow abruptly ended, and Rocky realized he was over Union Station. From Union Station it was a heading of almost exactly 315 degrees to Lambert Airport. Rocky steered into that heading, then began searching for the flashing lights that marked the water tower.

The palms of his hands were sweating, and he could feel a tension in the back of his neck and in his legs. His breath came in small gasps as he leaned over the side and looked for the small red blinking lights of the tower.

"There!" he shouted excitedly, though Kendra couldn't hear him over the engine noise and wouldn't have known what he was talking about even if she could.

The lights were no more than a slight red glow, barely discernible through the fog. If they hadn't been flashing, he probably wouldn't have noticed them at all. He flew toward them, then turned his airplane so that the tower passed just off the tip of his left wing. When he was even with it he throttled back and put the airplane into a gentle descent. Within seconds he was inside the fog bank, and everything disappeared in a thick, gray haze.

The fog was even worse than the cloud had been. He could barely see the back of Kendra's head, let alone his wing tips. He alternately wiped the palms of his hands on his legs and continued the descent, gradually flattening out the plane. At the last minute he saw the big orange tetrahedron and knew that he was only a few feet above the ground. He quickly chopped the throttle, and the airplane settled the rest of the way down. He felt a slight bump as the wheels touched the ground, and he let the plane roll until it came to a stop. There, no more than ten feet in front of him, was the yellow glow of a light shining through the hangar window.

Rocky let out a long, slow breath, as if he had been holding it the entire time. He wanted to get out and kiss the ground, but he wouldn't dare do it in front of the young woman passenger. He knew that she had to be terrified, and he couldn't afford to show her that he, too, had been worried.

To his surprise, Kendra turned toward him with a broad smile on her face. "That was fun!" she exclaimed. "I was a little frightened when it was so bumpy, but the last part—where we came down through the cloud— why, that didn't frighten me at all. That was just like settling down on a big, soft featherbed."

No, Rocky told himself, she hadn't been afraid because she had no idea of the danger they'd been in.

"Like a featherbed? Yeah, I suppose so," Rocky said dryly.

Having arrived back in St. Louis with plenty of time to spare, Kendra Mills decided to have dinner before heading for Jefferson University.

By the time she left the restaurant, the fog had begun to lift. She hailed a taxi, and when she stepped out at the front gate of the university, the moon was shining down brightly on the buildings of what was known as the Hilltop Campus. Spengeman Hall, the administration building, had only a few lights on; in contrast, "Billy Books" had all its lights burning brightly, filled with students cramming for upcoming exams. Most of the windows in the dormitories were also glowing.

As Kendra walked across the quad, the clock tower at Spengeman Hall started its eight-note prelude, then began chiming the hour. Kendra counted the ninth *bong* just as she opened the door to the women's dormitory. The housemother, sitting on a sofa and reading a magazine, looked up in surprise.

"Good evening, Mrs. Pynchon," Kendra said. She set her suitcase down long enough to get her breath.

"Good heavens, dear, what are you doing down here?" Mrs. Pynchon asked. "I just saw you in your bed a few minutes ago."

"You saw me in bed?"

"Yes, I told Miss Hunter that I was beginning to get worried that you wouldn't return in time, and she told me you were already here. She pointed to your bed, and I saw you sleeping. That is, I *thought* I saw you sleeping." Mrs. Pynchon's eyes narrowed suspiciously. "Who was it, if it wasn't you?"

Kendra knew then that Demaris, her roommate, had been covering for her. "Oh, it was me," she said quickly. "But I had to go back for my suitcase. You must have missed me when I walked through." It was a lame excuse—it didn't even make much sense, if one thought about it even for half a moment—but it was the best Kendra could come up with, unprepared to lie as she was.

"Yes, I suppose I did," Mrs. Pynchon replied, seemingly mollified. "At any rate, I'm glad you made it back on time. I do hate it so when I must get one of my girls in trouble, but it *is* my job to report you, after all, if one of you misses bed check. I hope all of you understand that."

"Yes, we do understand," Kendra said. "I don't think anyone holds it against you. Well, good night, Mrs. Pynchon."

"Good night, dear," the housemother replied absently, already reabsorbed in her novel.

Once upstairs, Kendra set her suitcase down and was about to open her door when it was opened from inside by her roommate.

"Jeepers, kiddo, I was getting afraid that you weren't going to make it back in time for ol' Eagle-Eye Pynchon's nightly bed check." Demaris Hunter reached out and took Kendra's suitcase. "Umph, this thing weighs a ton. What have you got in it?"

"Just my things," Kendra said. "By the way, how did you make Mrs. Pynchon think I was already back?"

"Oh, it wasn't me. Dora did it," Demaris quipped.

Kendra laughed, for Dora was the name she had given her dress dummy. She walked over to her bed and pulled the covers back. "Dora, what do you mean sleeping in my bed?" Kendra asked sternly as she took the dress form out of the bed and carried it over to the closet. "Don't you know you have your own place?"

"Don't be so mean to her," Demaris said with a laugh as she put the suitcase on Kendra's bed. "She was just trying to help you out."

"Oh, I appreciate it, I really do," Kendra said. "You're a dear, Dora," she called, blowing a kiss toward the closet. She began unpacking her bag.

"Hey! How did you get back from Chicago? You weren't on the eight o'clock train. I know, because I checked."

"Oh, Demaris!" Kendra exclaimed, feeling the excitement all over again. "You'll never believe it. I *flew* back!"

"You *flew* back? What do you mean, you flew back?"

"In an airplane," Kendra explained. "I bought a fare on the mail plane from Chicago to St. Louis."

Demaris gasped and put her hand to her mouth. "My God, you aren't serious!"

"Yes, I'm perfectly serious. You see, I missed the train, and— Oh, it was wonderful fun! I've never experienced anything quite like it in my entire life!"

"Tell me about the pilot."

"The pilot?"

"Yes. Was he dashing and handsome? If he had asked you to fly to Borneo with him, would you have gone?"

"No, don't be silly!"

"I would've gone," Demaris said. Using the thumb and forefinger of her right hand, she made a motion as if she were twirling a handlebar mustache. "My dear," she said enticingly, "come with me. I want you to fly with me to Borneo."

Dropping the pose of the dashing aviator, she then became the willing female. "Oh, yes, my hero," she said in a simpering tone, "I will go anywhere with you . . . although I don't even know where Borneo is," she added in her normal voice.

Kendra laughed. "You are a nut," she said. "You wouldn't really go anywhere with him."

"I am *not* a nut, I am a romantic. And I would love

to fly off somewhere with a handsome aviator," Demaris insisted. She smiled. "He *was* handsome, wasn't he?"

"I suppose so," Kendra said.

"You *suppose* so? Don't you know?"

"I don't look at men that way."

"How *do* you look at them?"

"The way I look at *everyone*. For what they are, not for their appearance."

"I'm not the nut, you are," Demaris said. "You're just lucky that Philip is so good-looking."

The smile left Kendra's face. "It's all over between Philip and me, Demaris. I told him I never wanted to see him again."

"You did?" Demaris gasped. "But I thought you two were about to be married?"

"Yes, we had made those plans. And Philip was still planning on it—in his way. But he didn't let a little thing like being engaged to me stop him from going out with every girl in Chicago."

"Oh, I'm so sorry, Kendra."

Kendra opened the drawer to her dresser and began putting away her lingerie.

"Actually, I'm not," she finally replied. "I've known for a long time that Philip was too young for me."

"Too *young* for you? What do you mean? He's two years older than you are."

"Chronologically, perhaps. But in every other way he's much too young. Besides, he never understood or appreciated my desire to be a journalist. That's why I came to St. Louis to go to school. Jefferson has the best school of journalism in the country."

"Yeah, I know. That's what you've been telling me. I just hope it's worth it, that's all. I mean, Philip Malone! What a dreamboat he is! And you let him get away."

"If it wasn't meant to be, it wasn't meant to be. That's all there is to it," Kendra said firmly. "It will all work out for the best, I'm sure."

"Well, I'm just glad you got back in time to avoid being expelled. I mean, with only three weeks to go, it would've been awful. Oh, and I almost forgot. You got a letter from *The Chronicle* today. It's over there on your desk."

"Do you mean to tell me I got a letter from *The Chronicle* and you're just now getting around to telling me?" Kendra asked excitedly. "What's *wrong* with you? Don't you know how important that is?"

"I'm sorry. What's the big deal?"

"What's the big deal? It's just about the biggest thing of my life, that's all. Where is it?"

"There, under the lamp."

Kendra saw the letter, then hurriedly tore open the envelope. She read a few lines and let out a whoop of excitement.

"What is it?" Demaris asked.

"It's from the personnel department. I got the interview! They want me to come in right after I graduate."

"So, my roommate is going to be a newspaper-woman," Demaris said. Suddenly she smiled and struck a pose. "I know. You can interview me after I become a movie star. You can ask me what it's like to kiss Alphonso Delavente."

"Lights out, girls, lights out!" Mrs. Pynchon called from out in the hallway.

Little by little, room by room, the dorm grew quiet as the students settled into their beds. Kendra climbed into her bed and pulled the sheet up under her chin, then looked across the moonlit room at her roommate, who was also crawling into bed.

"Demaris, do you ever stop to think that when we graduate in three more weeks, our lives will be changed forever?"

"How?"

"Well, for one thing, we'll be out into the world, on our own. Our girlhood will be over."

Demaris snorted. "Honey, I lost my 'girlhood' when I was sixteen."

"You're awful," Kendra said, laughing. Then a moment later she asked, "To Morris?"

"To Morris? That drip? Heavens no."

"Then who?"

"Why are you so curious?"

"I'm gong to be a newspaperwoman, remember? Curiosity is my stock-in-trade."

"And you are going to write about it?"

"Of course. You're going to be a movie star, aren't you? People like to know such things about movie stars."

"No, they don't really want to know. Once they find out some scandal on a movie star, they drop them. I don't want that to happen to me."

"Then I shall write only sweetness and light about you," Kendra said.

"Oh, no, you mustn't do that, either. You must give them a *hint* of scandal. After all, they do like to fantasize, you know."

"Yes, don't we all?" Kendra mused.

"You fantasize? I thought I was the only one around here who did that."

"Of course I do. It's just that our fantasies take different paths," Kendra explained. "In my fantasy, I write a story that's picked up by the Associated Press and run on the front pages of newspapers all across America. In your fantasy, you are the toast of Hollywood."

Demaris chuckled. "Not always," she said. "Sometimes I fantasize about Mario."

"Mario?"

"Mario Conti."

"Who is he? I've never heard of him."

"He used to work for my father. He had dark hair and black, flashing eyes. He was about twenty-two or twenty-three then."

"Then?"

"When it happened," Demaris said.

"Oh!" Kendra gasped. "*He* was the one!"

"Yes."

They were silent for a long moment; then Demaris spoke again, this time in a quiet, almost contrite voice.

"Kendra, you'll never say anything about it, will you?"

"No, no, of course not," Kendra promised.

"I've never told a soul," Demaris said. "There have been times when I wanted to, but I've kept it secret all these years."

"Demaris?"

"Yes?"

"Thank you for trusting me."

CHAPTER FOUR

Demaris Hunter was easily the most popular girl in school. It wasn't just because she was beautiful, though she certainly was that. She had blond hair, crystal-blue eyes, fashionably high cheekbones, and the lean, sleek, almost boyish figure so sought after by all the other girls. It wasn't because she was rich, either, because Jefferson University was full of the daughters of wealthy men. Demaris was so popular because she was funny without being offensive, daring without being foolish, and friendly without being gushy. Her smile was genuine, and her compliments were sincere. She was totally democratic in the relationships she cultivated, and those students who came from the poorest circumstances didn't feel in the least patronized by her friendship.

If someone—male or female—wanted to select a person who they felt best represented the quintessential student in the marvelous decade of the twenties, they might well have chosen Demaris. She was not only pretty and popular, she also epitomized a sense of the fun of being young. Nothing exemplified that fun more than Demaris's car—a rakish little canary-yellow two-seater Auburn that had red leather seats, balloon tires, and chrome exhaust headers snaking out of each side of the sloping hood. Its six-cylinder engine made the car capable of doing over one hundred miles per hour on a suitable road, and though Demaris had never driven the car that fast, there was no doubt in anyone's mind that she might try it if dared.

The car was a gift from her father, an investment broker who had made millions of dollars for his clients and himself in the booming stock market. He had hoped by his gift to persuade Demaris to conduct herself in a more decorous manner. The very nature of the gift, however, proved to be counterproductive to his plan, and the sight of the sleek, yellow Auburn racing about with a wildly beautiful girl at the wheel and laughing young men and women hanging on for dear life became quite a common sight on the streets of St. Louis.

Such as now.

Demaris turned off Lindell Boulevard with her tires squealing and Kendra Mills, her only passenger, holding on to keep from bouncing out.

"Are you okay?" Demaris shouted into the wind.

"I'm fine," Kendra answered. She laughed. "I don't know which is the bigger thrill, riding with you or flying with Mr. Rockwell. Must you go so fast?"

"Yes, I must," Demaris said as she slid to a stop in the gravel-covered student parking lot at the university. "Don't forget, we have to get ready for the dance tonight."

"*You* have to get ready, you mean," Kendra said.

Demaris turned off the key, and the engine died. The sudden quiet after all the engine and wind noise seemed almost alien. "You're going too, aren't you?" she asked.

"No, I don't think so."

"Kendra, don't be silly. It'll be loads of fun, really."

"I don't have a date. And I've no intention of going alone."

"Oh, pooh, is that all that's bothering you?" Demaris asked. "Well, don't you worry about that. I can fix you up in no time."

"No, thank you. I don't need to be 'fixed up.'"

"Listen, a blind date is no big deal," Demaris said reassuringly. She giggled. "I've been on lots of them. They're scads of fun; you never know who you're going to get, or what he's going to look like."

"That's my point."

"Silly girl! I'm going to take care of it for you," Demaris insisted. "Do you think I'd let my roomie get stuck with a flat tire? Not on your life, kiddo. Trust me."

"I don't know . . . ." Kendra hedged.

"Come on; what do you have to lose? Even if you don't hit it off, you'll have fun. And you have to admit, it'd be better than staying in the dorm, studying, wouldn't it?"

Kendra laughed. "I guess you're right," she said.

"Of course I'm right. Now, come on. Let's beat it over to the dorm. I'll make a few calls, and you'll be all set."

The girls had to cross the campus to get to their dormitory. The center lawn of the campus, a grassy plaza called the quad, was crowded with students. It was a beautiful spring afternoon, perfect for lying or sitting around on the grass, and hundreds were taking advantage of the opportunity. Over near the sidewalk a group of students was gathered around a radio, its tulip-shaped speaker spilling out the music of Rudy Vallee.

Other students were gathered around what was known as Statue Circle, an area set off from the rest of the plaza by a one-hundred-foot-diameter circle made of whitewashed stones. Its name came from the two statues inside the enclosure, the dominant one that of Jefferson's founder, Professor Henry Spengeman, and a smaller one of Spengeman's successor, Professor William Bateman.

The Spengeman statue, done by Rodin in the style of his own famous work, *The Thinker*, was three times life size and depicted the professor sitting in a chair, resting his chin upon his right hand, while in his left he held a book. The chair was sitting on a large concrete pedestal on which a brass plaque was mounted that read: IN MEMORY OF PROFESSOR HENRY R. SPENGEMAN, OUR BELOVED FOUNDER AND FIRST PRESIDENT, 1853-1881.

Bateman, the man generally credited with turning the school from a small regional college into a nationally recognized university, had been honored with a life-size statue. Also made of bronze, it depicted him standing and leaning forward slightly, his hands resting on a brass rail as he stared out over the campus. A brass plaque said: PROFESSOR WILLIAM T. BATEMAN. KEEPING WATCH. PRESIDENT, 1881-1918.

The area inside Statue Circle was hallowed territory that was reserved for seniors only, and several of them were enjoying the privilege. A young man in a raccoon coat was singing and playing a ukelele, entertaining those who had gathered around him. Kendra saw a hip flask being passed between the students. Laughing, one of the students held it up toward the statue of Spengeman by way of a toast; then he held the flask up to Bateman's lips, as if the professor were taking a drink with them. By tradition, no one ever bothered Spengeman's statue. Bateman's statue, however, was fair game and was almost always decorated in accordance with the times. He was ideal for pranks, and during the rush season he could inevitably be found wearing the beanie of one of the fraternities. At other times there might be a Jefferson U. pennant tucked under his arm, or he might be wearing a green sweater with a red letter J. Today he was holding a pennant, wearing a raccoon coat, and sporting a red and green scarf.

Another reason no one ever bothered the Spengeman Statue was that it was under the special watch of an elite group known as the Quad Quad. The Quad Quad had been started over twenty years ago by four young men who, by popularity, social position, and athletic and academic achievement, had established themselves as the crème de la crème of the senior class. Because the foursome regularly gathered at the campus quadrangle, they took to calling themselves the quad quad. Now, a far cry from the informal, self-appointed group, membership in the Quad Quad was the greatest honor that could be bestowed on any senior, and the four young men holding that honor were elected by their class from among a list of candidates put forth by the faculty. Under penalty of demerits, only a member of the Quad Quad could even touch the statue of Professor Spengeman.

When Kendra and Demaris reached their dormitory, they found it a madhouse of activity, with its residents running up and down the hallways, borrowing hairbrushes, stockings, and tubes of lipstick. Music spilled out from the record players of two or three of the rooms, each song different and fighting for dominance not only with the other songs, but with the rest of the noise. The two young women hurried into their room, leaving open the door so they could partake in the shouts and laughter and bits and pieces of conversation and banter that flew back and forth between the rooms.

"What do you think about this dress?"

"Oh, you are just too, too divine!"

"Wear these shoes. They're the bee's knees."

"They say Ellen broke up with Joe Harvey. I wonder if he'll be there. Oh, he is such a dreamboat!"

Suddenly there was a loud squeal of delight; then footfalls came running down the hall and an excited face poked inside Kendra and Demaris's room.

"Demaris! Kendra! Guess what?" the girl shouted. "You'll never guess!"

"What?" Demaris asked, looking up from the mirror.

"I just heard from my father! He's on the Veiled Prophet Committee. You and I have both been selected as Veiled Prophet handmaidens! Just think, Demaris, one of us might be the next Goddess of Love and Beauty! Isn't it wonderful?"

"Yes," Demaris said, smiling brightly.

"I've got to go tell the others!" The girl continued on down the hall, while Demaris turned back to the mirror to resume applying her makeup.

"I must say," Kendra said, "*you* don't seem too excited about it."

"I'm not," Demaris replied.

"But isn't it quite an honor?"

Demaris shrugged. "Not particularly."

"Oh, but I'd think that it would be."

"You aren't from St. Louis, so you don't understand the concept. The Veiled Prophet Ball is just a game played by wealthy fathers to make certain their daughters are introduced into *proper* society, make the *proper* connections, and then marry *properly*." Each time Demaris said the word "proper," she came down hard, mocking it.

"What's wrong with that?"

"Nothing, I suppose, if you want to stay in St. Louis and be *proper* for your whole life." Demaris shrugged again, then turned back to the mirror and began plucking an eyebrow—though, as far as Kendra could see, Demaris's brows were already perfect.

"And you don't want to be proper?" she asked.

"No longer than I have to be."

"I know. You want to go to Hollywood and kiss Alphonso Delavente."

Demaris smiled. "Not just Alphonso Delavente. I want to kiss *all* of them," she said. She pursed her lips and mugged into the mirror. "I want to be known as Hollywood's hottest kisser."

"Hollywood's hottest kisser," Kendra repeated. "Hardly a suitable ambition for someone of your intelligence."

"By suitable, don't you mean proper?" Demaris asked.

Kendra laughed. "Well, I suppose I do. Although I could also say mature."

"You're the mature one, Kendra Mills, not me," Demaris said, examining her reflection critically. "Sometimes you act as if you're twenty years older than the rest of us."

"Is that so bad?" Kendra asked, shaking her head in confusion.

"It's very bad," Demaris answered. She peered at her roommate's reflection, then asked, "You haven't learned the secret yet, have you? Men don't want mature women. They want little girls and no responsibility. Playthings," she added. "Why do you think we go to so much trouble to flatten our breasts? It's because big breasts remind men of their mothers, and mothers they absolutely do not want."

"Well, thank you Miss Hunter for my lesson in psychology," Kendra said coolly, pushing up her glasses.

"Don't be upset," Demaris said. "I'm just telling you this for your own good. You can call it psychology if you want. I call it practical advice on landing a modern man."

"Suppose I don't want a modern man?"

"Of course you do," Demaris said. "Everyone does. Oh, that reminds me. Guess who your blind date is?"

"I have no idea."

"Mark Peters. You know who he is, don't you? He played halfback last year."

"Yes, of course I know who he is."

"Didn't I tell you I'd pick a dreamboat for you?"

"I thought he was engaged."

"No more. That's all over," Demaris said. "He's on the market, kiddo, and you are the first shopper."

"My, my. Well, will I get to examine his teeth and pat him on the derriere?"

Demaris laughed loudly. "I think that would be a great idea," she said.

"By the way, what does Morris think of you going to Hollywood?"

Morris Montgomery was Demaris's "steady," and Kendra thought them a natural pair, for Morris matched Demaris in popularity and was considered the BMOC— Big Man on Campus. He was extremely handsome and, because his father was a very successful criminal lawyer, came from a background of wealth.

"He knows it's what I want to do," Demaris said. "But I don't think he thinks I'm really serious." She chuckled. "Of course, neither do my parents nor anyone else. But I tell you, kiddo, there are going to be some shocked people around here when I make my big departure."

"Come on, you two!" someone shouted from the hall. "You're going to be late."

The dance was held in the gymnasium. The Art Club had decorated it, using "The Haunted Mansion" as their theme. The place was filled with bed-sheet ghosts, painted skeletons, and cardboard witches and tomb-stones, strategically located around the dance floor. The centerpiece was a large, papier-mâché black widow spider that hung from an elaborately woven spiderweb. The red hourglass on the black widow's abdomen was a red lightbulb that blinked on and off.

Technically there was no liquor, for this was Prohibition, but liquor had always been against the rules at college dances, so this was no different from any other time . . . and, like every other time, liquor was available, concealed in long, thin bottles slipped down inside canes, or in neat silver flasks that were flat enough to ride inconspicuously in one's hip or breast pocket.

Kendra's date for the evening, Mark Peters, was a handsome man and, because he had been a football hero, very popular. He was also wealthy. His father was president of the River Commerce Bank, so he was considered a very good catch. Several of the other girls looked at Kendra with envy when she arrived at the dance on Mark's arm. Halfway through the evening, however, she would have willingly given Mark up to any of them. He was, she decided, far too full of himself.

When Demaris and Morris left the dance later that night for a forbidden but exciting tour of the city's "speaks," Kendra and Mark went with them, though if she had been given her choice, she would have gone back to her room. It wasn't that she was opposed to going to a speakeasy; it was the idea of going with tittering, squealing college kids that she found disagreeable. In truth, though Kendra was no older than the rest of them, Demaris was right. In Kendra's attitude and demeanor she was, and always had been, much more mature than her peers.

"I think I should warn you that the fellows who run this place are genuine gangsters," Morris whispered as they found a table in the Purple Orchid club. Because of his father's profession, Morris could truthfully claim some intimacy with the facts of who was a gangster and who wasn't.

"Oh, how scandalous!" Demaris exclaimed excitedly.

"But, if you stop to consider it, we're gangsters too," Morris continued. "After all, drinking is illegal."

"Morris, is it true that the owner of this club has actually had men killed?" Mark asked.

"That's what my father says," Morris replied. "And he ought to know."

The others shuddered with excitement.

The Purple Orchid was almost as large as the gym had been, though half of it was covered with tables, leaving only half open for dancing. A full pit orchestra, complete with strings and oboes and an entire array of percussion instruments, provided the music. A huge mirrored ball hung from the ceiling, and as it rotated, it projected hundreds of tiny stars around the ballroom. The band, the people who were gyrating on the dance floor, and even those patrons just sitting at the tables became participants in this man-made galaxy.

"Isn't this the cat's pajamas?" Demaris asked breathlessly. "Don't you just love coming here like this?"

"What's the difference between this place and where we just were?" Kendra asked. "We had music, liquor, and dancing there, just like here."

"Oh, Kendra, really. As if you don't know," Demaris chided. "Come on, Morris. Let's dance," she urged, leading her date onto the dance floor.

"Kendra, I want you to know that you don't have to

be frightened," Mark said solicitously. "I'll protect you."

Kendra looked at Mark and for a moment had a mental image of him doing battle for her. She found the idea humorous and she grinned. "Thanks," she said dryly.

Mark, misinterpreting the smile, swelled importantly. "It's only right that I should do so."

The opportunity for Mark to make good on his promise came much sooner than he had undoubtedly anticipated when a pock-faced man with red hair and beady gray eyes came over to the table to ask Kendra to dance.

"Thank you for asking me," Kendra replied politely, "but I feel it wouldn't be correct for me to leave my friends."

"Your friends can wait," the man said gruffly.

"Thank you, no."

"What's the matter? Somebody like me not good enough for a bunch of rich college kids like you?"

Mark stood up then. He was bigger and stronger than the man who was making a pest of himself and obviously felt no fear in expressing himself.

"You heard the lady, mister," Mark said. He pointed to the table where the man had come from. "Now, why don't you just go back over to your table like a good fellow, and leave us alone?"

"I wasn't talkin' to you, sonny," the man snapped. "I was talkin' to the dame, here. How about it, honey? Just one little dance." He reached out for her, but that was as far as he got.

"I said, go away and leave us alone!" Mark said, more sharply this time. He gave the man a shove, pushing him so hard that he fell against the next table.

Seeing the trouble, Demaris and Morris left the dance floor and returned to their friends. Their presence seemed to add fuel to the gangster's fire. "Well, now, aren't you the snot-nosed, Joe-college son of a bitch?" the man growled at Mark, getting up quickly. "I'll just bet you play football, don't you, sonny?"

"As a matter of fact I do," Mark answered. "So if you

know what's good for you, you'll be smart and leave us alone."

The man put his hand inside his jacket pocket. "You don't know who you're messin' around with, Mr. Football Hero."

"Maybe the young man doesn't know who you are, but I do," a new voice said. "Your name is Eddie Quick. And now that I've said it aloud, Mr. Quick, everyone else in here knows who you are, too. Under the circumstances, do you really want to do something in front of so many people?"

Kendra turned toward the voice. The man who had just spoken was, she guessed, in his midfifties. He was a small man, nearly bald, with an oversized nose and close-set eyes accented by wire-rim glasses. In appearance he was totally unimpressive; but his voice had the quiet confidence of someone who was used to being listened to.

"You'd best be stayin' out of this, mister," Eddie Quick said. He pointed to Mark. "I'm goin' to teach this here college boy a lesson he won't be learnin' in no class."

"Try it and I'll mop up the floor with you," Mark countered. He had either not seen Eddie Quick's hand dip to the inside of his jacket or didn't know the significance of it. "And you, sir," Mark said to the man who had intervened, "I appreciate your concern, but I don't need any help. You'd better stay out of it, or you'll get hurt."

"Mark," Kendra said, pulling on her date's sleeve. "Mark, leave it alone." She had recognized the small man. He was Thomas Petzold, publisher of *The St. Louis Chronicle*. She had also understood Eddie Quick's maneuver.

"No," Mark said. He grinned, clearly relishing his moment upon the stage. "This fellow started it. I'm going to give him the chance to finish it."

"Well, now, punk, that's just what I'm plannin' to do. I'm goin' to finish it!" Quick reached inside his jacket

again, and when his hand came out this time, it was
wrapped around a gun.

"Oh, my God!" Demaris gasped. A few other women
screamed when they saw the gun in Quick's hand, and
the band, just now realizing that they had lost their
audience, quit playing. The music fell off in a few
ragged, discordant bars, and the huge room, which a
moment before had been full of music and the excited
buzz of conversation, was silent except for the heretofore
unnoticed squeak of the rotating mirrored ball. The
hundreds of tiny dots of light now played on faces drawn
into expressions of anxious intensity.

"Well, now, what about it, sonny? Are you still the
hero?" Quick asked, opening and closing his fingers on
the butt of his pistol.

"Mr. Quick," Petzold said to the gangster, "how
many of us are you prepared to shoot tonight?"

"Just the football hero here," Quick replied, pointing at Mark.

"Uh-uh," the older man said, shaking his head.
"That won't do. If you shoot him, then you're going to
have to shoot the young people with him as well. And
then you'll have to shoot me and the guests at my table.
After that, you'll have to shoot everyone in this room.
Otherwise, someone is sure to identify you. Do you have
that many bullets, Mr. Quick? Do you think you can get
everyone before they get away?"

"Who the . . . who the hell are you?" Quick asked
in frustration.

"My name is Thomas Petzold."

"Well, let me tell you, Petzold. You've got a bad
habit of buttin' in where it's none of your business."

"Oh, but butting in *is* my business," Petzold corrected. He smiled. "You see, I own *The St. Louis
Chronicle*, and unless you want everything you do here
tonight published in tomorrow's paper, you will put your
gun away."

"What the hell do I care what's published in tomorrow's paper?"

"Maybe you don't care, Eddie, but I certainly do,"

another, authoritative voice said. "Would you kindly be puttin' your gun away and quit makin' a bigger fool of yourself than you already have? These are our customers you're botherin'." The man giving the orders was short and stout, with a red face and thinning hair.

"That's Paddy Egan," Morris whispered to the others. Kendra had heard of him; he was the most notorious underworld figure in St. Louis.

"Mr. Egan, I'm not goin' to be takin' guff off some young punk like—"

"I said they're our customers, Eddie," Egan interrupted, his light-blue, piercing eyes boring into Quick. "And we'll not be frightenin' our customers. What kind of business would that be, now? You be a good lad and do what I tell you. Put the gun away, and go back into my office and cool yourself for a spell."

Eddie sighed, then put his pistol away as directed. "Whatever you say, Mr. Egan." He pointed at Mark. "But you. You'd better be watchin' that smart young mouth of yours. One of these days you'll say somethin' to someone when you don't have a bunch of people around to protect you." He flashed an evil grin. "And I hope that someone'll be me."

"Eddie," Egan growled.

"Yes, sir, Mr. Egan, I'm goin'," Quick said compliantly.

Egan arranged his face in what might have been a smile. He held out his hand toward Kendra's table. "You folks please sit back down and enjoy the evenin'," he urged. "I'm goin' to send over a bottle of our best champagne with my compliments."

"Thank you, Mr. Egan," Morris said. Nervously, the four sat back at their table and the band, after a short, insistent signal from Egan, resumed playing.

"Wasn't that Mr. Egan a nice man?" Demaris asked.

"A nice man?" Kendra replied, snorting. "Demaris, did you see his eyes? They were the most frightening eyes I've ever looked into. That man is evil—pure and unadulterated evil."

"Oh, he isn't so bad," Mark said. "What do you think, Morris?"

"He's one of my father's clients," Morris said. "It would be inappropriate for me to comment."

Thomas Petzold walked over to their table then and told them, "I'm about to leave. But before I do, I want to apologize for butting in like that."

"You don't have to apologize, Mr. Petzold," Morris said. "We appreciate your help."

"It's just that I know a little something of Eddie Quick, and it looked to me as if he was getting a bit hot under the collar. And to be quite honest, I was getting frightened."

"I appreciate what you were trying to do, Mr. Petzold," Mark said. "But as I said, I could have handled him all right."

"Oh, Mark, don't be a goose," Demaris said. "The man had a gun."

"He wouldn't use that gun," Mark insisted. "It was only for show."

"Do you read my paper, Mr. Peters?" Petzold asked. "You *are* Mark Peters, aren't you? The football player?"

"Yeah," Mark said, smiling broadly at being recognized. "Yeah, that's me."

"Do you read my paper, Mr. Peters?" Petzold asked again.

"Sure, I read it. That is, I read the sports page and the funny papers." He laughed. "I like *Mutt and Jeff.*"

"Yes, well, if you ever read any of the rest of the paper, you'd know that Eddie Quick has already used his gun several times."

"Then why isn't he in jail?"

Petzold chuckled, then nodded toward Morris. "Oh, because Mr. Egan, the owner of this club, is able to hire very good lawyers like this young man's father to keep his men and himself out of jail," he said.

"It makes no difference. I'm sure that if anybody wants to start anything, I can take care of myself and my friends," Mark insisted.

"Mark, you *are* an overbearing oaf, aren't you?" Kendra said. "Thank you, Mr. Petzold. We really do appreciate what you did for us."

"Yes, that goes for me, too," Demaris added.

A waiter arrived then, carrying a silver ice bucket. With a dramatic flourish he pulled away the towel, revealing a bottle of bonded champagne.

"For you and your friends, Mr. Montgomery, compliments of Mr. Egan," the waiter said.

"Ah, good. And now the fun begins," Morris said, lifting the bottle.

"Listen, I'm afraid all of this has given me a terrible headache," Kendra muttered. "If you don't mind, I think I'd like to go home."

"Go home? What do you mean, go home? Kendra, the party is just getting started!" Mark complained. "Do you expect me to just take you home and leave our friends like this?"

"You don't have to leave," Kendra said. "I'll call a cab."

"Young lady, I'm about to take my guests home," Thomas Petzold put in. "They live out on Lindell Avenue, quite near the university. You *are* going to the university, I assume?"

"Yes, I am."

"Then would you allow me to drop you off?"

"Oh, would you, Mr. Petzold? Yes, thank you, that would be very nice," Kendra said.

"Kendra, do you want me to come with you?" Demaris asked.

"Wait a minute, Demaris. You aren't going too, are you?" Morris protested.

Kendra smiled and put her hand out to her friend's shoulder. "You don't need to, Demaris," she said. "Stay and enjoy yourself." She looked over at Mark. "I'm sure you'll all be perfectly safe. After all, you do have Mark to look after you," she added, unable to resist the gentle gibe.

"Yeah, you'll be fine," Mark said, clearly not catching the sarcasm.

If it had been lost on Mark, it was obvious to Petzold, who smiled broadly, then asked, "Shall we, Miss . . . ?"

"Kendra Mills, and I'm ready when you are."

Kendra didn't actually have a headache; she simply had no desire to stay and had used that as an excuse to get away. The fact that Thomas Petzold had offered her a ride home was a bonus. Since he was the man she hoped to work for, this would be an excellent opportunity to meet him.

"Allow me," Petzold said, offering her his arm and escorting her out of the club.

Petzold's car was a Lincoln limousine. His chauffeur sat in an open front seat, while the rear of the car was enclosed. The "saloon" part of the car had two facing, plushly upholstered sofa-type seats. Kendra sat beside Petzold facing forward, while Petzold's two guests—a distinguished-looking older man and his wife—sat across from them, facing to the rear.

"That was very close to being unpleasant," the gentleman who was Petzold's guest said. It was the first time Kendra had heard him speak, and she noticed that he spoke with a decided accent, more specifically a Yiddish accent.

"Yes, it was," Petzold agreed. "Miss Mills, I realize that you're probably wondering what such fine, upstanding people as us were doing in a place like that," Petzold remarked as the car started off. "And the only way I can answer that is to say that, like many Americans, we sometimes wink our eyes at the noble experiment of Prohibition. I hope you'll not think evil of us."

"How could I find fault with you for being there?" Kendra replied, laughing. "I was there, too, remember?"

"Ah, yes, to be sure. Then, to avoid any further embarrassment, suppose we all pretend that we were there only to listen to the fine orchestra," the publisher suggested. Kendra laughed appreciatively. Petzold introduced her to his guests, Mr. and Mrs. Chaim Gelbman. Gelbman was the owner of Gelbman's Department

Stores, generally considered St. Louis's largest and finest.

"Have you shopped in my husband's stores, young lady?" Golda Gelbman asked.

"Yes, I have, Mrs. Gelbman, and you'll be happy to know that I'm a most satisfied customer," Kendra said. "Though I'm afraid my father feels that I spend far too much money in your family's stores," she added.

Chaim Gelbman chuckled. "I hope I have not made an enemy of your father," he said. "Enemies I do not need."

"Your merchandise is good and fairly priced," Kendra said. "You can't make enemies that way."

Gelbman beamed. "You are a smart girl who knows the right words to say," he told her. "So, you are studying at Jefferson University?"

"Yes."

"It is a fine school. Our son, David, is a graduate of Jefferson."

"Oh, David Gelbman. Yes, of course. I know him. That is, I know *of* him. He was one of the founders of the Quad Quad," Kendra said.

"Yes, the Quad Quad. I remember him speaking of it. But it was a thing of such little consequence. How is it that you know of it?"

"Like many things with simple beginnings, the Quad Quad has become quite an honored institution at our school," Kendra explained. "As a freshman I had to learn its history. Where is your son now?"

"He lives in Vienna with his wife and family," Gelbman answered. "I wish he would return to America, but he likes it there, and he must make his own life. His friend, Bob Canfield, was also a part of this group. Do you know about him?"

"Oh, yes," Kendra replied. "Everyone knows about Mr. Canfield—*and* about his generosity to the school."

"Did you know, also, that one of the original Quad Quad members worked for me?" Petzold asked.

"Terry Perkins, you mean," Kendra replied. "Yes, of course I know that. After all, you endowed the School of

Journalism in his name. I've often been curious about him. I've read some of his stories, of course."

"I believe Terry Perkins would have become one of the finest newspapermen ever, had he lived long enough to realize his potential," Petzold said, sighing sadly.

"You can say that, even though he worked for you for such a short time?" Kendra asked.

"Yes, unequivocally."

"Do you believe he was better than Eric Twainbough?"

"Well, now, what do you know of Eric Twainbough?"

Kendra chuckled. "For one thing, I know he married Tanner Tannenhower and they have a baby," she said.

"Yes, they did, didn't they? Do you know her, by the way? I believe she graduated from your school."

"Yes, I do know her. She's a lovely person. I can see why Mr. Twainbough was taken with her."

"But don't you think she's a bit young for him? She is barely twenty-three, and he's in his midthirties, I believe."

Kendra shook her head. "I don't believe chronological age has anything to do with whether or not two people can fall in love. Do you?"

"I don't know. I've never fallen in love," Petzold admitted.

"Neither have I," Kendra said. "I was speaking in the abstract."

"I'm sorry. I didn't mean my response to be flippant," Petzold said quickly. "And I do hope you're right, for I very much want them to have a successful marriage. I like Eric very much. And, as a matter of fact, I am Tanner's godfather. But, to get back to Eric's work, are you familiar with it?"

"I studied his articles in the journalism file at school. That's why I'd be interested in your comparison of him and Perkins."

"I'm not sure I can make such a comparison. They're vastly different types of writers, so comparing them may be like comparing apples and oranges. You see, Twainbough's real ambition is to be a novelist, and his writing reflects that style. Terry, on the other hand, never wanted to be anything more than a good newspaperman."

"Some of the pieces Twainbough wrote while he was in Russia were absolutely brilliant," Kendra said.

"You're right, those pieces were brilliant, and I'd have to say that he is the best writer I've ever employed."

"But I thought you just said Terry Perkins was."

Petzold smiled and held up his finger. "No, my dear, I said Terry was the best *newspaperman*."

"Oh, I see." Kendra smiled. "Yes, I think I understand."

"Do you? Really?"

"Yes. If you want to know who, what, and where, read Terry Perkins. If you want to know how and why, read Eric Twainbough."

Petzold laughed. "What a perfect way to put it. Yes, you *do* understand the difference between a writer and a newspaperman. And now that brings up the question, which are you?"

"Which am I?"

"You *are* the same Kendra Mills who has an appointment for an interview with my personnel staff, aren't you?"

Kendra gasped. "You know about my interview?"

"Yes, of course I know. I'm the boss, remember?"

"I just didn't expect you to . . . I mean, with so many important things to do, I wouldn't have thought you pay attention to every application."

"Your application was particularly called to my attention by the head of the Journalism Department," Petzold said. "Now, answer my question: Are you a newspaperman or a writer?"

Kendra smiled. "I'm a newspaper*woman*," she said.

"Then you have the job. Report for work as soon as school is out."

"But the interview?"

"My dear, it sounds to me as though you just had it," Chaim Gelbman put in, chuckling. "And, Thomas, as long as you continue to hire bright people like this young lady, my advertising business you will always have."

The car soon stopped in front of the Gelbman house.

"Well, so quickly we are here," Golda Gelbman said. "Thomas, we thank you very much for the entertaining evening. And it was a pleasure to meet you, Miss Mills."

"I could not agree more," her husband added, smiling at Kendra.

"The pleasure was all mine," Kendra responded.

The chauffeur was holding open the rear door for the Gelbmans, and they stepped out. When the car started up again, Petzold instructed his driver to head for Kendra's dormitory, six blocks away.

"The Gelbmans are very nice," Kendra remarked.

"They are very lonely," Petzold replied.

"Lonely?"

"They are Jewish, and family is very important to them. But their only son and their grandchildren are in Austria. They are all alone here."

"Do you have family here, Mr. Petzold?"

"Me? Oh, uh, no." He coughed, and Kendra had the feeling it was to cover his embarrassment. "But I've never been married, and I have no children, so it isn't the same."

"I'm sorry. Please forgive me for asking such a personal question," Kendra said.

Petzold smiled. "You are a young woman; such questions are the privilege of youth," he said.

"You say that as if you're an old man."

"I'm in my fifties," Petzold said. "Certainly too old to be worrying about such things as children now."

"Oh, but that's not true," Kendra countered. "Why, lots of men in their fifties have fathered children."

"If I were going to do something like that, don't you think it would be better if I had a wife?"

Kendra slapped her hand over her mouth. "I'm

sorry," she said. "I suppose that was a rather foolish pronouncement, wasn't it?"

"Not at all, my dear, not at all," Petzold said, laughing. "I'm finding this conversation absolutely delightful. In fact, I would have to say that meeting you has made this evening extremely pleasant. I only hope your boyfriend doesn't get himself into more trouble tonight."

"My boyfriend?"

"Mr. Peters."

"Oh. He was my date to the graduation dance, but he isn't my boyfriend," Kendra explained.

"He isn't? Well, I guess I just assumed that all young, attractive people had boyfriends and girlfriends. Now it's my turn to apologize for being presumptuous."

"That's okay."

The car slowed, then stopped, and Petzold looked out the window. "Oh, we're at the university already."

"Yes. Thank you very much for the ride," Kendra said. The rear door was opened suddenly by the chauffeur. Kendra started to exit, then paused. "Mr. Petzold, before I take the job you've offered me, I must tell you that I'm not at all interested in writing about women's teas and garden parties and such. I want to do real stories."

"Do you have any ideas about the kind of things you'd like to do?"

"Yes, I have several ideas."

"Listen, would you like to go someplace and have a nice, quiet cup of coffee?" Petzold asked abruptly. "We could talk about this."

"I'd love to," Kendra replied, settling back in.

Petzold smiled at her, then waved his chauffeur back to the driver's seat. The publisher pulled the speaking tube up from the side of the car and instructed, "Wilson, find some café or something that's open. The young lady and I would like to have a cup of coffee."

The car was put in gear, and they drove off.

Petzold leaned back in the seat and looked over at the young woman beside him, and the expression on his face indicated just how much he was looking forward to the prospect of drinking coffee with her.

BERLIN, GERMANY

"Here you are," Simon Blumberg said, handing a bank note to the taxi driver. The fare from Simon's apartment to the cabaret was hundreds of marks. Inflation was progressing at such a pace that the printing presses were barely able to keep up with it, as evidenced by the fact that this particular bank note was printed on one side only. Worse, nearly everyone in Germany had lost their life's savings.

There were many, however, who managed to benefit from the situation. The major industrialists who were involved in international business and finance were able to eliminate long-term debts by paying them off in the worthless German money while maintaining their personal wealth in one of the healthier foreign currencies. And Simon Blumberg, though not an international financier, was, nevertheless, able to live quite comfortably in Berlin on a very small amount of money because his source of income was from outside the country. Once a month Simon received from his cousin David Gelbman in Vienna a letter containing Swiss francs in the equivalent of two hundred American dollars. This money was very stable, and the more inflated Germany's economy became, the more purchasing power Simon's francs gained.

Because of his family connections, Simon was a junior partner in David's very successful Vienna department store. Simon lived in Berlin ostensibly as the Berlin representative for David, and whenever David needed a Berlin contact for something, he would notify Simon. But the truth was, Simon was a representative in name only. He was in Berlin because he was unable to settle down in Vienna.

Simon had lost a leg during the war, but like many other veterans of the Great War, the visible wound was not the most serious wound. Simon had come back from the war moody and morose. He had lost faith—in God, in humanity, and, most of all, in himself. All of his relatives and acquaintances—and they were only acquaintances, for he had no friends left—were as ready to see him leave Vienna as he had been *to* ready to leave. They didn't know how to cope with someone who had gone to war an idealistic young man and had returned an empty shell.

Though he was Austrian, Simon had fought in the German Army during the war because he had been studying at a university in Germany when the war began. It hadn't been unusual for Austrians to find themselves in the German Army—the two nations were closely linked politically, culturally, and, of course, by language—and there had been other Austrians in the unit Simon had been assigned to. The most notable of these was Adolph Hitler, who was now beginning to make a name for himself as a beer hall speaker in Bavarian politics.

Simon had been fitted with an artificial limb, which allowed him to get around quite well, though it was still necessary for him to use a cane. He also walked with a very pronounced limp, but that didn't prevent him from enjoying all that Berlin had to offer. And right now Berlin offered a great deal.

Like the scarred psyches of so many veterans of the war, Berlin, too, had lost its soul. Once the Imperial capital and seat of culture, it was now the hottest fleshpot center since ancient Rome. Its racy nighttime entertainment dealt more openly in sex, liquor, and drugs than anyplace else in the world.

Young cabaret patrons indulged in cocaine, morphine, and torrid sexual affairs with both genders. There were special clubs that catered to lesbians, and there were homosexual clubs where Berlin's leading businessmen and politicians could come and select young male lovers. Far from being underground clubs, they advertised their specialties on posters prominently displayed on billboards and kiosks throughout Berlin.

All over the city nudity flourished in nightclubs, on the stage and screen, and at exclusive small cabarets where topless waitresses in filmy panties allowed themselves to be openly fondled for generous tips. Prostitutes worked the streets without shame. Some wore boots and carried whips, others wore pigtails and carried schoolbooks.

"Ah, good evening, Herr Blumberg," the maître d' said, holding the door open for Simon when he stepped out of the taxi at his favorite cabaret. "It is so good to see you again tonight. I have your table for you, and the show has not yet started."

"If you know where to look, the show never ends," Simon said, pointing to a couple in a booth in the darkened corner. The two were in a tight embrace with their hands groping inside each other's clothes. One wore male clothing, the other female. On the surface it looked like one of the more normal relationships, but Simon knew them both and knew that the one in men's clothes was a woman, while the one in women's clothes was a man.

"Absinthe, as usual?" the maître d' asked.

"Yes," Simon said. He crossed to the table that was now reserved for him on a nightly basis. Moments later a waitress brought him his drink, then leaned over the table, inviting him to put the money between her breasts. Instead, Simon reached up under her skirt and slipped the money into her panties, feeling her pubic hair with the back of his hand.

"Oh, *mein Herr*! You are naughty, naughty tonight," the girl said with a giggle.

"I am naughty every night," Simon said. "Why should this night be any different?"

A few minutes later the members of the band came out. After setting up their music stands and instruments, they played a fanfare; then the room darkened except for a spotlight focused on the center of the stage. The master of ceremonies—wearing a tuxedo, lipstick, rouge, and eye makeup, his hair slicked back—came out from behind the sparkling curtains and held up his hand.

"And now, ladies and gentlemen, for your special entertainment, a new show—presented for the first time tonight—a very special chorus line, consisting of Monica and Ursula, and their friends! So that you will know who is who, Monica is the blonde, Ursula is the brunette." The emcee started to leave, but then he stopped and looked back toward the audience. "Oh, and you must look up here to see who is the blonde and who is the brunette," he said, pointing to his head. He moved his hand to his crotch. "Down here, where all you naughty people will be looking, they are the same."

The audience roared with laughter.

The curtain opened. Monica was on one end of the stage, Ursula on the other. Both women were nude. Between them was a harness arrangement to which was attached a series of full-sized, cardboard-cutout dolls. The arms and legs of the dolls pivoted so they could move, and the harness stretching between Monica and Ursula allowed the figures to move in exact unison with the women's movements. Monica and Ursula could cavort about the stage in such a way as to make it appear as if they were a full chorus line, dancing to the music.

The number continued for several minutes, with Monica and Ursula unabashedly presenting themselves in full-frontal and rear-view nudity to the audience. Finally, to the cheers of the many patrons, the performance ended.

After the show, Simon called the waitress over and, tipping her handsomely, told her he would pay generously to visit one of the women who had just performed.

"Which one, *mein Herr*?"

"I don't care," Simon said.

"I'll make the arrangements."

A few moments later the waitress returned to Simon's table and reported, "The arrangements are made, Herr Blumberg. Go to the end of the hall, the last door on the right."

"Thank you."

Simon picked his way through the smoke-filled and crowded room to the hallway, then down the long, narrow corridor to the door the waitress had indicated. It was closed, and he knocked once, rather sharply.

"Come!" a woman's voice instructed.

Simon stepped into the room, then closed the door behind him. At first he saw no one; then he heard a woman giggle.

"Silly boy, we are over here, behind the curtain," a woman's voice said.

"We?" Simon asked.

"Yes, we. Come over here."

Simon walked over to the beaded curtain and pushed his way through. There, on the double bed, were Monica and Ursula. Both were still nude. Ursula was lying alongside her partner with her head on Monica's shoulder and her hand on one of Monica's breasts. Monica was twisting Ursula's pubic hair around her fingers.

"We are a team," Monica explained. "I hope you don't mind."

"As long as your other friends don't join us," Simon said, pointing to the harness and cardboard cutouts that made up their act.

Monica laughed, then kissed Ursula, sliding her tongue into Ursula's mouth. Ursula returned the kiss and the two women were oblivious to Simon long enough for him to get undressed. By the time the kiss ended, Simon was sitting on the foot of the bed, removing the artificial leg from his left stump.

"Oh, *mein Herr!*" Ursula said, raising up on her elbows and looking at Simon in surprise. "You have no leg!"

"I know," Simon said dryly. He stood on his good leg and faced them, now as naked as they, his aroused condition readily apparent. He smiled broadly. "But, as you can see, I *do* have a cock."

CHAPTER FIVE

"Come babe, come babe, come babe! Fire it in here! Shoot that old apple across the plate!" the catcher shouted.

"No batter, no batter!" the shortstop called.

"Throw it past him, Lenny! You can do it! Throw it past him!" the center fielder yelled, following his command with a series of piercing whistles.

Nearly one thousand spectators jammed the bleachers at Sikeston's Fairground Ballpark, and they leaned forward expectantly as Lenny Puckett went into his stretch.

The Barnstorming All Stars led the Sikeston Stags, one to nothing. The All Stars were made up of professional players, all of whom had played several years in the major leagues, but most of whom were now past their prime. Too old to play in the minor leagues where

86

much younger players were waiting for their own chance to move up, over-the-hill players often formed all-star groups to travel around the country and play local teams. For this they received two thirds of the gate.

The Sikeston Stags, like most local teams, were composed of amateurs, men who played baseball on Saturdays and Sundays but held other jobs during the week. One or two of the Stags had played a little professional ball, but for the most part the team was composed of men who had never received a dime for their efforts and played baseball solely because they loved the game. The star of the Sikeston Stags was Lenny Puckett.

At nineteen, Lenny was the youngest player on the team, a high school graduate who now worked at the Canfield Sawmill, the only surviving sawmill of what had once been southeast Missouri's leading industry. Lenny had won thirty-six games for the Stags last year and twelve so far in the young season this year. Against the All Stars today he had given up only one hit, to a man said to be one of the barred 1919 White Sox players and now playing under an assumed name. That hit had produced the only run in the game. It was now the top of the ninth, and there were two outs.

Lenny already had one strike on the batter, and he was trying to close the door on him so the Stags would have one more chance to make up the run. He whipped the ball toward the plate, but he was a bit too anxious and his throw was high—so high that Del Murtaugh, the catcher, had to stand quickly to make the grab.

Del tossed back the ball with a slow shake of his head.

Lenny grooved the next ball in, and the batter swung from his heels. The ball took off like a shot, heading deep for left field. The left fielder broke toward the ball, then pulled up short as he watched it sail over the fence. Fortunately, it was foul by a couple of inches. Lenny, who had held his breath for the entire flight of the ball, now let it out in a long sigh of relief.

"You were lucky, kid," one of the old pros called

from the visitors' dugout. "But not for long. Gabby's just playing with you."

Determined not to give Gabby Spradling something else to hit, Lenny threw another one that the catcher had to stretch for.

"Ball two!" the umpire called.

The catcher pulled off his mask and, tucking it under his arm, made a slow stroll toward the mound. "Settle down, Lenny," Del said as he handed over the ball. "You've faced this guy three times already today, and you struck him out three times."

Instead of responding to the catcher's words, Lenny looked anxiously toward the stands and asked, "Where's that scout, Del? I heard there was going to be a scout from the big leagues here today, watching us play. Have you seen him?"

"They don't always come up and identify themselves like that," Del said. "Not till after the game's over. They don't want to make you nervous."

"I'm already nervous," Lenny said.

"No need for that. You can handle this guy. Listen, I've got an idea. You've got one to waste, so throw it low and outside—so far out that he won't reach for it. Then come back with your fast ball, high and inside, and put everything you've got on it. I'll try and hang on to it."

"Okay," Lenny agreed.

The catcher went back behind the plate and got into position. Then Lenny threw the ball low and outside.

"Good fast ball, Lenny!" Del called as he tossed the ball back to the pitcher.

"Ha!" Gabby, the batter, said. "Is that what you call his fast ball?"

Lenny stretched, then fired again. This time the ball smoked by the batter so fast that it was already in Del's glove before Gabby was halfway through his swing.

"Steeerike three, you're out!" the umpire shouted, and the spectators in the stands cheered wildly.

"No, *that's* his fast ball," Del said, laughing and rolling the ball back toward the mound as the Stags started coming in from the field.

"Shit! Where'd that come from?" Gabby muttered in disgust as he threw his bat toward the visitors' dugout.

"It came from the cannon this boy has for a right arm," the umpire quipped.

"Lookin' good, Lenny, lookin' good," Max Heckemeyer, the team manager, shouted as the Stags came trotting in from the field. Max worked at the shoe factory now, but he had once played a season with Connie Mack's Philadelphia Athletics.

"Mr. Heckemeyer, where's that scout?" Lenny asked. "Have you seen him?"

"Yeah, I've seen him," Heckemeyer said. "He's here."

"Where?"

Heckemeyer chuckled. "Oh, no, I can't tell you that. He made me promise. But you don't need to worry about him just now. I'll introduce you to him after the game is over."

"Yeah, well, a lot of good it'll do me if we lose," Lenny grumbled. He walked to the end of the dugout, then started studying the bleachers, trying to find an unfamiliar face in the crowd. "I wish I could pick him out," he said, more to himself than aloud.

"Murtaugh, you're up," Heckemeyer called.

"Get a hit, Del," one of the other players said, and Del selected a bat, spit out a wad of tobacco, then started toward the plate.

He hit the ball deep into left field, but the left fielder drifted back in time to haul it down for out number one.

The next player hit a line drive sharply to the right, and the crowd started to cheer, but then they groaned when the All Stars' second baseman made a dive to his left to come up with a sensational catch.

The third batter then struck out, and the game was over.

The crowd began filing out, shouting encouraging remarks to their local nine. But most of the Stags threw their bats or kicked at the dirt. In contrast, the All Stars showed no emotion as they left the field. It was just

another day's work for them. By nightfall they'd be on
the train, heading for another town, another local team,
and another cut of the gate.

Disgustedly, Lenny walked out to the mound to
pick up his glove. If the big-league scout really was here,
he hadn't come down to the dugout to see him. And why
should he, Lenny thought. Scouts wanted winners, and
Lenny hadn't won his game today.

Gabby Spradling, the All Stars' third baseman,
approached Lenny. "You pitched a good game, kid," he
said.

"Thanks," Lenny replied, getting a good look at the
last man he had faced. He hadn't realized until this
moment how old Spradling was. He looked at least forty.
Were all the All Stars that old? It was bad enough losing
today. Had he lost to a bunch of old men? "It wasn't good
enough," he added.

Gabby chuckled. "Depends on what you're talking
about," he said. "It wasn't good enough to win this game
for you, but it was good enough to get you a contract
with the St. Louis Grays. That is, if you're interested."

"What?" Lenny asked, astonished. He looked toward the dugout and saw Heckemeyer walking toward
him, a big grin spread across his face.

"Lenny, I want you to meet Gabby Spradling."

"Yeah, I already met him," Lenny said, confused.

"You met Gabby Spradling the player. Now I want
you to meet Gabby Spradling the scout for the St. Louis
Grays."

"You? But you can't be a scout! You're one of the
players!"

"Where do you think scouts come from?" Gabby
asked with a chuckle.

"I don't know. I guess I never really thought about
it."

"But you *have* thought about playing in the big
leagues, haven't you?" Gabby asked.

"Yeah, sure! I mean, yes, sir," Lenny said. "That's
just about all I *ever* think about."

"Well, so how about it? Would you like to play with the Grays?"

"Yes, sir, you bet I would!" Lenny exclaimed.

"We'll give you twenty-four hundred dollars to finish the season with us. If you do a good job, we'll renegotiate the contract next year."

"Twenty-four hundred dollars? That's . . . that's two hundred dollars a month! That's four times more money than I make working at the sawmill!"

Gabby laughed. "Don't be such a hard bargainer, kid."

"What do you think, Mr. Heckemeyer?" Lenny asked.

"Yeah, Max, what do you think about it?" Gabby asked.

"I can't see St. Louis paying the boy that kind of money for the rest of the season, just to play for one of their farm teams," Heckemeyer said.

"Pretty smart observation," Gabby said. "But the truth is, I don't think they'll be sending Lenny to one of the farm clubs. Hogan's arm is beginning to bother him pretty much regularly now. Mr. Norton wants to try and keep him until after the fourth of July, and then he's got a place for him managing one of our farm clubs. That'll open up a spot in our rotation, and, unless I miss my guess, Lenny can fill it. In the meantime, Lenny, you may as well stay here and work out with Mr. Heckemeyer's team until we call you up. Is that all right with you?"

Lenny bent down and picked up a baseball that was lying on the ground. "Yahoo!" he shouted, throwing the ball toward center field. The ball sailed over the center field wall with as much authority as if it had been energized by Babe Ruth's bat.

"I'll consider that a yes," Gabby said. He smiled broadly and stuck out his hand. "Then we've got a deal. You'll be getting a letter from our home office in St. Louis, confirming the deal. There'll be a contract enclosed, along with traveling money. Your salary starts when you report to the team on July fifth."

"Can I tell the fellas at the sawmill?" Lenny asked.

Heckemeyer chuckled. "Lenny, somethin' like this travels fast. I reckon they'll know all about it long before you get there."

Sikeston, Missouri, was a town that identified itself by the sounds of its industry. As the terminus for one of the earliest railroads west of the Mississippi, the sound of chugging locomotives, clanging bells, and steam whistles was long a part of its heritage. In the fall there was the cannonading of the cotton compress, the booming sound coming from the steam release after the compression of a half-ton of loose cotton into a tightly compacted and banded bale. And there was another sound that had been so much a part of the scene that people noticed it only when it was gone, the screech of saw blades biting into timber.

There was a time in southeast Missouri's history when lumbering was its number-one industry, for practically the entire bootheel of the state was covered with swamp, and that swamp was filled with trees. For a forty-year period following the Civil War woodcutters worked from dawn to dark, standing in small boats and chopping down the trees. America's demand for hardwood had been insatiable, and southeast Missouri produced more of it than any other place in the country.

Reforestation was impossible, however, and the demand eventually exhausted the supply, leaving the swampland barren of just about everything but ugly stumps, infestations of mosquitoes, and cottonmouth snakes.

Southeast Missouri could have become a desolate area had that land not been drained, cleared, and planted, turning land once considered worthless into productive farmland. And though timber was no longer a major industry, enough of it remained in isolated spots to keep at least one sawmill working. That sawmill belonged to Robert Canfield. It had been in his family for three generations, and lumber was the initial source of the Canfield money.

Lenny Puckett worked in that sawmill, and when he went to work the next day, he discovered that Max Heckemeyer had been right. Everyone *did* know the news of his signing with the scout for the St. Louis Grays, and they all found an opportunity to come by and congratulate him.

"You'll be turnin' into a rich baseball player and forgettin' all 'bout us down here at the mill," Julius Coleman shouted over the scream of the giant saw blade. Julius, a big black man, was one of the men who loaded the large logs onto the chute.

"No, I won't forget, Julius," Lenny yelled back. He smiled. "Anyway, don't you want my job? When I leave here for the big leagues, they'll be having to move somebody up. You might as well be the gang foreman."

The log finally split into two pieces, and the piercing wail of the saw died down, replaced by the quiet hum of the big round blade spinning without purchase. The split pieces were repositioned and started through a second time, and the spinning blade bit into wood again, sending out a spray of sawdust and emitting another ear-piercing noise.

"What are you talkin' about, Mr. Lenny? Mr. Travis ain't goin' to be makin' no colored man gang foreman," Julius shouted. "There are white folks workin' on this line, an' he ain't goin' to have no colored man bossin' white folks."

"Sure he will," Lenny said. "You're the best man for the job."

The log was split a second time, and the noise level dropped.

"Don't mean no disrespect, Mr. Lenny, but I'm already the best man for the job. I been here six years, you ain't been here but two."

"You're right," Lenny said. "Which is all the more reason you should have the job. I'll talk to Buddy about it."

"Won't do no good to talk to him about it. Don't you

know he's the Grand Dragon of the KKK? Ain't no need in you talkin' to him about it. Ain't no need at all."

The saw screamed again.

The Ku Klux Klan was very active in southeast Missouri, and several of the white workers at the mill were enrolled as members. Lenny had been approached about joining, and he had even considered it because so many of his friends belonged. He hadn't, though, basically because he wasn't a joiner. And, anyway, the idea of a bunch of grown men running around in sheets seemed rather silly to him—though he had never said as much to Buddy Travis. Travis was his boss, and Lenny figured it probably wouldn't be a very good idea to let him know what he really thought.

But he wasn't afraid to speak his mind to Julius. "What is the KKK anyway," he shouted, "except a bunch of grown men acting like it's Halloween? Actually, it's sort of childish, don't you think?"

"No, sir, Mr. Lenny," Julius replied. "It may be lots of things, but it ain't somethin' I'd call childish."

The last log of this bunch was cut and trimmed, and the saw was shut off for lubrication. The sawmill was silent as Lenny walked into Travis's office, intending to talk to him about moving Julius up when he left.

"Hello, Lenny," Travis said, smiling broadly and greeting him with outstretched hand. "I can't tell you how proud you made all of us. Yes, sir, when you go up to St. Louis, all of us down here are goin' to be listenin' to them ball games on the radio every time you play."

"Thanks," Lenny said. "Listen, Buddy—"

"Wait," Travis said, holding up his hand. He picked up the top piece of paper from a stack on the corner of his desk, and Lenny saw that it was a flyer of some sort. "Next weekend we'll be inductin' some new members into the Klan," Travis explained, giving the flyer to Lenny. "It'd be mighty pleasin' to me if one of 'em was to be you."

Lenny read the flyer. DEFEND LIBERTY AND THE AMERICAN WAY OF LIFE! it proclaimed. JOIN FOUR MILLION OF YOUR WHITE BRETHREN! KEEP AMERICA PURE!

"Thanks, Buddy, but I'm not much of a joiner," Lenny said, handing back the flyer.

"Well, if you change your mind, we'd like to have you," Travis urged. "It'd sure be a feather in our cap, havin' you in our Klavern." He put the flyer on the pile with the others. "Now, what can I do for you?"

Lenny looked out toward the saw line at the workers, black and white, who were taking their short break. He realized then that he was wasting his time. Julius was right. There was no way Buddy Travis would let Julius be the boss over any of the white men, even if Julius was more qualified. And if Lenny broached the subject, he would just make Travis angry.

"Nothing, Buddy." He walked over to the scuttle marked WHITE ONLY and scooped up a dipper of water. "Just came in for a drink is all," he said. At that particular moment Lenny Puckett didn't feel very good about himself.

The big burning cross in the middle of the open field projected a wavering orange light onto the nearby trees.

Boyd McMullen, president of the Commercial Bank of Sikeston, was wearing the white silk robes of the Ku Klux Klan. He was seated with the other officers of the SEMO Klavern on a raised platform in front of the burning cross. Standing in a loose formation to either side of the platform were the rank-and-file members of the Klan, while at rigid attention in front of the platform were the fifteen candidates being presented for membership.

McMullen had been a member of the Klan for just over a year, and he had had mixed feelings when he joined. In the first place he was in his forties now, and, as he had said when he declined the first invitation to join, he was a little too old to be running around in the middle of the night dressed in some Halloween costume, burning crosses, and "howling at the moon." Also, the Klan had a bad name. The state of Oklahoma had actually outlawed the Klan, and if *The St. Louis Chronicle* had its way, Missouri would, too.

However, the Klan was very popular in the Missouri Bootheel, and McMullen liked the things it stood for. He liked the idea of America for Americans, maintaining the purity of the races, and the defense of the Bible. And with such lofty ideas to build upon, he was certain that the image of the Klan could be improved. However, it could never be improved if only the lowest class of people filled its ranks. The Klan needed people like Boyd McMullen—good, solid businessmen with noble ideas and honorable intentions—if it were ever to really become a respectable organization.

Though he didn't speak of it much, McMullen had joined the Klan for another reason: Membership would be good for his bank. Nobody from any of Sikeston's other banks belonged to the Klan, which meant that his bank had the business of every Klan member.

The Grand Dragon of the Knights of the White Gardenia, as the SEMO Klavern called itself, was Buddy Travis. To McMullen, Travis was a perfect example of the improving image of the Klan. Buddy Travis was foreman at the Canfield Mill, and any association with Robert Canfield was good. In addition to the man's responsible job, he was also a Sunday-school teacher at the Salvation Church of Redemption, and he refereed high school basketball games. If the Klan had more people like Travis, McMullen thought, and fewer like the McCorkle brothers—two hooligans from East Prairie—there wouldn't be an image problem. Last week the McCorkle brothers beat up a colored man and burned his barn for no good reason other than that the victim was colored.

Even though Travis worked for Bob Canfield, that didn't mean Canfield approved of the Klan. In fact, McMullen had known Canfield all his life and knew very well that the industrialist hated the Klan and everything it stood for. Nevertheless, having the foreman of his sawmill be the Grand Dragon gave the illusion of

Canfield's approval, and most people wouldn't look beyond that.

The banker thought about his boyhood friend. Twenty years ago Boyd McMullen and Bob Canfield had been business adversaries, each buying up worthless swampland to convert to rich delta farmland. In the intervening years Canfield had built a tremendous fortune. Now, though McMullen was a moderately wealthy man, he was a pauper compared to Canfield. McMullen thought it ironic that he was partly responsible for Canfield's phenomenal success, for by purchasing a piece of land that had blocked Canfield's access to a drainage canal, he had forced Canfield to get control of another access by buying the Puritex Corporation. Now the Canfield-Puritex Corporation was one of the nation's biggest businesses, and Robert Canfield, as the owner and president of the company, was one of the most influential men in America. Boyd McMullen, on the other hand, was just a small-town banker.

"Boyd, are you listenin' to me?"

"What?" McMullen asked, jerked out of his reverie by the question that had been loudly whispered by the man seated beside him.

"I said it's too bad we couldn't get Lenny Puckett to join up," the man whispered. "Folks'd sure sit up and take notice of us if we had a big-league baseball player with us."

"Puckett's not in the big leagues yet," McMullen said.

"Yeah, but he soon will be."

"Shh!" one of the others ordered. "The Grand Dragon is about to speak."

The Grand Dragon, whose scarlet robe identified his lofty position, stood at the front of the platform with his right hand raised. "Would the worthy candidates who are presentin' themselves for admission to our order please raise their right hands and repeat after me?" he intoned.

Immediately, the hands of the candidates were raised. They then repeated in unison the oath administered by their Grand Dragon: "In taking this oath, I hereby accept membership into the mystical realm of the Invisible Empire. I do so in full awareness of my responsibilities to God, country, family, and the white Protestant race. I swear to always be true to the Klan and to my fellow members, to obey its laws and tenets, and to ever hold high the ideal of white supremacy."

"Gentlemen," Travis said at the conclusion of the oath, "it gives me great pleasure to tell you that you are now honored members of the Knights of the White Gardenia, SEMO Klavern, of the National Order of the Knights of the Ku Klux Klan. It is my duty to charge you to keep yourself vigilant and ready always to perform such duties as may be required of you for the good of the Realm. Welcome, boys," he added.

"Yahoo!" one of the candidates shouted.

"Hell, John Henry can wear that mask all he wants," one of the older members said dryly. "All he's got to do is come out with that yell one time, and everybody in the Bootheel'll know who he is."

The others laughed.

"Okay, fellows, we're among friends now," Travis said. "You all can take off your hoods."

Everyone in the field removed their hoods, and the new candidates were revealed for the first time. McMullen looked them over carefully. Four of them, he noticed, did their banking somewhere else. He'd have to pay a call on them tomorrow, to speak to them about loyalty to fellow Klansmen.

ST. LOUIS, MISSOURI

The day dawned clear and clean. Even the smoke emitted from the chimneys did so in tight, twisted ropes so that the entire city sparkled under the morning light.

In an industrial area overlooking the Mississippi River, Bob Canfield stood at the window of his office on the top floor of the Canfield-Puritex Corporation. The window afforded a wonderful view of the river, but more importantly to Bob it overlooked the busy yard five floors below. A network of railroad tracks ran into the complex, and on each of the tracks were dozens of boxcars, some filled, others waiting to be filled. Several trucks were also backed up to the warehouse platform, and like the railroad cars, they were being loaded with outgoing shipments of Puritex products: Corn Toasties, Wheat Flakes, and Rice Pops—products proclaimed in the advertising that Bob purchased in magazines, newspapers, and on billboards across the country as "America's favorite breakfast cereals." More recently Bob was experimenting with advertising on the radio, already sponsoring the radio broadcasts of the St. Louis Grays' baseball games.

In addition to breakfast cereals, Canfield-Puritex produced a full line of animal-feed products for farm and domestic animals. Puritex Puppy Grub and Puritex Cat Banquet were now two of the most popular pet-food products in America.

On the sides of the railroad cars and trucks, painted on the upper corner of the building, and imprinted upon the label of every product to leave this building as well as the four other manufacturing plants across the country was the Canfield-Puritex logo: a square consisting of blue-and-white stripes running diagonally from the lower left to the upper right. Bob had wanted a trademark that could be instantly recognized and easily remembered, and one of Bob's employees had come up with the trademark a few years before. The man, a veteran of the Great War, recalled how easily he could pick out the shoulder patch of his division—the Third Infantry—among all the other shoulder patches. It was simple and striking, and, in fact, a recent newspaper poll had placed the Puritex logo number three in recognition, behind Nipper the curious dog listening to "His Master's Voice" for the Victor Talking Machine Company and the maid brandishing a stick on behalf of Old Dutch Cleanser.

When the breakfast product went national, Bob had seen the need to buy factories in other locations, though St. Louis was still the national headquarters. Actually, it could properly be regarded as an international headquarters since there was also a Canfield-Puritex factory in Canada. But though the company was international in scope, it still hadn't gone public, meaning its stock wasn't being traded on the New York Stock Exchange. Bob Canfield was the sole owner of the company.

The company occupied all of Bob's time now, but he had never lost his interest in agriculture and still owned many acres of prime farmland in southeast Missouri. That land, now managed by Bob's farm manager, L.E. Parker, was broken up and rented out to several individual farmers.

Bob was grateful for his success, and over the years he had managed in one way or another to share his success with others. One of his biggest personal interests was Jefferson University, some three miles across town. Besides building the library named after his brother, Bob was also the largest single contributor to the university's annual fund drive.

He could also be counted on to support other worthy programs within the city of St. Louis, such as the symphony orchestra, the Art League, and the Forest Park Beautification Committee, and he provided money to the half-dozen charitable organizations that helped feed and clothe the needy people of the city.

Bob's wife, Connie, had been a leader in the women's suffrage movement a decade earlier; with the right to vote now granted to women, she had turned her energies toward other deserving programs, such as the Committee for the Preservation of St. Louis Landmarks. While those activities had won the approval of her friends in the country club, some others, like the Committee for Freedom of Artistic Expression, a euphemism for anticensorship, met with somewhat less enthusiasm. Connie was also a member of the D.A.R., having established her right of membership through a great-great-grandfather who had served as a private in a Virginia battalion of Brigadier General Anthony Wayne's brigade. At first Connie was a little embarrassed that her ancestor hadn't been a general or colonel or, at the very least, an officer. But now Connie took a sort of perverse pleasure in the fact that her lofty membership in the organization was founded upon such lowly beginnings as a foot soldier.

Bob and Connie had two sons, John, seventeen, and Willie, who was a year younger. John was solid and practical, like his father; Willie had an irrepressible streak of independence about him, more like his mother. Both boys were excellent athletes, an attribute they got from both their parents.

The buzzer on Bob's desk sounded, interrupting his moment of reverie, and he walked back to the desk to push down on the intercom lever.

"Yes, Miss Thompson?"

"Mr. Tannenhower and Mr. Shaw are here, Mr. Canfield, wondering if you might have time to see them."

Bob hadn't been expecting his visitors and was a bit surprised and curious as to why they were here. "Yes, of course. Send them right in," he replied after a moment.

He walked over to the door to greet them as they arrived. Bob knew them very well, both socially and professionally. John Shaw, in fact, was one of his fellow parishioners at Christ Church. For a moment Bob thought that might have something to do with their visit; then he remembered Ludwig Tannenhower was a Lutheran.

"Hello, Bob," John Shaw said, extending his hand.

"Hello, John . . . Ludwig," Bob responded, shaking their hands in turn. "Come on in and have a seat. Coffee?"

"Yes, thank you," John said.

Bob leaned his head out the door. "Miss Thompson, would you bring us some coffee, please?"

"Right away, Mr. Canfield."

Bob showed his visitors to the seating area in a corner of his large office. The two men opted for the brown leather couch, while Bob took one of the matching chairs opposite them.

"So, Ludwig, what do you hear from your daughter? How does she like married life?" Bob asked.

"Evidently she likes it very much," Ludwig said, easing his big frame onto the sofa. "Her mother and I would like her to come home, of course. Why, we haven't even seen the baby yet! We've offered Mr. Twainbough a good job with our company, but he's determined to be a novelist."

"And Tanner? What does she think of it?"

"She seems to be happy, so what can I do? She won't even take the money I try to send to her. It's almost as if living in near poverty is a great adventure for her."

"Well, I've known Eric Twainbough a long time," Bob said. "If you want my opinion, your daughter has found herself a very good man."

"I am glad to hear you say that," Ludwig replied. "I know who he is, of course. I remember when he wrote stories for the newspaper. Still . . ." Ludwig let the word hang for a moment, then sighed, as if dismissing that subject. "But, John and I didn't come to speak of Tanner and her husband or even of my grandson. We have something else we want to talk to you about."

"Wait," John Shaw abruptly said. He looked toward the door to make sure it was closed. "Is there any chance we can be overheard, Bob?" He pointed to the intercom on Bob's desk. "I mean by that machine?"

"No," Bob answered, "it's off. Why? What's the big secret? What's this all about?"

"Go ahead, Ludwig," John said. "You tell him."

"Bob," Ludwig began, "John and I have been given a singular honor. We have been provided with a list of worthy names, candidates from whom will be selected this year's Veiled Prophet." He paused, then asked, "You do understand the concept of the Veiled Prophet, don't you?"

"A little," Bob said.

"Well, this is the forty-fourth year of the reign of the Veiled Prophet," Ludwig explained, "and as I'm sure you know, each year a worthy St. Louis man is chosen to don the robe and veil of the Veiled Prophet. He is then honored in a gala parade of bands, floats, and marching units, and thus receives his subjects, the citizens of St. Louis, since the entire city turns out for the festivities.

"After the parade the Veiled Prophet chooses, from among a hundred suitable young ladies, the Goddess of Love and Beauty. She reigns at the Veiled Prophet Ball, which is, as you know, the social event of the year, for it's at this ball that young ladies are presented into society." Ludwig sighed. "I had intended that my daughter be introduced this year. But no matter; there are many other worthy young ladies eligible."

Confused, Bob shook his head and shrugged. "Well, as both you gentlemen know, I have no daughters. So I'm not sure where I fit into all this."

"We're coming to that," John said, smiling.

"As you also know, Bob, only the most worthy men are selected as candidates to be the Veiled Prophet," Ludwig continued. "Men who have lived their lives in such a way as to be an inspiration to all others."

"To be selected as the Veiled Prophet is the greatest honor that can be bestowed upon a citizen of St. Louis," John added.

"Yes, I'm sure it would be," Bob agreed.

"And what makes the position truly unique," John went on, "is that the identity of the Veiled Prophet is kept eternally secret. No one, except the Veiled Prophet himself and the two men whose duty it is to make the selection from the list of candidates, will ever know who he is, for he and the selection committee are sworn to secrecy."

"You see," Ludwig explained, "in that way the honor is truly in the event and not in the recognition."

"Yes, I do see," Bob said. "And I approve. So, you want to ask my opinion of some of the names on the list, is that it?"

"No," Ludwig replied. He smiled. "*Your* name heads the list, Bob. We want to appoint you to that exalted position."

"We would like you to be the Veiled Prophet for 1923," John added.

"With the stipulation that no one will ever be told," Ludwig reminded him.

Bob thought about it for a moment; then he smiled broadly. "Gentlemen, never in my life have I been able to keep a secret from my wife."

John laughed. "This is not a problem unique to you, so in their infinite wisdom the originators of the idea decreed that the Veiled Prophet *could* share the honor with his wife."

"Then in that case, if you truly consider me worthy of such an honor, I would deem it a privilege to accept."

Ludwig and John reached out to shake Bob's hand. "The reign of the 1923 Veiled Prophet has begun," Ludwig said solemnly.

CHICAGO, ILLINOIS

Kerry O'Braugh and Johnny Torrio were driving down Michigan Avenue, with Kerry at the wheel. Torrio often asked Kerry to take him for a drive when he had something he wanted to talk over in private, since that way they could say anything they wished without fear of being overheard.

"You like this car?" Johnny asked.

"Are you kidding?" Kerry replied. "A red Dusenberg? What's there not to like?"

"It's yours," Johnny said.

"What?"

"Yeah, go ahead and take it," Torrio said. "I'll have the papers transferred to your name so that it's all legal."

"Gee, Johnny," Kerry breathed. He reached out and touched the dash, then looked through the windshield at the long, polished hood. "It's beautiful! I don't know what to say."

"You've earned it, kid," Torrio said. "You've *more* than earned it. No matter what I asked you to do over the last few years, you've done it. And you've done a good job. Like that liquor-warehouse business at Fusco's

Garage a couple of months ago. That was a neat, clean job. You made me real proud."

"Thanks," Kerry said, feeling emotions he rarely felt. "And not just for the car. Thanks for . . . for everything."

Torrio reached over and ruffled Kerry's hair. "I know what you mean," he said. "But now, kid, comes the hard part."

"What's that?"

"I want you to do somethin' for me. Somethin' you might not understand at first, but believe me, it's important. It's real important, or I'd never ask you to do it."

"I'll do it for you, Johnny."

"You haven't even heard what it is I'm askin' you."

"It don't matter," Kerry replied. "Whatever it is, I'll do it."

"All right, here it is: I want you to get outta Chicago."

Kerry's head whipped around. "What?"

"Hear me out," Torrio said, holding up his hand to still any protest. "I want you to leave Chicago and go down to St. Louis."

"Johnny, if that's what you want I'll do it," Kerry said. "I said I would and I will. But I'd like to know why."

"All right, that's only fair. A few years ago when I brought Capone out here from New York, I figured he'd be my right-hand man. Not my equal, my right-hand man. But Capone"—Torrio paused for a moment, then sighed before he went on—"Capone's an ambitious man. Already he's maybe a little more than my right hand, if you know what I mean. He considers himself my partner."

"Yeah, I've sometimes wondered about that," Kerry said. An idea entered his mind, and he barely paused before plunging on. "Johnny, listen, there's just the two of us in this car right now, so nothin' anybody says ever has to go any further. What about Capone? You want me to rub him out?"

"What?" Torrio asked, askance. He looked at Kerry

for a moment, and then he laughed, softly. "You'd do that for me, wouldn't you, kid? You'd do it, or you'd die tryin'."

"I might die," Kerry admitted, "but Capone'd be dead, too."

"You know, I just believe you could do it. If anyone could, you could." Torrio sighed again. "But, no, I don't want Capone dead. He's where he is 'cause he's good. And even sharin' the operation with him, I'm a lot better off than I ever dreamed I'd be. To be honest with you, kid, I'm lucky to be hooked up with Capone. But the problem is, he may get—" Torrio broke off and stared out the window. A policeman standing on the corner, obviously recognizing him, gave him a little salute. Torrio waved back.

"He may get what?" Kerry prompted.

"He may get a bit greedy," Torrio finished. He sighed. "And if he does, I've got two options. One, to fight him—in which case, I don't mind tellin' you, I'd lose—and the other is to get outta town and let him have the entire operation, lock, stock, and whiskey barrel."

"We can beat him, Johnny," Kerry said firmly.

"No," Torrio said. "No, we can't. Not everyone who works for me is as loyal as you. I've got you, and Capone has Frank Netti. In my book you're every bit as good an enforcer as Netti. But Netti has a hundred torpedoes working for him, and you have no more than a dozen that you can count on."

"I'll put my dozen against Netti's hundred any day," Kerry boasted.

Torrio laughed. "I know you would. But I'm not goin' to fight him. I'm goin' to get along with him for as long as I can."

"All right, but what has that got to do with me leavin' Chicago and goin' to St. Louis?" Kerry asked.

"If I have to leave town in a year or two, I'd like to think I had some place to go," Torrio replied. "I want you to go down to St. Louis and open it up."

"Okay," Kerry said, nodding. "Is there anybody workin' down there now?"

"None of *our* people," Torrio said. "A handful of Irish are runnin' the show. The head man is someone named Paddy Egan. I figure havin' an Irish name might come in handy for you down there."

"You may be right," Kerry agreed.

Torrio was silent for a moment, then said, "Listen, Kerry, before you go, I want you to take the oath."

"What?" Kerry gasped, his eyes wide in surprise as he stared at Torrio. "Johnny, do you mean it?"

"Yeah, I mean it," Torrio said. "You're one-half Sicilian. As far as I'm concerned, one-half Sicilian is worth a whole Neapolitan anytime, you know what I mean?" he added, referring to the fact that Capone was from Naples.

"Capone's never taken the oath, has he?"

"No. He ain't never been invited," Torrio said. "But I'm invitin' you. You want to join La Cosa Nostra or not?"

Kerry blinked his eyes very rapidly, several times, but he couldn't prevent the tears from forming, and his eyes were wet with emotion when he looked back at Torrio. "My entire life I've dreamed of bein' in the Family," he said. "I never thought I'd be allowed."

"If you were still in the old country, maybe you wouldn't be," Torrio admitted. "But we're in America now. And once you're in, you're in, kid. You can never leave . . . and you can never be expelled. You got to make your choice right now, 'cause it'll never be offered to you again. Now, what's it to be?"

"Yeah, Johnny," Kerry said. "Yeah, I want to join."

Torrio smiled broadly. "That's what I thought. Okay, you drive over to Dominick's Pasta House now," he instructed. "Me and you, we got some friends waitin' there. We'll have the ceremony. After that, you take this car, a little expense money, and five or six of your best men. In a few days you'll leave for St. Louis."

"How much expense money?" Kerry asked.

"A couple of grand is all I can manage without makin' Capone suspicious," Torrio said apologetically. "You'll have to set up somethin' as soon as you get there.

Whatever you can set up is yours . . . yours and your gang's, to do with as you see fit."

"I'll take care of it," Kerry promised. "But what about Capone and the others? What are they goin' to say when they see me and a few of my boys gone?"

"You don't worry about them. I'll tell them some people were beginnin' to ask questions about the Fusco business, and you had to get outta town."

Twelve men were sitting around the table in a back room of Dominick's Pasta House when Kerry O'Braugh and Johnny Torrio walked in. Kerry knew all twelve of them, for they were members of the Torrio-Capone organization. They were also all members of the Mafia.

Torrio took his place at the head of the table, indicating that Kerry should sit to his left. Dinner was immediately served and consumed lustily.

The guests had eaten and were convivially talking over their glasses of wine when Torrio stood up and tapped on his glass. The others fell silent.

"Guido," Torrio said. "You want to make certain the door is locked?"

The man sitting closest to the door went to check, then nodded at Torrio as he returned to his seat.

Torrio nodded back. "Gents," he said, "you all know Kerry O'Braugh. You know the work he's done for us and the loyalty he has shown—and you all know that I regard Kerry like a brother. You also know that he's Sicilian. More Sicilian than most of us at this table, because Kerry, he was born there. His mother was Sicilian, and his grandfather was a *capo di regime*. Kerry's father died in a vendetta at the side of his *capo di regime*, even though he wasn't a member."

Torrio raised his glass toward Kerry. "Kerry, your father died an honorable death, and I drink to him." He took a sip of wine, as did everyone else around the table.

"Now," Torrio continued, "Kerry's father couldn't be a member, no matter how loyal he was, because he wasn't Sicilian. This man that I love like a brother, Kerry

O'Braugh"—Torrio put his arm on Kerry's shoulder—"*is* Sicilian. I don't intend that he should be denied membership in the order any longer, just because he has a mick name. So I propose that, tonight, we accept him into our brotherhood. Are there any objections?"

Torrio studied the faces of the men around the table, but no one raised an objection.

"All right, then," Torrio went on. "Kerry, are you ready?"

"I am ready, *Padrone*," Kerry said.

"Kerry, your parents had you baptized when you were a baby; now we're goin' to baptize you into the Family. Stand up."

Kerry stood.

"Hold out your trigger finger," Torrio ordered.

Kerry did as he was instructed, and Torrio picked up a knife, then made a small cut in Kerry's finger. Under the finger he held a card bearing the picture of St. Michael, Kerry's family's patron saint. The blood dripped onto the picture, staining it a deep crimson.

In Italian, Kerry took the oath: "I want to enter into this organization to protect my family and to protect all my friends. I swear not to divulge this secret and to obey with love and *omertà*."

"Okay, Kerry, you have taken the oath," Torrio said. "A man, he gets into the organization alive; the only way he gets out is by death. There ain't no Jesus, no Madonna, no one who can help any of us if we ever give up this secret to anyone. This thing we got here, it cannot be exposed. Ever. You know what I mean?"

"Yes, *Padrone*."

"Okay, you seal the bargain now."

Torrio struck a match and held the flame to the corner of the card that bore the bloodstained picture of St. Michael. As the card burned, Kerry held it in his hand and took his final vow.

"As burns this saint, so will burn my soul if I betray this organization. I enter it alive and leave it dead."

Kerry held the card in his hand until it was entirely

consumed by fire, wincing with the pain but not dropping it even when he got a whiff of burned flesh.

"Okay," Torrio said, smiling broadly and embracing Kerry, "you're one of us now."

"This is the proudest day of my life," Kerry answered quietly.

CHAPTER
SIX

LATE JUNE 1923, ST. LOUIS, MISSOURI

The hotel ballroom was a study in purple and
yellow, the colors of the Veiled Prophet. The throne sat
upon a dais covered with purple velvet, and the chair
itself was gilded and cushioned with yellow silk pillows.
Hundreds of potted purple and yellow chrysanthemums
adorned the room, and clusters of purple and yellow
balloons, ribbons, and drapery filled the corners and
cascaded down the grand staircase.

Admission to the Veiled Prophet Ball was by invitation only, and it was the supreme honor of the social
season and a highly sought-after prize. Though only the
most affluent would attend, a healthy bank account
would not in itself guarantee an invitation, for more than
money was required to grace these halls. Only someone
inhabiting the top echelon of St. Louis society could
expect the cream-colored, engraved envelope that con-

tained the prized invitation, and the guest lists of the
year's subsequent important social events were predi-
cated upon who attended the Veiled Prophet Ball.

Although the ball was in honor of the Veiled
Prophet, he would actually make only a brief appearance
when, dressed in ceremonial robes of purple and yellow
and a concealing veil, he would deliver his prophecy to
his subjects and extend his scepter toward the debutante
who would be crowned Goddess of Love and Beauty for
1923. The brevity of his appearance ensured that he
wouldn't be gone long enough from his fellow guests to
allow someone to put two and two together and come up
with an identity. And to prevent the possibility of anyone recognizing his voice, the prophecy of the Veiled
Prophet, though written by him, would be delivered by
his Public Crier.

That time had come in this evening's festivities, so
the Public Crier, dressed in the garments of a page of the
court, banged his large, heavy staff three times on the
floor to get the attention of the elegantly attired men and
women in the ballroom.

"Hear ye, hear ye, hear ye! Draw near, O loyal
subjects of the Veiled Prophet, and attend my voice. I
am pleased to deliver His Majesty's prophecy."

The Public Crier cleared his throat, then unrolled a
scroll from top and bottom.

"Progress and prosperity," the Crier read, "are the
things I see for the city of St. Louis and for her worthy
citizens. The legacy of St. Louis as a center of transportation, begun with wagon trains and continued with river-
boats and railroads, has been brought into the twentieth
century with the automobile. Concrete roads connect St.
Louis with Chicago and points east; a fine gravel road
now extends west to Kansas City; and with the establishment of airmail and airline service between St. Louis
and Chicago, our fair city stands upon the threshold of
the future. These are the marks of progress, and atten-
dant to this progress is the promise of another year of
prosperity. This is the legacy that I, your Veiled Prophet,
in the forty-fourth year of my realm, bequeath to you."

A round of applause greeted the conclusion of the prophecy. Though the prophecy was supposed to be the most important part of the Veiled Prophet's reign, the announcement of the Goddess of Love and Beauty was a subject of much greater anticipation. Out of the one hundred young ladies who were the original candidates, ten had been selected as his handmaidens, and from these ten one would be selected as the Goddess of Love and Beauty.

Again the Public Crier banged his staff three times. Three trumpeters then appeared from behind a curtain, and like the Crier the trumpeters were dressed in purple and yellow silk. As the players raised their trumpets— the very long instruments used for playing court fanfares— banners unfurled from beneath them. The banners were embossed with the seal of the city of St. Louis, over which had been printed the initials *VP*.

A stirring fanfare was played in three-part harmony. At its conclusion the Veiled Prophet rose from his throne and walked over to the Circle of Love and Beauty, where his ten handmaidens waited full of hope and anxious expectation. He stopped in front of one of the girls and pointed his scepter.

"Hear ye, hear ye, hear ye!" the Crier shouted. "The Goddess of Love and Beauty for the year of our Lord nineteen hundred and twenty-three, and for the year of the reign of the forty-fourth Veiled Prophet, has been chosen. Bow down and pay honor to the beauty and grace of Miss Demaris Hunter!"

The crowd broke into loud applause as last year's Goddess rushed forward to place the crown on Demaris's head and last year's First Handmaiden put the royal cape around her shoulders. Photographers from all the city's newspapers filled the room with brilliant flashes as they took their pictures. The reign of the Goddess of Love and Beauty of 1923 had begun.

"You missed it, Dad," John said, when Bob Canfield returned to their table a few moments later.

"Missed what?"

"While you were out calling the plant manager, the VP selected the new Goddess of Love and Beauty."

"Oh, no. Wouldn't you know it?" Bob said with convincing disappointment. He looked at the whirl of dancers who, now that the business was over, had invaded the ballroom floor. "Did he pick a pretty one? Someone I'd approve of?"

"Yes, dear, she's very lovely," Connie said, smiling knowingly and backing up her husband's act.

"I'll tell you one thing: If she ever wants to go parking she can be my Sheba, and I'll be her sheik," Willie said.

"Go parking?" Bob asked, confused.

"Yeah, in my strugglebuggy," Willie replied.

"Strugglebuggy?" Bob was even more bewildered.

"Jalopy, Dad. You know . . ."

"Car," John finally explained.

"The automobile?" Bob said. "Well, if you mean an automobile, why don't you call it an automobile?"

"No one calls them automobiles anymore, Dad," Willie said.

"Why not? That's what they are, isn't it?"

"I guess we're lucky he calls it an automobile," John told his brother, grinning. "He could be calling it a horseless carriage."

"Horseless carriage is a more appropriate term than strugglebuggy or jalopy," Bob insisted. "Now, what do you mean by 'parking'?"

"Ooo, la, la!" Willie said, and both boys laughed.

"Ooo, la, la?" Bob asked.

The boys laughed again at Bob's confusion, and this time Connie laughed with them. "Oh, darling, really, you are so behind times," she said. "Don't you know anything? When a boy takes a girl parking, it means he's sparking her in a car. Do you get it? Sparking? Parking?"

"Necking," John interpreted.

"Yeah," Willie added. "Making whoopee."

John laughed. "No, you only make whoopee if the girl is willing to go all the way."

"Go all the way?" Bob interjected. "What does *that* mean?"

"You know, Dad," John began. "It means to, uh"—he glanced at his brother—"fornicate."

"Now, boys, don't be so brazen," Connie ordered.

"I swear, fifty years from now the English language as we know it will be as dead as Latin," Bob complained.

"But kids will still be studying it in school," Willie predicted, "just as we study Latin."

"And wondering why," John added.

"Doesn't it bother you to think of our language dying?" Bob asked. "Especially since people like you two are helping to kill it?"

"Look at it this way, Dad. We're not killing English," John explained, "we're giving birth to Jive."

Willie laughed. "Yeah. Maybe I'll become a professor of Jive." Holding his tuxedo lapels, he adopted a pompous tone and asked his brother, "Tell me, little Johnny, what does the term 'spiffy' mean?"

"Spiffy," John repeated, his hands clasped in front of him and looking straight ahead. "To be spiffy means to be smart in appearance or dress. In other words, to be stylish, as in, 'My, you do look spiffy today, William.'"

"That's swell, little Johnny. For that you get an E for Excellent."

Connie joined the boys in laughter, which grew even richer when Bob demanded to know what they found so all-fired funny. He was scowling good-naturedly at his family when one of the bellboys from the hotel stepped up to their table and cleared his throat to get Bob's attention.

"Mr. Canfield?"

"Yes," Bob replied.

"You have a long-distance telephone call at the front desk, sir," the bellhop said. "I believe the gentleman calling said his name was Mr. Parker."

"Parker? L.E. Parker?"

"Yes, sir, I believe so."

"That's very odd," Bob said to no one in particular. "Why on earth would L.E. be calling me here?"

L.E. Parker, Bob's farm manager down in Sikeston, lived in the same house Bob had once lived in. He had no telephone in his home, so it was unusual for him to call Bob at any time; to track him down at an event like the Veiled Prophet Ball was unheard of.

"Bob, what do you think it is?" Connie asked, her voice showing her concern.

"I don't know," Bob said. "But whatever it is, it can't be good."

The bellboy led Bob to the small office behind the hotel's front desk. "I'll have the operator put the call through to here," the bellboy offered. "It will be quieter, and you'll have a little more privacy."

"Thanks," Bob said, handing the bellboy a dollar bill.

"Thank *you*, sir," the bellboy replied, smiling broadly.

Bob waited for the phone, then picked it up on the first ring.

"Mr. Canfield?" the telephone operator inquired.

"Yes, this is Bob Canfield."

"Would you hold the line, please, for a long-distance telephone call from Mr. L.E. Parker?" she asked.

"Yes, operator, I'll hold."

"I have your party in St. Louis now, Mr. Parker," the woman's voice said a moment later. "You may go ahead."

"Mr. Canfield?" Bob heard Parker shout.

"Yes, L.E. What is it?" Bob asked, lifting his own voice.

"It's the Klan, Mr. Canfield," L.E. replied.

"The what?" Bob asked.

"The Klan. You know, them fellas that go around dressed up in bed sheets? The Ku Klux Klan?"

"Yes, I know who they are," Bob said, "but what do they have to do with this call?"

"They're all gettin' together to go out to George Summers's place."

George Summers, now in his midseventies, had worked for the Canfields all his life. His father had been a slave on Bob's grandfather's farm, and George had himself been born a slave. He now owned the house and farm where he had been born—a gift from Bob's father.

"Why in heaven's name would they be doing something like that? George has never given anybody any trouble over anything."

"It's because of George's nephew, Julius Coleman," L.E. explained. "The Klan is after Julius 'cause he hit a white man. They think he's hidin' out at George's house."

"*Is* he hiding there?"

"I don't know."

"Has the Klan already gone out to George's?"

"No, sir, not yet. But they're fixin' to go. They're meetin' out at Miner Switch right now, listenin' to speeches and gettin' themselves all worked up into a frenzy."

"Then the thing to do is to call the police. Tell them to get out there and break up the meeting."

"That won't do no good, Mr. Canfield. The police don't have no jurisdiction out in Miner Switch. They don't have none at George's place, either."

"Then call the sheriff," Bob suggested.

"I tried that, too. Him and his deputies is up at Jefferson City."

"Damn," Bob spat. "All right, look. If Julius really is at George's house, maybe you can get to him before the Klan does. Try and talk him into going somewhere else. He has no right to put George in danger."

"I'll do what I can," L.E. promised.

"In the meantime, I'm coming down."

"Tomorrow?"

"No, tonight. Right now. I'll have Rocky fly me down. How's Blodgett Lane? Is it in pretty good condition, or is it all muddy and full of holes?"

"Well, yes, sir, it's in pretty good shape," L.E. said. "But, Mr. Canfield, you're not goin' to have Rocky try and land on it tonight, are you?"

Blodgett Lane was a long, straight road that ran between St. John's Bayou and an adjacent cotton field.

When Rocky flew Bob down to the farm the last time, they had used Blodgett Lane for a landing strip.

"I've no other choice," Bob said. "And you're going to have to get some light out there for me."

"I'll come up with somethin', but I don't rightly know what it'll be," L.E. replied. "Hey, wait a minute, I got an idea. Joyce has about a dozen smudge pots out in her orchard. She fires them up whenever she's afraid the frost might damage her peaches."

"Smudge pots? Yeah, that might work. What are they made from?"

"Oil drums, cut in half."

"Okay, they'll have to do," Bob said. "Line them along both sides of the lane. When you hear us pass overhead, light them."

"Yes, sir, I'll do that," L.E. promised.

With an angry sigh, Bob replaced the telephone receiver and left the hotel office, hurrying back to his family.

Though L.E. Parker had nothing to do with the operation of the sawmill, he did have an office there that he used for the management of the Canfield farms, and as soon as he had heard what the Ku Klux Klan was planning, he had gone to the office to use the phone. Unable to get any help from the police or the sheriff's office and feeling he had nothing left to try, he had done the only thing he could think of and called Bob Canfield.

With the call completed, L.E. reached up and snapped off the desk lamp, plunging the office into deep shadows. It wasn't totally dark in the building because some light came from the bright silver splash of the moon as well as a wavering, yellow glow projected into the mill from the lumber yard outside. But while that light provided some illumination, it also distorted and twisted the huge saws, log chutes, and work platforms into such bizarre shapes and shadows that the familiar surroundings took on an unfamiliar and eerie atmosphere.

L.E. suddenly felt his hair stand on end when he noticed that one of the shadows was moving.

"Who is it?" he called, standing up quickly and walking to the office doorway. "Who's out there?"

"It's me, Mr. Parker," a voice replied from the darkness of the mill. "Lenny Puckett."

"Lenny?" L.E. said, feeling relief wash through him. "What are you doin' here?"

The shadow moved closer, passing into a patch of light so that L.E. could see him quite clearly.

"I saw your car," Lenny replied. "I figured you were in here."

"Yes. I had to make a telephone call," L.E. said, offering no further explanation.

"Mr. Parker, have you heard what the Klan is doing?" Lenny asked.

"Yes, I've heard."

"We can't let them do that, Mr. Parker. They've got no right going after Julius like they're doing."

"I don't understand what the devil brought this on, anyhow," L.E. said. "Julius has been workin' here for two or three years with no problems. What happened? What in Sam Hill made him suddenly decide to take a poke at Travis?"

"It's all my fault," Lenny said glumly.

"How is it your fault?"

"I don't know whether you've heard or not, but I'm going to be leaving Sikeston pretty soon. I'm going to play baseball in the big leagues."

"Hell, Lenny, the whole town has heard that," L.E. said, smiling at the young man. "We're all very proud of you."

"Yes, sir, well, I'm honored by all that. But when I leave, someone's got to take my place, and I figured the best man would be Julius. I first thought that it'd be best not to say anything, but I finally decided to give Buddy Travis my opinion. I guess Buddy didn't like the idea too much, because he set out to prove I was wrong. For more than a week now he's been riding Julius something awful, finding fault with everything he does, yelling at

him, picking on him, calling him a dumb nigger and all
sorts of things.

"None of that bothered Julius, though," the young
man continued. "He just kept his mouth shut and kept
on working. But his keeping quiet got to playing on
Buddy's nerves, so this morning Buddy moved right up
into Julius's face and started yelling at him.

"'What's the matter with you, nigger?' he shouted.
'Can't you hear me?' Well, I guess that was when Julius
had enough, because he answered, 'Yes, sir, I can hear
you. You sound just like a brayin' mule. And I never pay
any attention to a brayin' mule.'"

"What happened then?" L.E. asked.

"Then Buddy got really mad," Lenny explained.
"He picked up a leather whip and told Julius that he was
going to take the hide off his body. He never got that far,
though. He no sooner picked up the whip than Julius
grabbed it from him, then punched him right in the
mouth."

"So, that's how Julius hit a white man?"

"Yes, sir."

"Well, I'll tell it to you true, boy. If there ever was
a man had a lickin' comin', it was Buddy Travis for doin'
somethin' like that in the first place," L.E. said. "Julius
had every right to hit him."

"Yes, sir, I agree with you. Only now Buddy's got
the Klan all stirred up. He says Julius has to be made an
example of in order to teach all the other coloreds that
they can't go around hitting a white man anytime they
want to."

"Yeah, I heard that they're after him. Tell me, just
what kind of example are they plannin' on makin',
Lenny? You got any idea?"

"Yes, sir," Lenny answered. "They're planning on
tarring and feathering him."

"Son of a bitch," L.E. muttered.

"We can't let that happen, Mr. Parker. We got to do
something about it."

"I'm goin' to do somethin' about it," L.E. said.

"Want to come with me, Lenny? It looks like I'm goin' to be needin' your help."

"Yes, sir, I'll come with you," Lenny said. "But what are we going to do? Are we going out to Miner Switch to try and talk them out of it?"

"No, we'd just be wastin' our breath," L.E. replied. "We're goin' to fix a place for an airplane to land."

At Lambert Field in St. Louis, Bob Canfield put on a leather flying jacket while the pilot—a tall, slim man in his late thirties—busied himself readying the plane, a DH-4 belonging to Robertson Aircraft. This would be the first time Bob had ever flown with this man, but he had no choice. He had been unable to locate Rocky Rockwell.

"I appreciate your flying me down to Sikeston, Mr. MacIntosh," Bob said.

"My pleasure, Mr. Canfield," the pilot answered. "I just wish I had a faster airplane. Seventy-five miles an hour is about all we're going to get out of this old crate, and at that rate it's going to take us a couple of hours."

The two men were suddenly caught in a pair of headlights as a car approached. The vehicle drove right up to the hangar before it stopped, and the driver got out and hurried toward them. When the driver stepped into the hangar's lights, Bob smiled.

"Hello, Rocky," he said. "I was told nobody knew where to find you."

"Oh, they found me all right. What are you doing with this guy? You don't really think I'd let you fly with someone else, do you?"

"But I hear Mr. MacIntosh is a marvelous aviator."

"He's all right, I suppose, but he comes down in a parachute about as often as he lands the plane," Rocky quipped, a reference to the fact that the other pilot had been forced to bail out of a crippled airplane a month earlier. "How're you doing, Mac? Why don't you come fly for us instead of Robertson? Our planes don't quit flying like his do."

"What planes? I thought you had only one, suitable for mail service."

"Vicious rumors, spread by our competition," Rocky said. "Anyhow, thanks for coming out, but I'll take him now."

"That'll work better for me anyway," MacIntosh said. "I have to take off for Chicago at four in the morning, and I might be hard-pressed to get back in time."

"Thank you, Mr. MacIntosh," Bob said, reaching out to shake hands. "I do appreciate you going out of your way to come out here tonight."

"You want to use this plane?" MacIntosh asked. "It's a spare, and it's already gassed up and ready to go."

"Thanks, but so is the McPheeters Racer," Rocky said. "I'd rather use it."

"The Racer? Not the RM-3?" Bob asked.

"You *are* in a hurry to get there, aren't you? Otherwise, you wouldn't want to fly out in the middle of the night."

"Yes, I am in a hurry," Bob confirmed.

"Then we'll use the Racer. There's nothing faster in America. Hold on to your hat, Mr. Canfield. I'll have you down there in less than an hour."

"I'll prop you and pull the chocks," MacIntosh offered.

"Thanks," Rocky said, already striding toward the Racer.

The aircraft sat on the flight line, poised and ready to go. As Bob approached it and saw its low wing, smooth skin, and long, rakish cowl gleaming softly in the moonlight, he thought it was as sleek looking as a bullet.

"Get in," Rocky said, patting the front cockpit. "I'll show you what this baby can do."

Bob strapped himself into his seat and adjusted the helmet and goggles. Then he watched as MacIntosh twisted the prop through until he found the compression stroke.

"Switch on!" MacIntosh called.

"Contact!" Rocky replied.

MacIntosh jerked down on the propeller, and the engine caught. Then he pulled the chocks from beneath the wheels and waved as the airplane began rolling across the ground.

Instead of going all the way out to the end of the runway then turning into the wind for a normal takeoff, Rocky opened the throttle to full power almost from the moment they began to move. Seconds later the airplane leapt into the air, and in no time at all the lights of St. Louis were falling off far below and behind them. By looking under the left wing as they headed south, Bob could see the long, silvery ribbon that was the Mississippi River.

Bob had flown enough times with Rocky now to be able to read some of the instruments, so he turned on the little light to examine the dials on the panel before him. The altimeter told him they were at 5,000 feet, and the compass read 185 degrees, but Bob was most impressed by the airspeed indicator, for its needle was quivering at the 200-mile-per-hour mark. Rocky hadn't been exaggerating when he said they'd be in Sikeston in less than an hour, Bob thought. He just hoped it wouldn't already be too late.

With his wife, Joyce, and his two children, Rubye, just turned thirteen, and Richard Edward, aged nine, helping, L.E. and Lenny soon had a dozen sawed-off oil drums spotted alongside Blodgett Lane. Blackened with soot, they were normally used to light fires that would fight off unseasonable frosts and protect Joyce's peach orchard. They would, however, work quite well to light the makeshift runway.

"Okay," L.E. said to the others when all the drums were in place, "the minute you hear the plane overhead, light these things. I'm goin' over to George's house."

"What are you going to do over there, L.E.?" Joyce asked anxiously.

"I don't know, but I've got to do somethin'."

"You be careful."

"I will. If I can hold that mob off until Mr. Canfield gets here, I'm pretty sure they'll listen to him. Hell, they'll have to. Most of them work for him in one way or another."

"I'm coming with you, Mr. Parker," Lenny insisted.

"No, you'd better not, Lenny. If the Klan's really got their dander up, I don't reckon they'll stop to see whose skin is white and whose is colored when they open the ball."

"Then that's all the more reason Lenny should be with you," Joyce said.

"What do you mean?"

"Well, think about it, L.E.," she said. "Lenny Puckett is a famous man around here, now that he's going off to play big-league baseball. Everyone's real proud of him. The folks in the Klan may not be quite so quick to do anything if he's with you."

"She's got a point, Mr. Parker," Lenny said. "I don't agree with what they're doing tonight, but I figure most of the fellas in the KKK are my friends. I don't think they'd do anything to hurt me—or anyone with me."

"All right," L.E. agreed. "If you want to come along, I won't try and stop you. Come on, we'll walk. That way we can leave the car here for Mr. Canfield to have a way up to the house."

George Summers's house was just a short distance up the lane from the Parker house, though set considerably back from the road up on a slight rise, and when L.E. and Lenny approached it minutes later, the house was a study in silver and black under the wash of the full moon. Not a light could be seen, and for all appearances the house was totally deserted, though L.E. knew that it wasn't.

"Wait," L.E. called out to Lenny when they reached the edge of the property. "You don't want to go bargin' up there unless you're plannin' to get your fool head shot off. George has a shotgun, and he knows how to use it."

"But I don't mean them any harm," Lenny insisted.

"How's George supposed to know that?" L.E. asked. Without moving another inch, he cupped his hands around his mouth and shouted toward the house. "George, it's me, L.E.! I got Lenny Puckett with me, and we're alone! Can we come up to the front porch?"

"Come on up, Mr. L.E.," George's voice replied smoothly.

L.E. and Lenny walked across the wide lawn, stopping just short of the porch step. The front door opened, and George stepped outside. When he moved into the moonlight, L.E. could see that he was wearing a pair of bib coveralls over long-handle underwear. His face was deeply wrinkled, and his gray hair and beard had thinned considerably in the past several years. Though George and his wife, Clemmie, were well into their seventies, L.E. had always felt that there was a look of permanence about them, sort of like the Rock of Gibraltar. Tonight, however, he could see signs of erosion, perhaps for the first time.

"Hello, George."

"Hello, Mr. L.E. What brings you out here in the middle of the night?" George's voice was soft, deep, and resonant.

"I come to warn you, George. The KKK is holdin' themselves a meetin' right now," L.E. said. "And from what I can gather, they're plannin' to come over here."

"Yes, sir, I 'spect they are," George replied calmly.

"You know about it?"

"Oh, yes, sir, I know about it."

"Then you might also know that they ain't really after you," L.E. said. "The one they want is Julius."

"Yes, sir, I know that, too."

"Is he here?"

"I'm here, Mr. Parker," Julius said. The voice came from the pitch blackness inside the house. The young man then stepped right up to the door, but it was so dark behind him that L.E. sensed more than saw him. "Hello, Lenny," Julius added.

"Hello, Julius," Lenny replied.

"Julius, you've got to get out of here," L.E. said. "Don't you know that by bein' here, you've put George and Clemmie in danger? Come on over to my house. They won't look for you there."

"I appreciate your offer, Mr. Parker," Julius said, "but I don't reckon I'll be goin' anywhere for a while."

"What do you mean?"

Julius pushed through the screen door out onto the porch, and L.E. saw that he was hobbling on a pair of makeshift crutches. "When I was runnin' from the sawmill this mornin', I fell and broke my ankle," Julius explained. "I can't walk."

"You can ride, can't you? Get in the back of George's car. George, you take Julius and Clemmie over to my house. I'll wait here and see what I can do about talkin' this mob into goin' home."

"No, sir, I can't do that," George said.

"You can't do that? What do you mean, you can't do that?"

"This place is my home, Mr. L.E.," George said, his voice resolute. "Mine and Clemmie's. Do you understand that? It ain't the place I rent, and it ain't the place I'm buyin'. It's mine, free and clear. There ain't nobody else in my family, goin' all the way back to Africa, I 'spect, what ever owned the place where they lived. Well, me and Clemmie, we own this place," he said proudly. "And now that we got it, there ain't no man alive, black or white, goin' to run us off our own place."

"Are you sure that's what Clemmie wants?" L.E. asked.

"Yes, sir, Mr. L.E. It's what I want," Clemmie's voice called from the darkness inside the house, making it obvious that she had been listening to the entire conversation.

"All right, George," L.E. said quietly. "If you and Clemmie are goin' to stay here, then I'm goin' to stay here with you."

"I am, too," Lenny said.

"Ain't no call for you folks to do that," George said. "It ain't your trouble, it's ours."

"We're neighbors, George," L.E. said. "The way I look at it, whenever there's trouble, neighbors help neighbors. When Joyce and the kids and I were down with the influenza some years back, you didn't stay outside, away from the sickness, sayin' that it was our trouble, did you? No, sir," L.E. said, answering his own question. "You and Clemmie nursed us back to health. You could have caught the sickness from us and died, but you never gave it a second thought. I figure it's about time I paid you back a little."

"Then you're welcome to stay, Mr. L.E.," George said. "And I'm mighty grateful for the company."

"I guess we should make some plans," L.E. said. "I know you have a gun. I wonder if I have time to go get mine."

"No, sir!" George said anxiously. "We won't be usin' no guns."

"George, we don't have a choice," L.E. countered, his voice exasperated. He pointed out into the dark. "Don't you understand what I've been tellin' you? In about ten minutes this place is going to be surrounded by twenty or thirty armed men. And you're sayin' we have to face them without so much as one gun?"

"I agree with Mr. L.E., Uncle George," Julius put in. "We ought to have at least one gun!"

"Why, Julius?" George asked. "Tell me what one gun would do 'sides get us killed?"

"Well, we could at least stand up here like men," Julius insisted.

"That's exactly what I intend to do," George said. "Stand up here like a man. But I don't need no gun to make me a man. And neither do you."

"Listen!" Lenny hissed. "You hear that?"

At Lenny's warning the other men hushed. For a moment they could hear nothing except the frogs and crickets. Then they heard a faint sound, high and thin, over the night creatures. When they looked in the direction of the sound, they saw a dim glow on the horizon.

"It's them," L.E. said. "That's their cars and trucks."

"Mr. L.E., if you're havin' second thoughts 'bout

stayin', now's the time for you to get goin'," George said. "You could use my car and go out the back way."

"I told you, we aren't leavin' you to face that mob alone."

"Then get up here on the front porch, back in the shadows, and try and stay out of sight," George ordered. "No sense in lettin' them see everythin' all at once."

L.E. and Lenny did as they were told. Then, as if transfixed, the four men watched the glow advance until it turned into individual lights . . . the headlights of cars. By now, also, the engines of the approaching automobiles were quite loud. A few moments later the cars turned off the main road and started down the lane, bouncing and bobbing on the uneven surface. Spears of light danced and jabbed through the dark, falling on George's car, lighting up the barn, and splashing against the front porch.

Finally the cars reached their destination. They were maneuvered into a large semicircle and stopped side by side, with the headlamps trained on the front of George's house. One by one automobile doors slammed, and rough voices called to each other as the men exited the machines and began to gather. Within moments there were at least thirty hooded men standing in front of the cars. They cast huge, ominous-looking shadows, backlit by the yellow headlights. Most were carrying what appeared to be clubs or baseball bats rather than guns.

"George?" one of the figures called. "George, are you in there?"

George didn't answer.

"George, we know you're in there," the voice called again. "We know you're in there, 'cause you got no place else to go. Come on out here, boy." Though he wasn't wearing the scarlet robe of his rank, Buddy Travis was given away by his voice.

"Maybe we need to get ol' George's attention," another voice said. "Let's get it up, men."

L.E. and the others stayed back in the shadows on the porch, watching as the hooded men worked diligently in the front yard, pounding something into the ground and then pouring something over the erected object. A breeze came up, carrying with it the scent of kerosene. Then the Klansmen all stood back, and one of their hooded number tossed a fluttering match toward the object. The kerosene-soaked form caught quickly, blazed up, and etched a fiery cross against the night sky.

"You son of a bitch," L.E. muttered and he started forward, but George reached out and grabbed him and pulled him back, showing an amazing degree of strength for a man his age.

"What do you men want?" George asked, stepping out of the concealing shadows and speaking for the first time. "You got no right to be burnin' that thing in my yard."

"Well, now, lookee here," one of the robed figures taunted. "All you got to do is light up a cross, and they'll come runnin' every time. Where is he, George?"

"Where's who?"

"You know who we're talkin' about," Travis said. "Where's Julius? We know he's your nephew, and we know he come out here to your house today after he caused all the trouble. Now, where is he?"

George didn't answer. For a long moment the only sound was the hissing, kerosene-fed flames and the cracking of the wood of the cross. Even the frogs and crickets had fallen silent.

Standing there on the porch, L.E. thought it was as unearthly a sight as he could ever imagine. Caught in the glare of the car headlamps behind them, the hooded mob looked as if they were glowing, and their robes reflected the orange and red of the flames. It looked for all the world as if a window had been opened to disclose the denizens of hell.

"Maybe he needs some more persuadin'," one of the men suggested.

"George, we ain't after you nor your wife," Travis said. "We don't even want to do nothin' to your house. All we want is Julius. You give him to us, and we'll leave you alone."

"Otherwise, you're likely to find out that your house just sort of 'accidently' burned down," another said, and several of the men sniggered.

"If you burn this house, you goin' to have to burn me with it," George said.

"Hell, you think that'll stop us?" one of the men called. He chuckled. "I'd just as soon burn a nigger as hang one."

"Then you goin' to have to burn me, too," Clemmie said, stepping out onto the porch to stand beside her husband.

"That ain't no problem. We can make it two."

"Wait a minute! Hold on here," one of the hooded men said. "What are you doin'? We didn't come out here to kill anybody. We just come out here to make an example, is all. There ain't no sense in lettin' this get out of hand!"

"Can you think of a better example than a couple of dead niggers?"

"You mean three," L.E. said, showing himself for the first time. "Because if you kill George and Clemmie, you're goin' to have to kill me, too."

"And me," Lenny added, stepping up to stand beside the others.

The sudden and unexpected appearance of two white men startled the Klan.

"What the hell? What are you two white men doing up there? You got no business up there," Travis said.

"We aren't white," L.E. said.

"What do you mean, you ain't white? 'Course you're white."

"I'm not white tonight," L.E. said. "Not if it means I got to be counted with the likes of you."

"You'd rather be counted with the niggers?"

"I'd rather be counted with my neighbors and friends," L.E. said. "And when someone starts threatenin' to kill my neighbors, I don't take to it too kindly."

"We ain't really plannin' on killin' anyone, L.E.," Travis said. "Hell, we ain't even after George and Clemmie. We know they're decent coloreds. No, sir. All we want to do is teach that young buck, Julius, a lesson. These niggers got to learn they can't go around hittin' white folks and get away with it."

"And if Julius isn't here?" L.E. replied.

"He's here. We know damned well he's here. And we plan to come up there and find him."

"You got no right to come onto a man's private property without him invitin' you," George said. "And I ain't invited you."

"I'm invitin' myself," Travis said. "Come on, men."

"Wait! Listen!" someone said. "What's that sound?"

Like the others, L.E. listened to hear what the man was talking about. When he heard the high-pitched snarl, he smiled. He knew exactly what it was. It was an airplane . . . and that meant Bob Canfield was here.

From thirty-five hundred feet the burning cross stood out boldly against the dark background. The moment Bob saw it, he knew what it was, and it made him sick to his stomach with anger.

"You bastards!" he shouted into the slipstream. "You miserable bastards!"

Rocky throttled the engine back, then banged on the fuselage to get Bob's attention. When Bob looked around, Rocky handed him the .38-caliber pistol he had to carry as an airmail pilot. Bob took the gun, though he didn't know what he would actually do with it. He soon learned, however, that Rocky had something in mind, because Rocky stood the airplane on its left wing tip, then started spiraling down toward the cross. In no time at all they were just a few feet off the ground, heading right for the burning cross. In the light of its flames, Bob could see nearly a dozen cars, all lined up in a neat row. That was when he got the idea.

"What the hell? He's comin' right for us! Who *is* that crazy son of a bitch?" one of the Klansmen yelled, pointing to the airplane that was now so low that they quickly dived to the ground in fear.

"He's shooting at us!" shouted one of the others, his arms protectively over his head.

From his position on the front porch, L.E. could see flashes of light coming from the cockpit of the plane, and he knew the Klansman was right: It was gunfire. Because of the noise of the engine, the gunshots couldn't be heard. The sound of shattering glass could be heard, however, as the bullets from Bob's gun smashed through the windshields of a couple of the Klansmen's cars. One of the bullets hit a front light, and it exploded in a brilliant flash, then went out, its passing marked by a wisp of smoke that curled up into the darkness.

When Rocky pulled up from his impromptu strafing run, he saw the twelve burning smudge pots that had been used to mark out the "runway" for him, and he turned the plane around to line up with the road. He let the plane down slowly, its wheels feeling for the ground. He had landed on Blodgett Lane before, but that was in the daylight and in a sturdy biplane. Now it was nighttime, and the little Racer he was flying had sacrificed a bit of sturdiness and maneuverability to gain speed. There was every chance, Rocky knew, that they would ground loop, or worse, flip upside down and slide along for three or four hundred feet before bursting into flames. But he had no choice now. He was committed to the landing.

Despite his worries the wheels touched down gently. Rocky chopped the throttle, then applied the brakes. The plane rolled on past the most distant drum of flame before it finally came to a stop. Rocky turned it around and taxied back to the first of the oil drums.

Joyce met the plane even before it stopped. "Please hurry, Mr. Canfield," she shouted, pointing to the car. "L.E. and young Lenny Puckett are over at George's, too!"

●　　●　　●

"Hold it! Hold it! Where are you all goin'? Get on back here!" Travis yelled to the several KKK men who had started for their cars. Startled by the sharpness of his command, the fleeing men stopped.

"Are you all gonna let some damned fool shootin' at us from an airplane stop us now? We've come too far to turn back," Travis said. "You know damned well they're hidin' Julius up there. Let's just go get him."

"No!" one of the hooded men shouted, and he broke out of the group and ran toward the house. L.E. felt George tense beside him, and he started forward to meet the attack. To his surprise, however, the KKK man wasn't coming to attack them. Instead, about halfway to the house he suddenly turned toward the others and held his arms up in the air. "Leave these people alone!" he yelled.

"What the hell's got into you? Have you gone crazy?" Travis called.

"Yeah," the man said. He reached up and pulled off his hood. There were several gasps from those assembled, for this was a violation of the highest order. The identity of a person was never supposed to be revealed during an actual operation. "I went crazy when I joined this group," he said. He turned toward the house, and L.E. recognized Boyd McMullen, the banker and one of the most prominent men in town.

"George, I want to ask your forgiveness," McMullen said.

"McMullen, what the hell's got into you? We'll have you up before the Court of Honor for this!" Travis screamed. "You'll be expelled from the Klan!"

By now McMullen was clutching at the robe itself, and a moment later he had it off. He threw it into the dirt, alongside his hood.

"Expelled, hell! I just quit!" McMullen replied.

Another car arrived at that moment, careening across the front yard until it reached the very edge of the porch. Recognizing it as his car, L.E. knew at once who it was. When the car stopped, Bob Canfield and Rocky Rockwell got out. Bob looked at the small group arrayed on the front porch of the house, then at the much larger group of hooded men out by the burning cross. He saw Boyd McMullen standing between the two groups, and Bob's face twisted into an expression of surprise.

"Boyd?"

"Mr. McMullen is with us, Mr. Canfield," L.E. said quickly.

"Then get back here with us," Bob said quietly. "Among friends," he added.

Suddenly one of the other Klansmen took off his hood and started walking slowly toward the front of the house. This was a much younger man, about Lenny's age.

"It's Del Murtaugh!" Lenny said happily. "He plays baseball with me."

Del reached the house, then turned to face the remaining Klansmen.

"Who else?" Bob asked. "Who else will join us?"

"Nobody else," Travis shouted back. "The rest of us are standin' firm for what we believe in."

One of the Klansmen went toward his car. "I'm goin' home," he said. "If anyone wants a ride, come along." Three others went with him.

"Come back here!" Travis shouted. "Come back here, you goddamned cowards!"

Another group started to leave, then another, despite Travis's shouts that alternated between pleas and curses.

"Travis, is that you behind that hood?" Bob asked. "That sounds like your voice."

"Let's get out of here," Travis mumbled, and the rest of the Klansmen began to leave.

"You're fired, Travis!" Bob shouted. "I won't have someone like you working for me!"

Just as Travis reached his car, he stopped and turned back toward the house. He jerked off his hood. "You don't have to fire me, you nigger-lovin' son of a bitch! I quit!" he shouted, pounding his fist on the top of his car.

"That's funny," Rocky said.

"What's funny?" Lenny asked.

"That fellow just quit a job he didn't have."

The others laughed, then stood in silence as one by one the cars drove away. Now only one car remained. It was Boyd McMullen's car. It was also one of those with a shot-out windshield.

"I want to thank you men for comin' over to our side," L.E. said.

"Shucks," Del said. "Me and Lenny've been on the same side too long. I reckon I just couldn't see myself out there with those guys while he was up here."

"What about you, Mr. McMullen?" Lenny asked. "That was a pretty brave thing you did, defyin' them like that. What made you do it?"

"You know that little talk L.E. gave about bein' neighbors?"

"Yes, sir."

"George is my neighbor, too. He saved my life a few years ago.".

"I never knew that," Bob said.

"It was during the big flu epidemic. George found me passed out in my car," McMullen said. "He could have left me. No one would have ever known, and no one would have blamed him if they did know."

"I would have known, Mr. McMullen," George said. "And I wouldn't've been able to live with myself if I'd done that."

"You're a good man, George Summers," McMullen said. "In fact, I'd have to say right now that you're a hell of a lot better man than I am."

Clemmie came out onto the porch then, carrying a kerosene lantern. She hung it on the front post, and its golden circle of light took in the group with a warm, friendly glow. "I got some coffee brewin'," she said softly. "I'd be mighty pleased if you'd all stay and drink a cup."

"We wouldn't want to put you out any," Del said.

"Ain't no puttin' out to it," Clemmie said. "I got it started."

"Maybe these other fellows don't know, Clemmie, but I remember what a good cup of coffee you make,"

Bob said. "I'd be very happy to stay. And I'm sure the others will be, too."

It wasn't until then that everyone noticed the way Bob was dressed. He had left the leather jacket in the airplane, revealing the formal evening clothes that he had worn to the Veiled Prophet Ball.

Clemmie chuckled, then commented on it first. "Lord, Mr. Canfield, you're dressed up mighty fine this evenin'."

"Yeah, how about that?" McMullen said, grinning. "Boys, I don't know if we can drink coffee with this man or not. I'm not sure the rest of us are properly dressed for the occasion."

"As I've always said, it doesn't hurt to look your best," Bob replied dryly.

ST. LOUIS

At that same moment, 150 miles north of Sikeston, a red Dusenberg was coming off Eads Bridge, having just crossed the river from Illinois into Missouri. The car belonged to Kerry O'Braugh, but Kerry wasn't driving. That task was left to Vinnie Todaro. Vinnie would also be the chief enforcer for the gang Kerry planned to put together in St. Louis. The remainder of Kerry's men had already arrived or were coming by train.

"Here it is, Vinnie," Kerry said, taking in the lights of St. Louis with a sweep of his hand. "St. Louie—a plum ripe for the picking."

CHAPTER SEVEN

LATE SUMMER 1923, ST. LOUIS

Every girl who worked in the Club Araby was beautiful. Paddy Egan would have it no other way. "When a man goes out for a good time, it's good-lookin' women he'll be wantin' around him," Paddy liked to say. "Even if he's got his wife along, there's no harm for him to have a wee look."

"What if his wife is a pretty woman?" someone asked.

"Sure an' that's all the more reason our women have to be beautiful," Paddy would explain, holding up a finger. "Havin' a pretty wife means that he has an eye for fine-lookin' gals."

One of the prettiest of the women who worked in the Club Araby was Rana McClarity. Rana was a hat-check girl, and Kerry had noticed her the first time he visited the club. He began paying a lot of attention to her, so much, in fact, that Carmine Brazzi and Vinnie Todaro started teasing him. Kerry didn't care. He was attracted to her and interested in seeing how far he could go in developing a relationship with her—and it wasn't just the possibility of sex that held his interest.

Kerry knew from his experience in Chicago that hatcheck girls, even those as beautiful as Rana, often blended into the background—which meant that important things were discussed in front of them as if they were no more than a piece of furniture. If Kerry played his cards right, Rana could be an excellent source of information.

But she was a hard sell. It took Kerry a number of visits to the club, a small fortune in tips, and many flirtatious remarks before Rana would give him her address. She lived in northeast St. Louis on Hodiamont Street in an area known as Kerry Patch—the center of the Irish gang that controlled all of St. Louis's underworld activities. Kerry O'Braugh thought it a good omen that this territory he planned to control had his name on it.

Only two types of people lived in Kerry Patch, the gangsters and the honest, middle-class factory workers and shopkeepers. The middle-class citizens drove Fords, Chevrolets, and Maxwells; the gangsters drove Cadillacs, Lincolns, Packards, and Dusenbergs. Kerry realized that if someone in Kerry Patch saw a bright-red Dusenberg that didn't belong to one of the known gangsters, it would arouse immediate attention. Since he didn't want that, he left his car at home and took a cab out to Rana's house.

When the taxi drove by Sportsman's Park on the way to North St. Louis, Kerry saw large crowds of people moving through the gates. Vendors on the streets and sidewalks around the stadium were hawking pennants, hats, and programs for the game between the St. Louis Grays and the Detroit Tigers.

"Everyone's wantin' to see this new pitcher go up against Detroit's Ty Cobb," the cabdriver explained. "Swampwater Puckett they call him." The driver laughed.

"I think his real name is somethin' like Larry or some such, but they say he comes from the middle of a swamp, so that's why they call him Swampwater. You seen him pitch yet?"

"No."

"I seen him. He beat the Yankees the day I seen him—and let me tell you, that ain't easy to do. Yes sir, I believe Mr. Tannenhower has absolutely got hisself a real crackerjack of a pitcher."

"I don't care much for baseball," Kerry said.

The driver briefly turned around, a surprised look on his face. "You don't like *baseball*?"

"No."

"I ain't never met no one who didn't like baseball. Hell, I grew up playin' it in the streets and empty lots. I thought every kid in America did."

"Not me."

A loud bell clanged, almost in Kerry's ear.

"Goddamned trolleys think they own the goddamned street," the driver groused as he reluctantly gave way to a streetcar that rumbled past. "What kind of work you do?" the driver asked.

"Investments," Kerry answered. "I represent a Chicago company."

"Oh, yeah? Me an' the wife got some investments. We buy a little stock about every month. You know, things like General Motors, U.S. Steel, Penn Central Railroad, and stuff like that. Good, solid stock. What kind of stock you handle?"

"Liquid assets," Kerry answered after only the briefest hesitation, smiling at his own joke.

"Liquid assets, huh? Well, I don't know much about that sort of thing," the driver said. He turned the corner and announced, "Okay, this here is Hodiamont Street. You got the address?"

"Yeah, it's twenty-one fifteen," Kerry said.

"That's a few more blocks," the driver said, picking up speed slightly.

Most of the houses looked alike, Kerry noticed, all very small and made of red brick and built so close

together that the space between the houses was little
more than a walkway. They had tiny front yards, some of
which sported carefully nurtured grass and flowers but
more often were bare dirt.

At one of the cross streets a fire hydrant had been
opened on the corner, and a group of kids was playing in
the gushing water. The taxi driver had to slow down, not
only for the water, but also to avoid the kids dashing
about, so involved with having fun that they were totally
oblivious to any vehicular traffic. A block farther down
the street the taxi encountered another group of kids,
this time following a horse-drawn ice wagon. They were
waiting patiently for handouts of slivers of ice from
broken blocks. The cabby honked, then steered around
the wagon. A moment later he stopped at the curb in
front of a long row of brick houses no different from any
of the other houses they had passed.

"Here it is. You want me to wait?"

"No," Kerry said.

"How you plannin' on gettin' back? There ain't that
many cabs cruisin' out here lookin' for fares. Folks out
here usually drive their own cars or else take the bus or
trolley."

"I'll manage," Kerry said.

"Have it your way. That'll be fifteen cents."

Kerry paid the fare, then got out of the car. After
the taxi drove away he turned to look at the houses. The
number that would have indicated 2115 was missing
from the front stoop post, but the building was sided by
2113 and 2117, so he knew which house it had to be.

Because it was hot, all the doors and all the windows
of the houses were open to let in what little breeze there
was. Kerry could hear the baseball game coming from a
radio playing inside one of the houses.

"*Lenny 'Swampwater' Puckett has three wins and
no losses since he came up to the majors in late July,*" the
announcer was saying. "*He has blazing speed, and he
can break a curve ball around the corner of a house. It's
the top of the third inning, and Swampwater has faced
only six men, including Ty Cobb. What a shame this boy*

*didn't come up at the first of the year, folks. If he had,
I believe we'd be challenging the Yankees right now for
first place."*

Rana met Kerry at the front door before he could
even knock.

"Hi," she said, opening the screen door for him.
"Come on in."

She was wearing a light, cotton housedress. It was
the first time Kerry had ever seen her in anything but
the very short skirts, figure-hugging halters, and mesh
stockings she wore at the club. For some strange reason
he found this innocent, almost housewifely, appearance
more seductive than the overtly sexy outfits he normally
saw her in.

They spent the afternoon talking, and though Kerry
had planned to lead the conversation in such a way as to
get information from her, he discovered that he was
actually enjoying himself. He told Rana things about
himself that he had never told another soul, talking
about his father and about his youth in Sicily, of the
humiliation of going through the immigration process at
Ellis Island, and of how it felt to see his mother
remarry—not for love, but for convenience. He told her
of the time he spent in a reformatory and of the tortures
he had endured there under the guise of "correctional
punishment." Rana cried at the sad parts and laughed at
the funny stories. Kerry didn't say anything about being
a member of the Mafia or about the men he had killed or
about any of his activities or associations in Chicago.

Rana's story was almost as involved as Kerry's. She
was a girl who had matured early and in the eighth grade
got caught in a compromising position with her math
teacher. She got that way because the teacher had
offered her an E, which in the Missouri grading system
was equal to an A, if she'd go to bed with him. Rana
wanted the E, and she was curious about sex. What she
was never able to understand was why, when they were
caught, she was expelled from school while the teacher
got off with no more than a mild reprimand.

Rana's home life had never been pleasant. Her mother had died, and her father was an alcoholic and a compulsive gambler. After she left school, Rana took a job in a pants factory, but she was never able to get ahead because it took everything she made just to keep the house going and pay her father's liquor bill and gambling debts. Then one night her father brought a strange man to her bedroom and suggested to Rana that if a pretty girl was smart, she could make a lot more money than she was earning at the pants factory.

Rana slammed the door to her room and tried to send them away, but her father pleaded with her and told her that he owed the man a great deal of money. If she didn't do this for him, her father said, the man would kill him. Rana accommodated her father's creditor, lying there beneath his sweating, grimy bulk, smelling his oniony breath and gritting her teeth against the pain and humiliation. Later that night, after the man had gone and her father had passed out in a drunken stupor, she left the house. That was four years ago, and she had neither spoken to nor heard from her father since. She had no idea whether he was dead or alive, and she didn't care.

Now she worked for Paddy Egan. She made good money at the Club Araby, and the working conditions weren't bad, though Paddy let it be known that whenever he wanted female companionship, any girl he chose would have to come around or lose her job. Rana had been with him three or four times. Doing it for him made her feel dirty, she told Kerry, and she hated him for making her do it. But as she wanted to keep her job, there was nothing she could do about it. Fortunately, Egan had turned his attentions toward a new girl, a singer with the band. Rana said that she had also heard he was seeing a colored girl on the sly.

There had been one man in Rana's life whom she really thought she could love. He used to pick her up after work and take her to an apartment that he had downtown. He was a businessman, a very respected businessman, Rana said, but he was married. He had told Rana that he was going to divorce his wife, and she stayed with him for eighteen months because she actually believed him.

About three months ago she had finally reached the conclusion that he had no intention of ever getting a divorce. She had confronted him, and he admitted it. He had told her he loved her but that family conditions and business circumstances made a divorce impossible. He had begged her to stay with him, but she refused. She had moved her things out of his apartment and told him she didn't want to see him again. Since that time she hadn't been with anyone, either socially or sexually.

"You aren't married, are you?" she asked Kerry as she finished her story. They were sitting together on the sofa, and at some time during the exchange of stories Kerry had draped his arm around her so that she was now leaning against his shoulder.

"No," Kerry replied with a little chuckle. "I'm not married."

"Good," Rana said. "I don't think I want to go through that again." She took his hand and placed it on her breast, then raised her mouth to his and kissed him. Kerry was surprised to discover that she wasn't wearing a brassiere, and he felt her nipple grow hard under the thin cotton dress.

"Come on," Rana said, standing then and tugging gently at his hand. "I know a place where we can be much more comfortable."

Kerry followed Rana down the hall and into her bedroom. Like all the rooms of the house, the bedroom was small, with barely enough room for the iron-frame double bed, a dresser, and a chest of drawers. The wallpaper was ivory-colored and imprinted with tiny blue flowers, and on the wall just above the bed hung a crucifix. On the opposite wall hung a print of a vase of flowers. Muslin curtains at the open window swelled with the gentle afternoon breeze.

"Get undressed," Rana said without fanfare, crossing the room. "I'll turn on the fan."

A black oscillating fan, the words "Emerson Electric" printed on the little red disk in the center of its blade guard, sat on the chest of drawers. Rana turned it on, and it began humming as it moved back and forth, sweeping the bed with its gentle current.

Kerry undressed quickly, then lay back naked and watched Rana undress. She was much slower. She wasn't teasing him; she was just being methodical, hanging up her dress, putting away her shoes, and folding her stockings. Then, with a smile that was almost shy, she slipped out of her panties and lay them on the dresser beside her hose.

"Was I taking too long to get undressed?" she asked. She sat on the edge of the bed and looked down at Kerry, blocking off part of the fan's sweep so that now it caught Kerry only when it was at the extreme left of its arc.

"No," Kerry said. "I liked watching you."

"Did you?"

"Very much."

"I can tell," Rana said dryly, looking directly at his erection. "Can I hold it?"

"What? Oh! Yeah, sure," Kerry answered.

Rana wrapped her hand around his penis. Kerry thought it was incredible how her fingers could feel hot and cold at the same time, like fire and ice. She squeezed it, then moved her hand up and down a few times.

"No, don't. I'm going to come," Kerry said in a strained voice.

Rana laughed a low, husky laugh; then she let go of his penis and moved her hands up to his shoulders. "No, you won't. You'll come when I decide you'll come." She leaned forward to kiss him, and he felt her nipples brush against his chest. He started to turn over, but she pushed him back down.

"No," she said. "You just lay there. I'll get on top of you."

"I don't do it that way," Kerry said.

"Sure you do. You just haven't done it that way *yet*,"

she replied as she straddled him. As she took him inside her, Kerry felt as if he were being drawn into a vat of warm wax. He felt exquisite pleasure from the soles of his feet to the top of his scalp, and all resistance to this less than manly way to make love left him. He lay back on the bed as defenseless as a milk-fed puppy and looked up at her—at her breasts swaying gently as they hung down, at the flare of her hips, and at the entangling of their pubic hair.

As Rana moved up and down on him, her eyes were closed and her hair was plastered to the side of her face by perspiration. She was biting her lower lip and her face was contorted into an expression of ecstasy. Kerry was aware of many sensations: of what he felt—the sheet against his back that he had never experienced during sex before and the caress that was almost like a lover's kiss of the sweeping breeze from the oscillating Emerson; of what he heard—the squishing sound of flesh against flesh, the little grunts and moans deep in Rana's throat, and the squeak of the bed springs; and of what he smelled—the detergent of the bed sheets from their last washing and her perfume, mingling with their musk in the hot room.

When he felt himself approaching the precipice of climax, he tried to back away, to maintain some authority over the situation if only for his own self-esteem. And yet even in that Rana maintained her dominance, for she so controlled his body and its sensations that she didn't let him have his way. Then her own climax burst over him with such a wave of energy that, with a gut-wrenching groan of complete submission and almost unendurable pleasure, Kerry felt himself exploding inside her. When she collapsed across him and he held her close to him—feeling her breasts press into his chest, feeling the sweat pool between their bodies, feeling her heartbeat against his—he was almost ready to say that he had never had sex before today. He had been with women, lots of women, but nothing had ever been like this. They lay together like that, under the sweep of the fan, until the evening shadows filled the room.

TWO DAYS LATER

"I've heard of some crazy things in my life, Kerry O'Braugh, but robbin' a funeral parlor is about the craziest thing ever," Vinnie Todaro said.

"Yeah, boss. You ain't serious, are you? Are we really going to knock over a funeral parlor?" Carmine Brazzi asked.

"That's what we're goin' to do, boys," Kerry replied, picking up the bolt assembly of the .45-caliber Thompson submachine gun that lay in pieces on the table in front of him. He was cleaning each part thoroughly, then reassembling the weapon.

"You're the boss," Vinnie muttered.

"That's right, Vinnie," Kerry said. "I'm the boss." He glanced up from the trigger housing. "Look, we need money, right?"

"Well, yeah, we do. But how much money can we get from a funeral parlor?"

"Yeah, what are we goin' to do, take the nickels off the stiff's eyes?" Carmine asked, and then he laughed at his own joke.

"Not exactly. I just found out that the McElwain Funeral Parlor is Paddy Egan's bank."

"His bank?"

"That's right. Every Sunday afternoon all the money from his speaks, gamblin' joints, and the rest of his operations gets brought to the funeral home. It's kept in a safe in the back of the mortuary."

"Jeez, Boss, where'd you hear that?"

Kerry thought of Rana and smiled. "Never mind," he said. "Just take it from me that the information's good."

"Is it a real funeral parlor?" Vinnie asked nervously.

"Yeah, it's real."

"No. What I mean is, are there likely to be any stiffs there?"

"It'd look kind of suspicious to have a funeral parlor and not have any bodies, wouldn't it?" Kerry replied.

"Yeah," Vinnie said. "Yeah, I guess it would. Look,

Boss, even if it is Egan's bank, do you think knockin' over a funeral parlor is really such a good idea? I mean, it's kind'a like robbin' a grave or somethin', ain't it? What if there are some bodies in there?"

"If there are, we'll be as quiet as mice so we don't wake 'em up," Kerry said. He laughed, and Carmine laughed with him.

"That ain't funny, guys," Vinnie said. "This kind of stuff gives me the creeps."

"Yeah, well, see if this'll help calm you down," Kerry said. "The person I got this information from tells me there could be as much as fifty thousand dollars in there."

"Fifty thousand?" Vinnie gasped.

"That's right," Kerry said. "If we pull this job off, it'll do two things for us. It'll get us some money for operatin' expenses, and it'll hurt Egan bad. Real bad." He smiled. "Plus, since it's dirty money, the cops won't be after us for it."

"Fifty thousand?" Vinnie asked again.

"Fifty thousand," Kerry confirmed. "Do you still have the creeps about goin' into a funeral parlor?"

Vinnie smiled. "For fifty thousand bucks I'd rob a bishop's crypt."

Vinnie struck a match, but Kerry reached over and slapped it out of his hand. The flaming match dropped onto Vinnie's pants leg, then fell to the floor of the car.

"Christ!" Vinnie yelped. "What'd you do that for?" He stepped on the still-burning match to put it out.

"Use your head, Vinnie," Kerry growled. "We're parked over here like we're supposed to be one of the cars for sale on this lot. Don't you think it might look just a little suspicious if somebody over in the funeral home looked across the street here and saw a light in what's supposed to be an empty car?"

"Oh," Vinnie mumbled. "Yeah, I guess you're right. But I need a smoke. Christ, I'm dyin' for a cigarette."

"If the wrong person sees you light one up, you just

might die for it," Kerry warned. He took out a package of chewing gum. "Here," he offered. "Chew some gum."

"Okay, thanks." Vinnie took a stick of gum, peeled it, and put it in his mouth. A moment later he was chewing it with his mouth open, cracking it between his teeth, while at the same time drumming nervously on the steering wheel.

"Shit," Carmine muttered. "Damned if I wouldn't rather let him smoke and take a chance on gettin' shot than listen to that. Will you, goddammit, chew with your mouth shut?"

"And quit your fuckin' fidgetin'," Kerry added.

"I can't help it," Vinnie said. "This deal's got me nervous. I mean, robbin' a funeral parlor, for Chrissake. Whoever heard of such a thing?"

"Shh!" Kerry abruptly cautioned. "It looks like the last mourners are coming out now. Be quiet."

"Didn't your Uncle George look good, Martha?" a woman's voice, floating across the street, asked. "He looked just like he was sleeping."

"Yes, Mama, in the arms of the Lord," a younger-sounding woman replied.

Two men followed the women out of the parlor. One of the men turned to lock the doors behind him.

"Thanks for holding the parlor open for us, Mr. McElwain," the other man said. "We had to drive all the way up here from Cape Girardeau, and I didn't know if we were going to make it in time or not."

"That's quite all right, Mr. Strayhorn. I knew you'd want to see your brother one last time before the funeral," McElwain replied.

Strayhorn and his wife and daughter got into one car and drove away, while McElwain, after trying the door to make certain it was locked, got into another. A moment later the car started up and drove away.

"Now?" Carmine asked, reaching for the door handle in the back seat.

"Not yet," Kerry replied. "Wait a few more minutes."

"What for?" Carmine asked. "He's gone."

"Just wait," Kerry said again.

The three men sat quietly for a few moments longer; then McElwain's car reappeared. It slowed down in front of the funeral parlor, McElwain looked over his building carefully, and then he drove away.

"Okay. Now," Kerry said.

"How'd you know he was goin' to come back like that?" Carmine asked, his voice filled with awe.

"Because *I* would if I thought someone might be waitin' and watchin' to see when I close."

"Son of a bitch. You're pretty smart," Carmine said.

"Yeah, that's why he's the boss," Vinnie reminded him.

Kerry turned the door handle. "Okay, Carmine, you and me are goin' to get in through the back window. Vinnie, you wait in the car. When you see us comin' alongside the building, start the motor. By the time we reach the street, I want you there to pick us up. You got that?"

"Yeah, Boss, I got it," Vinnie said. "I'm just glad I don't have to go in there."

"What's your problem?" Carmine asked, giggling. "Didn't you hear the woman say it looked just like old George was sleepin'? Of course, we could always wake him up."

"You got a smart mouth, you know that, Carmine?" Vinnie said.

"Cut it out, both of you," Kerry hissed. "Come on, Carmine, let's go."

The two gangsters ran across the street, then down the side of the funeral parlor, disappearing quickly into the shadows. When they reached the back of the building, they found a window that was just about waist high. Kerry tried it, but it was locked. He took off his jacket and wrapped it around a rock, then broke out the window. The cloth of his jacket deadened the sound somewhat, though it still made quite a noise.

"If that don't wake the dead, nothin' will," Carmine quipped, and Kerry glared at him. Kerry reached through

the window and released the latch; then he slid it open
and slipped inside, Carmine right behind him.

The first thing they were aware of was an overpow-
ering smell—a combination of flowers and formalde-
hyde. Taking their flashlights from their pockets, they
played the beams around the room, illuminating porcelain sinks and a lead-lined embalming table.

"We're in the embalming room," Kerry said.

"Oh, shit! Look at that!" Carmine gasped. His beam
of light had fallen upon a second embalming table and
the body of a young woman. She was totally naked, and
her skin was bluish-white. There were terrible wounds
all over her body, though the wounds were bloodless,
almost yellow in appearance.

"Auto accident," Kerry said. "I read about it in the
paper."

Carmine crossed himself as they left the embalming
room and walked into the display parlor. Here, on a
catafalque surrounded by banks of flowers, rested an
open coffin. A man lay in this coffin, his hair neatly
combed, his face powdered and rouged, his eyes closed,
"just like he was sleeping."

"That must be Mr. Strayhorn," Kerry said. Again,
Carmine crossed himself.

The two men hurried through the display parlor and
down the hall to the director's office. They found the safe
in a far corner.

"Think you can blow it?" Kerry asked.

"Piece o' cake," Carmine replied. He taped a tiny
vial of nitro to each of the two hinges, then ran a wire
across the room and connected it to a small, hand-
operated generator.

"Help me get this carpet draped over the safe, will
you?" he asked.

Together Kerry and Carmine moved the desk and
chairs so they could pick up the carpet. They spread the
carpet over the top of the safe, not only to protect them
in the event a large piece of the safe should chip off in the
blast, but also to deaden the sound. When the carpet

was in place, Carmine signaled for Kerry to get down while he twisted the handle to the generator.

Both vials went off together, a sign that Carmine had done his job well. Inside the room the explosion was loud enough to make Kerry's ears ring, but he knew from experience that the carpet would muffle the explosion enough so that any neighbor who might hear it could easily mistake it for boxcars bumping together on the nearby train track or even a distant rumble of thunder.

Rushing to the safe, they removed the carpet, and a thick, noxious cloud of smoke billowed up around them, causing them to cough. They waved their hands in front of their faces, warding off the smoke, then looked at the safe. The door had been blown loose at the hinges and its insides exposed.

"Holy shit! You were right!" Carmine said. "Look at that!"

Inside the safe were several stacks of bills, all neatly banded in bundles.

"Let's clean it out, then get the hell out of here," Kerry said, producing a sack from his pocket. Carmine had a similar sack, and in less than a minute both sacks were full, and the safe was empty.

"Let's go!" Kerry ordered.

Vinnie met them in the street in front of the funeral parlor, just as planned, and they hopped inside the car. The car sped away without so much as a sign of the police or any of Paddy Egan's men.

"Yahoo!" Carmine shouted as they drove off. "That went slicker'n pigeon shit! You should've been in there, Vinnie! I mean, it was slicker'n pigeon shit!"

"Were there any bodies in there?"

"What? Yeah, but it was no problem. I mean, me an' Kerry, we didn't even hardly notice 'em, did we, Boss?"

"These are thousand-dollar packets," Kerry said, handing Carmine a number of bundles without answering him. "Let's count 'em."

Kerry and Carmine began counting the packets of money while Vinnie kept looking back anxiously in the rearview mirror. A few moments later they finished the count.

"I got fifty-two packets," Kerry said. "How many do you have, Carmine?"

The gangster finished his tally and looked at Kerry in surprise. "I got forty-five of 'em. That makes ninety-seven. Ninety-seven thousand dollars!" Carmine exclaimed. "I thought you said there'd only be about fifty thousand. Why so much?"

"They must have two weeks' count here," Kerry said.

"Son of a bitch! We're rich!" Vinnie shouted.

"No, we're not," Kerry replied, taking all of the money and putting it back in the two sacks. "Not yet, anyway," he added. "But this is goin' to give us the chance to *get* rich."

CHAPTER EIGHT

It was Kendra Mills's idea to do a piece on the International Air Races being held in St. Louis. Thomas Petzold told her that he already had the story assigned, explaining that he had a sportswriter covering it from the sports angle and a science writer covering it for any breakthrough that might occur in the aviation industry. He asked Kendra what was left. When Kendra asked him who was covering the human side of the event, Petzold smiled and held up his hands in submission, then told her it was her assignment if she wanted it.

Petzold would have assigned a driver from the newspaper to take Kendra out to the airport had she wanted him to, but she knew that Demaris Hunter would probably enjoy the event, so she called her former roommate and asked if Demaris would like to drive her out. Demaris thought it would be, in her words, "a

153

hoot," and she agreed to pick Kendra up at the newspaper office a couple of hours before the race was to begin.

The traffic on the road leading to the airport grounds was extremely heavy, and when they got there several hundred cars were already parked behind the fence and more than a thousand people were milling about. A policeman was directing the arriving cars to a specific parking area, and when he indicated that Demaris should turn right when she wanted to turn left, the young woman shook her head.

"I don't want to go that way," she called out to him.

"I'm sorry, miss, but I have instructions to park everyone over here."

"I'm with the press," Kendra said, holding up her press card. "And I have a very important interview with Mr. Rockwell of Rockwell-McPheeters Aircraft."

"Oh, please be a dear and let us through," Demaris said, fixing her large blue eyes on the policeman. "We'll both lose our jobs if we don't get to see Mr. Rockwell."

He stroked his chin for a second, ignoring the honking horns from the drivers growing impatient behind them.

"All right," he finally conceded. "I could lose my own job for doing this, but go ahead."

Demaris smiled broadly. "Thanks," she replied, putting the car in gear.

The police officer held up his hand to stop the oncoming traffic and allow Demaris to turn in the opposite direction. She scooted through, gunning the engine.

The car slowed, and Kendra laughed. "We could both lose our jobs, huh?" she said.

"Well, your job is interviewing him, isn't it? And my job is driving you. If you lose your job, won't I lose mine?"

"I guess if you put it that way . . ." Kendra agreed, grinning.

After Demaris left the main road, she drove around behind one of the hangars. A moment later she pulled the little yellow Auburn onto a concrete ramp that was already crowded with airplanes and aviators.

"There he is," Kendra said, pointing to a man working on the engine of a sleek-looking, low-winged monoplane. "That's the man I flew down from Chicago with. Hello, Mr. Rockwell," she called.

"Oh, he *is* handsome, isn't he?" Demaris said.

Rocky looked up from the plane at the two young women in the car, then started toward them. He rubbed the back of his hand across his cheek, and as he did so, he left a small smear of grease on his face.

"Well, hello there, Miss Mills. I wasn't sure you'd come."

"I said I would," Kendra replied. She had a camera with her, and she raised it to take his picture.

"Don't they usually send a photographer along?" Rocky asked.

"Only for the veteran reporters," Kendra said with a smile as she removed the glass plate. "When you're just starting, as I am, you pretty much do everything for yourself."

"And who is this lovely young lady? Is she your assistant?"

"Oh, I'm sorry. How rude of me," Kendra said. "No, this is my friend, Demaris Hunter."

Rocky smiled and extended his hand. "I know who you are," he said. "I recognize you from your pictures. You're the . . . let me see, what do they call it? The Queen of Beauty?"

"Goddess," Demaris corrected. "Don't confuse me with a mere queen," she joked. "I am the *Goddess* of Love and Beauty."

"Well, all I can say is, it looks to me like they chose the right one," Rocky said.

"Why, I thank you, kind sir."

Rocky turned his attention back to Kendra. "Now, you said you wanted to do a story. So, what do you want to do, interview me?"

"I don't need to."

"You don't need to? Why not? I mean, how are you going to do a story if you don't ask me questions?"

"Oh, I may ask a few questions now and then. But mostly I'm just going to observe."

"Okay, if you think you can get a story that way," Rocky said, shrugging. He held up his finger. "But don't forget to mention Rockwell-McPheeters Aircraft. I mean, the whole reason I'm in this race is to get some publicity for our business."

"I'll give you some publicity, I promise," Kendra said.

"Mr. Rockwell, is that the airplane you're going to fly today?" Demaris asked, pointing to the plane Rocky had been working on.

"Yes. But call me Rocky, will you? Seems to me that anyone named Mr. Rockwell would have to wear a suit and tie. Somebody named Rocky can wear a leather flying jacket."

Demaris laughed. "Okay, Rocky. Are you going to win the race?"

"If I didn't think I'd win, I wouldn't be entered in the event," Rocky replied.

"Pretty sure of yourself, aren't you?"

"Well, no. Actually, I'm more sure of the airplane," he explained. "This is the McPheeters Racer, and I guarantee that it's the fastest job on the field. But I had very little to do with it. It was designed by my partner, Bryan McPheeters."

"Still, it takes some skill to pilot the plane, doesn't it?"

"I guess not just anyone could come in off the street and do it," Rocky admitted, shrugging.

"Could we have a closer look at the plane?" Kendra asked.

"Sure," Rocky replied. "That's what it's all about. Come on over. Isn't she a beauty?" he asked as they approached the ship.

"But how can this plane be faster than the others?" Demaris asked. "This one has only one wing; all the others have two. Doesn't that put it at a disadvantage?"

Rocky laughed. "Oh, no. That's one of the things

that makes it faster. You see, with only one wing there's less drag."

"Drag?"

"Resistance to the air," Rocky explained. "The more things there are sticking out into the air, the more chance the wind has to work against the craft and slow it down. That's called being clean, and this aircraft is very clean."

"Is that why the nose is pointed?"

"Yes," Rocky said. "Now you're beginning to catch on. And here. Feel this." He held Demaris's palm against the skin of the airplane, rubbing back and forth gently. "Do you feel how smooth the skin is?"

"Yes," she answered.

Seeing them, Kendra raised her camera and took a picture of Rocky sliding Demaris's hand over the skin of the plane.

"Doesn't that feel good?" Rocky asked.

Demaris looked directly into Rocky's eyes and smiled broadly. "It feels all right to me, honey," she bantered. "How does it feel to you?"

Rocky coughed to cover his obvious embarrassment. "Uh, fine," he said noncommittally, and then he continued his explanation. "But what I was trying to say is that a smooth skin helps move the wind over the surface more quickly."

"Demaris, I'm going to walk around and take a few more pictures and meet a few more people," Kendra interjected. "You want to come with me?"

"No, I'll stay here, if you don't mind," Demaris said. "In fact, I think I'll find a telephone and call Morris. I'll bet he'd like to see all this," she added, the sweep of her hand taking in the roughly one hundred planes gathered. The aircraft, parked in several long rows, were of all different sizes, shapes, and colors, though most of them, she noticed, had at least two wings. She smiled. If Rocky was telling the truth about drag, and she had no doubt but that he was, then the McPheeters Racer represented quite a departure from the accepted norm.

Rocky said his partner had designed the plane. Was he being innovative, or was he being foolish?

"Good idea. I'm sure he would," Kendra agreed as she started down the flight line.

"Anything I can do for you, Miss Hunter?" Rocky asked Demaris after Kendra left.

"Perhaps there is. Do you have a telephone, Rocky?"

"We sure do," Rocky answered. "But it's in the office, and the office is locked up. I'll have to let you in."

"Would you mind terribly?"

"No, I wouldn't mind at all."

Demaris followed Rocky through the hangar past a number of other planes and to a locked door that led to a small office at the back of the building.

"That big airplane there is the mail plane," Rocky pointed out as he put the key into the door lock. "That's the one your friend flew in."

"Oh, I'd love to take a ride someday."

"How about tomorrow?"

"Tomorrow?"

"Sure, if you'd like."

"Yes," Demaris breathed. "Yes, I'd like very much. Thank you."

Rocky opened the door and pointed to the telephone on the desk. "Be my guest," he said. "I need to return to the plane."

"I'll only be a minute," Demaris promised.

She put through the call, and as she waited for Morris to come to the phone, she studied the wall inside the office. On one part of the wall was a large, square piece of fabric, decorated with a number of black crosses. For a moment she didn't know what it was; then she remembered once reading that during the war the aviators painted little crosses on the side of their airplane for every enemy plane they shot down. That meant that Rocky had shot down—Demaris counted the crosses—twenty-six? My God, he had shot down twenty-six airplanes!

A shudder ran through her.

"Hello?" came a voice over the phone.

"Morris, hello," Demaris replied, quickly pulling her attention away from the wall and its chilling account of Rocky's wartime triumphs. "Listen, I've got something you ought to do today."

Demaris went on to tell Morris Montgomery about the upcoming air races and convinced him that he should round up several of their friends and bring a picnic lunch out to the airport. Morris agreed that it sounded like a good idea and promised to be there before the races began.

As Demaris was hanging up the telephone, something sitting on a shelf in the corner of the room got her attention. She went over to look at it more closely and saw that it was a parachute. What would it be like, she wondered, if she not only took a ride in an airplane, but also made a parachute leap from one?

Above the parachute were several pictures of planes: planes flying, planes on the ground, planes alone, and planes with men standing in front of them. In one picture a younger-looking Rocky had his arm draped across the shoulders of another man. They were standing in front of an airplane, and both were holding up champagne bottles toward the camera. Noticing that there was an inscription, Demaris leaned in to get a closer look.

THE LAFAYETTE ESCADRILLE'S THREE ACES: ROCKY ROCKWELL, BILLY CANFIELD, AND DOM PERIGNON, the caption read.

Billy Canfield? William Canfield. This was Billy Books! It was funny, Demaris thought, but she had never really thought of Billy Books as an actual person. He was just a name and a plaque, part of the school's background, like Spengeman Hall, the Bateman statue, and the flowers in the quad. And yet it was obvious from this photo that to Rocky, William Canfield was more than just a person, he was a friend. She took the picture down from the wall and studied it.

"He's the cause of all this," a voice said from the door. Startled, Demaris looked around to see Rocky standing there. He pointed to the picture in her hand. "Billy Canfield," he said easily. "This company, Rockwell-McPheeters Aircraft, it was all his idea."

"It was?"

"Sure," Rocky said.

Demaris held up the picture. "The library at school is named after him."

Rocky chuckled. "Yeah, I know. And I'll bet ol' Billy is getting a kick out of that. Not that he didn't like books, mind you. The truth is, he was a pretty smart fellow. He just wasn't the type you'd expect to find hanging around a library."

"What was he like?"

"Smart, brave, handsome—all the French girls went for him—loyal, dependable . . . and old."

"Old?" Demaris asked, her face screwing up in confusion. "What do you mean, old? He doesn't look very old to me."

"He's dead," Rocky said. "You can't get older than dead." He smiled sadly. "That's a joke that made the rounds in France."

"How did he die?"

"Quickly, I hope," Rocky said softly.

"I mean—"

"I know what you mean, Miss Hunter. And I don't mean to be flippant with my answer, really I don't. But there were so many young boys like Billy who were turned into old men that the only thing left we can hope for is that when they died, they died quickly."

"What did you mean when you said this was all his idea?"

"Billy was a Canfield. You can't live in this town without knowing what that means, can you?"

"Corn Toasties," Demaris said.

Rocky laughed. "Cereal, yes, but mostly money. Lots of money. Only Billy wasn't interested in cereal or feed or land or any of the dozens of other ways Bob Canfield has of making money. All Billy was interested in was flying. Even before the war he was sponsoring a few experimental airplanes, designed by a man who is, I think, the most brilliant aircraft designer in the business."

"Bryan McPheeters?"

"Yes, my partner," Rocky said. "Anyway, Billy used to tell me about the great airplanes Bryan had in his mind, and he swore that as soon as the war was over he was going to come back to St. Louis and build an aircraft manufacturing company. I was to be a part of it, he said." Rocky smiled and shook his head slowly. "I couldn't understand why he felt he needed me. I certainly had no money to invest in the project. I had no design ideas. And Billy was as good a flyer as I was. So why did he need me?" Rocky was silent for a moment before he continued. "I asked him why. And do you know what he answered?"

"No."

"He said, 'Because I know you'll make it happen.'" Rocky shrugged, then swept his hand around, taking in the office, the hangar, and, by implication, the airplanes involved. "So, that's just what I did. When the war was over, I came to St. Louis. It's funny. I mean, I had other things in mind, my own ideas. But with Billy gone, I was no longer my own man. Nothing I had planned seemed to matter. I was suddenly compelled to *make it happen* for Billy. I met with Bryan McPheeters, and I met with Bob Canfield. Bryan is giving the business his brilliance, Bob is giving it his money."

"And you?" Demaris asked.

"Me, Miss Hunter? I am giving it my life," Rocky replied solemnly.

Demaris looked back down at the picture of Billy, smiling at her from the photograph she was holding. She stared at it for a long moment. "Billy Books" would never mean the same thing to her again. When finally she looked up at Rocky again, there were tears in her eyes.

"I think Billy would be very proud," she said.

Morris Montgomery arrived at the airport an hour or so later with several other young people, having convinced them that a picnic on the grounds of the airport during an actual air race would be much more enjoyable than anything else they might have planned for their weekend outing. Meeting Demaris where she had instructed, Morris parked his roadster and hopped out.

"Oh, this is going to be great fun," he said to her, giving her a quick kiss. "To think of actually watching airplanes race against each other."

"But won't they fly so high that we won't be able to see them?" Mark Peters asked. Mark wasn't there for Kendra's sake. He was now keeping steady company with another young lady, and she was there, too, hanging on possessively to his arm lest Kendra decide she wanted a second opportunity at him.

"No, they won't be too high," Demaris explained. "They'll be flying around those markers there. They're called pylons," she added, pointing to one of them. "So they'll be flying low enough for us to see them quite well."

Having been here an hour longer than any of the others, Demaris was now the "expert" they turned to when they had questions. To her credit she had spent the time well, so she actually was able to answer most of the queries with some degree of accuracy.

"Say, suppose we set up over here?" Morris suggested. "We could spread out our lunch basket and listen to some radio broadcasts."

"You brought your radio!" Demaris exclaimed. "Good idea. Oh, and we have someone to root for," she told her friends. "We know one of the pilots who'll be flying in the races. His name is Rocky Rockwell."

"Then we shall all cheer for Rocky Rockwell," Morris said. "But tell me, how on earth did you meet such a fellow?"

"Kendra is doing a story about him for the newspaper," Demaris replied. "She met him last spring, when he flew her back from Chicago."

That was the first time any of the others knew of Kendra's experience, and they began asking all sorts of questions about it while Morris experimented with the radio. After several squeaks and squawks he finally managed to tune it in to a station, and broadcast music began to pour forth from the tulip-shaped speaker.

A portable radio cost nearly as much as a small car, and many of those who had come to watch the air races had never even seen one. For the moment hearing music come out of a box not much bigger than a picnic hamper was an experience in itself, and the crowd began to gather around, moving in as close as they could without being too forward.

"Let's dance!" one of the boys suggested, and, to the amusement of those who had been drawn by the spectacle of a portable radio, the group began gyrating to the music.

The dancing continued for a while, finally losing momentum and dissolving after the novelty wore off. Besides, the roar of aircraft engines being tested out on the airfield not only drowned out the music, it also drew attention so that soon the group of young men and women were as fascinated by the upcoming proceedings as were the other thirty thousand spectators lining the airfield.

"Good afternoon, ladies and gentlemen," a voice suddenly said from the radio. "This is station KSLM, broadcasting from Lambert Flying Field in St. Louis, Missouri, where today the fastest airplanes and the most skilled aviators in the world have gathered to test their skills."

"Oh, how wonderful!" one of the girls said. "We'll be able to watch the races and listen to the radio broadcast at the same time! This is going to be thrilling!"

One pilot didn't find the event at all thrilling, leastwise, not the outcome. Rocky Rockwell did not win. He hadn't even come close. The problem was that his plane had been *too* fast. During the straight part of the course, the McPheeters Racer was quite clearly faster than anything else on the field. Unfortunately it was so fast that at the end of each straight leg it was unable to make the turns within a radius that would bring it back on the course. Had they raced from St. Louis to Chicago and back, Rocky would have been the obvious winner. But they had raced around pylons set up within the confines of Lambert Field, and Rocky finished well down in the middle of the pack.

Rocky smiled and congratulated the winning pilot and joked with the others, then visited for a while with the two girls he had met with earlier and their friends. He cheerfully answered all their questions and kept up a good front, but when night fell and the day's festivities were over, and the cars began streaming away from the airport, looking like a string of glowing beetles, Rocky went into the office of the Rockwell-McPheeters Aviation Company and threw his chair against the wall, smashing it to pieces.

"Son of a bitch!" he screamed.

"Here, now!" Bryan McPheeters called in his soft Irish brogue, coming out of the back room. "What's goin' on?"

"Oh, Bryan, I'm sorry. I didn't even know you were in here," Rocky said. Still, he threw his leather helmet after the chair—but since it merely hit the wall quietly before bouncing to the floor, it didn't give him nearly the same satisfaction that the now-splintered chair had.

"And would you tell me what's wrong, now?" Bryan asked.

"*What's wrong?* Damn! Do I have to tell you? You did *your* job . . . you built the fastest plane here today. But I didn't do *my* job. All I had to do was fly it, and I couldn't even do that. I failed you."

"Don't go puttin' yourself down, lad," Bryan countered. "This so-called race was an abomination. The whole idea of making an aircraft go fast is to design it in such a way as to slip through the air cleanly. And yet 'tis these self-same clean lines that're the downfall of one who tries to negotiate such a short course. No, I'm afraid this race proved nothin'. The one who walked away with the trophy today did so at a speed of barely over one hundred fifty miles per hour."

"Maybe so," Rocky conceded glumly, "but I'd hoped that after today everyone would have heard of the Rockwell-McPheeters Aviation Company."

"That time will come, Rocky," Bryan said. "One day the sky will be filled with our planes."

"You know that, do you?"

"Aye, lad. As surely as if God whispered it in me ear."

Suddenly Rocky laughed. "All right. If God's been talking to you, who am I to disagree?" He started for the hangar.

"Where're you goin'?" Bryan asked.

"Out to the RM-3," Rocky said. "I promised a young lady a ride tomorrow, and I want to make certain that the plane is ready."

Demaris Hunter, dressed in as reasonable a facsimile of what an aviatrix would wear as she could find in her wardrobe, was walking through the preflight inspection with Rocky the next morning when he asked her, "What kind of ride do you want?"

"Well, I like to live dangerously," Demaris answered. "So I want everything. I want you to do loop-the-loops, fly upside down . . . anything and everything you can think of."

"Are you sure?"

"I'm sure."

"All right, if that's what you want. I'll just make certain you're well strapped in before we take off. But if it gets too rough for you, put both your hands on top of your head like this"—he demonstrated—"and I'll stop."

"It won't get too rough for me," Demaris promised.

Rocky assisted her into the front cockpit of the big biplane, then began strapping her in. While he was doing so, Demaris felt his hands moving around on her body, looking for the strap on one side and the buckle on the other as he cinched the belt down tightly. It was all perfectly innocent, but in the excitement of the moment Demaris could almost believe that Rocky's hands were a lover's hands, caressing her. As a result, she began to experience a tingling sensation throughout her body and a hot moistness between her legs.

Rocky climbed into the cockpit behind her, then gave a signal to one of the men working on the flight line. The man came over, stuck a crank in the side of the engine, and began to turn it. When the engine coughed and then caught a moment later, it was the greatest thrill Demaris had ever known in her life.

She leaned back in her seat and looked through the tiny windshield at the silver blur of the propeller as Rocky began to taxi away from the hangar. When the plane had reached the far end of the field, Rocky turned it around and, with the engine roaring at full speed, started back down the runway—faster, then faster still, faster even than Demaris had ever gone in her car. She felt the tail of the airplane lift up, then the main wheels. She looked over the side of the plane to watch the row of orange-painted baskets that marked the runway falling away below them. Then, suddenly and unexpectedly, she found herself looking straight up at the sky as Rocky pulled the airplane into a swooping climb. When they reached the top of the climb, Rocky leveled off by rolling upside down and Demaris was hanging by the lap belt. She looked up—or, rather, thought she had looked up—only to see the airport looming over her head.

Rocky rolled the airplane right side up, then whipped it into a snap roll, and the horizon whirled around in front of Demaris. Rocky headed southwest for a while, away from the city; then, when he was well clear of any other airplanes, he began wrenching the biplane around the sky. He put it through a series of loops, then let it fall off into a spin. Each maneuver was more exciting than the one preceding, and Demaris discovered, to her surprise, that she was actually on the edge of sexual orgasm.

Finally Rocky stopped the aerobatics and throttled back the engine. Demaris heard him banging on the fuselage, and when she twisted around in her seat, he held up the speaking tube, indicating that he wanted to talk to her.

"Did you enjoy it?" he asked, when she held the speaking tube to her ear.

"Yes! Oh, yes!"

"Do you want to land?"

"Oh, do you mean it's over?"

"No," Rocky replied. "I don't mean go back to the airport. I mean do you want to land down there?"

"Where? I don't see any place to land."

Rocky smiled at her. "I don't need much of a place," he said.

Demaris gasped as Rocky suddenly cut the engine, then stood the airplane on one wing. The roar of the engine was gone now, replaced by the rush of wind whipping across the wings and whistling through the bracing and guy wires. The airplane started slipping down toward the ground, and Demaris peered intently through the windshield and to each side, trying to find where he was planning to set down. The city of St. Louis, though visible, was now several miles behind them. All she could see ahead and below was a solid canopy of trees.

The plane continued to lose altitude, heading down toward the trees, lower and lower, though Demaris still had no idea where he could land. She picked up the speaking tube. "What are you doing?" she asked.

"I'm landing," he shouted, and because the engine was relatively silent, Demaris realized that she was hearing him without the tube, so she twisted around to look at him.

"You're going to crash into the trees!" she called back to him.

"I thought you said you liked to live your life dangerously!"

"Dangerously, yes—but not foolishly."

"Don't you trust me?"

"Of course I trust you! What other choice do I have?"

"If you're afraid, we can go back to St. Louis now."

For a moment Demaris thought he might be trying to test her. She considered it, then smiled at him. "No, thank you," she shouted at him. "I think you're just bluffing, trying to get me to say I'm afraid."

"You mean you aren't afraid?"

"Do your worst," she said. "I'm not afraid!"

"Then hold on, because we're going into the trees!"

Demaris turned around to face front again to see what Rocky had in mind. If he was trying to bluff her, he was doing a good job of it. It looked as if he had no intention whatever of adding power and climbing back into the sky. By now they were so low that the upper branches of some of the taller trees were slapping against the airplane's wheels. Then, in front of her, she saw an opening no bigger than a football field. Surely he wasn't planning to land there!

That was exactly what Rocky had in mind, for as soon as they cleared the last tree, the airplane dropped like an elevator.

"My God! You're crazy!" Demaris screamed.

Halfway across the opening, the wheels hit the ground. It was not until they were actually on the ground that Demaris saw a long, wide path stretching out in front of them. The path hadn't been visible from the air because it was completely covered by a canopy of large, spreading elm trees. The plane was still going at a pretty good speed when it slipped in under the trees onto the path, and by the time Rocky got it stopped, they were nearly a thousand feet into the woods. It was exactly as if he had landed at the mouth of a tunnel, then used the tunnel itself as a runway to let the plane roll to a stop. But stop it finally did. For a moment there was absolute silence.

"I discovered this place a couple of years ago," Rocky told Demaris. "But you're the first person I ever brought here."

"I'm honored," she said. "I *think*," she added dryly.

"You want to get out and take a walk?" Rocky asked.

"I don't know if I have the strength," she replied.

Rocky chuckled. "I guess it *was* sort of frightening."

"No, that's not it," Demaris said. "It's . . ." How could she tell him? She couldn't explain it herself, but it wasn't fear that made her weak. It was exhilaration and, yes, *sexual excitation*.

Rocky climbed down from the plane, then stood alongside the fuselage and reached up toward the front cockpit.

"Come on," he said. "Lean over the edge and I'll help you down."

Demaris felt Rocky's hands clasp her just under her shoulders, and she felt his strength as he lifted her over the padded rim of the cockpit well. She slid down, her body against his. The prolonged body-to-body contact, coupled with Demaris's awareness of Rocky's virility and her own aroused state, stimulated a hunger she could not suppress. As if by their own volition her arms wrapped around Rocky's neck, and she glued herself to him, grinding her pelvis tightly against his, pressing her lips to his lips, teasing him with the darting tip of her tongue.

If Rocky was surprised by what she did, it didn't slow his reaction. Demaris felt an almost instantaneous bulge grow at the front of his pants. He put his arms around her and pulled her to him even more tightly, returning her kiss with an ardor that quickly matched hers. Demaris felt her head spinning faster and faster with dizzying excitement, and for one frightening moment she actually thought that she was going to pass out.

Finally Rocky found the strength that she didn't have, and he broke off the kiss, though he didn't move away from her, and she could still feel the pounding heat of his erection. He looked down at her with a puzzled expression on his face.

"Little girl," he whispered, "I'm not one of your college classmates sparking with you on a moonlit date. Hell, I never even went to college. I have to warn you, you're playing a dangerous game."

Somewhere, deep within one of the chambers of her mind, the rational Demaris watched with a quickening concern over the consequences of her actions. This rational Demaris screamed for her to stop—now!— before things went any further. But reason and sanity had fled before the terrible fires of longing that licked at her body, and it was the reckless Demaris, not the rational Demaris, who was in charge.

"I told you," she said, unbuttoning Rocky's shirt. "I like to live dangerously."

"Damn you, girl," Rocky said, as, almost angrily, he scooped her up and carried her away from the airplane. Demaris now dissolved into a quivering mass of jelly, unable to initiate any action, unable to even think for herself. She was only barely aware that he was carrying her away as she wrapped her arms around his neck and kissed him again. He then lay her down, and she realized that he had found a soft bed of grass. He lay down beside her, and she felt his tongue at her lips and in her mouth as his hands spread over her body, undressing her. She was aware of the caress of a gentle breeze against her naked skin, and a part of her told her this was an unusual sensation while another part of her found increased excitement in the idea of being totally naked outdoors.

Rocky quickly and matter-of-factly took off his own clothes; then he moved over her. He held himself rigid above her for a long moment, as if offering her one last chance to say no.

"Do it!" she gasped through clenched teeth, reaching for him and feeling the throb of his erection. She pulled him to her, then thrust her hips up at the same time he pushed down.

"Oooohh!" she moaned as she felt him drive deep inside of her. One thrust was all it took to bring her to her first orgasm, a shattering explosion of sensation that flashed through her body like a sudden bolt of lightning.

Rocky continued to make love to her, and Demaris's sensations of ecstasy were redoubled. A second wave of pleasure burst over her, so intense as to be even greater than the one she had felt the first time, and she couldn't hold back the moans and whimpers of pleasure as she tried, desperately, to pull Rocky even deeper into her body.

Demaris felt Rocky grow tense, pause for a moment, and then, with a gasping moan, make one final, convulsive jerk as he spent himself inside her. At that moment Demaris attained the most wrenching orgasm of them all, hanging precariously balanced on a precipice between consciousness and unconsciousness for several seconds, experiencing repeated waves of pleasure, one bursting upon another until all conscious awareness was redirected to accommodate the sensations.

"Here," Rocky said, handing a tin cup of water to Demaris. Dressed again, she was sitting under a tree with her back against the trunk and her legs drawn up in front of her. She reached for the collapsible cup being offered.

"Thanks," she said. "Is it safe to drink this?"

"Oh, yes, the water's pure enough," he replied. "It's from a fast-flowing stream over there. I've drunk from it many times."

"In this cup?" She held it up and examined the side. It was engraved with a pair of wings, and she read the slogan aloud: "'Above the Best.' What does that mean?"

"That was our motto in France," Rocky answered. "It has sort of a double meaning. We were aviators, and we flew over the American Expeditionary Force. They called themselves the best army in the field, so we were 'above' the best." He grinned. "And, of course, it also means that we were even better."

"Is it exciting?" Demaris asked, taking a drink of the water. "I mean being in war . . . shooting down enemy airplanes."

Rocky got a faraway look in his eyes. "Yes," he said. "God help us, war is the most exciting thing a man can do."

"I wish I could experience it."

Rocky shook his head. "No," he said firmly. "Believe me, you don't want to experience the horror of war."

"Not the horror of it," Demaris said. "I know that war has its moments of horror. I saw the picture on the wall in your office, the one with you and Billy Canfield. He was your friend, and he was killed in the war. What

I'm talking about is the excitement. I wish I could experience the excitement."

"Excitement means a lot to you, doesn't it?"

"I guess it does."

"Why?"

"I don't know. It's like a craving of some sort. Sometimes I do very irrational things."

"You mean like what we did?"

Demaris smiled. "Yes, like what we did," she admitted.

"What about afterward? Like now, for instance. Are you having second thoughts about what happened? Are you worried?"

"Worried? Worried about what?" she asked.

"I don't know. Maybe getting pregnant."

"Are *you* worried about it?"

"Maybe I am."

"You're a big boy; I know you've been around. Do you worry about getting someone pregnant every time you're with a woman?"

"No," Rocky said. "But then I've never—"

"You've never what?"

"I've never done it with anyone like you before."

Demaris laughed. "What are you trying to say, Rocky? That I was so wonderful, you heard violins? That I altered the course of the heavenly bodies?"

Rocky chuckled. "No, nothing like that."

"Oh?" Demaris pouted. "And here I thought it was the most wonderful thing I had ever felt."

"Me, too," Rocky said quickly. "I mean, I liked it. A lot. It's just that, well, you're a high-class girl, and I've never . . . done it . . . with a high-class girl before. I'll do the right thing by you if you're pregnant but . . ."

Demaris laughed, then reached out and touched Rocky's hand. "I know you would, Rocky, and you're a dear for thinking it. But don't worry. I'm not only a 'high-class girl' as you say, I'm also a wealthy girl. Wealthy girls have ways of taking care of such things."

"What do you mean? Do you mean . . . My God, you don't mean an abortion, do you?"

"Yes," Demaris said.

"But those things are dangerous! I've heard stories of women who died from abortions!"

"That happens if you see a butcher in some dingy, dirty hotel room somewhere. But if you have enough money and know where to go, an abortion is a perfectly safe procedure."

"How do you know? Have you ever had one?"

"No," Demaris replied. "But I have friends who have."

"I can't let you do that," Rocky said. "You won't need to. I'm serious. If you're pregnant, I'll marry you."

"Rocky, don't you understand?" Demaris asked in an exasperated tone of voice. "I don't *want* to marry you."

"Yeah," Rocky said. He barked what might have been a laugh. "Well, I know I'm no great catch, especially for someone like you, but . . ."

"It isn't that," Demaris said quickly. "You're a wonderful man! My God, you're the kind of man girls like me fantasize about. But I don't want to marry *anybody* right now. I have plans for my life, and they don't include getting married—and they don't include being pregnant."

"But what if you are?"

"Will you quit worrying about it, for God's sake? It isn't even the right time of the month for me to get pregnant."

"All right," Rocky said. "All right, if you say so." He took the empty cup from her and collapsed it, then put it in his pocket. "Come on. We'd better be getting back. No one knows we stopped here. If we're overdue, folks will begin to get worried." He reached down to offer a hand to help Demaris stand up.

She took it, stood, then brushed off the back of her trousers, peering at him intently. "Are you all right?" she asked.

"Me? Yeah, of course I am. Why do you ask?"

"I don't know. I guess I have the feeling that what

happened today seems more traumatic for you than it was for me."

"Traumatic. Is that one of your college words?"

"I guess it is," Demaris said, smiling.

"What does it mean?"

Demaris laughed, then kissed Rocky on the cheek. "I think it means I'm a pretentious ass. Listen, Rocky, I'm not going to say let's just forget about everything that happened here this afternoon, because it was an experience I don't ever want to forget. But I don't want it to ever happen again, either. I want us to be friends—always—but not lovers. That complicates things, and I don't have room in my life for complications."

"You and me both, kid. You and me both." Rocky stuck out his hand and smiled. "Friends."

CHAPTER NINE

Karl Tannenhower took another swallow of beer, then set his mug down. He wiped the back of his hand across his mouth and looked over the table at his friend, Paul Maas.

"All right, I'm here, Paul. Where is this savior of Germany you've been telling me about? This Herr Hitler?"

"He'll be here," Paul promised. "The Party has rented the hall in the back of the beer house. Hitler is going to speak tonight. Will you stay and listen?"

"That's why I've come. I want to see with my own eyes this man I've been hearing about."

"You'll make a wonderful addition to the party," Paul said. "You were a zeppelin captain, and many people look up to you. Herr Hitler likes war heroes. He was himself a winner of the Iron Cross, First Class, you know. And there is Goering, who, like you, was awarded our country's highest honor, the Blue Max. There are many such soldiers in the movement, including, of course, the most famous soldier of them all, General Ludendorff. As I told you, he and Herr Hitler share the leadership of the party. So be assured, Karl, that when you join, you will be in good company."

"I didn't say I was going to join," Karl replied. "I said only that I would come to hear Hitler speak."

"But you might consider joining?"

Karl cupped his large hands around his beer mug, staring at it for a long moment. "I will consider it," he finally said. He sighed. "Something has to be done. You know, Paul, I attended a university in America, in the city of St. Louis. I could still be there, living the life of an American. But when the war started, I returned to Germany because I felt it was my duty to do battle for my Fatherland. And for what, I ask you? Not only did we lose the war, we are losing the peace. Our money is now worthless. The savings of generations have been wiped out by the mismanagement of the madmen who are in authority. And worse, Berlin has become the international cesspool of perversion and decadence. I am ashamed to claim the city as German."

"Yes, yes, you are absolutely right, Karl," Paul said enthusiastically. "And wait until you hear the speech tonight, for this is what Herr Hitler believes and talks about. You and I and Hitler and Ludendorff and Goering and the others who have joined the National Socialist German Workers' Party have no stomach for such things as go on in Berlin. We are soldiers and professionals and working men and women of every class. But, Karl, it is *we* who are the real Germany, not those perfumed dandies and whores and Communists and Jews who've taken over Berlin. It's time for Germany to awaken and that is why '*Deutschland Wach Auf*' has become our battle cry."

"What bothers me about all this," Karl remarked, "is that when someone asks one of our government officials about it, what do they say? They ask us to be patient."

"Of course they ask us to be patient," Paul replied, his voice caustic. "And why shouldn't they expect us to be patient? Didn't we give them our backs so they could stab us in the first place? Our army was undefeated in battle, our navy ruled the seas, and our airplanes controlled the skies. We had the Allies on their last legs, but the Jews and the Communists corrupted our government, poisoned our people, and undermined our will. You see now that we are living with the result."

"I'm not sure I can agree with you that we controlled the skies," Karl said. "During the last days of the war, the British and Americans made air raids against our bases with impunity. And I must confess to you, Paul, they hurt us very badly. It did not seem to me at that time that the Allies were on their last legs."

"Nor were *we*, nor were *we*!" Paul insisted. "We could have carried on the fight and negotiated a peace with honor. Instead, we are saddled with reparations that we, our children, our children's children, and *their* children will be paying until the end of the twentieth century."

"I agree with you. The reparations must be renegotiated."

"Renegotiated? Hah! Herr Hitler says that when the Nazis are in power, they will be *renounced*. The Allies have gotten their pound of flesh. They will get no more!"

There was a sudden commotion near the front of the beer hall then, followed by a scraping of chairs.

"It is Hitler!" someone shouted.

"Herr Hitler!" another called.

"Hitler is here!" a third declared.

Soon Hitler's name was on everyone's lips, and Karl looked over to catch a glimpse of him.

This was the first time Karl had seen the man, and he thought there was certainly nothing very impressive about him. Hitler was short, with a wild shock of hair hanging across his forehead and a small, closely cropped mustache. He was wearing a cheaply cut brown suit and a forest-green tie. He acknowledged the greetings with a nod, but he spoke to no one. Instead, he moved quickly through the beer hall and into the meeting room at the back.

"Come on," Paul said, hurrying his friend toward the meeting room. "I want you to sit as close to the front as possible so you don't miss a word he has to say."

They managed to find seats in the very front row. Karl looked around at the others who had filed in to listen to the speech. He was not surprised by the number of ex-soldiers that he saw, but he was surprised by the others—the shopkeepers and accountants, the mechanics and schoolteachers, the students and the housewives, the old and the young. A few were wearing the red, white, and black rosettes of the Hapsburg monarchy, while those who were already members of the Nazi party advertised their membership proudly by wearing swastika armbands, also in red, white, and black. Nowhere did Karl see the red, gold, and black colors of the Republic.

Hitler stepped up onto the platform at the front of the room and stood there for a moment, letting his arms hang, holding his hands together just in front of him. He didn't ask for quiet, and neither did he raise his hands in a signal. Nevertheless, the hundreds of conversations stilled and the room grew quiet except for an occasional clearing of the throat or the scrape of a chair.

Hitler had been looking down all this time, almost as if he were in prayer—though Karl would have bet that he wasn't. He kept the crowd waiting, even beyond the point at which they had grown silent, effectively building the tension. Finally Hitler looked up and let his gaze rake across everyone present. His eyes were light blue and penetrating, with an intensity unlike anything Karl had ever experienced.

Then Hitler began, his words almost a mumble. "Ladies, gentlemen, workers, students, my former comrades in arms, fellow party members, you have come here in Germany's hour of need—and for that I thank you," he added, almost in a grovel.

There were a few more coughs, another scraping chair. Those who had never heard him speak before were clearly puzzled as to how this quiet, almost timid man had gained such a reputation. The others, however, clearly knew and waited expectantly.

"On November eleventh, five years ago, I lay blind and crippled in a hospital bed on the Western Front. My one thought then was to have my sight and the use of my limbs restored so that I could return to the front and continue to do battle for the Fatherland. This thought and this thought alone sustained me, and when the doctors came and told me that the war was over, that everything I had fought for and bled for and suffered for was gone, I wept."

So far, Hitler's words had been soft, almost caressing, and the words "I wept" were spoken at little more than a whisper.

"*I cried for Germany!*" he abruptly shouted at the top of his voice, and the words cracked over the heads of the audience like a sudden peal of thunder. "I cried for my comrades who lay dead and unburied in the mud of France! I cried for the widows and orphans of these brave soldiers of the Fatherland! And then I learned that my tears, like the blood and sweat we and our comrades had shed, *were for nothing!*" he boomed, and the words echoed back from the walls of the chamber.

"Why? Because we had been stabbed in the back. The cowardly and incompetent government officials— not one of whom had ever heard the crack of a British Enfield rifle, not one of whom had ever heard the dull clank of the warning bell or smelled the sharp and life-smothering odor of gas, not one of whom had ever spent one night in the rain and the cold and the mud—*these so-called leaders of our country had had enough suffering and hardship.*"

Hitler minced the last few words, playing it for maximum sarcasm, and he was rewarded with the raucous laughter of his audience.

"And who were the people behind these cowardly, incompetent government officials?" Hitler chided. "First, there were the Communists, undermining the morale and the weal of our people; then there were the incompetent bureaucrats and government officials; and, finally, standing far to the rear, up to his ass in the dung heap, stood the international criminal of all that is vile and evil and filthy in the world . . . *the Jew!*"

The room erupted in a thunderous ovation of cheers and applause.

Hitler's speech continued for another forty-five minutes, and the whole time he manipulated the audience with the virtuoso of a master conductor directing his orchestra. He got tears when he wanted tears, laughter when he wanted laughter, and ear-splitting cheers when they were called for. When at last the speech was concluded, Hitler stood on the platform with his arms hanging limply at his side and his head bowed, drenched in sweat and breathing as hard as if he had just completed a ten-kilometer race—but his audience was fired up. Every man and woman in the hall had Hitler's name on their lips and a determination in their hearts to right all the wrongs that had been done to their country.

"Well! What do you think?" Paul asked, clapping wildly.

"Your Hitler is quite an impressive man," Karl agreed.

"He isn't my Hitler," Paul said. "He is Germany's Hitler. Would you like to meet him?"

Karl looked toward the platform and saw that scores of people had rushed forward and were reaching out their hands to touch the man who had just electrified them.

"No," Karl said. "I mean, yes, I would like to meet him, but I don't want to fight off the crowd."

Paul laughed. "Oh, don't worry about them," he said, waving at them dismissively. "Later tonight, Hitler is having a private meeting with some of the leaders of the movement."

"Well, if it's for the leaders, we wouldn't be able to get in, would we?"

"Who says we wouldn't?" Paul asked. He pointed to himself. "I am one of the leaders," he said. "And you can go with me."

"Then in that case, yes. I would like to meet him."

"Do you want to join the party?"

"I don't know," Karl replied, shrugging his massive shoulders. "I don't want to rush into anything."

"Just let me ask you this, Karl. Are you satisfied with the way things are now?"

"No. I am not satisfied with the way things are."

"Then you'll think about joining the Nazi Party?"

"Yes," Karl said. "I'll think about joining the Nazi Party."

They made their way out of the meeting hall and back into the beer house, where they slowly drank a stein of beer. After a while Paul checked his watch, then set down the stein. "Come. It's time," he told Karl and led him over to a side staircase.

After climbing the stairs, they walked down a narrow corridor to a room at the end of the hall. Paul knocked twice and opened the door. Adolf Hitler was standing there with several other men.

"Herr Hitler, I would like you to meet Commander Karl Tannenhower," Paul said, ushering his friend into the room.

"I have heard of you," Hitler said, taking Karl's hand and staring into his eyes. "You commanded an airship during the war."

"Yes," Karl replied, surprised by Hitler's statement.

Hitler smiled. "You must wonder how I know this," he said.

"Yes, I confess that I do wonder."

"I know everyone who won the Blue Max. Since it is Germany's highest award, it should be the patriotic duty of all Germans to know and honor these men."

"I am very flattered, Herr Hitler," Karl said. "And impressed."

"Ah, Commander Tannenhower, the human brain is

a wonderful and mysterious thing," Hitler said lightly, tapping the side of his head. "On some things it absolutely fails to work. Ask me, for example, about the mechanism that provides an automobile with its motion and I will confess to you that I haven't the foggiest notion. But I can name all the officers who served on the staff of Frederick the Great. I can hum every bar of every piece of music Wagner ever wrote and tell you when and where it was first publicly performed." Hitler smiled again. "And I can tell you that you have a lovely wife named Uta, the niece of Commander Mathey, and you have a son whose name I have never heard."

"It is Max, Herr Hitler."

"Max, is it?" Hitler laughed loudly. "Well, now, you have made it too easy for me. Since you are a holder of the Blue Max, it shall be a simple matter of association for me to remember the name of your son. Tell me, Commander, have you come to join the party?"

"Yes, Herr Hitler," Karl replied. If he had not been fully prepared to do so before this moment, he was now totally certain. The people of Germany needed someone to lead them out of their misery, and he was convinced that Adolf Hitler was the man who could do it.

"Well, then, go and see Herr Mueller over there. He will take your money and assign you a party number and give you a swastika armband to wear."

"That's all there is to it?" Karl asked.

"That's all there is to it," Hitler replied. He laughed. "Did you expect to be initiated in some mysterious rite? If so, I'm sorry to disappoint you, but we leave such things to the Freemasons and Jews. We are an open society . . . we wear our badge of membership proudly. No hiding our candle under a bushel basket. Herr Mueller, what is the party number of our newest member?" Hitler asked.

"Number twenty-five thousand, six hundred and eighty-three, Herr Hitler," Mueller answered.

"This is a good time for you to join the party," Hitler told Karl. "When the time comes, and it will, that we number ourselves in the millions, you will be proud and honored to have such a low number." He smiled and shook Karl's hand. "No doubt you have somewhat missed the excitement of your wartime exploits. Well, don't worry, Commander. Our duty is to awaken Germany, not lull it to sleep."

CHAPTER TEN

When Kerry O'Braugh and his crony Vinnie Todaro pulled up in front of a run-down-looking grocery store, a little black girl was standing in front, staring longingly at a jar of stick candy sitting in the display window. She was barefoot, her dress was dirty and torn, and the several tightly plaited braids that her hair was done up in were tied with ragged strips of cloth that might have once been ribbon. At the sound of the car door slamming shut behind her, the child turned and looked at Kerry and Vinnie through big brown eyes wide with wonder.

"You want a piece of that candy in there, little girl?" Kerry asked, striding across the sidewalk toward the store. "Tell me what kind you want, and I'll get it for you."

Instead of answering him, she turned and ran.

"What the hell did she do that for?" Kerry asked in

surprise, watching her quickly disappear down the street.

"Shit," Vinnie snorted. "She's probably never seen a white man before."

"What are you talkin' about? They have white people in East St. Louis."

"Not too damned many," Vinnie said. "I ain't seen nothin' but coloreds since the moment we come off the bridge." Vinnie put his hand in his jacket pocket. "You ask me, we shoulda brought our choppers with us."

"We're over here to talk business," Kerry said, "not get ourselves killed."

"What does a spook know about business?"

"Watch your fuckin' mouth, Vinnie. That kind of talk over here really *could* get us killed." Kerry took a piece of paper from his pocket and looked at the address, then compared it with the address painted on the glass front of the store. The numbers matched.

"This is it," he said and pulled opened the door.

The store smelled of flour, molasses, cured bacon, and dried apples. A dozen flypaper strips hung from the ceiling, displaying the evidence of their efficiency. A hand-lettered sign advertised pork chops at seventeen cents a pound, pork steaks at twelve, bacon at twelve, and chitterlings at five. An old black man was sitting on a stool behind the counter, and before Kerry even said anything, the man pointed to a door at the back of the store.

"We're supposed to go back there?" Kerry asked.

"You're the fella lookin' for Heavy Hart, aincha?"

"Yes."

"You find him back there."

Kerry and Vinnie walked between two long shelves of canned goods. When they reached the back of the store, someone stepped through the door to meet them.

"You totin'?" the man asked.

"What?" Vinnie replied.

"A gun. Are you totin' a gun?"

"You're goddamn right I'm carryin' a gun. You think I'd come over here without one?"

The man held out his hand, palm up. "Let me have it," he said.

"The hell you say. You ain't gettin' my gun."

"Give it to him," Kerry said, taking his own gun out gingerly and handing it over.

"Boss, what the hell you doin'?"

"We're in their territory now," Kerry said. "That means we play by their rules. Give him your gun."

"Goddammit!" Vinnie growled, giving up his gun.

"In here," the man said, gesturing into the room. "That's him, sittin' over there behind the table."

Heavy Hart more than lived up to his nickname, for he was one of the largest men Kerry had ever seen, black or white. He was nearly seven feet tall and he weighed well over three hundred fifty pounds. He was very dark—so dark that his skin shone. He was also completely bald, so it didn't take too much imagination to think of his head as being an enormous cannonball. He was eating spareribs, and the huge pile of bones lying on a separate plate gave mute testimony to the amount he had already consumed.

Two women were standing—or, more accurately, draped—on either side of him. They were young, pretty, and provocatively dressed.

"I'm sorry," Kerry said. "I didn't intend to break into your lunch."

"This ain't lunch, it's just a snack," Heavy Hart said, not bothering to interrupt his eating. He burped without apology. "You white boys come here to talk?"

"Yes."

"Talk," Heavy invited.

"Mr. Hart," Kerry started, but Heavy Hart laughed.

"What is it? What's wrong?"

"Listen to this shit, ladies," Hart said. "This white man callin' me 'mister.' You got to figure I got somethin' he wants."

Both women giggled appreciatively.

"Call me Heavy," Hart said. "That way I know you ain't tryin' to hide nothin' behind all the bullshit."

"Okay, Heavy," Kerry said. "I want us to form an alliance."

"A what?"

"Partners," Kerry said. "I'd like for us to team up to run Paddy Egan out of business."

"I'm goin' run that ofay out of business—and I don't need you to do that."

"Yes you do," Kerry said. "You're not strong enough by yourself."

"You tellin' me you are?"

"No," Kerry said. "I'm not either . . . at least, not by myself. That's why I've come to you for help."

"Why should I help you, white boy?"

"Because after we get rid of Egan, you and I can divide up the spoils. You take this side of the river, I take the other side."

"I already got this side of the river."

"No. You've got the coloreds in East St. Louis. But Egan has a half-dozen speaks over here. We get rid of him, you can take 'em all over."

"Boss, you givin' him the white speaks?" Vinnie asked.

"The folks who drink the booze don't care what color the hand is that delivers it," Kerry said. "Yeah, he can have the white speaks . . . and the numbers."

"What about the whores?" Hart asked.

"The whores over here? Yeah, of course."

"No," Heavy said. "I mean the whores in St. Louis."

"No," Kerry said. "The girls are a big part of my business."

Heavy put down a cleaned bone, then wiped the back of his hand across his mouth and smiled. "Ain't talkin' 'bout white whores," he said. "I'm talkin' about colored girls. All the colored whores in St. Louis belong to me. You do that, and you got yourself a deal."

Kerry thought a moment, then shrugged. "Colored whores? Sure, you can have the colored whores."

Hart laughed. "You don't know it, white boy, but you just give away a big part of your business," he said.

"The colored girls gets as many white customers as colored customers."

"Why would they do that?"

"Oh, honey," one of Hart's women said, throwing her hip toward Kerry in an exaggerated grind. "You mean you never done it with a colored gal?"

"No."

"Then, honey, you ain't never done it," the other woman said, and both laughed.

"Hush, you two," Hart said. "And you," he told Kerry, "you get to wantin' to try it, you try it with one of my whores over in St. Louis. These here women belong to me."

"No, no!" Kerry said quickly, holding his hands out. "Don't worry about that, Heavy. I wouldn't do nothin' now that'd cause trouble. We're just gettin' started good."

"Okay. What you want me to do?"

"Nothin' yet," Kerry said. "Leastwise, not until I tell you. We've got to plan this thing out. When we hit the son of a bitch, I want him hit hard."

Hart put his elbow on the table and made a fist as big as the head of a sledgehammer. "White boy, hittin' hard is just about what ol' Heavy Hart does best," he announced.

JEFFERSON CITY, MISSOURI

It was awards night at the Jefferson City Colored High School, and those who were to be honored for academic and athletic achievement were sitting on the stage. Andrew Booker was being honored in both areas. It wasn't even midway through the football season of his senior year, but he had already been recognized as an all-state colored high school football and basketball player.

So far three speakers had extolled the virtues of academics and academic athletics. Andrew, who was sitting in the front row, listened to the current speaker with half an ear. The good-looking youth glanced up at the scoreboard used for the basketball games. Unlike the electric ones that many of the white schools had, the information on this scoreboard had to be posted by hand. Andrew smiled as he remembered the night, last year, when he had single-handedly kept the scorekeeper so busy that the man could barely keep up. Andrew scored twenty-two points that night, leading his team to a thirty to twenty-six victory over Columbia Colored High School.

He then gazed around the gym. It was decorated tonight just as it was for basketball games, with twists of red-and-white crepe paper snaking around the hoop posts and affixed to the walls. Earlier, members of the school band had played several fight songs in honor of the awardees, and they sat now in uniform, just as they did during the basketball and football games. Six empty chairs were interspersed among the band's seats, their usual occupants now also among the honorees, and the empty chairs were marked with either a red rose or a white carnation—the roses signifying the girl band members being honored, the carnations signifying the boys.

One of the roses belonged to LaTonya Welles. Because her last name began with a W, LaTonya was sitting in the very back row of the honorees. Andrew twisted around in his chair to look back at her. He found her looking at him, and when their eyes met, she smiled broadly, the dimple in her cheek deepening.

"Better get ready, Andrew," the student next to him whispered. "They're about to announce the name of the Senior Honor Student."

Andrew turned toward the speaker. In addition to being an outstanding athlete, Andrew had also excelled in academics and was one of two students in competition for Senior Honor Student of the Year, the award given to the senior with the highest grade average. At the last grade check, Andrew was just a half point behind the first-place student, William Simmons. There had been an exam since then, and though Andrew was reasonably certain he had scored a perfect one hundred, if Willie had as well, Willie would still be in the lead. However, those grades hadn't been released, so no one knew for sure who the Senior Honor Student would be.

"The selection of Senior Honor Student was very hard this year," Dr. Tucker, the school superintendent, announced. "In fact, only one-half point separated the two. With the competition so fierce, we owe a sense of admiration to both. However, only one person can be designated Senior Honor Student of the Year, so we had to make a choice. I call both of these young people up now, in alphabetical order." He paused and looked over at the honorees. "Andrew Booker and William Simmons."

There was a round of applause for both boys as they stood. The classmates sitting around each of them offered their hands and wished them good luck. William Simmons was much shorter than Andrew—so short, in fact, that his classmates often called him "Wee Willie." He was not at all athletic, and even when he went to one of the games he would sometimes take a book. He adjusted his glasses as he reached the podium, then stuck his hand out toward Andrew.

"Good luck," he said.

"Same to you," Andrew replied.

"Ladies and gentlemen, I am pleased to announce that the Senior Honor Student for 1923-1924 is . . . William Simmons!"

The parents and guests applauded the announcement, while all the students in the school stood in honor. Willie, smiling broadly, took the certificate from the superintendent, then walked back to his chair, beaming under the congratulations offered him by the others.

After the awards ceremony was over, Andrew and LaTonya walked out together. Andrew saw his father standing near the flagpole, his arms folded across his chest and a smile on his face. A remarkably handsome man with silver hair, bronze skin, wide shoulders, and penetrating eyes, Loomis Booker cut quite an imposing figure.

"Hello, Pop," Andrew said.

"Hello, Professor Booker," LaTonya added.

"My, my, Miss Welles, you look particularly lovely tonight," Loomis said.

"Thank you."

"And you, young man," Loomis told his son, putting an arm around the boy's shoulders, "I am very proud of you. And your mother would be, too, if she were still alive."

"I wish you could have beaten Wee Willie," LaTonya said.

"Oh, I don't mind," Andrew said. "Actually, I think it's better this way."

"Why?" LaTonya asked, clearly surprised by Andrew's comment.

"Because I get to do a lot more things in school than he does. I play football and basketball, I run track, and I'm president of the senior class. Wee Willie doesn't get to do any of those things. In fact, Wee Willie didn't even have a date for the dance tonight"—he grinned—"whereas I have a date with the prettiest girl in school."

LaTonya smiled at the reference.

"So I'm glad Willie won," Andrew insisted.

"Oh, there you are, LaTonya," a woman called.

The threesome looked in the direction of the voice. A woman in a billowing yellow dress and a wide-brimmed hat that she held on to with her hand was charging toward them, smiling.

"I've been looking everywhere for you," she said.

"I was with Andrew, Mama," LaTonya replied. "I told you we were going to the awards dance."

The woman was young-looking and pretty and seemed much more like LaTonya's older sister than her mother. She leaned down slightly to kiss LaTonya on the cheek. "Well, yes, I know, honey, but I thought you would at least come by to say hello."

"Hello, Mrs. Welles," Andrew said.

"Hello, Andrew."

"Mrs. Welles, I'd like you to meet my father," Andrew said. "Loomis Booker."

"*Professor* Loomis Booker, Mama," LaTonya added

quickly. "He's the dean of students at Lincoln University."

"Yes, dear, I know who he is. I've heard all about this distinguished-looking gentleman," Mrs. Welles said. "I'm Della Welles, Professor. It's a pleasure to make your acquaintance."

"The pleasure is all mine," Loomis replied in a deep, resonant voice. "And I can clearly see why your daughter is such an attractive young lady."

"My goodness, Professor. Such talk will turn my head," Della Welles said dryly.

"We're going to the dance now, Mama. We won't be too late," LaTonya said, taking Andrew in tow.

"Bye, Pop. Bye, Mrs. Welles," Andrew called back as they hurried away.

Della laughed a deep, throaty laugh. "Don't they make a handsome couple, though?" she asked.

"Well, I hope not too handsome a couple," Loomis remarked.

"Why do you say that?"

"I'm afraid LaTonya just doesn't fit into my son's plans right now."

"Oh? And what's wrong with my daughter, Professor?" Della challenged.

"Please don't misunderstand, madam. I'm not singling out LaTonya. It's just that my son's plans don't allow for *any* women."

"And just what *are* your son's plans?"

"He wants to be a doctor."

"A colored doctor? Oh, heavens, Professor, he needs to change his plans. Don't you know colored doctors can't make any money? Their only patients are other colored folks, and that means that most of the time they never get paid. And if they *do* get paid, it's in chickens or jars of home-canned plums or some such thing as that. No, sir. If that boy ever plans to marry my daughter, he had better find himself something else to do."

Loomis laughed loudly. "Mrs. Welles, you do cut to the heart of things, don't you? I didn't realize we had already reached the point of negotiating a marriage between your daughter and my son. Actually, Andrew isn't as interested in being a general practitioner as he is in medical research."

"Medical research?"

"Yes."

"Hmm. 'This is my son-in-law, the medical researcher,'" she said, trying it on. She smiled and nodded her head. "Yes, that sounds pretty impressive."

Loomis laughed again, then asked, "Is there a Mr. Welles?"

"Never has been."

"Oh," Loomis replied, embarrassed that he had put her on the spot.

"I started calling myself that right after LaTonya was born," Della said. "I figured it'd be easier on her. Of course, she started asking questions about her daddy a long time ago so I finally had to tell her, 'Girl, your papa was a fancy-dressed, high-steppin', travelin' preacherman from Kansas City. I met him at a revival fish fry on Friday night, fell in love with him Saturday afternoon, and never saw him again after the Sunday morning services. He told me his name was Welles, but I never was able to find such a person in Kansas City, so I had you all by myself.' That's the truth of it, and that's what I told her. Do you find me shocking, Professor Booker?"

Laughing again, Loomis found himself attracted to a woman and feeling things he hadn't felt since his wife, Pearl, had died five years earlier. "I find you . . . fascinating," he replied. "By the way, have you had your dinner?"

"Yes," Della said. "But if this is an invitation, I'll eat again."

ST. LOUIS, MISSOURI

Two weeks later, more than six hundred people gathered in Sheldon Auditorium to hear Professor Loomis Booker speak, the third in a fall series of lectures given

by Jefferson University. The season's first lecture had
been by Elizabeth Custer, widow of General Custer, and
her subject was "Custer's Campaign, Victory through
Defeat." The second lecture was delivered by Colonel
Billy Mitchell on "Airpower, the Indispensable Arm of
America's Defense."

Loomis Booker, too, could have spoken on a military theme, for during the war he had been commis-
sioned in the Transportation Corps and assigned to duty
at the War Department level. America had responded to
the war in Europe with men and matériel on a scale far
surpassing anyone's wildest expectations. The efficient
use of America's vast system of railroads had been a
major part of that miracle, and Loomis Booker had
played a significant role in the successful outcome. Both
General Pershing and President Wilson had recognized
Loomis's contribution to the war effort by writing him
personal letters of commendation.

But Loomis's lecture wasn't about the military or
about the efficient utilization of America's railroads,
though he was still considered one of the country's
leading experts in that field. The year before he had
been asked by Congress to conduct a study of the
current status of America's railroads. He had been
chosen because a staffer to the head of the Congressional
Railways Committee had found in the archives several
references to, and praises of, the wartime work done by
one Loomis Booker. When Loomis had submitted his
study, the Congressional Committee was so impressed
with its content and thoroughness that they accepted it
without a single change. They had been about to ask him
to come to Congress and personally read it into the
record when someone noticed that Loomis Booker was a
Negro.

The fact that Loomis was colored had not lessened
the importance or the quality of his report, though a few
congressmen had suggested that his report be returned.
Fortunately, wiser heads prevailed, and a compromise
was struck. Loomis Booker's report was read into the
Congressional Record by one of the clerks of the Rail-

ways Committee. Loomis was given full credit for its authorship and received a letter of thanks signed by the Speaker of the House and President Coolidge. No mention was made of the fact that he was colored.

No mention was made of Loomis's color for the lecture series, either, though it was hardly a secret since he was well-known in the area—and, besides, the subject of his speech was "The White Man and the Negro: Their Destinies Are Linked in America's Future."

To Bob Canfield had gone the honor of introducing the speaker, for Bob had known Loomis since attending Jefferson University twenty years before. Officially, Loomis had just been the janitor there; to Bob, Loomis had also been tutor, mentor, and friend. Though denied enrollment in the all-white institution, Loomis had embarked on a course of self-study and had managed to educate himself to such an extent and with such distinction that he was eventually awarded a Doctor of Humanities degree by the university's trustees.

"Americans truly admire the self-made man," Bob began. "Therefore, Americans must truly admire Professor Loomis Booker, for he educated himself and obtained his academic accolades with just his reason and intellect for his faculty. Dr. Booker has the distinction of being the only Negro ever to be granted a degree from Jefferson University. If we turn that around, however, we may say that to Jefferson University went the honor of recognizing this brilliant and gifted man. Ladies and gentlemen, I give you the Vice-Chancellor and Dean of Students of Lincoln University, the Honorable Professor Loomis Booker."

As Loomis stood up and walked to the podium, he was greeted with a warm round of applause. But that applause was dramatically interrupted when three robed-and-hooded Klansmen suddenly burst in through the back door.

"Go back to Africa, nigger!"

"Keep America pure! America for the white man!"

"Get out of here, nigger!"

Guards rushed at once to grab the Klansmen as they

began to parade down the center aisle, chanting their slogans of hate. The guards hauled the three intruders out of the auditorium, though the men continued to scream oaths and obscenities even as they were being dragged away.

The crowd reacted in shock to the sudden and unexpected disruption. A murmur of uneasiness spread through the auditorium and a few wondered aloud if, in the interest of harmony, it might not be best to cancel the evening. Others demanded that Professor Booker be allowed to speak, pointing out that he had that right whether anyone agreed with him or not.

Loomis had said and done nothing throughout the entire disturbance. He had stood quietly and majestically at the front of the auditorium, his hands grasping each side of the podium and his eyes staring out at the audience. As the crowd gradually grew quiet, some supposed that it was the result of Loomis's commanding appearance.

Loomis waited until one could literally hear a pin drop. Then, speaking softly so as to force the audience to remain quiet, he began to speak.

"We are very nearly a quarter of the way through the twentieth century, and what a marvelous century it has been. We have stolen from the birds the power of flight. We have captured lightning and forced it to do our bidding. We have learned to use the very ether itself to transmit radio signals across great distances. The fastest horse cannot match the speed with which we travel, and all of these magnificent advances have been made within the lifetimes of most of us present in this room.

"There are scientists who tell us of even more wondrous things to come: of television—by which not only our voices, but our images will conquer distance—and of airplanes big enough to compete with the ships at sea and fast enough to cross the ocean in a single day. Some say the time may even come when man will travel to the moon and beyond.

"These are marvelous things to contemplate, and just as I was here at the birth of this century, so will my grandchildren be here at the century's conclusion to pass judgment upon the accuracy of these predictions. It is that distant point, the close of this century, that will be the subject of my discussion tonight. However, I won't be speaking about science and technology. Instead, I will speak of a world in which all social evils have been conquered, a world in which everyone, regardless of nationality, regardless of religion, and regardless of the color of their skin, will strive with equal opportunity toward the betterment of mankind.

"This does not mean that I see a color-blind society, for that would not be desirable. One who is truly color-blind sees only in shades of gray. How dreary would be a field of flowers if every blossom sprouted the same color. How drab would be the rainbow if the water's prisms produced only a single shade. No, my friends, what I pray my grandchildren will find at the end of this century is an America that delights in the many hues of its fabric as Joseph did in his Coat of Many Colors.

"I believe that when historians look back at the twentieth century to decide upon its greatest contribution, they won't choose the automobile, the radio, or even the airplane. When future historians speak of our century they will say, 'This was the century that all of God's people—white man and black man, red, yellow, and brown—came to sup at the table of universal brotherhood.'"

For a moment nothing but stunned silence greeted Loomis's speech. Then someone began clapping, then another, and then another still, until finally the entire auditorium joined in respectful, if not enthusiastic, applause.

After the speech Bob Canfield hosted a formal dinner in Loomis's honor. It had been his intention to have the dinner at the country club, but Loomis would not have been allowed, even as a guest. Therefore, Bob rented the banquet room at one of St. Louis's finest hotels. Even so, there were several guests who were clearly surprised to see a Negro, elegantly dressed and obviously among peers, dining with the most influential men and women of the city.

"Tell me, Bob," one of the businessmen at their table asked, "did I hear you correctly when you introduced Dr. Booker and said that he had a degree from Jefferson University?"

"Yes."

"How can that be? My daughter attended Jefferson University, and I know that it's for whites only."

"Dr. Booker, would you like to explain how that came about?" Bob invited.

"I'd be glad to," Loomis replied. He looked at the businessman who asked the question. "I worked at the school, Mr. Ingersol. I was a combination janitor, gardener, handyman, and errand boy. One of my duties was carrying away the trash. Before I disposed of the trash, however, I searched through it very carefully, looking for old, discarded textbooks. Whenever I found one, I restored it to a usable condition, eventually building a library of sorts."

"Of sorts?" Bob asked. "Excuse the interruption, Dr. Booker, but I want to give your library more credit than that. Gentlemen, over a period of several years, Dr. Booker created a personal library of those salvaged books that rivaled the library then in existence at Jefferson."

"The Booker File!" a young, recent graduate of the university exclaimed. "There's a special shelf at Billy Books—" The young man broke off and blushed. "Excuse me, Mr. Canfield. I mean at the William Canfield Library . . ."

Bob chuckled. "I know the students call it Billy Books," he said. "And to tell the truth, that would have suited my brother just fine. He enjoyed poking holes in pompous attitudes—my own occasional one included. And you're quite right. The Booker File is composed of those books Dr. Booker salvaged. I asked that it be established as a way of honoring Dr. Booker's achievement."

"I . . . I didn't know there was such a thing," Loomis said, obviously touched.

"Even so," Ingersol continued. "One can't get an education just by reading discarded textbooks."

"No," Loomis agreed. "In addition to discarded texts, I also managed, by culling through the trash, to construct a curriculum, complete with study guides, term papers, and midterm and end-of-term exams. Oh, I assure you, I was quite thorough."

"So thorough, in fact," Bob put in, "that he wound up with what would be considered a major in every discipline the university taught."

"Did anyone know about this while it was going on?"

"Oh, yes," Bob said. "There were a number of us students who discovered, quite early, that there was a ready source of help available. Dr. Booker was always very generous with his time, and his tutoring helped many a student through the dialectics of Latin and the confusion of calculus."

"But, how did he obtain a degree?" Ingersol asked.

"Professor Bateman felt that he deserved it," Bob said. "And he—"

"Excuse me, Mr. Canfield," Loomis interrupted. "You are leaving out your own contribution here. Gentlemen, Mr. Canfield prevailed upon the Board of Regents to grant me a special degree. I owe everything to him."

"Good for you, Bob, good for you," someone said, and the others around the table applauded.

"My son will be starting college this fall," Loomis continued, "but, as things stand now, Andrew can't attend classes here. He won't be able to follow in my footsteps and graduate from Jefferson. Instead, he'll be attending Howard Univerity. After that, he'll attend medical school in Boston . . . even though Jefferson University has a fine medical school. It is my fondest wish that Andrew's children, when they are of age, will be able to matriculate at Jefferson University or Washington University or even the University of Mississippi, if that's where they choose to go."

"That's a noble idea, to be sure, Dr. Booker," one of

the diners said. "But I don't think it will happen in our lifetime, the lifetime of our children, or of our grand-children. You saw what happened tonight, how much of an uproar was caused just by your speaking. And if you'll pardon my rudeness in pointing it out to you, sir, your speech, while it was beautifully delivered, met with a less-than-enthusiastic response. You give too much credit to the basic goodness of man when you say all those things will be accomplished in this century. On the contrary, I'm afraid we are at least one hundred years away from a complete mixing of the races—if, in fact, the races are ever mixed."

"I don't want a mixture," Loomis said.

"What? What do you mean? I thought that was the whole purpose of your speech tonight."

Loomis smiled. "Let us use an analogy from chemistry," he said. "In chemistry, a compound is something formed as the result of the union of two or more distinct elements. Our society is composed of a number of hyphenated Americans: the German-Americans, the Polish-Americans, the African-Americans, and so on. Gentlemen, I would much rather that the many races and ethnic groups of our nation create an entirely new compound: an *un*hyphenated American."

After the formal dinner Loomis returned home with Bob as his guest. It was the first time Loomis had ever stayed with the Canfields, and he enjoyed reminiscing and catching up with Connie, Willie, and John. Connie and the two boys finally went off to bed, while Bob and Loomis sat in Bob's library, smoking cigars and talking.

The library was nearly dark, lighted only by a lamp sitting on Bob's desk on the far side of the room. Bob sat on the end of a leather sofa, while Loomis sat in a big leather chair. Their cigars glowed in the semidarkness, and the room filled with the exhaled smoke.

"This is nice," Bob said, "sitting in here, puffing away to my heart's content. I couldn't do it if Connie were in here, you know."

Loomis chuckled. "No, I guess not. Ladies don't care that much for cigar smoke. Although, I must say, Pearl didn't nag me too much about it."

"Do you still miss her terribly?"

"Yes," Loomis said, the word as much a sigh as a statement. He leaned his head back on the chair and stared up at the ceiling for a long moment. "It's been five years now since she died," he said. "Yet sometimes, in the middle of the night, I'll realize that she isn't in bed with me, and it still takes me a moment to know why."

"Pearl was quite a woman," Bob said. He chuckled. "She was quite a young girl, too. I remember the time . . ."

Bob began telling stories of Pearl's adventures as a young girl, and before he was finished, both of them were laughing so hard that they were wiping away the tears. Pearl was George Summers's daughter and had been raised on the same farm with Bob. As they had been the same age, in the very early days they were playmates.

"I used to be jealous of you," Loomis admitted.

"Jealous of *me*?"

"Not in any sexual way," Loomis explained. "I was just jealous that you had known her as a girl and I hadn't. It seems now, in retrospect, that I had so little time with her."

"I know, my friend, I know," Bob said. He got up and walked over to put his hand on Loomis's shoulder for a moment. Then he crossed to the bookshelf, removed a couple of volumes of Shakespeare, and took out a bottle of brandy that had been hidden behind them. "How about a little violation of the Volstead Act?" Bob suggested, pouring two snifters.

"An excellent idea," Loomis agreed.

A moment later, with both men holding snifters of brandy, Bob raised his glass in a toast. Loomis touched his rim to Bob's, and they both took a sip.

"I want to thank you for what you did for my father-in-law," Loomis said. "He told me how you stood up to the Klan."

"I wasn't the only one," Bob replied. "If I had been, I would have been so sick in my soul that I'd never be able to go back down there. But there were several who stood up for George, and if they'll stand up for one colored man, I believe they'll stand up for all colored men. It may take a generation or two for it to come about, but the seeds of understanding are there, and I believe with all my heart that someday they will germinate."

"To that day," Loomis said, holding out his glass.

"To that day," Bob echoed.

LATE OCTOBER, ST. LOUIS, MISSOURI

"Okay, Demaris!" Rocky shouted, throttling back and pounding on the fuselage to get the attention of the young woman riding in the front cockpit. "If you are really serious about doing this, we're ready!"

Demaris looked out of the airplane. "Where's the golf course?" she called back.

"Down there, to the right. Do you see it?" Rocky asked.

"Yes, I see it," Demaris replied. She laughed. "I hope my father is playing a round this morning."

"Now, look at the smoke over there," Rocky called. "It'll tell you which way the wind is blowing and which way you're going to drift."

"I see it," Demaris shouted, nodding. "So, if I start here, the wind will cause me to drift over that way and I can come down directly on the golf course, right?"

"Right."

"Okay, I've got it," Demaris said. "I think," she added. She loosened the seat belt holding her in, then stood up and stepped out of the cockpit well and climbed down onto the bottom wing of the biplane, a DH-4 that she had rented especially for the occasion. Squatting there and holding on tightly to brace herself against the seventy-five-mile-per-hour wind, Demaris looked up at

Rocky and smiled. "Just pull on this thing, right?" She put her hand on the parachute retaining strap.

"No, no!" Rocky shouted excitedly, waving his hand back and forth. "For God's sake, you pull that and everything is going to come off! That's the release for your parachute! You pull the D-ring, right there in front. The D-ring! It's that silver thing. Do you see it?"

"This?" Demaris put her hand on the appropriate device.

"Yes, that."

"Yeah, I know," Demaris said, grinning. "I was just teasing you, that's all."

Rocky shook his head disapprovingly. "Don't tease," he called. "Listen, are you sure you want to go through with this? Why don't you just climb back in and let me take you back to the airport? Jumping out of a plane in a parachute isn't exactly like stepping off a chair, you know."

"Look at it this way," Demaris shouted back. "At least this time you won't have to worry about whether or not I'm pregnant."

Rocky laughed. "Yeah, I guess you have a point at that," he said. "I'll tell you this, girl: When you said you craved excitement, you weren't just whistling Dixie."

"Hey, I've got an idea! Why don't I jump naked?"

"What?" Rocky yelped.

"Just kidding!" Demaris laughed, then turned and stepped off the wing.

When she first jumped, she felt her stomach come up to her throat. The sensation of falling only lasted for a moment or two, however, and then it settled down and she had no sensation of falling at all. In fact she felt as if she were flying, and she spread out her hands and feet and looked down at the ground far below, like a bird soaring gracefully above it all. A great calmness came over her, and she had a curious sense of detachment as she looked down at the patterned formation of the ground—the clumps of trees, the golf course, the houses and their yards, and, toward the river, the city itself. The houses, trees, cars, and roads didn't appear to grow any larger, and she was ready to believe that she could stay up here for as long as she wanted.

Demaris turned her head to look back toward the airplane she had just jumped from, and when she did, the change in aerodynamics flipped her over onto her back. She could hardly believe her eyes, for the plane was now very small and very high, far above her. She had just left it! How had she come so far so quickly?

She managed to roll back over so that she was once again looking down at the ground. Now the features below her were noticeably larger than they had been, and she determined that she had come at least half of the way down. It was almost as an afterthought that she moved her hand to a strap and started to yank on it, only to remember that this was one of the straps holding her attached to the parachute. Laughing at the near mistake, she corrected herself, found the D-ring, and pulled it.

The chute streamed out behind her, then opened with a loud pop. She felt the opening shock all through her body, especially in her legs where the main support straps were. She looked up to see the big white canopy billowing above her. By the time she looked down again, she was no more than a hundred feet or so above the ninth green of the golf course. True to Rocky's promise, she had drifted across the woods and the road and was right where she wanted to be.

Demaris landed in one of the sand bunkers guarding the green. She fell to the ground and rolled, just as Rocky had instructed her to do, pleased to find that the landing fall wasn't all that bad. When her rolling was spent, she slipped out of the parachute harness, then stood up and began recovering the parachute by wadding up the cords and canopy silk. It had been an exhilarating experience.

And now, a voice in her head announced, as if speaking to an audience, *Miss Demaris Hunter, daredevil extraordinaire, is ready for her next adventure . . . whatever and wherever it may be.*

CHAPTER ELEVEN

NOVEMBER 8, 1923, MUNICH, GERMANY

Karl Tannenhower stood by the window in Gauleiter Paul Maas's small office, which had been provided to the National Socialist German Workers' Party free of charge by the owner of the tobacco shop on the ground floor. The building was on a street with the unlikely name of Im Tal—In the Valley.

It was about three o'clock in the afternoon, and Karl was looking out on a gray day that held the promise of snow. A gust of cold wind swirled up a small storm of littered paper. When one of the pieces of paper blew close to the window, Karl saw that it was a banknote worth fifty million marks.

Out on the street a pedestrian was standing at the corner with his hands thrust deep into his coat pockets, waiting to cross to the other side. He glanced at the money blowing by him but made no effort to pick any of it up, and when several bills were pressed against his leg by the wind, he shook his leg to be free of them, as if they were so much litter. The bills sailed and skipped and tumbled down the street, unclaimed by anyone.

Karl fixed that picture firmly in his mind. The sight of a German citizen standing on the corner while millions of marks swirled unwanted—worse, deemed an annoyance—was symbolic of all that was wrong with the country. Decent men and women had been destroyed by inflation and incompetence; and while families were ruined, Germany's capital city of Berlin sank deeper and deeper into a morass of perversion and corruption.

Something had to be done, and Karl believed in his heart that joining the Nazi party was a step in the right direction. In all of Germany, perhaps in all of Europe, only the National Socialists seemed to have an understanding of what was wrong with the world. And only they had a plan of action to make things right again.

Though it was General Ludendorff's prestige that had drawn Karl to the party in the first place, it was Adolf Hitler who gave him confidence in the party's ultimate success. Karl had never met anyone who made as much an impression on him as did Hitler. It wasn't just the man's power with the spoken word, it was the passion he had for what he was doing and the intensity with which he shared that passion, not only with hundreds of listeners in packed beer halls, but with individuals as well. If, in the recruitment of new converts to the party, a candidate was wavering, a personal meeting with Adolf Hitler was all that was required to "reel him in." Hitler would shake the candidate's hand, look at him squarely with those magnetic, almost hypnotic eyes of his, and speak to him. Hitler knew what to say and how to say it. He had the uncanny ability to put into words exactly what the candidate was thinking. After a brief discussion the candidate for party membership was absolutely certain that his ambitions, pride, loyalty, hopes, fears, and prejudices were one and the same with the ambitions, pride, loyalty, hopes, fears, and prejudices of the party.

"How have Uta and Max taken your move to Munich?" Paul Maas asked. Paul was sitting on a sofa in the room behind Karl, reading the *Völkischer Beobachter*. The day's headline in the paper was: SHALL WE FIND A SECOND GENERAL YORCK IN OUR HOUR OF NEED?

Karl turned to answer him. "There was nothing left for us in Hamburg," he said. "Max is young enough that the move was an exciting new adventure for him, and Uta agrees with me. If I am going to be active in the Nazi party, then I should be where the action is. And Munich seems to be that place."

"You've got that right, my friend," Paul said. He looked up and smiled knowingly. "Perhaps more action than you supposed."

"What do you mean?"

"I called you down here for a reason," he said. "Herr Hitler will be dropping by the office after a while. I think he will have some exciting news for us . . . news that will require men of resolve. Are you game?"

"Yes, of course I am," Karl replied. "I joined the party, didn't I?"

"Yes, and you have been a tremendous asset to us," Paul said. "Although, I must say, you don't seem to embrace the party's Jewish policy with unbridled enthusiasm."

"I suppose not," Karl agreed.

Paul folded the newspaper and put it aside. "You should, you know. Karl, I'm afraid that's a shortcoming you must address. Our position on the Jewish question is a very important part of the Nazi doctrine."

"Must we lean so heavily on the prejudices?"

"Yes, we must. Do you have difficulty with that?"

"I find it . . . distasteful," Karl admitted.

"I know you find it distasteful, but that's because you are a person of intellect and principle. But intellect and principle such as you possess are for the extraordinary man. For the ordinary man, the millions to whom we must appeal in order to swell our ranks and give our party power, prejudice becomes the common denominator."

"The lowest common denominator," Karl suggested.

Paul laughed. "Indeed, yes, the lowest common denominator. Nevertheless, it's a powerful force for cohesion. Workers and management, farmers and artisans, politicians and soldiers, housewives and students all have their prejudices. If we can organize those prejudices, unite them against one common enemy, then it will serve as the mortar that holds us all together."

"And we have chosen the Jews."

Paul laughed. "Yes, the *chosen* ones. It's really rather funny when you think about it."

"It seems to me as if we're working so hard to make everyone hate Jews that sometimes we let the more important things go. Why Jews? Why not Hottentots? Or Eskimos?"

"Well, we must be realistic, after all. We have to choose as our target someone who actually exists in German society, or our hate will be wasted. There are no Hottentots or Eskimos, but there are Jews, and Jews are clannish. They stand out by their dress, their culture, and their attitude of superiority. And have you ever done business with a Jew? To a Jew, a smart business deal is a moral imperative. It matters not if their success is gained at the misfortune of another. And if the one wronged is a Christian, all the better. Why Jews? I'll tell you why Jews. Because they have no one to champion their cause. While not everyone hates the Jew, no one really likes them . . . and that makes our job very easy."

"But haven't you ever known a Jew that you liked and who didn't at all fit the stereotype you just described?" Karl asked.

"No. Have you?"

"Yes, of course, several. For example, there is a doctor in Hamburg—"

Paul held up his hand. "No," he said. "Don't tell me his name. It would be better for you—and for your Jew doctor—if no one knew."

Karl shook his head. "I'd like to see the day come

when we can unite everyone in the name of a common good, and not in the name of a common hate."

"Perhaps at some point in the future that day will come," Paul suggested. "But, in the meantime, we must use whatever method is most effective, and our campaign against the Jews seems to fill that bill."

Outside, a group of uniformed men marched by, singing in lusty voice while their jackbooted feet pounded a staccato rhythm on the paving stones of the street. They were dressed in the brown shirts of the *Sturmabteilung*, or Storm Troopers—commonly called the SA—and they wore red, white, and black swastika armbands. At the head of the troops a flag bearer carried the flag of the party: a red banner with a black swastika inside a white circle. In Munich this flag was more prominent than any other, including the national flag.

"Was that another column of our troops?" Paul asked.

"Yes, and it's the fifth unit to march by here in the last hour. What's going on?"

Paul smiled. "They're marching all over the city," he said. "We've instructed them to march by the police barracks, then form up and march by again and yet again. We'll be doing that all day long so that hundreds will look like thousands and thousands will look like tens of thousands. It's all a part of the plan."

"What plan?"

"I'll tell you when it's time," Paul promised. "Don't worry, my friend. There is an important role for you. This day—and the names of all who take part in the events of this day—will be eternally etched in German history."

A car pulled up to the front of the tobacco shop. Inside were Putzi Hanfstaengl, Hermann Goering, and Adolf Hitler. Karl related to Putzi because, like Karl, he had attended an American university. Putzi had been a student at Harvard at the same time Karl was at Jefferson, and Putzi could remember watching Karl play American football.

"I must confess that my Germanic pride was stronger than my school ties, for I cheered every time you tackled a Harvard player," Putzi had told Karl the first time they met.

Sometimes the two men talked, almost longingly, of their days in America. Both were against the experiment of Prohibition, however, and they agreed that an America without beer would be a much less pleasant place to be than the America they had known.

Karl and Paul stood at attention when the three men entered the office.

Hitler was wearing a pistol over his tightly belted trench coat, and he nervously tapped the riding crop he carried against the side of his leg.

"You must both swear you will not mention this to a living soul," Hitler said urgently.

"We swear, *mein Herr*," Paul promised.

"The hour has come," Hitler announced. "Tonight General Commissioner Gustav von Kahr, General Otto von Lossow, and Colonel Hans Ritter von Seisser will be at the Bürgerbräu Keller to make a dedication to the war dead. They are the three most important men in the Bavarian government. Tonight we act. We are going to have them declare that Munich, and not Berlin, is the seat of German government."

"Herr Hitler, will they make such a declaration?" Karl asked in surprise.

Hitler smiled. "They will have no choice," he replied. "Now, I want you both to be at the Bürgerbräu Keller at seven o'clock. Wear your uniforms and armbands. And bring your pistols."

"Yes, sir," Paul said.

"Oh, and Commander Tannenhower, you once lived in America, did you not?"

"Yes," Karl said.

"Good, good. I am told there are many American correspondents in Munich now. I shall want them particularly sympathetic to our action; therefore, I would like you to assist Hanfstaengl. I have assigned him to take care of the foreign press."

"I shall provide all the assistance I can," Karl promised.

Hitler turned to leave, but then he stopped and stroked his chin for a moment. "I am told there is a powerful organization in America called the . . ." He looked at Putzi for help.

"Ku Klux Klan," Putzi supplied.

"Yes, yes, the Ku Klux Klan." Hitler laughed. "It's a rather funny name, don't you think? At any rate, I would like to know more about this Ku Klux Klan. Perhaps there is a way we could become allies. I understand that they are against the Communists and Jews, just as we are. And the Negro."

"They are against the Catholics as well," Putzi pointed out. "I am Catholic, as are you. And we have many Catholics in our movement."

"Yes," Hitler said. "Well, I'm sure we could work something out. At any rate, now is not the time to concern ourselves with such questions. Now is the time to take Germany for the Germans. Gentlemen, soon there may be blood on the paving stones of Munich's streets. If so, let us make certain that it is our enemies' blood, not our own."

Karl and Paul went to the SA headquarters shortly after six that evening. The second-floor office was crowded with dozens of key members of the party: gauleiters, troop commanders, and propagandists. The gray day had delivered on its promise of precipitation, and a heavy, wet snow, mixed with rain, had begun to fall. The office was heated by a small potbellied stove, which burned furiously in the corner. Karl walked over to hold his hands above the stove and warm himself. Though most of the men present were dressed in the light-brown shirt and dark-brown pants that was the uniform of the party, Karl was dressed in the uniform of a Navy commander. At his neck he wore the Blue Max, which garnered instant respect from the others gathered so that even though Karl's rank within the party was not impressive, the uniform and decorations he was wearing this evening were.

Hermann Göring looked even more impressive than Karl. He, too, wore the Blue Max, but he was also the head of the SA and was dressed accordingly. The left sleeve of his uniform bore a specially embroidered swastika armband, and a large white swastika—not tilted but sitting in the upright position—had been painted on the front of the helmet he was wearing. Like the others, Göring was wearing a pistol, but he had also added a ceremonial sword. It was typical, Karl thought, that Göring's uniform was a bit more resplendent than anyone else's, for Göring had a penchant for such things.

Karl thought that Hitler, on the other hand, was almost embarrassing looking. He was wearing a cheaply cut, poorly fitting morning coat and baggy pants. To the left breast of the coat he had pinned his Iron Cross. He looked more like the headwaiter of a run-down restaurant than the head of a party of several thousand members.

Göring came over to stand beside the stove. He knew of Karl's Blue Max because there were so few of them awarded that the recipients formed a very exclusive fraternity.

"On your way over here, did you notice many Storm Troopers?" Göring asked.

"Not as many tonight as earlier in the day," Karl answered.

"I'm worried about whether or not they'll all report for duty."

"Didn't you send out notices?"

"Yes, but the notices were white for routine drill rather than red for emergency. Hitler insisted we do it that way so as not to give away the element of surprise. But I'm afraid that too many of them will not realize the urgency of the call and will choose to stay out of the wet and the cold."

"Göring!" Hitler called from the other side of the crowded room. "Where are the Storm Troopers? Are they mobilizing?"

"Yes, Herr Hitler, I am certain they are," Göring answered. "As soon as I get my raincoat on, I am going to the barracks to see to it that they are issued their weapons."

"Then do it, man, do it," Hitler said excitedly. "We can't hold up a revolution just because you don't want to get your fancy uniform wet."

The laughter of the others followed Göring down the stairs.

"Karl," Putzi said, calling to him from across the room, "come with me now. I've just learned there are some American reporters who were denied entry into the Bürgerbräu Keller. We must see to them."

"Putzi, would you drive me to my meeting place? It's quite near where you must go," Paul asked, and Putzi nodded that he would.

Saluting the others, Karl and Paul tramped down the stairs with Putzi.

"I must say that with that uniform and medals, you should make quite an impression on our American friends," Putzi remarked to Karl.

"I feel awkward wearing the uniform of a Navy commander when I am no longer in the Navy."

"That doesn't matter," Paul said. "This is a patriotic meeting, a dedication to the war dead. That means any veteran can wear the uniform of his service."

"Yes, including Hitler," Putzi added. "Though he chose to wear that awful monstrosity of a morning coat rather than his uniform because he is ashamed that he was only a corporal."

"He served his country honorably and well," Karl said. "Why should he be ashamed?"

"Good point," Putzi said. "Why should he be, indeed?"

As the three men stepped outside, they heard the rhythmic tramp of boots coming down the street, followed by three dozen male voices bawling out a marching song. It was a troop of SA members, all wearing the special brown-shirt uniform of their organization. Around the corner they saw Göring's car driving away, and Karl got the distinct impression that Göring had instructed the unit to march by just to show Hitler that the troops were being mobilized.

Karl, Paul, and Putzi climbed into Putzi's waiting car and drove to where Paul's uniformed troop had assembled in an alley behind the Torbrau Hotel.

Paul got out of the car and, with Karl and Putzi listening before driving off, instructed his men, "If any of you are not committed to this, heart and soul, now is the time for you to leave. I will tell you now that we are the shock troops, and we will bear the brunt of what happens. It is our job to run the old government out so that we can establish a new one. Are all of you with me?"

"*Yes, sir!*" the men exclaimed as one.

"Good. Now, trucks will be waiting for us on the corner of Blan and St. Martin streets. Inside them you will find rifles, hand grenades, and machine guns."

"Let's go!" someone shouted, and the men formed into ranks, ready to march off.

Karl and Putzi wished Paul good luck, then bid him farewell and continued on to their destination. A crowd was in front of the Bürgerbräu Keller, forcing them to continue up the street for another block before they found a place to park. Exiting the car, they headed back up the street when a thin, stoop-shouldered little man with rimless glasses and a closely cropped mustache approached them.

"Is it true, Hanfstaengl, what I am hearing about tonight?" the man asked. "Is Hitler really about to make his move?"

"Yes, it's true," Putzi replied. "Will you be joining him?"

"No. No, I think not." The man started to leave, but before he did he turned back to shake both men's hands. "However, I do wish you all the luck," he said.

"Thank you," Putzi said.

"Who was that?" Karl asked when the man had walked away.

"Anton Drexler," Putzi said. "After tonight, I'm sure he'll be a footnote in history."

"A footnote in history? Why? What did he do?"

Putzi looked at Karl and smiled. "What did he do? Well, I'll tell you what he did, my friend. He founded the Nazi party."

Arriving at the Bürgerbräu Keller, Karl and Putzi became the object of attention of a group of American and English newspaper reporters who were standing outside, having been denied entrance.

"Putzi, darling," one of the women reporters said. "What is this? They won't let us in. I showed them my press credentials, but they were absolutely immovable. They are being very beastly about it."

"Dorothy, has Putzi ever failed you?" Putzi asked. "I'll take care of it."

"And who is *this* adorable creature?" the woman asked, referring to Karl while fitting a cigarette into a long holder, then posturing while one of the other reporters lit it for her.

"This is Lieutenant Commander Karl Tannenhower," Putzi said.

"Karl Tannenhower?" one of the men reporters asked. "There used to be a pretty good football player in America named Karl Tannenhower. He played for Illinois, I think. Or the University of Missouri."

"Jefferson University," Karl corrected.

"In St. Louis, yes!" the reporter said. "You! You're the same one?"

"In person," Putzi said. "Entertain them with tales of your gridiron greatness, would you, Karl? In the meantime, I shall see to it that they are granted admission."

"I saw you against Northwestern," the reporter said. "You were great in that game. You and . . . Who was that running back you had?"

"Billy Canfield."

"Yes, Billy Canfield. What ever happened to him?"

"He was killed," Karl said. "During the war."

"What a shame. Say, I can see from your uniform and medals that you were also in the war. It's ironic, isn't it? I mean Billy Canfield was an American, and you're a

German; before the war you were teammates and friends, and during the war you were enemies."

"No," Karl said firmly.

"No? What do you mean no? Surely you fought on opposite sides?"

"We did fight on opposite sides, yes. But we were never enemies."

"What a delightful way to put it," the woman named Dorothy said, writing Karl's comment in her notebook. "May I quote you?"

"I didn't say it to be quoted."

"That's even better," she said cynically. "It's a quote from the heart. So few quotes nowadays are."

"Okay," Putzi said, coming back to the group, rubbing his hands together. "Didn't I tell you Putzi would make things right for you? I've taken care of everything. You can go in with me."

"Oh, but Putzi, darling, must we *stay* with you?" Dorothy asked. "You are a dear, dear boy, but I do get better stories when I'm on my own."

"Dorothy, once we're inside, you may go anywhere you wish."

"And who said all Germans were Teutonic beasts?" Dorothy quipped.

The hall was packed with members of the Bavarian provincial cabinet, leaders of society, German newspaper editors, and military and police officers. At the head of the room, on a raised platform, General Commissioner Kahr had already begun his speech. His voice was high, screechy, and full of pompous references to such things as the "edification of the Germanic spirit."

"We've got them inside," Putzi said to Karl. "That's all we were told to do. No one said we would have to listen to this boring bag of wind, so how about a beer? I'll buy. I see that they cost only one billion marks each," he added sarcastically.

"Yes," Karl said. "A beer would be nice."

Karl and Putzi stood at the back of the room, drinking a beer and waiting. From this point on they would be witnesses only.

Suddenly the main door swung open, and in burst Hitler and Göring, followed by Paul Maas and the special shock wave of Storm Troopers. Göring had his sword in one hand and his pistol in the other. Hitler, too, had his pistol drawn.

Chairs and tables were overturned as Hitler, swept along by the shock troops, moved swiftly down the aisle. Men shouted in anger, and women screamed as the Storm Troopers cleared the way by shoving people aside, even using the butts of their rifles when necessary. Some of the men were holding hand grenades aloft, as if indicating they would use them if need be.

Munich's chief of police had been completely caught by surprise by the unexpected entry. Thrusting his hand into his pocket, he stepped forward to stop the intruders, but Hitler immediately turned his pistol on him, pressing the barrel right against the man's forehead.

"Take your hand out of your pocket," Hitler ordered.

The chief of police did as he was told.

Hitler climbed up onto a chair then and turned to face the crowd. There was so much noise and protest going on that when Hitler opened his mouth to speak, Karl couldn't hear him, even though he was just a few feet away. Hitler fired his gun into the ceiling and the explosion silenced the three thousand people. Now the crowd looked toward him expectantly, waiting to hear what he had to say.

"I announce to those present that a revolution has broken out in all Germany," Hitler said. "Six hundred armed men are occupying this room, and no one can leave. The Reichswehr and the state police are marching from their barracks under our flags. A German national and Bavarian government is being formed. The Knilling government and the Reich government are deposed."

"What? What are you saying?" somebody called out.

Ignoring the question, Hitler turned to the dais and shouted in a harsh, commanding tone, "His Excellency von Kahr, His Excellency von Lossow, and Colonel von

Seisser, I must ask you gentlemen to come with me. I guarantee your safety."

"Karl, how would you like to be a witness to history?" Putzi asked as soon as Hitler and his hostages had left the room.

"Yes, of course."

"Then let's go see what's going on. We shall have ringside seats."

Karl followed Putzi into the bare, cold room where von Kahr, von Lossow, and von Seisser were being guarded by a Storm Trooper with a drawn pistol.

Hitler was waving his own pistol around, and he stated, "No one will leave this room alive without my permission. Please, forgive me for proceeding in this manner, but I had no other means. It is done now and cannot be undone."

"What has been done?" von Kahr asked. "Herr Hitler, what is all this about?"

Hitler lowered his pistol. "Why should you even have to ask?" he replied. "You have seen the condition of things in Berlin. You know how worthless our money is. Our country cannot suffer any longer. We will wind up on the scrap heap of history. Now, something has been done. As I said, a new Reich government has been formed, and the old has been deposed. I have appointed Pöhner minister-president with dictatorial power in Bavaria." Hitler pointed to von Kahr. "You, Excellency, will be the state administrator." Hitler then continued, "I will be in charge of the Reich government, General Ludendorff is in charge of the national Army, von Lossow will be Reichswehr minister, and von Seisser will be the minister of police."

"You have made all these appointments, have you, Herr Hitler?" von Kahr asked. "That's a bit presumptuous, isn't it?"

"I know that this step is difficult for you gentlemen, but the step must be taken. Each of you must take your place; if you do not, then there is no justification for your existence. You must fight with me, be victorious with me, or die with me. If this undertaking fails, I have four bullets in my pistol; three are for you if you leave me, and the last bullet is for myself." Hitler still had the pistol in his hand, and to illustrate his point, he raised it to his head, held it there for a second, then let it drop.

Von Kahr stared at Hitler for a long moment before he spoke. "Don't make idle threats, Hitler. You can arrest me, you can have me shot, or you can shoot me yourself. To die or not to die is meaningless."

"Do you consider this threat idle, Herr von Kahr?" Hitler asked, bristling with quick anger. "I assure you, it is not!"

"Then kill me," von Kahr said calmly. He nodded his head toward the other two. "Kill them as well. But by all means, Hitler, *do not forget to kill yourself,*" he added dryly.

"It is clear that you don't understand the seriousness of the situation," Hitler snapped.

"And you don't understand the meaning of honor," von Seisser said, speaking for the first time. "You gave me your word of honor that you would *not* make a revolution. Yet, here you are, in the midst of one."

Hitler turned toward von Seisser and shrugged. "Yes, I did promise that. But it was in the interest of the Fatherland. Please, forgive me."

General von Lossow rose from his chair and stepped toward a window that looked down into the garden of the beer hall. Looking up at him from under the brims of their helmets, their rifles pointed at the window, was a group of Storm Troopers. Hitler glanced out and saw what von Lossow was looking at, then waved his hand, and the men slipped back into the shadows.

"As you can see," Hitler said, "we are all committed to victory."

"How does Ludendorff stand on this matter?" von Lossow asked.

"Ludendorff is squarely behind us," Hitler replied. "He is available and will be fetched immediately." Hitler put his pistol back in its holster then. "I will leave you gentlemen alone for a few minutes," he said. "I think you should be allowed to discuss this among yourselves. But consider it carefully, for I tell you this: For the next one thousand years, Germany will remember the action you take tonight."

When Karl returned to the main hall with Putzi, he saw a crowd of people frightened and uncertain as to what was going on. A few had tried to leave, only to be turned back by the Storm Troopers and the machine gun that had been mounted in the main door. The crowd was approaching hysteria, when Göring shouted for silence in a loud voice conditioned by commanding large formations of the SA. When the people grew silent, Göring began to talk.

"This is not an assault on von Kahr, von Lossow, von Seisser, the police, or the Army, who are already marching out of their barracks with flags waving. It is directed solely against the Berlin government of Jews. It is merely the preliminary step of a national revolution desired by everyone in this auditorium. We have dared this step because we are convinced it will make it easier for our leaders to act. But until that step is completed, you must all stay seated and follow the orders and instructions of the guards."

The crowd was silent for a moment, as if digesting Göring's remarks. Then Göring shouted, "Long live the new Reich government—Hitler, Ludendorff, Pohner, von Kahr!"

The exhortation by Göring brought rousing cheers from every corner of the hall.

The crowd was still cheering when Göring left the platform and found Putzi Hanfstaengl. "Putzi," he instructed, "conduct a press conference. That will hold them for a while. In any case, there is beer to drink." He glanced over his shoulder at the crowd, then added contemptuously, "Give a Bavarian a stein of beer, and he's content."

Putzi obediently climbed up on a nearby chair and began apprising the members of the foreign press that a new government had, indeed, been formed and that all persons and property would be respected. He also assured the reporters that order and discipline would be restored in the country.

At the conclusion of Putzi's press conference, Hitler appeared and mounted the dais. He started to speak, but there was so much conversation going on that no one could hear what he was saying. Angrily, he drew his pistol and again fired a shot into the ceiling.

"If you do not remain calm and listen to what I am saying, I will order a machine gun erected in the balcony with instructions to open fire at my command!" he screamed.

The hubbub quickly subsided.

"In homes all across Germany tonight," Hitler began, "children are crying because they are going to bed with empty stomachs. In homes all across Germany tonight, housewives are sobbing because they have no food to set before husbands returning from a day of back-breaking labor. In homes all across Germany tonight, husbands are weeping because, though they toil from dawn to dusk, they are unable to provide their families with the sustenance needed to hold body and soul together." He paused momentarily, then shouted, "Is it too much to ask for the right to live our lives in productivity and harmony?"

"*No!*" the crowd roared back.

"Are we beggars, to go to the nations of Europe with hat in hand, asking for bread?"

"*No!*"

"We have the resources," Hitler shouted, bringing his hand down sharply with this and each succeeding statement. "We have the skills! We have the energy! We have the will! We have the way! And, most of all, we have the *right* to live lives of respect!"

"*Sieg!*" Göring shouted.

"*Heil!*" the Storm Troopers responded.

"*Sieg!*"

"*Heil!*"

"*Sieg!*"

"*Heil!*"

"Outside this room are von Kahr, von Lossow, and

von Seisser," Hitler went on. "They are struggling hard to reach a decision. May I say to them that you will stand behind them?"

"*Yes! Yes!*" the crowd roared.

"In a free Germany," Hitler shouted, "there is also room for an autonomous Bavaria. I can say this to you: Either the German revolution begins tonight, or we will all be dead by dawn!"

The crowd exploded in cheers and applause, which continued long after Hitler had left. The noise spilled over into the room where the three Bavarian state ministers were being held prisoner. There could be no doubt in their minds but that the crowd had just endorsed the revolution.

Shortly after Hitler won the crowd to his side, General Ludendorff appeared, and Putzi hurried to him.

"Ah, General, you are here," Putzi said. "Herr Hitler wants you to speak to von Kahr and the others."

"I have heard that in the government Hitler has formed, he has made himself dictator of Germany, while I am given command of an army that doesn't exist," Ludendorff said. "Is this true?"

"I . . . I don't know," Putzi replied. "I'm not privy to the makeup of the new government."

"General, does this mean you won't support us?" Karl asked.

Ludendorff, who unlike the others was in civilian clothes, took off his glasses and polished them vigorously for a moment. "No," he finally answered, "that is not what I mean. I am a man of honor. I promised my support, and I shall deliver it. Herr Hitler can count on me."

Karl and Putzi followed Ludendorff into the back room where von Kahr and the others waited. When General von Lossow saw Ludendorff, he stood and saluted.

"General, what say you of all this?" von Lossow asked.

"I say this is a great national event," Ludendorff replied. "I advise you to collaborate."

"We can't turn back now, gentlemen," Hitler said. "Our action is already inscribed on the pages of world history."

"Very well," von Kahr sighed. "Let us go back into the hall and address the people. We will assure them of our support."

Hitler smiled broadly and reached out to shake the hand of each of the men.

"Thank you," he said. "I shall never forget this moment."

Arm in arm, Hitler, Ludendorff, and the triumvirate walked back out into the main hall. Karl started to follow, but he looked over at Putzi, who just stood there, a deep frown on his face.

"What's wrong?" Karl asked.

"I have a feeling we are about to be betrayed," Putzi said.

"By whom?"

"Von Kahr, von Lossow, and von Seisser."

"What? What do you mean?" Karl asked, puzzled. "They said they were going to go along with us."

"They had to say it," Putzi said. "We held them at gunpoint. But did you see their faces? Did you look into their eyes?"

"I thought I did."

"Then you didn't look deeply enough. I tell you, we are about to be betrayed."

Neither Karl nor Putzi could hear the short speeches each of the men gave from the platform, but they could hear the enthusiastic cheering of the crowd. A short time later—exhorting "On to victory!"—Hitler gave the orders to open the doors and allow everyone to leave. As the crowd left, von Lossow excused himself on the grounds that he had to go to his office to issue new orders, based on the night's events. No longer under the control of Hitler and his men, the other two ministers went with him.

•   •   •

All through the night Hitler and Ludendorff tried to call von Lossow, von Kahr, and von Seisser, but the phone was never answered. When they sent messengers, the messengers never returned. By dawn it was clear to everyone that despite their promises to the contrary, the three Bavarian ministers had deserted. The attempt to establish a new government around the framework of the old had miscarried. As someone who had made numerous tactical decisions, Karl Tannenhower knew what must come next.

"We have no choice now but to take the offensive, Hitler," General Ludendorff said, coming to the same conclusion that Karl had. "We must mobilize our forces and go to the streets."

"If the Army is against us, it will mean open warfare," Hitler said.

"Trust me. The Army will never fire upon their old commander," Ludendorff insisted. "They will throw down their arms and come to our side."

"We'll wait," Hitler said. "Röhm has taken charge of Army headquarters. We have the better position; we'll let the Army make the first move."

"You have opened the ball, Hitler. You can't turn back now. It would be disastrous to wait," Ludendorff insisted.

Hitler shook his head. "We'll see what happens with Röhm."

By eleven o'clock, Hitler received word that Ernst Röhm had been surrounded by the regular Army. Though neither Röhm's forces nor the troops of the regular Army wished to open fire, the situation was a standoff, with Röhm effectively neutralized. Now Hitler realized that what Ludendorff had been telling him was true. He had no choice. If he did not move now, and move decisively, the short-lived revolution would fail.

"We march!" Hitler shouted.

Taking up his shout, the Storm Troopers rushed outside to the street, then formed up for the march to the center of the city.

"Here, Karl!" Paul Maas shouted to his friend,

handing him the flag of his troop. "To you goes the honor of carrying our banner!"

Karl moved to the front of the column and raised the banner high. Hitler was in the middle of the front row with Ludendorff on one side and Scheubner-Richter on the other, and they, along with everyone else in the front row, had their arms linked. The men marched down Perusastrasse, then into Max-Joseph Platz. From there they moved north on Residenzstrasse, which ran alongside the Residenz, the huge palace of the ancient kings of Bavaria. At the far end of this street, just before it opened onto the Odeonsplatz, was the Feldherrnhalle— the Hall of Generals.

Ludendorff began singing "O Germany, High in Honor," and the others joined in with him.

"Paul!" Karl called back over his shoulder. He pointed to the Feldherrnhalle. "Look up there, in front of us!"

A small group of police and regular Army men were standing at the head of the street, waiting to meet the marchers. The police and soldiers were armed with rifles, which they were holding across their chest, with the butts pointed forward. The real object of Karl's attention, however, was a machine gun that had been erected at the Feldherrnhalle. Just beyond in the Odeonsplatz, an armored car sat, its turret-mounted machine gun also pointing down the Residenzstrasse.

"Look at those bastards!" one of the Storm Troopers shouted. "They're pointing machine guns at us!" The Storm Trooper raised his pistol.

"No!" Karl shouted over his shoulder. "Don't shoot! Don't shoot!"

Despite Karl's shout the Storm Trooper fired his pistol at the small group of regular Army soldiers who were standing at parade rest. The pistol shot hit one of the soldiers in the head, killing him instantly.

The other soldiers immediately returned fire, supported by the two machine guns.

Karl felt a numbing blow to his leg and fell to the pavement. The men behind him were falling as well.

Some of the marchers, like Scheubner-Richter, the man to Hitler's immediate right, were fatally wounded. Others, like Hitler and Ludendorff, dropped flat to the ground to escape the hail of bullets.

Dragging the flag with him, Karl crawled back to the front rank. There, Ulrich Graf, Hitler's bodyguard, had thrown himself over Hitler to protect him, and as Karl lay there, he saw little sprays of blood flying up from Graf each time he was hit. He was shot several times, though none of the wounds were fatal. Göring, too, had been shot and was bleeding profusely from wounds in the leg and groin. He was dragging himself toward a stone lion that stood in front of the Residenz.

Everywhere Karl looked, people were going down, writhing on the ground in agony, dead and dying, while the guns continued to fire. Blood flowed across the paving stones and soaked into the flag Karl was carrying. At that moment he recalled, with irony, Hitler's comment of the day before: *"Gentlemen, soon there may be blood on the paving stones of Munich's streets. If so, let us make sure it is our enemies' blood, not our own."*

After more than a full minute the shooting finally stopped, though the cries of the wounded did not. Many of those SA men who were not wounded were getting up and running back down the Residenzstrasse. Hitler, too, was struggling to rise, but he was held down by his wounded bodyguard. Karl crawled over to them and moved Ulrich Graf off Hitler, then rolled him gently onto his back.

"Graf, how badly are you hurt?" Karl asked.

Graf tried to laugh, but it came out more like a choking cough than a chuckle. "Did every damned one of them have to use me as a target?" he managed to ask.

The bodyguard was bleeding profusely, and Karl used the flag he had carried to try to stop the flow of blood. When he was finished, he looked up at Hitler, who was standing and holding his right shoulder.

"Are you hit?" Karl asked.

Hitler looked at Karl with an expression of confusion, almost detachment, and it was obvious that the man was in shock. Without answering, Hitler turned and started down the street after the others. Karl saw one of the SA officers go after Hitler and lead him into a yellow Opel that was parked on Max-Joseph Platz. A moment later the small car sped away, even as the police began their search for Hitler.

"You!" one of the policemen shouted to Karl. "What are you doing?"

"I am tending to this man's wounds," Karl replied.

"Leave him! We have doctors coming."

Karl stood up and looked around the plaza at the dead and the wounded. He saw General Ludendorff being led off by a group of regular Army men.

"Karl!" Paul Maas called, running from across the street. "Karl, are you all right?"

"Yes," Karl answered, but then he remembered that he had been shot in the leg. It was funny. At the moment he couldn't even feel it. "I've been shot in the leg," he added.

"Come with me," Paul said. "I'll get you to a doctor."

"Will they let us go?" Karl asked, gesturing toward the soldiers and police.

"Yes. They don't want us," Paul answered. "They only want Hitler and Ludendorff."

As Karl started limping away he heard Paul groan.

"Are you all right?" Karl asked.

"It's over," Paul sobbed. "Our beautiful dream of a new Germany is over."

CHAPTER TWELVE

Right after Ham was born, Mr. and Mrs. Eric Twainbough and their son had moved down one flight of stairs to a small apartment on the fourth floor. The flat wasn't as large as Eric's garret had been, but it was more appropriate for a family, for they now had a combination living room/kitchen, which Eric also used as a studio, two small but separate bedrooms, and—a particular luxury—their own private bathroom. From the kitchen table, which was also Eric's desk, Eric could look out over the rooftops of the surrounding houses with their clutter of dormer windows and collections of clay chimney pots. Beyond the rooftops was the lacy ironwork of the Eiffel Tower against the gray Parisian sky, and tendrils of mist spewed forth from its peak as if the tower itself were the source of this damp, dismal day.

Tanner Twainbough appeared in the bedroom door-

way, and Eric looked over at her. Just behind her, off the
bedroom, the door to the bathroom stood ajar, and Eric
had a clear view of the bidet, the bathtub, and the
kerosene-fired hot water tank. Tanner ran her hand
through her hair, mussed by the midmorning nap she
had just awoken from.

"Hi," she said sleepily.

"Hi, yourself," Eric replied.

"I had a good time last night," Tanner said. She
walked over to him, and he put one of his arms around
her and pulled her to him.

"Leave it to me to show you the hot spots," Eric said
dryly.

"No, I'm serious," Tanner insisted. "I like the kind
of nightlife you show me."

The nightlife he showed her was not high living and
champagne cocktails; it was small bistros and sidewalk
cafés and deep, introspective conversations with other
American, English, French, and even German veterans
of the Great War. They were all men who had shared a
profound experience, and they closed ranks around
themselves, even if they had fought on opposite sides of
the trenches. They spoke with feeling of the social
changes needed to ensure a world of peace, harmony,
and freedom from want. Some espoused the virtues of
Communism, while others were equally vocal for their
own social cause. But even those who were at diametric
ends of the spectrum in their political thinking were
closer to each other than outsiders because of their
common wartime experience. Most were artists of one
sort or another—painters, musicians, or writers. Tanner,
who had no artistic ambition of her own, thought it
wonderful to be with them and listen to the passion of
their conviction when they spoke, especially when they
discussed their art. Sometimes they even took Ham with
them—though their concierge's wife adored the child
and offered to babysit free of charge whenever they
wished—feeling that such intellectual exposure would
somehow leave an imprint, even though Ham had

absolutely no understanding at his age of what was being said.

Although Eric was not much older than the other expatriates, he occupied the undefined but very real position of group sage. The position fit him well, for he *seemed* a lot older than the others, and in terms of experience he was. Since their marriage Tanner had learned that Eric had lived a life full of adventure, having been at various times a working cowboy, a hobo, a performer for the Buffalo Bill Wild West Show, a professional boxer, and a merchant seaman. He had also panned for gold in Alaska, covered the war on the Eastern Front before the United States became involved, and was an eyewitness to—and in some ways an unwilling participant in—the Russian Revolution before finally winding up the war as a doughboy in the American Expeditionary Force.

Having read his aborted novel, Tanner wasn't at all surprised to learn that, like his protagonist, Eric had even had a love affair with a Russian princess. In fact the princess had been pregnant with Eric's baby when the Bolsheviks took her away. Eric never learned her fate and didn't know to this day whether she was alive or dead or whether the baby had ever been born. Tanner discovered very early in their marriage that a part of Eric was still in love with Katya and always would be. But Katya was his past while she and the baby were his present and his future, so she had learned to live with it without challenging it or being dismayed by it.

"How's the writing going?" she asked.

"Oh, I'm having a wonderful day," Eric replied sarcastically. He pointed to the paper and the pencils on his desk. "Do you see? I have three sharpened pencils and a pile of clean paper. The hardest part is done."

Tanner ran her fingers caressingly through Eric's hair. "Would you like to go down to Marcel's?"

"No, I don't think so."

"But, Eric, you work so well there. You've said often how you like to sit at the sidewalk tables while you work so you can watch the pretty girls walk by."

"Now, where would I see anyone any prettier than you?" Eric asked.

She laughed. "Oh, come now, this is Tanner you're talking to, remember? I'm not jealous. I know that pretty girls are just a part of your inventory. How can you write about beautiful young girls and handsome young men if you don't look at them from time to time? Besides, I'd like to have our lunch there."

"But won't that cost too much?"

She shook her head. "We can have the potato salad and a loaf of bread, so it won't cost much at all. Marcel will sell us yesterday's bread for very little, and the potato salad is cheap and filling."

"And a beer," Eric put in. "I'd like a beer for lunch." He looked up at Tanner. "But you're the one keeping up with the money. Can we afford a beer?"

"Of course. I wouldn't even suggest that we go to Marcel's if we couldn't drink a beer, would I? I'll just get my coat," Tanner said, buttoning her sweater. "We'll have a very pleasant outing, just the two of us."

"What if Ernest is there?" Eric asked. "If he is, he'll claim that I've come to steal from his aura . . . whatever the hell that means."

"I like the Hemingways," Tanner called from the bedroom, where she was getting her coat from the closet. "Especially Hadley. I knew the Richardsons in St. Louis, and I remember Hadley. We weren't close friends or anything like that—after all, she's older than I am—but I did know her and I liked her, even then."

"You aren't the only one younger than Hadley. Ernest is younger too."

Tanner came back across the room and put her hands on Eric's shoulders. "Don't be cruel, dear; she's not that much older. And besides, she's a very delightful person. I wish you could get along better with Ernest."

"Maybe I could if I didn't have to listen to those interminable bullfight stories. To hear him, he practically discovered the sport. Don't you just know he'd have a wonderful time in Milwaukee or Chicago? Anytime he wanted to, he could just go down to one of the meat-packing plants and watch a muscular Negro hit a cow in the head with a sledgehammer."

Tanner laughed. "You are awful," she said, buttoning her coat. "Listen, after you finish work for the day, if you'd like, we can stop by to visit Miss Stein."

"That's quite a concession for you, isn't it? I didn't think you liked Gertrude."

"Oh, my liking her isn't the problem. It's the tolerance factor she has for wives that's the problem. She tolerates wives . . . but she doesn't like them. Any of them."

"Except her own," Eric joked.

"Alice isn't her wife; Alice is her friend."

"Life mate," Eric said.

"Companion," Tanner suggested.

"Lover," Eric insisted.

"I never knew about such things until I met them. But I like Alice. You can't help but like her."

"I'm glad you do. It gives you someone to talk to when we stop by," Eric said. He began putting his pencils and the tablet into a worn leather briefcase. "By the way, I received a cable from Thomas Petzold yesterday. He's asked me to do three stories for him."

"But, Eric, I thought you weren't going to write for him anymore."

"I know I said that, but we really should think about it. Petzold is a good man, and he's always treated me fairly."

"I know he's a good man," Tanner said. "He's my godfather, for heaven's sake. And *The St. Louis Chronicle* is a good newspaper. But when you're writing for the newspaper or a magazine or for anything else, you don't do good work on your novel. At least, that's what you've always said."

"Yes, that's true," Eric agreed. "Even though I tell myself that I'm going to save my best stuff for my own stories, I can't write that way. I have to write everything the best that I can—and when I expend all my energy and creative juices on articles, I have nothing left for the book."

"Well, then, that settles it, doesn't it?" Tanner insisted. "You won't be writing for Thomas or anyone else until you've finished your novel."

"Before we decide that, I think you should know that he offered to pay me two hundred dollars per story," Eric said. "And he'll let me write about anything I wish."

Tanner inhaled sharply. "Six hundred dollars! Oh, Eric, that's a fortune! We could live for six months on that money."

"Then you agree with me? I should do them?"

"No," Tanner said resolutely, without a moment's hesitation. "It would get in the way of your novel. If we get desperate for money, we can always go to my father."

"Absolutely not!" Eric insisted.

"No matter; we won't have to. We can dip into the money my grandfather left me."

"No, that's *your* money," Eric countered.

"What do you mean, *my* money? Eric, when you sell *A Time for All Things*, will that be your money only? Or will it be ours?"

"Of course it'll be ours."

"Then what's the difference?"

"The difference is, you have this money already, whereas *A Time for All Things* has not yet sold."

"It will sell."

Eric kissed Tanner. "My foolish, wonderful, trusting girl," he said. "How do you know I'll ever sell that book?"

"I just know that you will," Tanner replied. "You've already proved that you're a wonderful writer. Even Uncle Rudolph loved your stories about the Russian Revolution."

Eric laughed. "Your Uncle Rudolph is prejudiced. He is a capitalist with a capital C, and he has a deep-rooted hatred of the Communists. I wasn't very sympathetic to the Bolsheviks, so of course he'd like what I wrote about them."

"You should be happy he's prejudiced," Tanner said. "When Papa learned that I wasn't coming home after Ham was born, he was ready to disown me. It was only

Uncle Rudolph's intercession on your behalf that saved the day. Anyway, he isn't the only one. Hundreds of thousands of people have read your writing, and they all like it."

"Then why haven't any of my novels sold?"

"They will. Someday you'll be a well-known author. They'll study *A Time for All Things* in English Lit at Jefferson University and at colleges all over the country."

"You think so, do you?"

"I *know* so," Tanner said firmly. She giggled. "But not unless you get it written. So, come on. I'll get Ham ready, and then we can go. Marcel's is waiting for us."

Marcel's Café was on rue du Bac. To reach it, Eric and Tanner pushed Ham's pram along the quays from Boulevard Saint Michel. It was a pleasant walk, taking them by the fishermen on the stone banks of the Seine and by the big river barges and tugboats that worked the river. They enjoyed watching all the activity, and Eric knew most of the fishermen and called to them by name.

Marcel's was a two-story building, painted white at the street level and yellow above. The top floor was an apartment for Marcel Aubron and his family. The café wasn't known to the tourists, though the big green tour buses did drive by quite often. Rather, it was frequented by native Parisians and by the handful of expatriates who had discovered it and claimed it as their own, secure in the fact that it was still a quiet place, unspoiled by visiting Americans and English. The café was known for its sausages and for the fish from the Seine that were breaded and deep fried until they were so crisp that even the bones could be eaten. There were as many tables outside as inside. During the summer, a large canvas awning covered the sidewalk tables; during the rest of the year, the canvas was rolled back, giving those who chose to dine alfresco the advantage of the sun. In the winter, when the outdoor tables were covered with snow and ice, they were empty, but in spring and summer and fall they were always filled.

By the time Eric and Tanner reached the café, several people were already at the tables, and one of them had a radio tuned to a station that was broadcasting a concert of Debussy's compositions.

"You sit here and write," Tanner said, finding a table that was warmed by the sun. "I'll take care of the baby and see to it that all of your friends keep away from you so that you won't be disturbed."

"If you keep them away from me, they won't be my friends any longer," Eric quipped.

"If they care no more for you than to disturb you while you're working, they aren't very good friends to begin with," Tanner rejoined.

Eric sat where Tanner had indicated and took out his writing tablet and a sharpened pencil. Smiling at him, Tanner opened the book of verse she had brought and began to read.

It took Eric a while to get back into the story, and he sat there for a long time, thinking about what he had written the day before. He still wanted to do a story about the war and felt certain that he had it in him. But he was now convinced that Tanner was right: He was too close to the war to be the objective author such a story required. Every time he tried to write the story, he found that he was writing himself into it, clogging up the flow of the narrative and squeezing the breath out of all other characters so that only he had an eye and a voice. Therefore, he had decided to lay the war story aside, letting it cool while he tried something entirely different.

A Time for All Things had nothing to do with the war. It was about the coming of age of a young man, and though this young man happened to be a working cowboy on a turn-of-the-century ranch, it wasn't a Western in the traditional sense. The story had the protagonist, fifteen-year-old John Logan, going off on a holiday with two older friends to "see the wonders of the St. Louis World's Fair"—but an ill-fated train robbery attempt along the way leaves his friends killed and John fleeing for his life, forced to abandon everything he had ever known.

The story was going very well, and Eric was exceptionally pleased with it. This book would sell. He had no doubt about it.

Another thing about doing this story pleased him: It made him even more certain that someday he'd be far enough removed from the war to be able to write about it. He knew this because *A Time for All Things* was his own life story. Eric *was* the orphan boy in the book who had gone off on a holiday to see the World's Fair with his two best friends, and he had been drawn into a train robbery attempt when his and his friends' money had been stolen soon after leaving the ranch. He had watched horrified as his two friends were cut down by shotgun blasts fired from the darkened interior of a mail car, and he had heard bullets whistle by his ears as he rode off into the night. That was twenty years ago, but as Eric wrote the story now, he could almost hear Jake Quinn and Marcus Parmeter talking to him.

"Come on, kid, you're tellin' that story like as if it was you them bar girls was after when we all know it was me they was lookin' at," Jake seemed to be saying into his ear.

"Yeah, he's right, kid," Marcus would likely reply. *"But they was only lookin' at him cause they hadn't never seen anyone as ugly as him."*

The writing flowed so well that Eric lost all track of time, not even breaking his concentration when the pencil lead would wear down so low that he'd have to stop work and pull out his penknife to sharpen it. After several pages he finally looked up at Tanner, sitting quietly across the table from him. She was absently rocking the pram with one hand while staring down at the river at a big black barge and at the barge captain's wife who was hanging her laundry out to dry.

"Hi," Eric said quietly.

"Hi," Tanner responded, turning toward him with a smile. "Is the writing going well?"

"Yes. Very well. Are you hungry?"

"A little," Tanner admitted.

"Well, why don't we eat? It must be nearly noon."

Tanner laughed.

"What is it? What's so funny?"

"It's after four," she said.

"*Four?* But how? It can't be."

"Look at the clock," she said, gesturing with her chin.

Eric leaned across the table to get a look at the clock on the steeple of a nearby church. "Why didn't you say something?" he asked, looking back at his wife. "You must be starved."

"I didn't want to disturb you." She grinned. "Besides, it made me feel very self-righteous. Starvation is my contribution to the great American novel."

"I'll order something for us," Eric offered.

"It's okay," Tanner said, raising her hand toward the owner. "I've already ordered. I told Marcel I'd signal him when we were ready."

A moment later Marcel brought their lunch—two large servings of potato salad made with olive oil and coarsely ground pepper, a bowl of mild peppers and pickles, and a loaf of bread. The bread was hot, steaming, and aromatic, and when Marcel put it down, Eric held up his hand in protest.

"We want day-old bread," he said.

"It's okay," Marcel replied, smiling. "Tomorrow, this will be day-old bread. I charge you the same."

"I appreciate that, Marcel," Eric said.

"And another beer for each of us, if you please," Tanner requested.

"Would you not prefer wine?" Marcel suggested.

Tanner giggled. "You're always trying to make me drink wine."

"But of course. Wine is very French," Marcel said.

"I like beer."

"That is very German," Marcel said.

"It's also very American. My father makes beer in America."

Eric laughed. "Not anymore, he doesn't," he said.

"Yes, that's true. Prohibition has put a stop to it," she agreed.

"I do not understand this Prohibition," Marcel said, shaking his head slowly. "Perhaps you can explain it to me."

"I'm sorry," Eric said. "We don't understand it either."

"Perhaps someone went a little crazy one time," Marcel suggested.

"Yes," Eric said, nodding. "That's as good an explanation as any."

Marcel smiled. "Oh, I nearly forgot. Hemingway left a letter here for you."

"Oh, maybe there's a picture of the baby," Tanner said, reaching for the envelope. She looked inside. "No, there isn't. Just a letter."

"Read it aloud," Eric asked.

Tanner cleared her throat and began to read:

"Dear Twainberries,

"No doubt you think I am a son of a bitch for leaving a letter for you at Marcel's, rather than being a civilized gent and sending it by post. But the thing is, we're still experimenting with living with a baby, etc. Hadley sick in bed for quite a while, me for a few days, baby hollers, etc., and on top of that I couldn't find your damn mailing address. Have I made enough excuses for you to forgive me?

"Hadley has the place under control now and doing all right. I not writing badly. Ford Madox Ford has a story in the *Transportation Review* for April. Several others he can't publish. Did you hear that Bunting was in jail in Genoa? I told Ezra I would write to anyone he suggested in Italy if it would do any good.

"Henry Strater left for America last week. Father forgive him for he knows not what he does.

"We christened the baby on Sunday—in an Episcopal Church, of all places. St. Luke's. But I didn't want to go the Catholic route, and the other Protestant Churches are too bland for my tastes. Besides, there is some connection there; James Joyce is singing in the St. Luke's choir. He's appearing in April's *Transatlantic*, by the way. His ms started at 7 pages but, by additions to the proof, eventually reached about 9 pages.

"Bill Bird is getting out my book *In Our Time* soon. He says soon. Actually, it was promised by the bindery 3 weeks ago. After awaiting various dates set by the binder, I have lost the fine thrill enjoyed by Benjie Franklin when entering Philadelphia with a roll under each arm. Fuck literature.

"I am writing some damn good stories right now, but I wish I had someone I could trust read them and advise me on same. Ford offers his services, but he is so goddamned involved in being the dregs of an English country gentleman that he does me no good. He has never recovered from having been a soldier. De Maupassant, Balzac, Stendhal, *they* were the literary creators of the war, weren't they? I think you and I should start denying we were in it for fear we'll become like those gentlemen. Down with gentlemen. All gentlemen are fakes anyway.

"Hem"

"Now, Eric, that was a nice, chatty letter. He's trying to be friends," Tanner said as she folded it up.

"Yeah, I guess so," Eric admitted. He chuckled. "Maybe being a papa has mellowed him somewhat."

"Papa Hemingway," Tanner said, laughing. "That's what we should call him now."

"No," Eric said, shaking his head. "I can't see him as Papa."

PASSOVER 1924, VIENNA, AUSTRIA

At the head of the table, David Gelbman raised his glass and began to chant the kiddush. "Blessed art thou, O Lord our God, creator of the fruit of the vine. Blessed art thou, O Lord our God, king of the universe, who hath sustained us in life and enabled us to reach this joyous season."

Anna, David's wife; Miriam, their daughter, who had just celebrated her twelfth birthday; Leo, their son, who at six was the youngest present and who would be called upon to recite the four questions; and Simon Blumberg, who was back from Berlin for Passover, picked up their cups and drank.

"L'chaim," Simon said, tossing the wine down as if it were a drink he had ordered in a bistro.

David let it be known by a reproving glance what he thought of Simon's lack of respect for the Seder meal, but he said nothing.

"Leo," he said, turning to his son, "are you ready?"

"Yes, Papa," Leo answered.

"All right, let's hear it."

Leo cleared his throat, then recited the four questions: "Why is this night different from all other nights? Why on this night do we eat only unleavened bread? Why on this night do we eat only bitter herbs and dip them twice? On all other nights we eat either sitting up or reclining; why on this night do we all recline?"

David answered each of Leo's questions; then they sang the "Daienu."

After that, one by one, David held up the Passover symbols on the plate in front of him and explained their meaning. Then Miriam was selected to open the door for Elijah, the prophet of the Messiah. A cup of wine sat on the table, waiting for Elijah, as it did on every Jewish table at every Seder meal.

"Is he there?" Leo asked innocently.

Miriam giggled. "No, he isn't here," she said. "Don't you know? He is never there."

"One day he will be," Anna promised.

"Will I see him?" Leo asked.

"Perhaps not in this lifetime," Anna answered.

Later, after the Seder meal had been concluded, David, Anna, and Simon sat in the parlor. Leo went outside to play, while Miriam went to her room to listen to records. Simon sat down in an easy chair and stretched his artificial leg out before him.

"Would you like a hassock?" Anna asked.

"No," Simon said. He smiled. "What I would like to do is take this wooden leg off, but that would be as unseemly as taking off one's socks."

"From the way you tossed down the wine at Seder, unseemliness doesn't exactly appear to deter you," David said tartly.

"I guess that's because I've spent more time in bars and bawdy houses than I have in homes and temples."

"Why do you do that?" David asked.

"Because that's where I get my religion."

"That's blasphemy."

"I consider life a blasphemy."

"You aren't grateful for life?"

"Not particularly," Simon answered, shrugging.

"Then I'm very sorry for you, Simon," David said. "There is more to your war wound than a missing leg."

Simon was silent for a long moment; then he sighed. "I'm sorry, David. I have no right to abuse your hospitality like this. Please, forgive me."

"No, you forgive me," David replied. "I have no right to abuse your privacy. What do you say we just talk about something else?"

"That's a good idea," Anna put in. "Oh, I know what we can talk about. What about this fellow Hitler? I see in the papers that he's going to serve five years in Landsberg Prison."

"Strange, isn't it?" David said. "I still see him as the brooding young man who carried my bags at the railroad station when I first arrived in Vienna. And later we met him at the opera house. You remember, don't you, Anna?"

"Yes," Anna said. "I remember him. But of course, Simon, you knew him. It must seem strange to think of someone you served with gaining such notoriety. We received a letter from David's parents in America, and they've even heard of him over there."

"Yes, I knew him during the war," Simon confirmed. "But the Hitler of today is nothing like that Hitler. And they say that none of his old comrades-in-arms can get close to him. But, of course, the fact that I am a Jew would make it even more difficult for me."

"Is he really as anti-Semitic as his rhetoric?" Anna asked.

"Yes," Simon replied. "That I know from the old days."

"But what does he want?"

"I think he'd like to see all Jews leave Germany," David said.

"More than that," Simon replied. "He would like to see all Jews leave the world."

"Leave the world? Don't be silly. How could we leave the world?" Anna asked with a little laugh.

"If we were all dead."

"Oh, come now," David said. "Do you really think his Jew-hating goes that far?"

"Yes, I really do."

"Well, in that case, I suppose we're lucky he was stopped in time," Anna said.

"Was he?" Simon asked.

"Of course he was. He's in prison, isn't he?"

"Yes, he's in prison," Simon admitted. "After a show trial, which he used as a podium for his speeches. And what of his prison? He doesn't have a cell, he has a two-room suite. And he has a doting staff to see to his every need. He's greeted every morning with the words 'Heil Hitler,' not only by his followers, but by the prison guards and the reporters who attend his weekly press conferences. I've heard he's even writing a book. And I'm told women often come around to the prison and ask permission to take a bath in the tub he uses so that they can feel closer to him. Now, you tell me, David, does that sound to you as if Adolf Hitler has been stopped?"

"Are you saying we will hear from him again?" David asked.

Simon nodded slowly. "Oh, yes. I am most definitely saying that."

CHAPTER

THIRTEEN

Sam Hamilton stood at the window of his office on West Forty-fourth Street, looking out through the gray drizzle at the grimacing gargoyle perched on the corner of the building directly across the street. The gargoyle and the other ornaments on top of the skyscraper had apparently been put in place for the enjoyment and appreciation of the occupants of the upper floors of the adjacent buildings, for certainly no one on the street twenty-two floors below would be able to see them. Sam had named this gargoyle "Mr. Melchoir" for no particular reason, and he sometimes talked to it on the theory that talking to a gargoyle was, somehow, better than talking to himself.

The window Sam was looking through was just behind his desk. On the wall to his right were the framed jacket covers of six of the books published by Pendarrow

House. During Sam's career at Pendarrow, he had edited over two hundred books, but only these few had made it to a position of honor on his wall. It was not that these six were the best selling of all he had done; in fact, many of the books *not* on the wall had sold much better, and one of the books displayed hadn't even sold enough to pay for itself. But these were the books he took the most pride in—and Sam had very exacting judgment.

A long narrow table against the same wall was piled high with manuscripts. At any given time as many as forty or fifty manuscripts were on that table, all unsolicited, "over the transom" works, and though it was rapidly becoming the policy of most publishing houses to allow the most junior assistant editors to move the slush pile through, Sam still insisted upon seeing each one. He couldn't honestly say that he read them, but he did glance through them, and while he wasn't able to judge the whole of a manuscript by such a brief perusal, within one or two paragraphs he felt that he could judge whether or not the writing itself had merit. When he found good writing, he would lay that manuscript aside and give it to one of the junior editors to read, with instructions to make a recommendation as to whether or not Sam should take the time to read the whole thing. One of the six books on his wall had come to him that way.

The third wall of Sam's office was occupied by a leather sofa, which faced a leather wing chair. Separating the sofa and chair was the kind of low table that some were now calling a "coffee table," and on the table, conspicuous by its prominent position, lay a typed manuscript. The title of the manuscript was *A Time for All Things*.

Like the manuscripts on the long table, this one had been an over-the-transom submission. What made it stand out from all the other unsolicited submissions was that this one had been accompanied by a letter of recommendation from Gertrude Stein:

"Mr. Twainbough has a marvelous facility with words, as you will discover if you take the time to read this wonderful ms. In *A Time for All Things* he has written a story both well crafted and entertaining. Although this is Mr. Twainbough's first novel, he has already enjoyed a distinguished career in journalism, and I feel certain that a sparkling literary career is just ahead."

Sam learned that Eric Twainbough lived in Paris but had come to New York to personally deliver the manuscript. He had brought the manuscript and Gertrude Stein's letter to Sam's office last Friday morning. Since the author had not bothered to make an appointment and was unexpected, Sam was not in his office when Eric had arrived. Undeterred, Eric had left the script and letter with Becky Cooper, Sam's secretary, telling her to inform Mr. Hamilton that he would hold himself available Monday morning at ten o'clock.

"He will 'hold himself available'?" Sam asked incredulously when Becky transmitted the message.

"That's what he said," Becky assured him.

The impudence of the man, Sam thought. He could not imagine the audacity of someone who would drop into a major publishing house and leave a manuscript, along with a message—not even a written note, mind you, but just a verbal message!—that he would "hold himself available" on Monday morning at ten o'clock. It was almost as if this Twainbough were granting an audience.

"What am I supposed to do when he shows up?" Sam had asked Becky. "Genuflect? Kiss his ring, perhaps?"

"How am I supposed to know?" Becky replied. "I'm just a secretary. Why don't you ask Mr. Melchoir?"

"He's no help. He never answers me."

Sam's first inclination had been to attach a form rejection letter to the script, then make it a point to be absent Monday morning when the author "made himself available." But he couldn't do that. Sam was basically a decent man, and he was willing to give the author the benefit of the doubt that he just didn't know any better. Also he knew of Gertrude Stein, and he respected her work, so her letter did carry some weight with him. Besides, he made it a point of honor to read at least a few words of every script that came in, so he could do no less for this one. The only concession he made to this author's audacity was to move his manuscript ahead of the others that had been waiting their turn on the long table.

At the end of the workday on Friday, Sam had decided to bring the manuscript home with him. That evening at the Harvard Club as he had waited for his dinner to arrive, he began casually looking through the script. He had become so immediately engrossed in the story that when, a half hour later, the headwaiter came over to inquire solicitously if something was wrong with the fillet of sole that had grown cold on Sam's plate, the editor had looked up in surprise. Until that moment Sam hadn't even realized that his meal had been served.

He had gone straight to his apartment after dinner, put on his pajamas, and sat up in bed reading until two o'clock in the morning. At ten o'clock on Saturday morning he had put through a long-distance call to Boston to Millie Pendarrow, owner of Pendarrow House, and informed her that on Monday morning he was going to buy a book that would be next year's runaway best-seller.

Now it was Monday morning, and as Sam waited in his office, staring out at the rain, something began to nag at him. He wasn't worried that he may have misjudged the quality of the writing in the excitement of the moment or in the exhaustion of reading it in one sitting in the middle of the night. He had gone back over parts of it Sunday afternoon and then again this morning, and the writing was as powerful on the second and third reading as it had been on the first. What was worrying him was something else, something that was potentially much more devastating: He could not shake the feeling that he had read some of Eric Twainbough's material before.

But where?

Surely something this powerful would have made enough of an impression on him that he would remember it. In fact, he couldn't believe that anything like this could have been published without it becoming as well-known as something by Melville or Dickens or even F. Scott Fitzgerald. Yet in the deepest recesses of his mind was a certainty that this reading wasn't for the first time.

"What do you think, Mr. Melchoir?" he asked the gargoyle. "Do I have something to worry about?"

"On the day that stone beast answers you, I'm changing jobs," Becky announced from the doorway.

"If he ever answers, I won't need you anymore," Sam replied with a grin, turning toward her.

"I thought you might like to know that Mr. Twain-bough is here."

"Show him in," Sam said. "No, on second thought, I'll go out and get him."

"This writer is going to be very important someday, isn't he?" Becky asked.

"What makes you say that?"

"Friday afternoon you were ready to chuck the manuscript out the window. But something made you change your mind, and now you've been waiting for him all morning."

"You're right," Sam said. "He could be a very important writer one day." If he's on the up-and-up, Sam thought but did not say.

Sam went into the outer office and found Eric Twainbough standing at a bookshelf, looking at the books on display. The author was wearing dark-brown trousers and a camel-colored jacket that was still spotted with drops of rain. His hair was sandy brown and flecked with gray, his eyes were brown, and he had a thick mustache that drooped past the corners of his mouth. Sam's first impression was that Eric was an exceptionally powerful man, tall and muscular with broad shoulders and chest, tempered by a slight belly.

"Mr. Twainbough," Sam said, reaching out to shake

hands. "Welcome to New York. Is this your first time in the city?"

"No," Eric said. He smiled. "I've been here several times . . . the first time in 1907. I was a member of Buffalo Bill's Wild West Show."

"Ah," Sam said, holding up his finger and smiling broadly. "Then you *do* write from experience."

Eric returned the smile. "That means you've read my book."

"Yes, I have."

"What do you think of it?"

"Let's talk in my office, shall we, Eric? May I call you Eric?"

"Sure."

Sam ushered Eric into his office. The author accepted a seat on the sofa and immediately noticed his manuscript on the table. From the slightly bemused look on Eric's face he seemed to be asking why the script was lying out like this.

"I understand you're living in Paris," Sam said.

Eric looked up. "Yes. I've been there since the war ended."

"Paris seems to be *the* gathering place for American artists and writers now," Sam suggested. "I know that Horace Liveright is very high on a young man who lives there. His name is Hemingsly, or something like that."

"Hemingway. Ernest Hemingway," Eric said.

"Yes, I believe that's it. Do you know him?"

"Yes, quite well. And Mr. Liveright should be high on him. Ernest is young, but he's a very talented writer."

"Harold Loeb and Sherwood Anderson also live in Paris, I believe," Sam said. "And they also write for Boni and Liveright. Do you know them?"

"Yes, I do."

Sam raised his hand to his chin and studied Eric for a moment. "I'm curious, Eric. Since you know all those writers, and since they all seem to be with Boni and Liveright, how is it that you sent your manuscript to us?"

Eric shrugged lightly. "I had to. I owed it to you."

"You *owed* it to Pendarrow House?"

"To *you* personally," Eric corrected.

"To me? I don't understand."

Eric smiled, then reached into his inside jacket pocket. He pulled out a letter, yellowed with age. "I've kept this ever since you wrote it. It went to war with me in Russia and later in the trenches of France." Opening the letter, he cleared his throat and began to read:

"Dear Mr. Twainbough.

"I have read your story *Glory Dust* with great interest but feel, unfortunately, that we must pass on it. It starts out well enough; the scenes on the ranch in Wyoming seem quite realistic, and the three cowboys' adventures on the way to the World's Fair are well wrought. I must say, however, that it loses credibility when they attempt to rob a train almost on the spur of the moment. I couldn't believe anyone would really try such a thing.

"I feel I would be remiss, Mr. Twainbough, if I did not give you some encouragement. You are obviously a man with a powerful imagination, which is good in a writer. You can also write about some subjects with the utmost believability; i.e., the ranch scene as I mentioned, life as a hobo, even what it must be like to pan for gold in the Alaskan wilderness. But though both your grammar and word usage indicate an obviously well-educated man, it may be that your education has conspired against you. It is my feeling, and my feeling only, I must stress, that your reverence for words has made you afraid to use them. I would advise this: Respect words, yes, but don't fear them. You must learn to be their master.

"I've never said anything quite like this in a letter of rejection, but I must tell you that a few lines here and there, a piece of a scene, a descriptive phrase, a snatch of dialogue, show absolute greatness. It is during those times that you have allowed your natural style to emerge. The rest of the time I feel that you aren't writing the way you *want* to write, rather you are writing the way you think you *should* write.

"Perhaps you should try writing for a newspaper for a while. I have some newspaper experience in my own background, and I know that the pressure of meeting daily deadlines will make you abandon the stilted style you have affected and force you into a more natural style of your own.

"In any case, I do hope you continue writing. I really do feel you have a great talent.

                                        "Yours sincerely,
                                        "Sam Hamilton"

"My God," Sam breathed. "You know, I *do* remember that letter. Not only that, I remember the book you submitted. And that's what's been troubling me. I thought I had read some of it before. Some of *Glory Dust* found its way into *A Time for All Things*, didn't it?"

"Quite a bit of it, yes."

"How long ago was that?"

"Ten years," Eric replied. "I took your advice, Mr. Hamilton, and went to work for a newspaper . . . *The St. Louis Chronicle*."

"I know it. It's a very good paper."

"Yes, well, I didn't plan on it taking me so long before I could get back to writing a novel," Eric said. "But a Communist revolution and a war got in the way."

"I must tell you, Eric, you used your time well," Sam said. "You have written a fine book . . . in fact, I would go so far as to say it's a wonderful book."

Eric smiled broadly. "Then you like it?"

"I like it very much."

"And you'll buy it?"

"Yes, I'll buy it."

"How much?"

Sam laughed. "You do get right to the point, don't you?"

"It's a matter of practicality," Eric said. "You see, I quit writing articles in order to do this book. I figure it has to make at least as much money as those articles were making, or it isn't worth my time."

"I see," Sam said. "And how much were you making from the articles?"

"The last offer I got was for three articles at two hundred dollars each," Eric replied.

"Two hundred dollars? For newspaper articles? Eric, that's a princely sum."

"I suppose it is," Eric agreed. "But at the risk of sounding immodest, I managed to develop a following while I was with the paper."

"What you are saying is, you gave up six hundred dollars to do this book."

"At least that much," Eric said. "There may have been one or two additional articles, had I agreed to do the first three."

"I see." Sam drummed his fingers on the arm of the chair for a moment. "We normally pay two hundred dollars for a first novel."

"Two hundred?" Eric said, falling back in his seat, obviously deflated. "That's it? That's no more than one article."

"I said normally. If the novel shows a great deal of promise, we may go to four hundred, and if it is exceptional, six hundred dollars—though for a first novel we've done that very rarely. But if we did that for you, it would match what you'd have gotten from the articles."

"Except it took me five months to write this book," Eric said. "I could have written all three newspaper articles in three weeks."

"The money you're paid for the newspaper articles stops there, doesn't it?" Sam asked. "What I mean is, you don't get any royalties?"

"No, of course not."

"Your book will sell for two-fifty. Eight percent, or a little over twenty cents of each book that sells, will be paid out in royalties. Once enough copies of your book have sold to earn back your advance, further sales earnings will go to you."

"How many books will I have to sell to pay back six hundred dollars?"

"About three thousand books."

"And how many will you print?"

"Twelve thousand five hundred."

"That would be twenty-five hundred dollars."

"Only if all the books were to sell. That's virtually impossible."

"I want twelve hundred dollars," Eric said. "I can live in Europe on a hundred dollars a month, and that'll give me a year to write my next book."

"Have you started your next book?"

"I started it four years ago," Eric said dryly.

"What makes you think you can have it finished in another year?"

"Because I know how to do it now."

Sam got up and walked over to his window. It had quit raining, and the gargoyle across the street was glistening in the newly emerged sun. On the street far below umbrellas had disappeared and open-top cars were reappearing in the traffic stream. Sam turned and looked back across the room at Eric.

"All right, I'll tell you what I'll do. I'll buy *A Time for All Things* for eight hundred dollars. And I'll give you the same amount for your next book, deliverable to me no later than one year from today. I'll pay you four hundred dollars now and another four hundred upon acceptance of the manuscript. That will give you the twelve hundred dollars you need right now. Have we a deal?"

Eric grinned with pleasure. "We have a deal," he said. He stood up and met Sam in the middle of the room, where the two men shook hands.

"Now that that's done," Sam said, "I'd like to invite you to a small reception being given tonight for Jay Rigdon, another of our authors. Several important people will be there whom I think you should meet, including Millie Pendarrow."

"May I bring my wife?"

"Yes, of course," Sam said. "It's being given in Jay's agent's apartment on Central Park West. . . . Here, let me write the address for you. It starts at seven o'clock," he added. "In the meantime, what are you going to be doing this afternoon?"

"We're going to the baseball game," Eric said. "The St. Louis Grays against the Yankees."

"Oh, yes, I read about that in the sports pages," Sam said. "I understand the Grays have a second-year pitcher named Swampwater Puckett who has never lost to the Yankees. It should be some game. Would you like me to see if I can get tickets for you?" He picked up the telephone, waiting for an answer.

"We have tickets, thank you."

"I believe I can get you a box seat."

"We're sitting in the owner's box."

"You know Jake Ruppert?" Sam asked, surprised.

"The *visiting* owner's box," Eric said. He grinned. "My father-in-law owns the St. Louis Grays."

Sam's eyes grew wide, and he put the phone back down sheepishly. "And here I was, the cosmopolitan New Yorker, trying to show off by getting you a box seat. I feel like a fool."

"Please don't," Eric said easily. "It was a very generous gesture, and I appreciate it." He held up the card with the address. "And I appreciate the invitation to the reception tonight. It'll be the first one I've ever attended. I'm looking forward to it—even more than I am to the game."

THE BRONX, NEW YORK

The Yankee Beanery restaurant was about three blocks away from Yankee stadium and was a regular stop not only for the players, but for the fans as well, particularly those headed to or coming from a game. The Beanery's walls were plastered with autographed pictures of baseball players, going all the way back to "Wee Willie" Keeler, Jimmy Collins, and Rube Waddel, who had been popular back at the turn of the century. Now, nearly every contemporary major-league player had his picture on the wall, including Lenny "Swampwater"

Puckett. The one notable exception was Ty Cobb. His picture was absent by the choice of Red Kirby, the owner of the Beanery, who had declared that he didn't like the son of a bitch and didn't want his picture around.

"All right, now," Pug Anders said, "here's the bet. My buddy Swampwater says he can eat more hot dogs than the Babe . . . and I got twenty dollars says he can do it."

"You're crazy. Can't nobody eat more hot dogs than Babe Ruth," one of the onlookers scoffed.

"I dunno," Pug said. "I've heard that Ruth can put 'em away, but I've never seen it. On the other hand, I've *seen* the kid, here."

Babe Ruth looked across the table at Lenny Puckett and smiled broadly. "That right, kid? Can you eat a hot dog or two?"

"Enough," Lenny replied.

"How many is enough?"

"Enough to beat you," Lenny insisted.

Several whistles and catcalls greeted Lenny's open challenge.

"Ooh, ya hear that, Babe?"

"He's callin' ya out."

"Send this punk kid back to St. Louis with a bellyache!"

"Whaddya say, Babe?" Pug asked. "Do we have a bet or not?"

"Show him, Babe."

Since the St. Louis Grays were the visiting team in New York, there were considerably more supporters for Babe Ruth than there were for Swampwater Puckett. In fact, if it hadn't been for Pug Anders, the St. Louis Grays' right fielder and Lenny's best friend, Lenny would have been alone in a hostile crowd.

"You really want to try this, kid?" Ruth asked.

"Sure, why not?" Lenny replied. "It's nearly lunch time, anyway."

"I gotta tell ya, kid, I can eat fourteen or fifteen of these things before I even get my second wind," Ruth warned. "Then, when the game starts, all I have to do is

just sort of stand around out there in the outfield.
Sometimes it's two or three innings before a ball's even
hit to me. That gives me plenty of time to let 'em digest.
But you have to pitch. That means you'll be working full
time."

"Ahh, don't let him worry you, Lenny. The way it
was rainin' this mornin,' there prob'ly ain't even gonna
be a game today," Pug said. "The Babe's just tryin' to get
you to back out, that's all. He's afraid he's going to lose
his twenty bucks."

"Is that what you're trying to do, Babe?" Lenny
asked. "You trying to make me back out?"

Ruth chuckled, and his eyes sparkled merrily. "Kid,
it'll be better for me if you *don't* back out," he said. "I
figure you're going to stay with me for at least ten or
eleven hot dogs. That means there's no way you can
really have your stuff working today. If you go up against
me, you're going to be a double loser—in here and out
at the ballpark."

The others laughed. "You tell him, Babe," someone
shouted.

"We'll see who loses," Lenny replied.

Pug, who had been Lenny's biggest backer and had
instigated the bet in the first place, now seemed to have
second thoughts. "Wait a minute, Lenny. I don't know;
maybe the Babe is right."

"Pug, what is this? Are you backing out on me?"
Lenny asked.

"No, I'm for you, kid. You know that. But you mess
around and start crampin' up, then lose the game
because of somethin' like this, you know what Mr.
Norton's gonna be like."

"Don't worry about it," Lenny said. "Once back in
Sikeston I ate twelve barbecue sandwiches, then went
out and pitched a double-header against the Poplar Bluff
Mules. Won both games, too."

One of the Yankee fans chuckled. "Well, hell, if the
boy can beat the *Poplar Bluff Mules*, he sure shouldn't
have any trouble with the New York Yankees."

The others laughed heartily at the gibe.

"Are you gonna fish or cut bait?" someone yelled.

"I aim to get on with it," Lenny said. He smiled at Babe Ruth. "But *you* can back out if you want to."

"I thank you for the opportunity, kid, but I guess I'll see it through. Let's do it." Babe sat down at the table and tied a napkin around his neck.

"You can do it, Babe!" someone shouted, and from all over the restaurant people began to crowd around the table.

"Leave a pathway, gentlemen," Red Kirby ordered those standing ten to twelve deep around the table. "You'll have to leave a pathway between the table and the kitchen."

A moment later two trays of freshly prepared hot dogs were brought to the table. One tray of ten was placed in front of Babe Ruth, and the other tray, holding an equal number, was put in front of Lenny. The hot dogs were wrapped in napkins, and little wisps of steam rose from the small, oblong packages.

"Begin," Red said.

Lenny ate very fast and had seven of them down before he even began to feel them. The next three he ate more slowly, and by the time he finished the last one, he was already wishing he hadn't gotten into this dumb contest.

"Make way, gentlemen, make way!" Red shouted, and those around the table opened up a path for the hustling waiters bearing two more steaming, aromatic trays. Like the first trays, these had ten each.

Lenny unwrapped the first one slowly and raised it to his mouth. Across the table from him Babe Ruth had already polished off number eleven and was opening number twelve. The fans were really getting into the spirit of it now, and they chanted and cheered as Babe began to chew.

"You know what would go really good with this, don't you?" Babe asked.

Some mustard began dribbling down his chin, and Lenny looked away so he wouldn't have to see it. Every bite Lenny swallowed now lay on his stomach like a lead ingot.

"Sauerkraut," Babe said, answering his own question. He belched. "A hot dog's not really a hot dog without sauerkraut. You got any sauerkraut, Red?"

"'Fraid we're out, Babe."

"How about some chocolate sauce? You got any chocolate sauce?"

"That we got."

"Okay, bring me a little of that."

Lenny looked up in amazement as Babe Ruth spooned chocolate sauce onto number thirteen and fourteen. The rotund Yankee began eating them with obvious, though perhaps feigned, enjoyment, while Lenny felt his stomach begin to churn.

"Of course," Babe continued, chewing on chocolate-covered number fourteen with as much gusto as he had number one, "some people like relish—you know, pickles and the like—on their hot dogs. Not me. Me, what I like most is sauerkraut. And horseradish. A good horseradish helps some, too. You got any horseradish? Horseradish and chocolate is good." He finished off fourteen and picked up fifteen.

"Sorry, Babe, no horseradish," Red said.

Lenny breathed a prayer of relief.

"How many's that make for you?" Babe asked, looking across the table at Lenny.

"This is twelve," Lenny said. So far he had taken only one bite.

"Twelve, huh? And this is what for me? Fifteen?"

"Yeah, Babe, fifteen," someone said.

The Yankee slugger polished off number fifteen, without chocolate sauce, then reached for his sixteenth. "I'll tell you what, Puckett," Babe said. "You need an edge. How about if I eat the rest of 'em like this?" Smiling broadly, he held up hot dog number sixteen, still wrapped in its paper napkin. He took a big bite and began chewing it up, napkin and all.

That did it. Lenny felt a sudden bubbling deep in

his bowels, then a searing heat that leapt up from his stomach and rushed to his throat.

"Excuse me," he gurgled, and, standing so quickly he knocked over the chair he'd been sitting in, he made a mad dash for the men's room. He barely made it.

Lenny stayed in the bathroom for about ten minutes, throwing up everything but his socks. Finally he heard the door open, and he looked up from his rather inglorious position of being wrapped around the toilet bowl to see Pug standing in the open doorway.

"I'm sorry, Pug," Lenny mumbled. "I guess I sorta let you down out there."

"Ah, it's all right," Pug said. "You gave it a good try. Listen, the reason I come in here, we just got a telephone call. The weatherman says it ain't goin' to rain no more today. The game's on. That means you're gonna have to pitch."

"Oohh," Lenny moaned.

"You up to it?"

"I've got no choice," Lenny answered, unwrapping himself from the bowl and getting to his feet. "You're right. I sure can't let Mr. Norton know about this. And if I tell him I'm sick, he's going to know why. How's Ruth, by the way? He can't be feelin' any too good himself."

"I don't know. When I left the son of a bitch, he was bettin' someone he could stand on his hands on the table."

"He was bluffing," Lenny said.

"Could be he was at first," Pug agreed. "But he done it. Twice."

"Oh, God, how I hate him," Lenny groaned.

As the visiting team, the St. Louis Grays batted first. They pushed in one run on three hits, so when Lenny Puckett walked out to the mound to throw his first pitch, his team had a one-run lead. With his stomach feeling like lead and his arms like rubber, Lenny put nothing into his fast ball, and the first batter nailed him for a double. He walked the second batter, then groaned as he watched Babe Ruth amble out to the plate. Two men were on base now, no outs, and Lenny was facing the most formidable slugger in all of baseball. The anvil in his stomach got heavier.

Just before Babe stepped into the batter's box, he grabbed his stomach, doubled over, and put his hand to his mouth as if he were about to throw up.

"Time!" the umpire called. "You all right, Babe?"

"Yeah," Babe answered. "I'm all right." He straightened up, then smiled and winked at Lenny. He stepped into the box and held his bat poised for the pitch.

Lenny raised his arms over his head, pulled them down to his chest, checked the runner on second, then delivered the pitch. He saw the bat leave Ruth's shoulder, then heard the crack as loud as thunder. The ball came back so fast it was nothing but a white streak going up and away. Lenny turned and watched it disappear way out and high up in the right center-field bleachers, into one of the shadowy rectangles marking the access ramps. No doubt the ball would momentarily be bouncing through the parking lot outside. Babe Ruth had just put the Yankees ahead three to one with one mighty swing of his bat. When Lenny turned back toward the plate, the Babe was just beginning to unwind from his swing. He smiled at Lenny, tipped his hat, then began trudging around the bases.

As Lenny watched the Yankee going through his orbit and listened to the roar of the crowd, he didn't know which he felt the more foolish about: thinking he could beat Babe Ruth over a plate of hot dogs . . . or thinking he could beat him over home plate.

317 CENTRAL PARK WEST, NEW YORK CITY

The party was in honor of Jay Rigdon's new novel, *Butterfly Ball*. As nearly as Eric Twainbough could gather, Rigdon's book was about a group of New York socialites who gave a series of balls during "the season," affairs that were supposedly to raise money for charity but were, in fact, very nearly wars that could make or break social careers.

Rigdon was being billed as "the next F. Scott Fitzgerald," but Eric had read Fitzgerald as well as Rigdon's first book, *Kites in the Night*, and he didn't agree with everyone's assessment of Rigdon's talents. However, the book was being published by Eric's new publisher, and he felt it would be disloyal to speak candidly.

Rigdon was a small man with a narrow face and delicate, almost feminine, features. He stood just inside the door of his agent's fifteenth-floor apartment, greeting the guests who had come to his fete. He was wearing an impeccably cut dinner jacket and a beautifully frilled white shirt. One hand held a long, ebony cigarette holder, while he offered the other to Eric, palm down, almost as a woman expecting to have it kissed.

"I'm Eric Twainbough, Mr. Rigdon," Eric said. "And this is my wife, Tanner."

"So you are the man Sam is so enamored of. You were all he could talk about today," Jay said in a voice that almost, but didn't quite, lisp. "My God, he didn't tell me you were such a large man. Everyone seems to be very high on you now, dear boy. In fact, I must say that the old green beast rose in my breast, and I became quite jealous. I had to remind them that this is *my* party, after all."

"It must be quite a thrill, attending a party for your own book," Eric suggested.

Jay pinched one cigarette out of its holder and replaced it with another. "It's a crashing bore, really," he said. "No one from the truly social set ever attends such things. Only publishers, agents, publicists, and occasionally other writers come. It's all rather incestuous, actually. But, tell me about your afternoon. I understand you went to a baseball match. Did you enjoy it?"

"Not too much, I'm afraid," Eric said. "We lost."

"I don't follow baseball much myself," Jay said. "We

have what . . . three teams in New York? Which one of them lost today?"

"Oh, the New York team won," Eric said. "It was our team"—he indicated Tanner and himself—"the St. Louis Grays, who lost."

"My. What a crushing disappointment that must have been for you," Rigdon said with unctuous insincerity. "Oh, you must excuse me, I see that Jon Kirby has arrived. He's been trying to woo me over to his literary agency. I have no intentions of leaving Phillip, but it doesn't hurt to make him think I might. And I do so enjoy the courtship." He looked at Tanner just before he left. "My dear, your dress is quite lovely."

"Thank you," Tanner said, but Rigdon was already walking away as she spoke.

Eric found Sam Hamilton and introduced Tanner to him. Sam "borrowed" Tanner to introduce her to several others, while Eric made his way to the hors d'oeuvre table.

Only one other person was at the table, an auburn-haired woman who was studying the hors d'oeuvres critically and holding her hand poised, ready to make a grab as soon as she found something that interested her. The woman was wearing a blue-green dress, simply cut, with a white sash.

"Do you see any stuffed artichokes?" she asked, without looking up. "I simply adore stuffed artichokes, but I don't see any."

Eric glanced around to make certain she was talking to him, then looked back at the table. "Uh, no, I don't," he said.

"Pity. Oh, well, the little pastry puffs are good, too." She took several of them and put them on her small plate, then, using a toothpick, popped one of them into her mouth. She smiled at Eric, holding her head tilted just so, as she examined him. Her eyebrows were perfectly arched, her lids were daubed with eye shadow that matched the shade of her dress, and her eyes themselves were nearly that color. Her cheeks were heavily rouged—a bit *too* heavily for Eric's taste—and her lips were a deep crimson, painted to give them a very full "bee-stung" effect. Eric wasn't sure how old she was, though he had the feeling that she was considerably older than she looked.

"Are you the wonderful new writer Sam is talking about?"

Eric smiled and nearly blushed. "Sam should be a publicist in addition to being an editor," he said. "He's sung my praises so much that I'm embarrassed. If such flattery wasn't a part of the business, I could easily have my head turned."

"Take it from me, dear boy, such praises coming from Sam Hamilton are true words of admiration and not mere flattery." She held one of the pastry puffs up to Eric's mouth, and he tasted it.

"It's good, thank you," he said. "Are you saying that Sam Hamilton is sincere?"

"Oh, yes, he's quite sincere," the woman replied. "Otherwise, I wouldn't have hired him."

"*You* hired him?"

"Well, my husband, actually, though it now amounts to the same thing since my husband died and left the publishing house to me."

"You are Mrs. Pendarrow."

"Millie Pendarrow, yes." She stuck her hand out, not palm down like Jay Rigdon, but ready to grip Eric's in a hearty handshake. "Sam tells me that you live in Paris."

"Yes."

"All the writers who are producing anything seem to live in Paris now. Why is that? Has America become a cultural wasteland?"

"No, it isn't that," Eric said. "It's something else . . . something that's difficult to explain."

"Try. You are obviously a man of words, as evidenced by the fact that I just paid you more for a first novel than Pendarrow House has ever paid anyone."

"I'll try," Eric promised, smiling slightly. He thought a moment, then said, "There's a restless discontent among the veterans of the war. Those of us who survived

the experience can't stop asking ourselves why? Why did
we survive? What capriciousness was there to God's plan
that allowed the Angel of Death to pass over the
battlefield, selecting some and leaving others?"

"You give God credit for that, do you?" Millie asked.

"Or the blame," Eric replied.

"Surely others have questioned the meaning of life
before . . ." Millie started, but she stopped when Eric
slowly but firmly shook his head.

"No. This is much more than some philosophic
consideration on the meaning of life," he told her. "Many
of us are artists—writers, poets, musicians, painters—
and we try to express through our art what we've been
through and what we feel. But we can't really do it. Not
even the most successful of us can *really* do it."

"Why is that, do you suppose?"

"Because no language in existence will make the
uninitiated understand—and no explanation is needed
for those who've experienced it. We are an entire
generation of men—English, French, American, German, Austrian, and Russian—cut off from the world and
isolated from history." Eric smiled sadly. "Gertrude
Stein calls us 'the lost generation.'"

"The lost generation. What a descriptive phrase.
Tell me, Eric, will your generation ever find itself?"

"No," Eric replied.

"No?" Millie pouted. "But isn't that a rather dismal
attitude to take? Are you doomed to eternal wandering,
like the mythical Lost Dutchman?"

"No, we'll make a few adjustments here and some
compensations there, so that eventually we'll come to a
rapprochement with society. But fifty, sixty, or even
seventy years from now, among the handful of veterans
who'll still be alive, there will be times when we'll hear
a sound or see a shaft of sunlight cutting through a puff
of smoke or get a whiff of an old fragrance, and we'll be
isolated again. Only by then our numbers will have been
so thinned that we'll no longer have anyone to share our
isolation."

"Heavens, I hope your book isn't this depressing," Millie said.

"It isn't," Sam Hamilton put in, approaching them. "It's a marvelous book, and next year, Millie, you're going to be bragging to all of your friends about being so clever as to be this young man's publisher."

"I'm sure I will," Millie said. "Uh-oh, here comes Jay. I had better spend some time with him. Bruised egos, you know."

"I'll help," Sam said, and the publisher and her senior editor hurried toward Rigdon, heaping effusive compliments on him.

Eric walked away from the hors d'oeuvre table and made his way through the swank apartment. The party flowed easily through four large rooms, and Eric moved from room to room, taking in the sights and sounds. He didn't know who any of the other guests were, but they were all full of the latest clever gossip from the publishing field.

". . . and they splashed around in the fountain as if it were their own private swimming pool," someone was saying.

"But, of course, fully dressed. Well, as fully dressed as Zelda and Scott ever get," another added, and everyone laughed.

"I don't approve of such behavior."

"Oh, I think their behavior is exciting. You have to admit that Scott and Zelda are wonderfully entertaining. And why shouldn't the literary world have stars the public can read about? The movie business shouldn't have all the glamor."

"I think Scott and Zelda are like moths, fluttering around the fire. One day they're going to get too close and go up in flames."

"But, oh, my friends, what a wonderful light it will make!" someone said, and they all laughed again.

Tanner materialized beside Eric just then and said, "Sweetheart, come look."

"Where have you been?" he asked.

"Oh, talking here and there," she replied. "But,

come here. I want to show you something." She tugged on his arm, leading him to the front room, where tall windows looked out over Central Park and the city beyond.

"Look," Tanner said, pointing to the great slabs of buildings whose lit windows created glowing, irregular patterns rising into the night. "Have you ever seen anything more beautiful?" she asked.

Eric realized then that this moment was the culmination of a lifetime of hopes and dreams. He was glad he had Tanner to share it with him, and he put his arms around her and pulled her to him, the top of her head landing just below his mouth. Nuzzling her hair, he looked out at the scene outside.

"No," he finally answered. "I have never seen anything more beautiful."

SPRING 1926, HOLLYWOOD, CALIFORNIA

For the making of the movie *King of the Sand*, the back lot of Goliath Studios had been converted into an encampment fit for an Arabian sheikh—or, at least, Hollywood's idea of one. A number of tents had been erected and an impressive-looking desert oasis built, complete with sand dunes, palm trees, and live camels.

King of the Sand was the most ballyhooed movie of the decade. Dozens of stories about it had already appeared in movie-fan magazines and newspaper articles, and Goliath Studios kept the fires fanned by conducting a nationwide advertising campaign. On rural highways and at choice locations inside cities huge billboards depicted a much-larger-than-life Alphonso Delavente, his sword raised, his silk robes flowing, and his perfect white teeth gleaming. Beneath the picture, in Arabian-looking script, was the legend, THE KING IS COMING!

Public excitement over Delavente's next picture had built to the point that theaters all across the country were reserving tickets, and many had already sold out for every performance date—some as far ahead as a full year after the picture was scheduled for release.

Alphonso Delavente was the biggest box-office draw in Hollywood. His lithe, muscular body and his almond-shaped black eyes, shining from vivid circles of white, appealed to the repressed sexual longings of every gullible coed and shop girl in America. His appeal wasn't limited to the young, either. Old maids and married housewives also flocked to his pictures to lose themselves in their own secret sexual fantasies as they watched him perform. When he leered at his helpless victim on the screen, every swooning woman in America exchanged places with her. And when the words "You little fool? Do you think you can resist me?" appeared on the dialogue board, each woman in the audience heard her own reply from deep in her heart.

"I confess this to you, Alphonso. At night, when my husband takes me, I close my eyes, and it is you ravaging me, as you have ravaged so many on the screen," one housewife had written him, in care of the studio.

King of the Sand was being directed by Guy Colby. Guy, who was forty-three, had begun his career as a playwright, but when no one in the legitimate theater seemed willing to produce any of his plays, he bought a train ticket to Hollywood and began making the rounds of the studios. Within six months he had sold four movie scripts, and in a town where success could be achieved overnight, Guy Colby became the writer of choice.

That was ten years ago. Four years ago Guy had gone into directing. He had also married twice, both times to movie stars. He was married now to Greta Gaynor, but they were separated. Greta lived in their mansion, Guy lived in a hotel apartment.

Of average height and weight, Guy had coarse sandy hair, blue eyes, and a face once described—by someone who was being kind—as "having character." He smoked too much, drank too much, and he had an ulcer. *King of the Sand* was his first major directing project, signifying that he had moved into the big leagues. Expanding on the baseball metaphor, he had said, "I don't have to hit a home run. All I have to do is get on base."

On the surface of it that seemed like a simple enough thing to do. After all, he had a strong script, an excellent production crew, and a successful studio behind him. But he also had Alphonso Delavente, as temperamental and difficult a person to work with as Guy had ever encountered. *King of the Sand* was already overdue and over budget, and, as a result, the ulcer in Guy's stomach burned as if he had swallowed a hot coal.

"We have the light, Mr. Colby," the head cameraman said. He pointed to a battery of mirrors that had been mounted on stands around the scene and placed in such a way as to focus the sunlight and eliminate the shadows.

"How long will we have the light before we have to reposition the mirrors?" Guy asked.

"Twenty minutes," the cameraman answered. "Half hour at the most. But we won't be able to reposition them again today. The sun'll be too low."

"Then I guess we'd better get it right the first time," Guy said. He raised his megaphone. "All right, places, everyone," he shouted. "Let's get rolling before we lose this light."

"Wait a minute, hold it!" someone called.

"What do you mean, hold it?" Guy asked tartly. "I thought *I* was the director of this picture."

"Well, of course you are, Guy. But if you start rolling the cameras now, you're just going to waste film. Alphonso isn't ready yet." The speaker was Manny Rosen, Alphonso's agent and personal manager.

Disgustedly, Guy lowered his megaphone. "Alphonso isn't ready? What the hell does he have to do to be ready? All I want the son of a bitch to do is to walk out of the goddamned tent! He can do that, can't he?"

"Please, Guy," Manny said, coming up to him, "you mustn't talk about Alphonso that way. He's very sensitive, and he knows you don't like him. Do you know how difficult it is for an artist—a true artist like Alphonso—to project when there's such antagonism in the air?"

"Project! What the hell does the son of a bitch have to project?" Guy asked. "He's not appealing to art lovers out there, you know. Goddammit, the women who are his fans don't need to be intellectually stimulated. Their stimulation occurs a little farther down, and all Alphonso has to do to reach that level is stand there while my cameramen do all the work. We'll film his smoldering eyes, his flaring nostrils, his slick black hair . . . and the bulge in the front of his pants. He does have a bulge in the front of his pants, doesn't he? If not, tell him to roll up a pair of socks. It works wonders for schoolboys."

"There is no need for such hostility, Guy. If you don't feel that you and Alphonso can work together, perhaps we'd better speak to the studio," Manny suggested coolly. "I'm sure they'd be glad to replace one of you, if necessary."

Smiling smugly, Manny made it clear that he knew he had scored with that one. Guy pulled out a package of cigarettes and extracted one while he studied the balding man before him, wishing he could smash him in the face but knowing it would cost him everything if he did. There was no question as to whom the studio would replace. Moviegoers weren't attracted to a picture by the name of the director; they were attracted by the name of the star.

Guy lit his cigarette and took a couple of puffs, fighting down the anger and the bile that rose in his throat. He forced himself to take a deep breath before he spoke.

"How long?" he finally asked.

"Not long," Manny replied. "Five or six minutes at the most. I'll go hurry him up," he promised, showing that in victory he could be magnanimous. "Trust me on this, Guy. If we can just work together, I have no doubt that we'll make a picture that will absolutely sing."

"Yeah, sing," Guy said sarcastically.

Manny hurried off to the small, wheeled dressing room where Alphonso waited while he got himself in the mood to project. Guy sat in his director's chair, smoked his cigarette, and tried to get his mind off the pain in his gut.

"What the hell?" someone suddenly said. "What is that?"

"I'll be damned," someone else declared.

"Look at that!" a third person exclaimed.

"Mr. Colby! Mr. Colby!" the gaffer shouted excitedly. "Look, up there!"

Following the gaffer's pointing finger, Guy saw a parachute coming down, heading straight for the set. "Watch the cameras and the equipment!" he shouted, standing up quickly. "Who the hell is that?" he asked. "Did anyone see an airplane? Was it in trouble? Did it go down somewhere?"

"I didn't see anything," someone replied.

"I saw the airplane. There wasn't any trouble. That fellow just jumped out of it," someone else said. "The airplane is still up there, see?" He pointed to a biplane that was circling at an altitude of about five thousand feet.

"Then what the hell did he jump out for?" Guy asked.

"Look out, here he comes!"

The parachutist hit just in front of the largest tent, fell, rolled once, then hopped back up as gracefully as a dancer.

"Bring that man over here to me," Guy ordered. He kept a tub of ice—now nearly all melted—beside his director's chair in which he kept several half-pint bottles of milk. Sticking his hand down into the cold water, he fished out a bottle and peeled off the pasteboard top. Guy had his head tilted back and his eyes closed, taking great, gulping swallows of the milk, when the parachutist was brought to him.

"My, you must really like milk," a woman's voice said.

Surprised, Guy opened his eyes and brought the empty bottle down from his lips. He wiped his mouth with the back of his hand as he studied the person standing before him. The parachutist who had dropped in on his set was, indeed, a woman—with blond hair, crystal-blue eyes, high cheekbones, and a lean, sleek, almost boyish figure. She was, in fact, one of the most beautiful women he had ever seen.

"No . . . uh . . . not really," Guy said, continuing to stare at her. "It's supposed to be good for my stomach when my ulcer flares up."

"And I made it flare up? I'm sorry."

"Who are you?"

"Demaris Hunter."

"Do you always drop in on people like that, Demaris Hunter?"

She laughed. "Only when I want to get their attention."

Guy looked around the set and saw that everyone had gathered in close to see the beautiful young woman who had fallen from the sky. No one, not even the most jaded cameramen who saw movie stars through their view finders day after day, was immune to the excitement Demaris had caused.

"Well, you did do that," Guy admitted.

"Miss Hunter, were you frightened?" somebody asked.

"No."

"What did it feel like?" another wanted to know.

"Exciting."

"Can you feel it in your stomach when you jump?"

"Yes. That's part of the excitement."

"Guy," Manny Rosen suddenly called. "Guy, if you would get everyone back in their places, Alphonso is ready now."

Guy looked over at the dressing trailer and saw Alphonso standing just outside, his arms folded across his chest, glaring with obvious annoyance at the excitement being created by the young woman parachutist and obviously resenting the fact that he was no longer the center of attention. The only reason Alphonso wanted the shooting to begin now was so he could recapture his accustomed role.

"It's too late," Guy said. "We'd have to reposition all

the mirrors now, and by the time we got them reset, there wouldn't be enough time to complete the shooting. I'm afraid we're through for the day."

"But you can't be," Manny protested. "Alphonso is emotionally ready."

Guy looked over at Alphonso. "Sorry, Alphonso," he called. "You'll just have to hold on to that emotion until tomorrow."

Muttering angrily in Italian, Alphonso started toward his car. Manny, suddenly realizing that he was about to be left behind, had to break into a run to catch up. He managed to jump into the car just as Alphonso roared off.

Guy laughed heartily, then turned back toward the mysterious and beautiful young woman who had broken up the afternoon's shooting session. Ordinarily he would have been furious. In this case, however, the intrusion—not to mention the intruder—was welcome.

Guy and Alphonso had been in a power struggle from the minute production started, and because of his star's box-office popularity, the director was playing against a stacked deck. Alphonso won today's round—or would have won it had Miss Demaris Hunter not literally dropped in on them at a fortuitous moment.

"I hope you didn't do this to make an impression on Alphonso," Guy said. "Because if you did, I'm afraid you managed just the reverse."

"Pooh," Demaris said, smiling sweetly. "I wasn't trying to impress Alphonso Delavente, Mr. Colby. *You* were the one I was after."

"I see," Guy said. He stroked his chin and studied Demaris for a long moment. "Then, if I asked you to have dinner with me tonight, there's a chance you'd say yes?"

"Oh, there's more than just a chance, Mr. Colby," Demaris said. "I'd be delighted to have dinner with you tonight."

"And if things go well between us, perhaps breakfast?"

Demaris laughed. "Are you trying to shock me, Mr. Colby?"

"Maybe."

"I'm afraid you'll find that I don't shock all that easily. I'd be glad to have breakfast with you."

"You will?"

"Yes. I know you're shooting, so you'll probably want to eat early. We could meet somewhere at, say, six in the morning?"

"Meet somewhere? That isn't exactly what I had in mind."

"I daresay it wasn't," Demaris replied with another easy laugh. "Suppose we just stick to dinner for now?"

Guy chuckled. "Okay, Miss Hunter. Dinner it is."

CHAPTER
FOURTEEN

FROM THE ST. LOUIS CHRONICLE, AUGUST 1926:

THE CANCER OF CRIME IN ST. LOUIS

by Kendra Mills

Perhaps it is the pervasive disregard of Prohibition. Or perhaps it is a product of the times; after all, we do live in an era of fast cars, high-flying airplanes, radio waves, and motion pictures. Whatever its cause, our fair city is suffering from an outbreak of lawlessness equal to the worst of any city in America. In addition to the normal criminal activities to which any city our size is subject, we are also afflicted with the malignancy of gangland war.

Three gangs are currently waging war on each other, two within the city itself and a third across the Mississippi River in East St. Louis. The East St.

Louis gang, composed entirely of Negroes, is controlled by one Charles R. "Heavy" Hart. If any nefarious operation is taking place in East St. Louis, Heavy Hart is the man behind it. On the Missouri side of the river, two gangs are at work. One gang, known as the East Siders, is led by Paddy Egan, a nightclub owner and known bootlegger. His name has been mentioned in connection with many unsolved homicides, including that of a federal judge. Mr. Egan has long been engaged in criminal activity in St. Louis but has avoided arrest because of the large number of police officers and state and municipal judges on his payroll. The third gang is known simply as the Kerry O'Braugh gang, named for its leader, who was a protégé of Johnny Torrio, one of Chicago's most notorious gang chiefs. Mr. Torrio was one of the victims of the recent war between the Torrio-Capone gang and the O'Bannion-Weiss gang. Nearly killed, Mr. Torrio recovered from his wounds, then emigrated to Italy. With his mentor no longer in Chicago, Mr. O'Braugh apparently decided not to return to the Windy City. That is good news for Chicagoans but bad news for the citizens of St. Louis, for Mr. O'Braugh has introduced to our fair city the same violence of gangland war that has for so long plagued Chicago.

An example of this new breed of violence occurred last week when four men walked into a florist shop belonging to Paddy Egan and began shooting up the place. Two of the men killed worked for Mr. Egan and had criminal records. The third victim, however, was a young man who, from all indications, was merely an innocent customer.

Yet though this was very obviously a gangland "rubout" and a skirmish in the gang war currently taking place in St. Louis, our city police are, incredibly, treating it as an attempted robbery. That means, of course, that the real perpetrators—members of a rival gang—will never be brought to justice.

As long as both the local police and judges are on

the payroll of the criminal elements, there is slim chance that honest citizens will ever regain control of the city or be entirely free from fear. It does little good to merely raise the alarm, for such warnings have no more authority than Chicken Little's cries that "the sky is falling." It is time for someone to take some action. Therefore, beginning next week and continuing each week thereafter, *The St. Louis Chronicle* will expose, by name and incident, two officials who are "on the take," those police officers and judges who are accepting bribes from criminals.

If the police officers and judges of the law-enforcement and criminal-justice systems dislike this approach, they can easily stop it. All they have to do is thoroughly clean their houses and throw out those corrupt officials who have violated the public trust.

When Kendra came to work the day after the article appeared, the other reporters in the newsroom stood up and applauded.

"Great article, Kendra," one coworker said.

"That took guts," another told her.

"Not too much," Kendra replied. "You see, I work in the bright lights, and the people I'm writing about are cockroaches who come out only at night."

Kendra sat down at her desk and began going through the mail. There were the usual number of letters from readers, some complimenting her on stories she had written, some taking issue with her, others offering suggestions for new stories. Kendra had brought a new type of journalism to the newspaper, an "exposé" style that looked in closets and under beds to find stories. Some readers called her a busybody, but there were many more who enjoyed her brand of journalism than those who didn't.

One of Kendra's biggest fans was Thomas Petzold himself. Because of her unique style of writing, the publisher had issued word that only he could kill a story she was working on. So far he had never turned down anything she wanted to do and had, in fact, even given her a couple of leads.

Mixed in with all the mail from her readers was a large brown envelope with the return address given as Demaris Hunter, 1598 South Gate, Hollywood, California. With a happy squeal, Kendra opened it and pulled out a glossy publicity picture of Demaris. It was an eight-by-ten head-and-shoulder "glamor" shot, and Demaris was staring straight at the camera through large, expressive eyes. Looking further inside the envelope, Kendra found a letter, which read:

Dear Kendra,

Don't let the address and the glamorous photograph fool you. I'm still not a movie star—heck, at this point I'd give anything just to be an extra. I haven't had any luck at all, though I do know the gate guards of every studio in Hollywood. That's because most of them have thrown me out at one time or another (ha ha).

What I thought would be a brilliant idea fizzled. I decided that by dropping in on a production set by parachute, I'd get noticed (and therefore signed) immediately. It turns out that my parachute leap was just one more in a long line of crazy stunts pulled by others trying to get noticed. Would-be actors and actresses have hired skywriters to write their name in the sky; others have tried flagpole sitting, marathon dancing, and goldfish swallowing. Like me, they all got their name in the paper one day, then disappeared from view the next.

I did make a friend in the business, though. His name is Guy Colby. Just in case you don't know of him, he's the director of *King of the Sand*. I guess you've heard of *it*. Guy says the only way to succeed in this business is to outlast everyone else. He says I shouldn't get discouraged and that I should develop a thick skin and keep trying for every picture. I'm following his advice.

Love, Demaris

P.S. I still haven't gotten to kiss Alphonso Delavente,
but I have met him. And now that I've met him, I
don't *want* to kiss him.

Kendra had just finished the letter when a copyboy
appeared at her desk.

"Miss Mills?"

"Yes?"

"Mr. Petzold would like to see you in his office."

"Thank you."

Kendra assumed Petzold wanted to discuss story
ideas or had a lead that could be developed, so she
grabbed her reporter's pad and pencil and hurried to the
publisher's office. When she reached it, however, she
found that Petzold wasn't alone. A tall, silver-haired,
dignified-looking man was with him. Kendra recognized
the visitor. He was Judge Matthew Bailey, a man whose
name had turned up several times during the course of
her investigations. Though she had no concrete evidence
against Bailey, Kendra was convinced he was crooked;
she just didn't have any way to prove it.

"Kendra," Tom said. "This is Judge Matthew Bailey."

"Good morning, Miss Mills," Bailey said.

"Good morning, Judge Bailey. Is there something I
can do for you?"

Bailey cleared his throat. "Yes, since you ask. You
could be a bit more circumspect in your writing."

"What do you mean?"

"Young woman, you have written a most irresponsible article," Bailey snapped, jabbing his finger at a
copy of the newspaper he was holding, the article folded
in full view. "It is not only irresponsible, it is inflamma-
tory and dangerous."

"Dangerous to whom?" Petzold put in.

"I beg your pardon?"

"Dangerous to whom?" the publisher repeated.
"Dangerous to the crooked officials who are about to be
exposed? Or dangerous to Miss Mills? I don't ask this
question idly, Judge. You see, if it is dangerous to the

crooked officials, then I say more power to her. If, on the other hand, it is dangerous to Miss Mills, then I say neither this newspaper nor any of my staff, including Miss Mills, will be intimidated by threats."

"It is dangerous to Miss Mills and to your paper, Mr. Petzold, because you are making accusations that cannot be substantiated. Don't you realize you could be sued for libel? Your paper could be shut down."

"We can't be shut down for printing the truth. If there are judges and police officers on gangsters' payrolls, our readers have a right to know."

"That's just it, Mr. Petzold," Bailey said. "There *are* no judges or police officers on their payrolls. If there were, don't you think I would know about it?"

"I'd like to think that you *wouldn't* know about it, Judge Bailey," Kendra noted dryly. "For if you did, that would implicate you as well, wouldn't it?"

"See here, young lady," Bailey blustered. "You are bordering on contempt."

"Contempt of what? We aren't in your court, Judge Bailey. We are in the court of the people," Petzold countered.

"The court of the people? Just what is *that* supposed to mean?"

"It means that this newspaper, like any newspaper, has a sacred obligation to the public, and we are bound by that covenant to bring to light any wrongdoing being committed against them."

"All I can say, Petzold, is that you had better keep a tight rein on your reporter here. Her zeal and enthusiasm for sensationalism could very well bring this newspaper crashing down on your head—and I, for one, will be watching her very closely. Good day to you both."

The judge left the office, slamming the door behind him, and Petzold and Kendra stood silently for a long moment. Then Kendra spoke.

"I hadn't thought about that," she said.

"Thought about what?"

"Thought about the fact that what I'm doing might

be dangerous to the paper. I'm sorry, Tom. I was just 'Damn the torpedoes, full speed ahead.'"

"You keep on doing exactly what you are doing," Petzold said.

"But if I'm putting the newspaper at risk . . ."

"Kendra, if it is *right*, do it," Petzold ordered. He smiled at her and took off his glasses to polish them. "Listen, until you came along, I had almost forgotten what a newspaper was supposed to be. I was more interested in how many column inches of space an advertiser was buying than I was in any story we were running. You've made me feel young again."

Kendra chuckled. "You say 'young again' as if you were old."

"I *am* old."

"You aren't even sixty."

"I'm not far from it."

"You know what they say—age is a matter of mind. If you don't mind, it doesn't matter."

He laughed. "I suppose it is. I know that before you came along, I never really thought about . . ." He stopped in midsentence, as if embarrassed at almost saying something.

"Before I came along you never really thought about what?" she prompted.

"Nothing. Never mind." He put his glasses back on, hooking them very carefully over his ears one at a time.

"You still have a spot," Kendra said. She reached up and pulled his glasses off, breathed on them to fog the lenses, then raised the hem of her skirt to wipe them clean. The action exposed her legs, but she did it so innocently that there was nothing overtly sexual about it. "There," she said, putting them back on for him. "Isn't that better?"

"Yes," Petzold agreed.

Kendra started to leave the office, but then she turned back toward him.

"By the way, do you like pot roast?"

"Pot roast?"

"Yes. Do you like it?"

"Yes, I do, as a matter of fact. Why do you ask?"

"Pot roast is one of the problems of living alone," Kendra said. "There's too much for one person, so I never cook it, even though I love it. However, if I had someone to share it with, I could enjoy it. Why don't you come to dinner tonight, and I'll fix us a pot roast?"

"Well, I, uh, would be happy to accept your kind invitation," Thomas Petzold stammered.

"Around eight," Kendra tossed over her shoulder as she left.

EAST ST. LOUIS, ILLINOIS

Kerry O'Braugh drove down to the riverfront, then stopped his car and waited. When the dark-green Packard arrived a few minutes later, Kerry flashed his lights at it. The Packard flashed back, and Kerry got out of his car, then walked across the cobblestones. He opened the back door of the Packard and slipped inside. As arranged, only Heavy Hart was in the Packard, but his tremendous bulk took up more than half the front seat.

"I don't know what you got in mind," Heavy said, "but I ain't interested. So far our partnership ain't done nothin' but get some of my folks killed."

"I've lost a few of my men, too, don't forget," Kerry replied.

"Yeah, well, if things don't change around here soon, I'm goin' to let you white boys fight it out among yourselves."

"I've got a plan," Kerry said.

"Good. You just go ahead and do your plan, and leave me out of it."

"I think I can do it without you," Kerry said. "But it'd be a lot easier with your help."

"Why should I help you?"

"Because if you do, there's a half-million dollars' worth of whiskey in it for you," Kerry said. "Bonded whiskey, mind you, not moonshine."

Heavy turned around for the first time and stared at Kerry. "Did you say a half million dollars?"

"At least. Maybe more."

"I'm listenin'."

ST. LOUIS, MISSOURI

At just before eight o'clock that night, Kendra Mills raised the two windows in the living room and the one in her bedroom. With the window fan operating in the kitchen, the warm, stale air was pumped out of her apartment and was replaced by the slightly cooler air outside. That plus the resulting breeze made her apartment quite comfortable, even on this hot summer night.

The pot roast she had cooked was done, though it continued to simmer slowly in its own juices, and the bouquet of roast beef and rising roll dough permeated the apartment, pulled through by the fan. Kendra walked over to the Victrola, which had an electrically operated turntable and an automatic record-changing mechanism, and stacked several records on the spindle. She had bought the record player a year earlier at the Gelbman's Department Store downtown, the first major acquisition she had made with money earned as a newspaper reporter.

A much more recent purchase was the yellow dress she was wearing this evening. She had also applied a touch of perfume—the proper use of which she had learned from Demaris.

"The thing to do is to wear perfume with such subtlety that your victim isn't even aware at first that he's being enticed by it," Demaris had explained in a melodramatic voice. "That way he'll know only that there's something maddeningly desirable about you, but he won't know what it is until it's too late."

At the time Kendra had laughed at Demaris's "instructions for capturing a man's heart." Now she sincerely hoped there was something to it.

Kendra was in love with Thomas Petzold—"Tom" to

her. She knew that on the surface of it such a thing was
entirely irrational. After all, she was only twenty-five
years old, and he was fifty-seven. And, as a matter of
comparison, Tom Petzold was two years older than her
own father.

But Kendra's emotional age had always been far
greater than her chronological age. Her father had once
told her that she was "born old," and he teased her on
her sixteenth birthday about being "sixteen going on
forty."

As a child she had always been much more interested in the adult world than that of her peers. College
had been important to her because of the educational
opportunities it offered, but she sometimes found it
difficult to cope with the infantilism of her friends and
classmates. She liked Demaris very much, but she had
regarded her roommate as something of a younger sister,
even though Demaris was actually one month older. The
football games, the dances, and the summer rush parties
had all been a part of her educational process . . . but,
always, such things had been secondary to the classes
themselves.

When Kendra began working at *The Chronicle*, she
was told that Tom Petzold was very much a loner and a
man who would have nothing to do with women. It
didn't take long for Kendra to see that the only reason he
was a loner was because there were so few others who
could match him in intensity. In that, Kendra and
Petzold were kindred spirits, and soon a relationship had
been established, though one carefully constructed to
stay within the bounds of propriety as dictated by the
differences in their ages and positions.

Recently, however, Kendra began to realize that
she wanted more from their relationship. What was
more, she was sure that Petzold did as well, though she
knew also that he was much too shy to make the first
move. She was equally shy, but, she reasoned, she was
younger and so perhaps a bit more flexible. Therefore, if
anything was to come of this thus-far unfulfilled relation-

ship, it would have to be as a result of her initiative. That was the reason she had invited him to dinner tonight.

Kendra had just put on a Gershwin tune when a knock sounded at the door to her apartment. Opening it, she found Tom Petzold standing there, holding a bouquet of flowers in one hand and a bottle of wine in the other.

"This is a very old, very good, bottle of wine that I've kept for a long time. If we drink it tonight, are we going to be exposed in your column?" he quipped.

"Don't worry. I can be most discreet when it's necessary," Kendra said, smiling. "Come in."

In the background the music was "The Man I Love." Kendra hadn't selected it with any devious purpose in mind, but she couldn't help but think about its significance as she took her guest's hat and the bouquet.

"These are lovely," she said. "I'll put them in water."

"I'm not exactly current on what's expected on a date," Petzold said. "I mean, if this is truly a date. In my day it was expected that a man would bring a lady flowers."

"Yes, I'd call it a date," Kendra said. "And I'm very pleased with the flowers."

"The pot roast smells good."

"It does, doesn't it? That aroma has been driving me mad with hunger. While I'm getting water for the flowers, I'll put the rolls on. We'll eat in a half hour or so."

"Sounds good," Petzold said. "Oh, you may be interested to know that I've rebudgeted the front page. From now on you're going to get as much space as you want. We'll adjust the other stories accordingly."

"Thank you," Kendra said. "But let's make a pact, just for tonight."

"What sort of pact?"

"Absolutely no discussion of the newspaper."

The publisher laughed easily. "That's going to be difficult for me," he said. "I don't know anything else *to* talk about."

"Sure you do. You've just hidden behind the newspaper too long, that's all. It's time someone drew you out a little."

"And you are that someone?"

"Yes."

Tom Petzold cleared his throat. "Well, I can't think of anyone I'd rather have drawing me out." He paused, then added, "By the way, I like that dress. You look very lovely in it."

"See? You *do* know the right things to say," Kendra teased.

During the meal, Petzold gave Kendra a bit of his own background—that he had come to America as a young man, teaching himself the language so well that he could speak English without the slightest hint of a German accent, and that shortly after the turn of the century he had bought *The Chronicle* at a bankruptcy sale and had since built it into one of the finest newspapers in America. Kendra already knew some of what he told her, but she graciously kept it to herself, giving him center stage.

"Have there been no women in your life?" she asked, after they had finished their meal and returned to the living room. As all the records had played through once, she began restacking them on the spindle for a second go-around.

"No," he replied, sitting on the sofa. "At first I told myself it was because I didn't have the time; I was too busy building my paper. Then I said it was because I could never find anyone who would put up with the passion I have for the paper. But now I'm ready to admit that perhaps I was never much of a 'catch' for any woman in the first place."

"Nonsense," Kendra retorted, coming over to sit beside him. "You'd be a wonderful catch for the right woman. You're like the treasures in King Tut's tomb. You've lain undiscovered for all these years, that's all."

"It's nice of you to say so," Petzold said with a laugh. "But if that's true, I certainly hope I don't have to wait three thousand years, like King Tut."

"You don't have to wait anymore at all. I have discovered you," Kendra said.

"You?"

Kendra reached up and took his glasses off, then placed them on the lamp table. She touched his temples with the tips of her fingers.

"Yes, Tom. Me."

For just a moment there was a question in Petzold's eyes; then it was clear that he answered the unasked question himself as he understood what she was saying. Kendra saw his sincere joy as he realized, perhaps for the first time, that the obvious feeling he had for her wasn't one-sided. She knew that he wanted to kiss her but was a bit hesitant, perhaps not yet sure of his position. So she moved her lips slightly closer to his, letting him know that she wanted the kiss as much as he did.

Kendra had orchestrated everything that had happened so far this evening, but when she felt Petzold's arms closing firmly around her and his lips pressing hard against hers, she lost all self-possession. She was made light-headed by the depth of his searching, hungry kiss and felt a whirlpool of desire pull her deeper and deeper into its powerful center of pleasure.

She wasn't sure when they decided to move into her bedroom; she wasn't even sure who had made the first move in that direction. What happened afterward seemed to come to her through a dream. She was cognizant once of catching her own reflection in the mirror of her dresser—and only slightly surprised to see that she was completely naked. She examined her body with what was almost detached interest, as if determining how it would appear to her lover. She was small and almost fragile looking, with firm little breasts topped with tightly drawn coral-colored nipples, thin hips leading down to a small triangle of pubic hair, and delicate legs. In the shadows on the bed behind her Petzold was busily slipping out of his trousers and hanging them neatly across the back of a chair, fastidious in his personal habits, even in this most intimate of moments. From the Victrola in the living room came a crooning voice:

>*"Although he may not be the man*
>*some girls think of as handsome*
>*to my heart he'll carry the key . . ."*

Kendra gave herself to the man she loved then, and there was a sweetness to the act, a warm intimacy as if what they were doing was right, was meant to be done. There were no awkward moments, no hesitancy, no holding back from embarrassment or inexperience. What they were doing was as familiar and comfortable as if they had been husband and wife for many years, loving and being loved.

A few minutes later Petzold raised himself up to look at her face and into her eyes, supporting his weight on the palms of his hands. Their bodies were still connected at the most critical juncture, and Kendra could feel the pleasure of him inside her.

"I love you, Kendra," he whispered.

"I love you, Tom."

"Will you marry me?"

Suddenly, inexplicably, Kendra laughed.

"What is it? Why are you laughing?"

"When I was a little girl I used to wonder what it was going to be like when my future husband proposed to me. I wondered if he would get down on one knee the way they do it in the romance stories. I never dreamed it would be during coitus."

He chuckled with her. "If I had my way, we'd call the preacher right now and stay just like this, all during the ceremony."

Kendra laughed again—a throaty, sensual, bawdy laugh that she hadn't known she possessed—and said, "Now, *that* would make quite a story for the paper, wouldn't it?"

EXCERPTS FROM THE ST. LOUIS CHRONICLE,
SEPTEMBER 1926

LEAGUE OF NATIONS ADMITS GERMANY

GENEVA—Germany has now been granted a permanent seat in the League of Nations, and its entry into the world body—created as a forum for discussions between countries—is the final step in the normalization of Europe after the late war. Ironically, though one of the original architects of the League of Nations was President Woodrow Wilson, the United States has never joined.

HURRICANE KILLS 1,000, LEAVES THOUSANDS MORE HOMELESS

MIAMI—This southeastern Florida community was nearly leveled two days ago when a tropical hurricane roared through with 130-mile-per-hour winds. The city itself was reduced to a pile of splintered wood and broken glass, while the streets are lined with more than a dozen beached ships.

AL CAPONE ESCAPES GANG-WAR ATTACK

CICERO, ILLINOIS—Eleven cars loaded with gangsters drove by Al Capone's base of operations in this Chicago suburb yesterday, firing machine guns, shotguns, and pistols. The gunfire broke several windows in the hotel where the gangster makes his headquarters and damaged numerous autos parked nearby. Despite the large amount of gunfire, however, only two people were injured and neither of them seriously. Capone, who wasn't in the hotel at the time, escaped the attack.

BOOK REVIEWS

THE SUN ALSO RISES, Ernest Hemingway, Scribners. $2.95.

Mr. Hemingway's novel is about a generation of restless, multinational men and women thrown together in Paris. It is absorbing, beautifully and tenderly absurd, and heartbreaking—and no review can convey the quality of this work. It is a truly gripping story, told in a lean, hard, athletic narrative prose. Quite simply, it is magnificent and compelling writing.

A TIME FOR ALL THINGS, Eric Twainbough, Pendarrow House. $2.95.

This coming-of-age story takes its central character on a worldwide journey of discovery and self-discovery. The author's ear for language, its rhythms and patterns, is quite remarkable, enabling the reader to not merely "read" what the characters are saying, but to "hear" them through dialogue that is almost musical.

A Time for All Things is a wonderfully crafted, exciting adventure told through writing filled with action and rich in characterization. This novel—a first by the author—is surely destined to be one of the biggest books of the season.

SOCIETY

THOMAS PETZOLD AND KENDRA MILLS WED

In a quiet ceremony attended by only a few close friends, Thomas Petzold, owner and publisher of *The St. Louis Chronicle*, and Kendra Mills, a *Chronicle* journalist, were married yesterday.

HOLLYWOOD CHATTER

Syndicated column by Babs Benedict.

Hundreds of thousands of weeping women crowded the streets around a small church in Hollywood, where funeral services for Alphonso Delavente took place. The great Latin lover suddenly fell ill last week with what seemed to be a mild case of la grippe. Then, quite unexpectedly, he developed pneumonia and died within twenty-four hours.

All of Hollywood—indeed, the world—was stunned by the shocking news. Alphonso Delavente was Hollywood's all-time greatest box-office attraction, and everyone was eagerly awaiting the beginning of production for *Prince of the Sand*, the sequel to his previous film and an epic that would have been his first talking picture.

As Alphonso's body was transported from the church to the cemetery, huge crowds of hysterically wailing women, eager for a chance to touch the hearse that was transferring the remains of their secret heart's love, pushed out into the street. This caused the procession to be halted many times while the police cleared the way.

"What use for me to live, now that he is dead?" one woman is said to have screamed as she threw herself in the path of the oncoming hearse. Only the quick action of a nearby policeman saved the distraught young woman from her own untimely death.

Greta Gaynor rode in a white limousine just behind the hearse. Miss Gaynor has just been selected to costar with Ken Allen in Goliath Studios' first talking picture, *Guns of The Mesa*, scheduled to go into production next spring. Sources close to this reporter say that she was also close to inking the contract that would have made her costar to Alphonso Delavente in his first-ever talkie.

Demaris Hunter had been in Hollywood for a year and a half when she returned to St. Louis to be in Kendra's wedding. At first she had been shocked to hear whom her friend was marrying. After all, Thomas Petzold was no spring chicken. But when she saw them together on their wedding day, she was convinced that there were no two people anywhere on earth better suited for each other. She didn't even have to ask Kendra if she was sure she was doing the right thing. It was obvious just by looking that Kendra was.

Demaris's father was very happy to have his daughter back home, though he was disappointed to learn that she planned to return to Hollywood. He tried to talk her out of it, but she was adamant. Finally he relented, giving her one more year to "get this movie silliness out of her system."

Agreeing, as much to keep peace in the family as anything else, Demaris secretly told herself that she would assess the situation in another year. If she thought there was still a chance of getting into pictures, she would stay in Hollywood—no matter what her father wanted. If she was no closer then than she was now, she might as well come home and do whatever it was he had in mind for her.

What Demaris's father had in mind, of course, was for his daughter to return to St. Louis, find a nice, "proper" young man, get married, and settle down. Whoever the "proper" young man would be, it wouldn't be Morris Montgomery. Demaris read in *The Chronicle* of Morris's engagement to Cynthia Brookings, the Veiled Prophet Goddess of Love and Beauty for 1926.

When Demaris returned to her Hollywood apartment a week after Kendra's wedding, she found a neat pile of mail on her kitchen table, left there by the apartment manager. One of the letters was from Goliath Studios, but because Guy Colby's name was written just above the Goliath imprint, she assumed the letter was personal.

It had been Demaris's original intention to use her relationship with Guy as a means of getting a part in a movie. But the more she thought about it, the tackier the idea seemed to her, so she abandoned it. She did, however, continue to see him and even slept with him a couple of times. Or at least she tried to.

Guy was impotent, a condition Demaris had never encountered—in fact, had never even heard of before. On both attempts, despite their best efforts, nothing happened between them. Their anxious bodies would grind at each other until finally Guy would fall to one side with a cry of frustration and an inert penis lying limply between his legs.

Demaris had wondered aloud one night if it was her fault, if he didn't find her attractive enough or if she wasn't doing something he wanted done. Guy had assured her tearfully that she wasn't to blame; it was because Greta Gaynor had castrated him—figuratively, if not literally. Not until the situation was resolved with her, he had said, would he ever be a whole man again.

Greta Gaynor was one of the most important stars in the business. Guy and Greta lived separately, and there was no hope of any reconciliation ever occurring between them, but Guy had told Demaris up front that he didn't plan to divorce Greta anytime soon. He couldn't, he had explained, because Greta had let him know that if he did, it would cost him a fortune in alimony and property settlement.

After a couple of months Guy and Demaris stopped seeing each other, though their drifting apart had been quite amicable. He had called her once or twice since then and even wrote her a few times, though this was the first time he had ever written her on Goliath stationery. Pleased to hear from him again, Demaris opened the letter, wondering what he wanted.

Dear Miss Hunter:

On April 1, 1927, Goliath Pictures will begin shooting *Guns of the Mesa*, starring Ken Allen and Greta Gaynor. There is a small but important role for another woman in the picture, and I would like to offer you that part.

If you feel that I am imposing on our friendship by asking you to take a role in a movie I am directing, then I ask your forgiveness and withdraw the offer. If, however, you would be interested, I am prepared, on behalf of Goliath Studios, to offer you a standard contract.

I think you should be advised that *Guns of the Mesa* is to be a motion picture with sound, the first full-length feature with sound that Goliath has produced or that I have directed. Please let me have your answer as soon as possible.

Sincerely,
Guy Colby

CHAPTER

FIFTEEN

OCTOBER 1926, WERTHEIM, GERMANY

Holding on to the doorframe to steady himself against the train's rocking motion, Eric Twainbough stuck his head inside the doorway of the small passenger compartment and smiled at his wife. He then gave a quick glance at the four other passengers who had shared all or part of the long trip with them: the overweight and gregarious priest, the professor who had kept his nose in a book and said nothing to anyone from the time he boarded, the woman with a basket stuffed full of aromatic sausages and cheeses that she willingly shared, and the woman's eight-year-old son, who was so active that after one of his many exploratory trips through the train, the exasperated conductor returned him to the compartment and delivered a stern lecture on how children should be disciplined.

"Tanner, we're coming in to Wertheim," Eric announced. "Come and look at it. It's such a beautiful little village."

Tanner got up and joined him in the corridor. "Do you feel guilty about leaving Ham in Paris?" she asked, her voice and expression reflecting her concern.

Eric put his hands on his wife's shoulders. "Tanner, Marcel and his wife have raised three children of their own. I'm sure Ham will be just fine with them. Besides, it isn't as if we had left him with strangers. They're like family to him."

Tanner sighed. "You're right. But, still, I know he wanted to come. It was hard to tell him that we were going to leave him for two weeks."

"You know how he loves being with the Aubrons. I'd be surprised if he even knew we were missing."

"Oh, how can you say that?" Tanner asked. "Are you suggesting he won't even *miss* us?"

Eric laughed. "Well, maybe a little," he admitted. "Though probably not nearly as much as you'll miss him. But this vacation was your idea, after all, so why not enjoy it? Come over here and take a look at what I wanted you to see."

Her concerned expression turned to one of delight as she looked out the window. "Oh, Eric, isn't it beautiful? We *are* going to have a fine time, aren't we?"

"Yes, we are—if you can quite worrying about the baby long enough," Eric replied. "Ah, we're coming into the station."

The houses and municipal buildings of the colorful Bavarian village of Wertheim clung to the sides of the hills like clusters of wildflowers and looked down over the Main River.

As the train drew to a stop, the sounds of numerous bands playing from various points in town filtered into the station. It was autumn, and all of Bavaria was celebrating the wine harvest. Like most other villages, towns, and cities in Germany at this time of year, the entire town of Wertheim was given over to a festival, and the streets were filled not only with the music of the competing bands, but with the shouts and laughter of thousands of people.

All over town there were decorated booths selling flowers, beer, sausages, sweet rolls, souvenirs, and a potent mixture called *neuweisswein* or "new white wine," a milky substance left over from the wine-making process. Sometimes there would be little sticks, seeds, bits of pulp, and husks floating around in the wine, but that didn't deter its consumption in great quantities. *Neuweisswein* wasn't bottled, but stored in large stone crocks and, when ordered by a customer, dispensed with a dipper and served in beer mugs.

Banners hung from second-story windows or floated in the breeze as they dangled from wires stretched across the streets. Like the streets themselves, the station platform was crowded with men and women of the village, welcoming the tourists who had come to share the festival with them. Most of the men were dressed in lederhosen and Tyrolean caps, while the women were wearing colorful dresses and aprons. Also scattered through the crowd were men in uniforms. Some wore the uniform of the local police, some wore state police uniforms, and some were wearing uniforms of the Army. The most dominant uniform, however, was the dark-brown trousers and light brown shirt of the SA.

"Oh, look! Look, there they are!" Tanner said, pointing to the crowd. "There's Cousin Karl and his wife, Uta. Karl!" she shouted, waving out the open window of the train. "Karl, hello! We're over here!" Karl was in neither the lederhosen costume nor a uniform. Like Eric, he was dressed in a simple business suit.

Because Tanner was speaking English in a sea of German, her call stood out above all the other noise. Karl looked across the heads of the crowd and saw her, then smiled and pointed her out to his wife and son. Uta was holding an infant in her arms, and she held the little girl's hand up to wave at Tanner.

"That's Liesl," Tanner explained. "Oh, isn't she adorable?"

The train came to a stop, and the two Americans

scrambled down the train's steps. Moments later Tanner, Karl, and Uta were embracing, while Eric stood by. Then Tanner introduced him. In deference to Eric's limited fluency in German, they all spoke English.

"I read the review of your book," Karl told Eric. "You must be very proud to be a published author."

"Yes, I do feel pretty good about it," Eric said, grinning. "Though I'm surprised that you found a review to read. How did you manage that?"

"It wasn't so difficult. There's a place in Munich that sells American newspapers. There I can buy *The New York Times*," Karl explained. "And sometimes even *The St. Louis Chronicle*. I like it when I can buy *The Chronicle* and read news of St. Louis. Often I see names of people, places, or things that I recognize."

"Yes. Karl follows everything American," Uta interjected with a laugh. "If someone did not know him better, they would think he is more American than German. I think sometimes he wishes he could go back."

"I wouldn't mind going back for a visit," Karl admitted. "But I am German. I should stay here."

"Of course you should stay here," Tanner said. "Germany is a beautiful country. And now that the inflation is over, things are being set right again."

"Yes, things are much better than when you were here last," Karl said, "though there is much left to do. But, come, we can't stand around on the station platform all day. We must collect your bags and then get you checked into the hotel. I have reserved a room for you in the same hotel where we are staying."

"Oh, I think it was wonderful that we could take our holiday together," Uta said. "It will be so much fun."

"And I'm happy to meet Liesl," Tanner said, chucking the baby under the chin. The baby smiled at her. "Oh, she is so beautiful! May I hold her?"

"Of course," Uta said, handing the baby over to Tanner. "I'm just sorry you couldn't have brought Ludwig."

"We call him Ham," Tanner said, rubbing noses with the baby girl she was holding.

"Ham? *Schinken?*" Karl asked, confused by the name.

Tanner laughed. "No, not the ham that you eat. Ham is short for Hamilton. We named him Ludwig Hamilton Twainbough. Sam Hamilton is the name of Eric's editor at the publishing house, and we took his name for luck." She handed the baby back to Uta, then smiled down at Max. "Max," she said. "What a fine young man you have become."

"Thank you," Max answered politely. "I am eight years old now. I am much bigger than I was when you saw me last."

"Well, I can certainly see that," Tanner said. She glanced along the station platform. "Oh, there are our bags being unloaded."

"Come, I'll help you with them," Karl said to Eric.

"Thanks."

The group walked over to the baggage cart, and Eric handed over his claim tickets.

"Tell me, Eric," Karl said as he easily hefted one of the suitcases with a muscular arm, "when you were in America last, did you get to see any football games?"

"No," Eric answered. "We were there during base-ball season."

"Too bad. I have read of a player from Illinois, a man named Red Grange. He's very good. We played against Illinois when I was at Jefferson. I'm glad they didn't have a runner such as Red Grange then. I think he would be a hard man to tackle."

"Yes, so I understand," Eric said. "But I also understand you were a very good tackler. Perhaps it isn't so much that Red Grange is a very good runner as it is that he hasn't encountered anyone who can tackle as well as you could."

Karl laughed. "My friend, if the writing ever runs dry for you, perhaps you should consider politics. You speak like a politician."

Tanner smiled at her husband affectionately as she responded to her cousin, "I don't think we need worry about a career change. Eric loves writing too much to ever give it up."

The several blocks' walk to their small hotel took a considerable amount of time because of the crowds and the festivities. After Eric and Tanner checked in, Uta suggested, "You two must be tired from your trip. Would you like the remainder of the afternoon to rest? The hotel provides sitters for children, so we could all go out together tonight."

"Yes," Tanner said. "Yes, I think that would be very nice."

"Then we will see you when? Nineteen hours?" Karl asked.

"Yes," Tanner replied. "Seven o'clock will be fine."

They bid one another good-bye, and Eric and Tanner climbed the stairs to their room, located at the front of the second floor. Tossing their suitcases on the bed, they crossed the room to the window and looked out at all the activity taking place on the street below. Even if they hadn't been looking outside, they would have been aware of the festival because whether open or closed, the window let through the sounds of laughter, music, and the barkers' shouts.

Their room was fairly spacious and bright. Its clean-scrubbed wood floor was bare, but the iron-framed bed, which was remarkably high, was covered with a colorful down comforter. There were no built-in closets, but there was a large pine wardrobe and a tall chest of drawers. Tanner began unpacking, hanging some garments and placing others in the drawers. A large porcelain pitcher and bowl sat atop a washstand, providing the only washing facilities, for there was no running water in the room. The toilet itself was down the hall.

Eric sat on the edge of the bed, then bounced up and down a couple of times, listening to the squeak of the springs.

"What are you doing?" Tanner asked, giggling. "Testing it out?"

"I might be," Eric admitted. He smiled. "By the

way, I got a letter from Sam Hamilton just before we left Paris."

"Did you now? And what did he have to say?" Tanner hung the last of her dresses up, smoothing the wrinkles out with her hand.

"He wanted to know if you might be interested in making love to the man who has the number-one best-selling book in America right now," Eric said almost conversationally.

"*What?*" Tanner asked, looking toward him.

"*A Time for All Things* has just moved above *The Sun Also Rises*. It's now the best-selling novel in America," Eric said, his face spread with a broad grin.

"Oh, Eric!" Tanner squealed. "Oh, that's wonderful! But, look here! You've had that letter with you ever since we left Paris, haven't you?"

"Yes."

"How could you have kept such a secret? Why have you waited so long to tell me? Didn't you think I might be mildly interested?"

"Oh, I was sure you might be interested," Eric answered, still grinning, "but I planned to make love as soon as I told you. Do you really think we could have done that in the compartment of the train?"

Tanner laughed. "I don't know why not. It wouldn't have bothered me any," she said. "But, of course, the priest might have been somewhat discomfited by it."

"Discomfited, huh?" Eric said. He reached out for her and pulled her to him, then rolled her over onto the bed. He opened her blouse, exposing her breasts. "I'll show you who's discomfited."

When the foursome walked along the streets that night, the air was redolent with grilling bratwurst from a nearby vendor. Though they had planned to find a café somewhere, they soon succumbed to the succulent aroma of the cooking sausages, and they ate a stand-up supper of bratwurst and Brötchen covered with sauerkraut and hot mustard. Later, after they had walked through the entire town, they wound up at the largest of all the festival concessions, located on the bank of the Main River. This was a huge tent, or, more accurately, a half-acre canvas awning that stretched out over a dozen or more very long tables. Each table sat at least fifty people, and every table was filled to capacity with revelers. In addition to those who were seated, scores of other customers were standing around, waiting for a place to sit.

Large-bosomed waitresses hurried to and fro through the crowd, delivering fresh beer to the tables and carrying the stone mugs back for refills. The waitresses were very skilled at their profession and could carry a remarkable number of mugs at a time, thus managing to keep the beer flowing freely. And all that beer resulted in two long lines for the toilets—the line for women being much the longer since men could go through faster.

Outside the canopied area a group of celebrants was shooting off fireworks. Occasionally Eric and his companions managed to get a direct look at one of the colorful aerial bursts, but for the most part the pyrotechnical displays were hidden from view by the canvas top. However, that didn't keep them from enjoying it, for they could see the reflection of the rockets, aerial bombs, and vivid bursting stars of fire on the surface of the black river.

Several pleasure boats and a couple of working barges were tied up on the riverbanks. The boats, and even the barges, were filled with people having a good time, and occasionally a toot from their horns would punctuate the other noises.

Under the canopy the hundreds of beer drinkers, men and women, had linked arms and were rocking back and forth to one of the songs the band was playing. Karl, Uta, Eric, and Tanner joined in.

"You must admit," Karl shouted above the noise, "we Germans know how to have a good time."

"Yes," Eric agreed. "Although in this, like everything else you do, there's an almost maniacal drive . . .

as if the entire country had been ordered to have a good time, and therefore you're bound to do it."

"What do you mean, maniacal?"

"Perhaps I chose the wrong word. It's as if you have a compulsion to have fun."

"Compulsion?"

"*Zwang*," Tanner translated.

Karl thought about it for a moment, then laughed. "Yes," he said. "Yes, I think perhaps you're quite correct. It is true that everything we Germans do, we do with determination. However, I regard that as our strength."

"As long as you don't confuse rigidity with strength," Eric suggested.

The band stopped its song and everyone unhooked arms, then drank their beer. A moment later the band started in again, and this time everyone cheered loudly. It was obvious that this particular music was a signal. Suddenly, as the band played, all the men sitting across the table from each other, in many cases perfect strangers to one another, began slapping each other's hands, right to right and left to left, all in rhythm to the song.

The man immediately across the table from Eric was as big as the American himself and was wearing one of the many SA uniforms that Eric saw sprinkled throughout the crowd. The uniforms didn't particularly disturb Eric. He didn't find them ominous, especially knowing the Germans' love for uniforms. And for the most part the Storm Troopers seemed like everyone else, just men determined to have a good time.

Scattered throughout the beer tent several pairs of men began climbing up onto the tables to carry the clapping game to the next higher level. At this level, instead of slapping the diagonally opposite hands of their partner, they would clap their hands, slap their knees, then slap their partner's face, all in rhythm to the band music.

"*Ich fordere Sie heraus*," the SA man said, grinning broadly. He pointed to one of the other tables.

"I'm not sure I understand what he wants, Karl."

"He is challenging you," Karl explained. "He wants
to dance with you."

"He wants to *dance* with me?" Eric asked.

The big German chuckled. "*Tanz, ja, ja,*" he said.

"Tell him thanks, but no thanks," Eric said. "He
isn't exactly my type."

Karl laughed. "I think you misunderstand. He's not
exactly asking you to polka. He wants to slap your face."

"What?" Eric gasped.

"Like there," Karl said, pointing to another pair of
men who had already begun the bizarre ritual of slapping
each other in the face.

"Now why on earth would I want to do something
like that?" Eric asked rhetorically, considering the idea
completely absurd.

Karl spoke to the man in German, explaining that
Eric was American and didn't understand.

"American," the SA man said, speaking in labored
English. "You are not a man?"

"It's not that," Eric said.

"Then we do," the SA man invited again.

"Eric, don't do it. You have nothing to prove,"
Tanner put in.

"Come," the German said, climbing onto the table
and reaching down toward Eric.

"*Ja, ja, ja,*" the other patrons around the table
urged.

"Okay," Eric finally consented, standing up. "But I
have to tell you, I think it's stupid to get up here and
invite another man to hit you in the face. I didn't enjoy
this even when I was a prizefighter and got paid for it."

"Then why in God's name are you doing it?" Tanner
asked anxiously.

"I don't know why," Eric admitted. He smiled
broadly, self-consciously, as he hopped up onto the table
amidst the cheers of everyone seated there with them.
"But I don't see any way out of it."

The German demonstrated, without words, what
they were to do. He went through the rhythm of
clapping his own hands, slapping his knees, then making

the motion of slapping Eric's face, though he didn't actually hit him this time. Then he took Eric's hands by the wrists and repeated the steps.

"We go now?" the German asked.

"Yes," Eric answered.

Eric clapped his hands, then let the German hit him. He wasn't prepared for the ferocity of the blow. He heard a sudden ringing in his ears, saw a flash of light, and was knocked sideways for half a step. He recovered quickly, however, and a moment later had the satisfaction of seeing the German blink in pain when he pelted him with two solid slaps, one on each cheek.

The smile didn't leave the German's face, but it did take on a rather frozen look as he went through the pattern to return the blows. He didn't hit Eric any harder this time, but he didn't hit him any easier, either. It was as if he had discovered the exact threshold, understanding that if he crossed it, it would turn the "dance" from a very rough game into a very real fight.

Eric tasted blood on his lip, but he saw a mouse spring up under the German's right eye, and he assumed he had, literally, made his point.

The others at this table realized now that what they were seeing between Eric and his partner was more than routine. Another pair of men had climbed up onto the table beside Eric and the German, but they soon stopped their own performance. It made no difference; no one was watching them anyway, for all eyes were riveted on Eric and the SA man and how hard they were hitting each other.

Soon the two tables closest to them noticed what was going on, and their own dancers stopped so they could watch; then others stopped, then others still, until, halfway through the song, everyone had sat down except Eric and his SA partner. As they continued to slap each other, the ferocity of their blows made loud, popping noises that could be heard throughout the entire assemblage.

By now the band had also picked up on what was going on between the two men, and to the delight of the audience, they prolonged the song to keep the entertainment going.

Eric wasn't sure how much longer he could continue. He could taste blood from both sides of his mouth, one of his eyes was puffed up, and his ear was so tender and painful that he felt it might have been partially torn away from his head. Still, he went on.

The SA man was in no better shape. Blood trickled from the corner of his mouth, one of his eyes was swollen completely shut, and the other eye nearly so.

Still the music went on.

By now those tables farthest away from Eric's had emptied, their occupants surging forward to watch. And new people crowded in from outside, hoping to catch a glimpse of the goings-on. The throng was so dense that not even the waitresses could get through to deliver their beer.

The blows continued to ring against the side of Eric's head, and he felt his knees getting weaker and his legs turning to rubber.

The music went on.

Then suddenly, unexpectedly, the German dropped to one knee. The man looked up through his barely open eye over a nose puffed up like a banana and streaming with blood. It also looked as though his cheekbone was broken. The German tried to stand up again, but he fell, this time falling onto his backside.

With that, the band played one loud crescendo, and the crowd exploded in applause and cheers. Several hands reached for Eric, and before he realized what was going on, he was hoisted onto several pairs of shoulders, paraded around the room, and presented to each table, where everyone sitting there held out their beer or wine mugs toward him and saluted with a loud "*Prost!*"

"I can't believe you actually did such a foolish thing," Tanner told her husband, her voice a mixture of exasperation and concern as she treated Eric's cuts with tincture of iodine. They, along with Karl and Uta, were sitting in the lobby of the hotel, which provided the only decent seating area in the small establishment.

Eric, sitting in a large, overstuffed chair with his head resting against the chair back and holding an ice-filled hand towel to his swollen eye, groaned slightly and said, "You could believe it if you were on this side of my face."

"Well, you won, if that means anything to you," Tanner muttered.

"It means nothing," Eric said. Then he chuckled. "Although, if I was going to make this much of an investment in it, I'm glad I didn't lose."

"That's what I thought," Tanner said. She wasn't being gentle with the iodine.

"Ouch, that hurts!" Eric protested.

"You deserve to hurt."

"Karl, did you know that fellow?" Eric asked.

"Yes, I know him," Karl said. "He is not a bad sort. Sometimes he is a little slow-witted."

Eric laughed. "Thanks. That speaks well for me, doesn't it? Tonight he managed to find someone at his own level. He's a Nazi, isn't he? I mean, that's what that uniform is that he was wearing."

"Yes, he's a member of the SA."

"I was surprised to see that the Nazis still have any strength to speak of. I thought it dissipated when Hitler went to jail, but I see their flags flying everywhere. Even here at the festival there are almost as many of those red flags with swastikas as there is anything else."

"Yes, but you must remember, we are in Bavaria. We are strongest here," Karl explained.

"We? Karl, you don't mean to tell me you're still a Nazi?" Tanner asked.

"Yes, of course I am. In fact, that is my occupation now. I am a gauleiter."

"I know you said you were some sort of district leader, but I thought that was a civil service job."

"No. That's a job for the Nazis. And, I must admit, I am quite well paid in this capacity."

"But why would you continue to ally yourself with

such thugs and bullies?" Tanner asked. "I mean, the inflation is over with now. There's no need to go around fighting in the streets anymore."

Karl smiled. "The street fighting is over," he said.

"Is it? Then why is it necessary to have brutes in the party, such as that man who did this to Eric?"

Karl laughed. "Did you get a good look at that brute, Brunhilde? He looks much worse than Eric, I think."

"Yeah, I did get him pretty good, didn't I?" Eric said proudly.

"I'm serious," Tanner said. "I just can't believe you're a Nazi."

"Tanner, there are many things you do not understand," Uta said. "I am proud that my husband is a Nazi. He fought for Germany during the war; now he must fight for Germany during peace."

"Are you guys planning another coup?"

"No," Karl answered. "There will be no more coup attempts. I think we made a mistake before, but that was a desperate measure, taken at a desperate time. Now we are spending our time building the party into a national political organization. I believe the time will come when the Nazis will have control of the national government, but that control will be attained by the ballot, not by bullets."

"There," Tanner said to Eric, finishing her doctoring. "You're all taken care of now."

"Ah, and just in time. Here is the schnapps I ordered," Karl said as a waiter approached them, carrying a bottle and four glasses on a tray. He put the tray down on a table, then withdrew. Karl poured, then passed the glasses around. The four touched their glasses in a silent salute.

Eric took a swallow, then smiled. "Ah, that's good. I can feel it all the way down to my toes." He looked over at Karl. "What makes you think the people will elect the Nazis, Karl?" he asked, getting back to their conversation. "I would think they'd be very complacent, now that Germany has recovered from the inflation."

"I'm not so sure we have recovered," Karl said.

"What do you mean? I bought a beer for fifteen pfennig. A couple of years ago it would have cost millions of marks."

"I must confess that I don't understand such things, but Hitler and the economists in our party tell us this is a false recovery," Karl explained. "True, the Dawes plan has restructured reparations and made credit available so that Germany could revalue its money. But we are now a nation living on credit. We haven't yet regained our industrial strength—and until we do, we are courting disaster. Soon there will be a depression, and that will be as bad, or worse, than the terrible inflation we have just experienced. When that happens, the people will cry out for a führer to save them, to lead them out of the mess. That führer is none other than Adolph Hitler."

"Do you really have that much faith in the man?" Eric asked.

"Yes, I do. You don't know him like I do. He is not only a political genius, he is the most dynamic man I have ever known. Perhaps he is the most dynamic man in history. I am certain he is the most dynamic man in German history."

"What is he doing now?" Eric asked. "We don't hear about him as much as we used to."

"He is living in Munich," Karl said. "He is often seen in the company of a young lady named Geli Raubal. Fräulein Raubal is Herr Hitler's half niece, and they say she has captured his heart. He is much more subdued than he once was. He goes to museums, attends the operas and the cinemas. There are some in the party who are disturbed by this, but I, for one, think it's a very good thing. I think it helps with the way the public perceives him. It isn't good that so many people remember him only for that foolishly inspired revolution we attempted."

"How does he make his living?" Eric asked.

"Well, like you, he's a writer," Karl replied. "He has published his book, and it's selling quite briskly, I believe."

"Mein Kampf, yes, I've heard of it."

"Have you read it?" Karl asked.

"No, I haven't read it. Have you?"

"Well, uh, no," Karl admitted. He laughed. "To tell the truth, it is a bit too heavy for my taste. But it *is* selling very well, and it's moving Hitler out of the streets and into the parlors. I think that is necessary. Also, Hitler is now courting the industrialists and the financial powers of Germany. This is a good move, too, I think. You know, the Communists are always talking about overthrowing the moneyed classes and redistributing the wealth. Hitler talks of letting them keep their wealth, while winning them over to our side."

"I have to admit, that seems to make more sense," Eric said. "However, I still have a difficult time seeing Adolph Hitler ever regaining the popularity he enjoyed in 1923. My belief is that the Nazi party is going nowhere. If I were you, my friend, I'd look for another star to hitch your wagon to."

"You underestimate the man," Karl said. "The whole world underestimates him. Just wait and see. One day he will be the most powerful man in all Europe."

"Enough politics, enough," Tanner said, clapping her hands together. "I say let's just enjoy the rest of our vacation with no more talk of politics and"—she looked pointedly at Eric—"no more trying to prove you are a man. You're worse than Ernest, running with the bulls."

"Please!" Eric said, holding up his hands in mock horror and laughing. "Don't compare me to that. I promise, I'll be good from now on."

CHAPTER

SIXTEEN

In 1909 an investor built a railroad spur line just outside
this small city in Illinois. At the end of the spur line this
same businessman constructed a large warehouse. The
purpose of the spur line and warehouse was to process,
store, and ship marijuana, then a legal commodity. But
the market that the would-be entrepreneur anticipated
for marijuana never materialized, so he abandoned the
idea—along with the spur line and the warehouse.
Eventually the U.S. government took over both as
compensation for delinquent taxes, intending to sell
them, but in the intervening years since the government
had confiscated the property, there had been no buyers.
Thus the warehouse was neglected, run down, and
posted with signs declaring U.S. GOVERNMENT PROPERTY/
KEEP OUT when Kerry O'Braugh discovered it.

This warehouse was where Kerry had asked Heavy

Hart to meet him. He was standing on the crumbling loading dock when four cars bringing Heavy and his entourage arrived, adding to the twelve trucks and two cars Kerry already had on the scene.

With two men to each truck and four to each car, Kerry had a total of thirty-two men. Heavy had sixteen. This was the first time the two gang leaders had ever met with the odds in Kerry's favor, and when Heavy pulled to a stop, he didn't even get out of his car. Kerry realized at once what the problem must be, so he hopped down from the loading dock and walked over·to the Packard to talk to the huge black man.

"Heavy, I'm glad you could come," he greeted.

"What the fuck is goin' on here?" Heavy asked. "What you have so many men here for?"

"Because it's goin' to take a lot of men to do what I have in mind," Kerry answered. He smiled encouragingly. "And you're part of it," he added. "Come on, Heavy. We're partners, not enemies." He laughed. "Besides, most of the men with me are workers—truck drivers and dockhands. You're the one with all the muscle here. I'd be a fool to try somethin'."

"What you have in mind?"

"Get out of the car, and we'll talk about it."

"You go on back over to the dock," Heavy said. "I'll join you in a minute."

"Okay. If that's how you want to do it, it's fine with me. I've got nothin' to hide here."

Kerry walked back over to the loading dock, then leaned against it and lit a cigarette.

"Why won't they get out of the car?" Vinnie Todaro asked, coming over to the edge of the dock and squatting down so that he was at about the level of Kerry's head. "What's the matter with them niggers?"

"I told you not to call 'em that," Kerry snapped.

"Why not? That's what they are, ain't it?"

"They don't like bein' called a nigger any more than you like bein' called a wop."

"Well, what do I give a shit what they like bein' called?"

"They're our partners," Kerry said, glaring at Vinnie. "If you can't accept that . . ."

"I can accept it," Vinnie said quickly. "I mean, I can work with niggers, all right. I just don't like 'em."

"Then keep your opinion about 'em to yourself."

"You aren't goin' to tell me you actually like the nig . . . coloreds, are you?" Vinnie asked.

"I'm goin' to follow my own advice," Kerry said, "and keep my opinion to myself. Believe me, it's much healthier in the long run."

The door to the Packard opened, and Heavy Hart got out, unwinding his enormous seven-foot frame. He closed the door behind him, and the car started up, then pulled away. The other three cars followed. Kerry watched Heavy amble across the cinder-covered lot toward him.

"What's goin' on?" Kerry asked. "Where are your men goin'?"

"Just over to the edge of the field there," Heavy said, and even as he spoke the four cars stopped and waited. "I told 'em to wait there out of the way. That way you can't try nothin' funny. And if somethin' happens to me, they know what to do."

Kerry smiled. "Good enough," he said. He offered the man a cigarette, but Heavy declined, pulling out a cigar instead. Kerry lit it for him.

"Okay, what is it?" Heavy asked, blowing out a cloud of smoke as his cigar caught. "How we goin' to make this half-million dollars you talkin' about?"

"Tannenhower Brewery," Kerry said.

"Shit," Heavy scoffed. He spit out a piece of tobacco from his cigar. "You call me out here for that? Folks been tryin' to get at those people ever since Prohibition come in. Them Tannenhower brothers is fine, upstandin' citizens. There ain't no way you goin' to reach them."

"I'm not goin' after the Tannenhower brothers," Kerry said. He flashed a self-satisfied smile. "I'm goin' after the liquor the government has stored in one of the Tannenhower warehouses."

"What kind of liquor?"

"The best. Bonded liquor from Canada, Ireland, and Scotland. Quality stuff."

Heavy's eyes narrowed. "You tryin' to tell me the government keeps stuff like that around?"

"What do you think the feds do with all the bonded whiskey they find?"

"They chop holes in it and let it pour out into the streets," Heavy replied.

"No, they don't."

"The hell they don't. I seen pictures of 'em doin' it."

Kerry laughed. "They do a little of that just for the pictures," he explained, "but most of the whiskey they impound. I figure they're plannin' on sellin' it off after Prohibition is repealed. Anyway, for right now they're keepin' it in no more than two or three warehouses across the country—and the biggest warehouse is the one they're rentin' from Tannenhower Brewery. They got more than twenty million dollars' worth of liquor stashed out there."

Heavy let out a long, low whistle. "Twenty million dollars?"

"That's right. 'Course, we couldn't move that much even if we had all night long. But I've got a dozen trucks here. I figure we ought to be able to take out at least two million dollars' worth tonight. Are you interested?"

"If there's two million dollars' worth of whiskey, how come you say we only get a half million?"

"I'm havin' to move it at fifty percent," Kerry replied. "We got to do that. We can't handle this much by ourselves."

"Yeah, I guess you're right." Heavy stroked his chin and studied Kerry for a long moment. "Okay, I'm interested, but I don't see you just invitin' me in like this. 'Specially since you got enough trucks and strong backs to handle the job yourself and a place to fence it. So, what's the catch? Why you lettin' us in?"

"I've known about this booze for a long time," Kerry said. "And I've been plannin' the operation for a long time. But I've also been lookin' for the right opportunity. Well, that opportunity has come. I've just learned that the Purple Orchid is goin' to be closed to its regular customers tonight. Paddy Egan is throwin' a big party for all his men." Kerry chuckled. "I think the reason they're havin' their meetin' is to decide what to do about us . . . you and me. Only, I've got my own ideas about you and me, if you're willin' to go along with it."

"You're doin' the talkin'," Heavy said. "Let me hear what you got to say."

"We're never goin' to get another chance like this. I'd like for you and your bunch to drop in on Egan's party," Kerry said. "There are sixteen of you, and he won't be expectin' you. You'll catch 'em with their pants down."

"Yeah," Heavy said. He smiled. "I'd like to catch that ofay son of a bitch with his pants down."

"That'll do two things for us," Kerry went on. "If you hit 'em hard enough, you can rub out so many of Egan's gang that he won't have enough people left to rob a gas station, let alone cause *us* any more trouble. And you might even get lucky and get Egan himself. In the meantime, that'll cause such a commotion that every cop in town—even the ones off duty—will be called out. Everybody will be rushin' over to the club to see what the hell's goin' on."

"And while we're havin' our party, you'll be cleanin' out the warehouse," Heavy said, grinning. "I got to hand it to you, O'Braugh. That's a pretty good plan. 'Course, you got the easy end of it. We're the ones goin' to be standin' around in the middle of all them flyin' bullets."

"That's true," Kerry agreed. "But I'm also the one that planned and organized it. And you're gettin' half for helpin'. Now, are you in or out?"

Heavy stuck the cigar in his mouth and settled it there. "We're in," he said.

"Do you have a watch?"

"Yeah, I got a watch. What's the matter with you? You think I ain't got a watch?"

"What time do you have?"

Heavy pulled out his pocket watch and examined it. "I got three minutes till four."

"I have five of four," Kerry said, looking at his gold wrist watch. "They're pretty close together so that means they're runnin' at about the same speed. We'll set 'em both for four. At exactly eleven o'clock tonight, you make your attack. By that time most of Egan's men will be good and drunk. Also that's late enough that most of the cops will be off duty. At exactly eleven o'clock, the same time you're startin' your attack, I'll start loadin' up the trucks. After we get all the trucks loaded, we'll bring the booze back here," he said, gesturing at the abandoned warehouse. "Tomorrow afternoon we'll count it together, then deliver it to the Commissioners."

"The Commissioners? You're dealin' with them?"

"Yeah. Why? You have any objections?"

"I've tried to deal with 'em a few times, but they don't deal with colored folks."

Kerry smiled. "Hell, that ain't no problem, Heavy. Maybe you haven't noticed, but I ain't colored."

"Yeah," Heavy said, smiling. "I did notice you're kinda pale."

"Don't worry about the Commissioners. I'll deal for both of us; then I'll give you your cut in cash."

"Maybe it'd be better if I just took my half in liquor," Heavy said.

"If that's what you'd like. But are you sure you want that much liquor on your hands?"

"No, I guess not. You go ahead and handle it for me. I'll see you tomorra'."

"Good luck tonight."

"Thanks," Heavy said. He turned and started to walk across the wide field to the cars. Then he stopped and grunted. "Shit, ain't no need of me walkin' that far." He held up his hand in signal, and the four cars started toward him. As they bounced across the field, Heavy turned and looked back at Kerry.

"You know, O'Braugh, there's more about me an' you that's alike than there is that's different. Ain't no reason we can't work together for a long time, if we could learn to trust each other full."

Kerry smiled. "If there's money in it, Heavy, we can learn," he said.

Heavy chuckled. "You got that right, O'Braugh. You sure do got that right." The Packard drew up alongside him, and he slipped into it; then the four cars started off.

"We ain't really goin' to share with 'em, are we?" Vinnie asked his cohort.

"Yeah," Kerry answered, watching the cars as they pulled away, "we're goin' to share with 'em. They're gettin' their full cut, just like I promised." He turned and looked at Vinnie. "It's called the cost of doin' business."

Part of the cost of doing business, Kerry had already discovered, was in getting rid of the whiskey once he had it. The "Commissioners" that he had mentioned were a group of high-powered fences who worked not only with liquor, but with stolen goods from furs to candy. The biggest single part of their business was supplying bootleggers and speakeasies. This they did over a six-state area, and Heavy was right about them: They dealt only with whites.

The Commissioners got their name from the connections they had. They owned enough judges, policemen, and city and state officials in their territory to make their operation virtually foolproof. And they would give a straight fifty percent—in quick, ready cash—for all the whiskey Kerry could deliver.

Kerry planned to sell off half of his share of the whiskey, keeping the other half to use as leverage to sign up all the speaks in St. Louis. After tonight he figured he'd pick up most, if not all, of the speaks Egan was now servicing. By this time tomorrow Kerry O'Braugh would control St. Louis.

Before it got that far, however, Kerry would have to pull off the job, and that required careful attention to all the details. Signaling his men, Kerry called them all together so he could explain, step by step, his plans for the operation.

Those plans called for a convoy of twelve trucks, divided into four groups of three, and two cars. The drivers of each of the four lead trucks had already cased the Tannenhower warehouse and studied the neighborhood. They knew every alley, every late-night operation, every gin mill, and every stop sign within a nine-block radius of the target. The warehouse could only accommodate three trucks at a time, so the loading operation was going to have to be very closely coordinated. Kerry figured that it was just as well all twelve trucks couldn't be there at the same time because so many trucks driving through that part of town that late at night were bound to catch somebody's interest.

Unlike the truck drivers and their loaders, Kerry and his remaining seven men, who would be riding in the cars, would all be armed. But Kerry gave specific instructions that no one was to shoot, under any circumstances, unless they were actually ambushed.

"All the shooting will be going on across town," he explained. "We don't want to give any cop any reason to come around and stick his nose into what we're doing."

While the feds kept none of their people at the warehouse, two night watchmen would be on duty. But they wouldn't pose any problem. Kerry had learned that they earned twenty dollars a week for working from ten till six every night. He bought both of them off for five thousand dollars each. That was almost five years' pay, and all they had to do to earn it was allow themselves to be tied up. It had been an easy sale.

When he was certain that his men perfectly understood what they had to do, Kerry dismissed them, telling them to go get a bite to eat while there was still time. "But no drinkin'," he warned. "I want everybody to have their full wits about 'em."

Sitting in his car that night, about four blocks away from the Tannenhower warehouse, Kerry turned on the flashlight he was carrying and looked at his watch.

"What time is it?" Carmine Brazzi asked.

"Two minutes to eleven."

"Think we'll hear anything when Heavy and his boys open the show?" Carmine asked.

"I doubt it. We're too far away from the club," Kerry said. "But that's the beauty of it. Nobody'll be botherin' us, you see, 'cause all the action'll be over there."

"I sure hope them niggers don't chicken out on us," Vinnie said. "If they decide to take a powder, we're goin' to be hung out to dry."

"They'll do their end of it," Kerry said. He looked at his watch again. "Okay, let's go."

The location of the big, sprawling redbrick building was ideal, for it was sheltered from the rear by two buildings, one a vacated warehouse that was two stories taller. That meant that the loading in the back would be completely shielded from the bordering street—and any curious eyes.

Kerry put one man on top of the vacant warehouse, two more on the ends of the narrow road running alongside the tracks of the loading area, and a fourth on the other side of the bordering building in the rear. That way, he figured, it would be impossible for anyone to surprise them.

One of the night watchmen met them at the rear loading door.

"Come on in," he hissed. "There's nobody around."

"Wait a minute," Kerry replied. He pointed to the lock. "We can't just waltz on in. We have to break that lock. Otherwise, the feds'll know right off the bat that you was cooperatin' with us."

"Oh, yeah," the night watchman replied. He laughed nervously. "Yeah, I guess I wasn't thinking."

"Take care of it, Vinnie," Kerry ordered.

Nodding, Vinnie put a crowbar to the hasp. It gave a protesting squeak, then pulled out of the door, leaving an ugly strip of splintered wood.

"All right, let's go," Kerry said. "Get the first trucks in here."

At a prearranged signal, three trucks came down the alley, then turned around and backed up to the loading dock. The drivers opened the tailgates, while the loaders rushed inside the warehouse to pick up the two-wheeled loading dollies. Kerry followed the loaders down inside, then stopped and gave a long, appreciative whistle. He had never seen anything like it. For what seemed like miles there were endless rows of whiskey, unbottled in barrels and bottled by the case.

"My God!" Carmine gasped. "There's enough booze here to keep everyone in America drunk for months."

"Don't stand around gawkin'," Kerry ordered. "Let's get busy."

Rana McClarity hadn't been scheduled to work the Purple Orchid tonight, but when Rosalie O'Toole called her and asked her if she would fill in for her, Rana agreed. She didn't have any reason not to. Kerry had already told her that he'd be too busy to come by tonight, so she had nothing else to do.

Paddy Egan was well aware of the fact that Rana was a frequent companion of Kerry O'Braugh's. Egan knew because Rana had told him. She had to tell him about Kerry, because Egan would have discovered it anyway. And if Egan believed Rana was giving Kerry useful information, it would have gone very badly for her. To Rana's surprise, however, Egan had actually encouraged her to see Kerry, so he could have "some eyes and ears in the enemy camp."

Rana was a survivor. If Paddy Egan wanted information about Kerry, then Rana would supply it. If Kerry wanted information about Paddy Egan, she would supply that, too. But of the two men, she preferred Kerry O'Braugh. So she compensated for her double-dealing, in her mind at least, by providing Kerry with generally better information than she provided Egan.

She had told Kerry, for example, that her boss would be throwing a special party for all of his men tonight, and Kerry had been very interested in that. He had also asked her to stay away tonight, and she had promised him that she would. She figured that he didn't want her at a party with Paddy Egan, and she thought it was cute that he was jealous. But she also figured a little jealousy wouldn't hurt. It would keep Kerry more interested in her. And, besides, attending this party tonight would provide her with another opportunity to get some additional information for him. She was sure that when she told Kerry tomorrow that she had attended the party, he would forgive her, especially if she had some good information.

It didn't take Rana long to discover that this was no ordinary party. Except for Rana, only two other women were at the club tonight, and the two who were, Jo Ann Reilly and Karen Thomas, were working waitresses, not good-time girls. There was no music, and though there was considerable drinking, it was hard, fast drinking, without the usual jesting and laughter. There was very little conversation. Instead, Paddy Egan was delivering what amounted to a lecture as he cursed Kerry O'Braugh and "the wops and niggers" that worked for him.

Then Rana overheard something that she felt certain justified her coming here tonight: Paddy Egan was planning an attack on Kerry O'Braugh. He intended to marshal all his forces together and take out Kerry and his whole gang in one fell swoop.

Rana had been sitting on a stool in the back of the hatcheck room, rubbing her feet, when she heard them begin to make their plans. Then, in what seemed like a stroke of luck, she discovered a small notepad and a pencil lying on a shelf just under the half-open Dutch door that separated the hatcheck room from the entry foyer. It would be very helpful, she decided, if she took a few notes on some of the things Egan was saying. That way there'd be no mistakes about what she told Kerry. She picked up the pad and began writing.

"I knew all along you was spyin' for O'Braugh," a raspy voice suddenly said. "I told Paddy if we left a pencil and pad lyin' around where you'd spot it, you'd use it."

Rana gasped and looked around behind her. Eddie

Quick had just let himself in through the back door and was now standing there smiling evilly at her.

"Eddie!" Rana said, feeling her stomach lurch.

"And guess what? Poor, dumb old Paddy didn't want to believe it," Eddie said.

"Believe what? What are you doing here?" Rana tried to put the notepad behind her, but Eddie reached for it.

"What am I doin' here? I'm here to take care of a rat, that's what I'm doin' here," Eddie said. He clamped down on her wrist with such force that Rana let out a little gasp of pain and dropped the notepad.

"Paddy's not going to like it, you hurting one of his women," Rana said, rubbing her wrist.

"Woman, man, female rat, male rat, it don't make no difference. You're all the same," Eddie growled. He started toward her, and Rana could see something deep and sinister in his eyes.

"Eddie . . . what . . . what are you going to do?" she asked. Her head began to spin as a quick, hot fear built up inside her, filling her veins and clogging her senses.

Eddie Quick put his hands around Rana's neck and began to squeeze. Her eyes bulged and her mouth opened wide, first in an effort to scream, then in a gasping, desperate attempt to breathe. She wasn't successful at either.

Still smiling malignantly, Eddie watched her face darken and her bulging eyes fill with terror as Rana realized that she was about to die.

Suddenly and inexplicably, Eddie got an erection. It had never happened to him like this before, but looking into Rana's eyes and seeing her life leave by degrees was the most erotic thing he'd ever experienced. Beneath his hands he could feel the throbbing pulse in her neck, which seemed to echo the throbbing pulse in his penis. He squeezed harder, and when she raised her weak, fluttering fingers to his hands to try to break his grip, her touch was as soft and ineffective as the brush of a butterfly's wing. Eddie's erection grew stronger, and he felt the hot, familiar buildup of energy in the small of his back, the pit of his stomach, and the soles of his feet. He squeezed harder and thrust his pelvis forward.

The pulse throb in Rana's neck finally stopped, and the light in her eyes went out. She went completely limp, and as she did so, Eddie felt the hot rush of his orgasm. He pulled Rana's body against his throbbing penis and began gushing semen, so caught up in the blissful sensations he was feeling that he was totally unconcerned that it was happening in his pants.

As the last quiver of Eddie's climax faded, the front door of the club burst open and several men charged through. For just an instant Eddie Quick was still in a semistupor from the most mind-boggling orgasm he had ever experienced. As a result, he was impassive, almost disinterested, as he watched Heavy Hart and his men dash in. Then he saw that they were armed and black, and he knew they had come to kill, so he came quickly back to his senses.

Heavy's men didn't see Eddie, because they surged right past the hatcheck room without so much as a glance through the open top half of the Dutch door. As soon as they reached the club floor, they fanned out and began firing.

Had Eddie started shooting at them from the coat-check room he might have broken up their attack. The attackers wouldn't have had any way of knowing how many were behind them, and Heavy would have found it necessary to take immediate steps to keep from being surrounded. At the very least it would have bought a little time for the rest of the East Siders to get to their guns and dive for cover.

But Eddie had no concern for the fate of the others; his only thought was how to save his own skin. Looking desperately around for a place to hide, he spotted a coatrack with several raincoats hanging on it. The coats were kept as a courtesy for guests who might get caught by an unexpected downpour, but Eddie had another purpose for them. Pulling the rack to the floor, he slid in

under the coats, biting on his own arm to keep from
whimpering out loud.

Eddie lay under the coats, listening to the firing and
the screaming for what seemed an eternity but was
actually less than ninety seconds. By then Heavy Hart
and his men had completely decimated the gang known
as the East Siders.

A few of the East Siders had been able to shoot
back, and two of Heavy's men went down. But most of
the East Siders had been dulled by whiskey and numbed
by fear, making easy targets for the shotguns and tommy
guns blasting away at them.

"Let's go!" Heavy shouted after the fusillade of
firing.

The small army of men withdrew as suddenly as
they had appeared, taking with them the two of their
number hit in the exchange of gunfire.

Eddie Quick had not been seen. He lay under the
raincoats, shaking uncontrollably for another full minute
after Heavy and his men had left. Finally he squirmed
out from under the coats and took a cautious look
around. Getting to his knees, he crawled over to the
Dutch door, then raised up and peered over the shelf.

The club was a shambles. Chairs were broken,
tables were overturned, and bullets had splintered the
bar. Behind the bar the shattered mirror hung in great,
jagged pieces, and in one of the shards Eddie could see
the grotesque reflection of a floor that was covered with
broken glass, pools of blood, and sprawled bodies.

"My God!" Eddie mumbled. "They killed 'em. They
killed 'em all!"

"No, they're not all dead," a woman's voice said.

That was when Eddie saw Jo Ann Reilly for the first
time. She was on her knees beside one of the bodies
nearest the coat-check room. "Come out here and help.
I'm going to call the police."

"The police?"

"We need ambulances."

"Tell Paddy," Eddie said. "He'll know what to do."

"Paddy's dead," Jo Ann replied. "But Duke's alive and so are Mickey and Tim."

"Gerry's alive, too," the other waitress, Karen Thomas, said from the other side of the room. Neither woman had been hit, and it was clear that they hadn't been targets.

"Tell Rana to get out here and help us," Jo Ann said.

"Rana . . . Rana's dead. One of the niggers killed her."

Jo Ann stared at Eddie for a moment, then spat angrily, "The bastard! I hope he rots in hell." She got up and walked over to the telephone behind the bar.

"What're you goin' to do?" Eddie asked.

"I told you. I'm going to call the police," Jo Ann answered. "We need ambulances."

"I don't know if we should do that or not," Eddie said. He picked his way numbly through the overturned chairs, splintered tables, shattered glass, and dead or dying bodies to an upright stool at the end of the bar. "Paddy won't like it if we call the police. He won't like it at all."

Jo Ann looked over at Karen and shook her head, then made the call.

"Rana! Rana, wait'll you hear!" Kerry O'Braugh called excitedly, letting himself into Rana McClarity's house the following afternoon. "Rana?"

Where the hell was she, he wondered. He had just made the split with Heavy Hart and his men, and now he wanted to share his good fortune with his woman.

"She isn't here," Jo Ann Reilly said, coming from the kitchen to meet Kerry.

Kerry knew Jo Ann from the Purple Orchid, but this was the first time he had ever seen her at Rana's house, and he was a bit surprised by her presence.

"What are you doing here?" he asked her.

"There are some things that need to be taken care of," she replied. "Since Rana didn't have any family that anyone knew about, I volunteered to do it."

"Didn't have?" Kerry asked. "What do you mean, didn't have? What the hell are you talking about? Listen, what the hell's going on here? Where's Rana?"

Jo Ann shook her head slowly. "I'm sorry to have to be the one to tell you this, Kerry. Rana's dead."

"Dead?"

"She was killed last night, at the club."

"Oh, Jesus!" Kerry moaned. He put his fist to his forehead. "Oh, sweet Jesus! She wasn't even supposed to be there! Why was she there?"

"Rosalie got sick and asked Rana to take her place."

Kerry sank onto the sofa and leaned his head back, fighting back the bile rising in his throat and willing himself not to scream.

"You sent them, didn't you, Kerry?"

"Sent who?"

"Oh, come on, for Chrissake! Give me a little credit, won't you?" Jo Ann said angrily. "You sent the coloreds out there, didn't you?"

Kerry nodded silently.

"I thought you did."

"But I swear to you, I didn't know Rana would be there," Kerry said. "They'll pay for it. Damn them! Goddamn them to hell! All they were supposed to do was take out Egan and his gang. What the hell did they have to shoot her for?"

"I shouldn't give you the comfort, you son of a bitch," Jo Ann growled. "But if it's any consolation to you, the coloreds didn't kill Rana."

Kerry opened his eyes and looked at Jo Ann. "What? What do you mean they didn't kill her? What are you talkin' about?"

"Rana wasn't shot," Jo Ann said. "She was strangled. Somebody choked her to death."

"Shit!"

"That's why I know it wasn't the coloreds," Jo Ann explained. "All they did was come inside, stand there, shoot until all the guys were down, then leave. It couldn't have been any of the coloreds who killed Rana,

because none of them ever went into the hatcheck room
the whole time they were there."

"Then how did it happen? Who did it?"

"Eddie Quick did it."

"Eddie Quick?"

"It had to be him. I saw him go into the hatcheck
room just before the shooting started . . . and he didn't
come out again until just after it ended. He didn't have
a scratch on him."

"I'm going to kill him," Kerry said in a quiet,
menacing voice.

"I thought you might," Jo Ann said. "That's the only
reason I told you." She fixed Kerry with an icy stare.
"Mister, in my book, you aren't worth a cup of warm
piss. But Eddie Quick needs killing, and if you take care
of it, then at least you'll have done one worthwhile thing
in your life."

CHAPTER
SEVENTEEN

"Don't you feel that it's a step down to be directing a Western again after your success with *King of the Sand*?" a reporter asked Guy Colby.

"No, of course not. Why should I?" Guy replied. "*Guns of the Mesa* is a big-budget Western and has big-budget stars in Ken Allen and Greta Gaynor. And it is my first talkie. I like the idea of directing a Western for my first talkie. It's a genre I'm very familiar with. And Ken Allen is extremely easy to work with."

The reporter grinned. "How about your ex-wife?"

"Gloria Gaynor isn't my *ex*-wife. We're still married."

"But you aren't living together."

"No, we aren't living together."

"Is she difficult to work with?"

"She's a professional."

"I just wondered if, under the circumstances, it might not be difficult to work with her. After all, you did say *Ken* was easy to work with . . . you didn't say anything about Greta Gaynor."

"You're trying to make trouble by putting words in my mouth," Guy groused. "Don't do that. I've got enough problems without you creating new ones for me."

"What sort of problems?"

"Technical ones. It used to be that all you had to worry about was the light. If you think the light is difficult to manage, you should try working with microphones. You have to arrange them to pick up what sound you *do* want while screening out the sound you *don't* want. It's damn near impossible, and the sound engineers who can bring it off are geniuses. I'm happy to say," he was quick to add, "that Goliath Studios seems to have acquired the best in that department."

"We're ready, Mr. Colby," someone shouted.

Guy glanced over at his assistant director, then back at the reporter. "If you'll excuse me now, I have work to do," he said, then turned his attention back to the set, which was a typical cattle ranch, consisting of a house, barn, and stable, that had been constructed on one of Goliath Studios' large back lots.

"Places, everyone," the A.D. called. "You extras, please get out of the way. Miss Hunter? Miss Hunter?" The A.D. lowered his megaphone and looked over at Guy. "Guy, this scene calls for Miss Hunter to come through the corral gate, but for reasons known only to her, she has chosen not to be in her place at the corral gate."

Demaris, who had been sitting on a wagon, jumped off quickly and started running toward the corral. "I'm here, I'm here," she called. "I'm sorry. The technicians told me to get back out of the way."

"Don't worry about it," Guy said. "Just take your place near the gate, and when we call 'action,' walk through it. Do you know your lines?"

"Oh yes. I know my lines . . . and Miss Gaynor's

lines, Mr. Allen's lines, the sheriff's lines, and the stable boy's lines," Demaris said, grinning.

"You know my lines, do you?" Greta asked caustically. "You've already got my husband; what are you doing now, bucking for my job?"

Demaris laughed self-consciously. "No, of course not. As I said, I know Mr. Allen's lines, too, but I'm not after his job, either. It's just that I was so excited about being in the movie that I learned the whole script."

"Did you now? Well, how fortunate we are that you've done that. If we forget a line, you can simply supply us with the correct words, like the prompter at a stage play."

"Yes, I suppose I could," Demaris answered hesitantly. Greta's voice dripped with sarcasm, and it was obvious that Demaris knew she had to walk a fine line to keep from making the situation any worse.

"Well, I have news for you, dearie," Greta said. "This *isn't* a stage play, this is a motion picture. So don't you worry about my lines. People don't pay money to hear us speak, they pay money to see us act. And a great many of them have paid to see me even though I've never spoken a line on the screen before now. This whole idea of talking pictures is absurd. If I had my way, no talking pictures would be made. The only reason I'm making this one is because my contract required it."

"Could we get started, please?" Guy asked.

"Of course. Don't let me stop the great director from working," Greta said, her tone acerbic. "Please, by all means, go on with the shooting."

"Thank you for your permission," Guy replied, equally caustic. "All right, let's go. Ken? Ken, where are you?"

"I'm up here, pardner. All ready," a foghorn voice answered. A big man with sparkling blue eyes and a wide, easy grin appeared in the open door of the hayloft.

"What the hell are you doing up there?"

"What am I doin' up here? Why, hell, pardner, the script calls for me to jump down from the hayloft. Remember?"

"Yes, I remember. I wrote the damn thing," Guy said. "But *you* aren't going to jump, are you? I thought that was what we paid the stuntmen for."

"Now, goddammit, son, before I became a star, I *was* a stuntman. I don't need somebody just to make a little old jump. Don't worry about it, I can do it."

"All right, all right," Guy said, waving him back. "If you want to do it, do it. Now, Demaris, you come through the gate and see Greta approaching the barn; then you call to her. Are you ready?"

"I'm ready," Demaris said.

"Are you ready, Greta?"

"I wasn't the one not on her mark," Greta reminded him.

"Quiet on the set!" Guy called.

The assistant director pushed a button that caused an electric bell to ring shrilly.

"Roll camera."

"Speed."

"Slate it."

"*Guns of the Mesa*, scene five, take one," the slate man said, holding the slate in front of the camera lens and snapping it shut.

"Action!" Guy called.

Standing by the corral gate, Demaris had been waiting expectantly, feeling her excitement rising. Then the camera began rolling, and she opened the gate and started through the corral. This was it! This would be the first time Demaris had appeared on camera. For as long as she could remember, this was what she wanted to do. It was the proudest moment of her life.

The scene called for Greta, playing the rancher's daughter, to come toward Demaris.

"Miss Johnson," Demaris said, speaking in character toward the other actress, "Buck is here!"

"Where—is—he?" Greta answered. Her words were a monotone, flat and emotionless.

"In the barn, hiding in the hayloft. He's been shot."

"Why—did—you—bring—him—here?" Greta continued. "It—will—just—make—trouble—for—my—father."

"I *had* to bring him here. I didn't know where else to go."

"He—cannot—stay—here."

"Please, you must hide him! He has no other place to go! If the posse finds him, he'll be killed!"

"Why—do—you—care—what—happens—to—Buck?"

"Because I . . ."

"Because—you—what?"

"I love him, Miss Johnson."

"You—love—him? I—had—no—idea," Greta droned. "I—thought—you—were—just—a—saloon—girl."

"I know I have no right to love him," Demaris responded, putting just the right feeling into the words. "I know you would be much better for him. That's why I brought him here. You see, I love him enough to give him up." The camera moved in for a close-up of Demaris's face and the tears that had sprung easily to her eyes.

"I—was—wrong—about—you. I—can—see that—you—really—do—love—him. I—will—keep—him—here. Don't—worry. He—will—be—safe—here."

"Cut!" Guy called. "Okay, let's do it again."

"What?" Greta screamed. She put her hands on her hips and stepped off the set to glare at Guy. "Would you mind telling me just why the hell we're shooting it again?" Greta asked. "I didn't miss one word! Not one goddamned word of my dialogue!"

"Come on, Greta, you're a pro. You know we never get it on the first shot," Guy said.

Greta pointed at Demaris. "*She* screwed it up, didn't she? For God's sake, Guy, if you must pay for your fun in bed, do it the way everybody else does. Go to a bawdy house. Don't bring your whores onto the set to screw up *my* scenes. Because I have news for you, buster. I was perfect in this scene, and I'm not doing it again!"

With a swirl of long skirt and hair, Greta spun around and left the set. For a long moment afterward there was absolute silence.

"Guy, what do you want to do now?" the assistant director asked.

Guy sighed. "That's it for the day," he said. "We'll try again tomorrow."

With production halted for the day, the other actors who had been standing by, waiting for their cues, turned to follow Greta toward the main studio building a hundred yards away. Almost instantly the set began to crawl with technicians, hurrying to take down the mirrors and lights and disconnect the various wires and microphones.

"Electrician! I need an electrician," someone called.

"Sound? Sound, you want to mark this mike location?"

"Would somebody from props please get over here?"

Demaris didn't move from her position as she watched the departure of the actors and the sudden activity of the crew. She was hurt and humiliated and she wished there were a hole she could crawl into. Her eyes welled with tears, and the lump in her throat felt like a baseball. She knew that everyone probably thought as Greta had intimated: that Demaris was in this movie only because she had slept with Guy Colby. The irony of it all was almost more than she could bear. She looked over at Guy and found him watching her, but he immediately shifted his gaze, as if unable to meet hers.

"Guy, I—"

"No, not now, Demaris, please," Guy said, turning away from her.

So he, too, had abandoned her. Fighting back her tears, Demaris watched him walk away a few yards to be joined almost immediately by the A.D. and the lighting and sound engineers. They began an intense and animated conversation, no doubt about some technical problem.

When Demaris looked back toward the set, she saw that the only people remaining behind were a couple of carpenters who were making some repair to one of the rails on the fence that encircled the corral.

With a sigh, she started toward the studio building. Halfway across the back lot, a custom-built Cadillac Sport Phaeton roared up, then slid to a stop in front of her. The car was midnight blue, with a shiny chrome grille. Mounted on the grille was a polished set of steer horns. The driver leaned over and opened the door on the passenger's side of the car, then patted the leather seat in invitation.

"Darlin', you look like you need your spirits lifted," the driver said. "Allow me to introduce myself."

"I know who you are, Mr. Allen."

Ken Allen held up his index finger and waved it back and forth. "You just think you do. But you know me only as Ken Allen, movie star. I am also Ken Allen, player of the guitar, singer of songs, teller of tall tales, connoisseur of beautiful women, soother of wounded spirits, and purveyor of truth and justice."

Demaris laughed.

"You see? I've already begun to soothe your wounded spirits," he said. "Get in. I'm takin' you to dinner."

"My purse and street clothes are in the dressing room," she said.

"Leave them there. You look good in your cowgirl dress. Get in."

"All right," Demaris said. She got into the car, and he reached across her to close the door.

"Did you see how everyone deserted you when the Bitch of Bayonne came down on you?" Ken asked as he put the car in gear and began driving away.

"Bitch of Bayonne?"

"Greta Gaynor. She's from Bayonne, New Jersey," Ken said. "If you can believe it, there are some people back there who are even proud of that fact."

"She's a very talented actress," Demaris said. "The people in her hometown should be proud."

"She's jealous. That's why she took it out on you today."

"I figured that, but I don't know why," Demaris said. "I haven't even seen Guy in quite a while. In fact, I was surprised when he offered me a part in this picture because I honestly thought he had forgotten all about me. Anyway, I thought they were separated. Why is she jealous of him?"

Ken laughed. "You really don't know, do you?" They were in traffic now, and he honked as he accelerated quickly to pass a car that was poking along in front of them.

"Really don't know what?"

"Darlin', she doesn't give a damn about you and Guy. As far as she's concerned, the two of you could crawl into bed together right there on the set, and she wouldn't care. That is, if poor old Guy can crawl into bed with *any* woman anymore. I've heard stories."

He looked over at Demaris, but she continued to stare through the windshield without giving him any indication that she knew what he was talking about.

"Good for you, darlin'," Ken said quietly, and Demaris realized then that somehow Ken knew definitely that Guy was impotent—and he was complimenting her for not betraying the director.

Demaris again refrained from acknowledging that particular line of thought and instead said, "I don't understand. If Miss Gaynor doesn't care for Guy, why is she so jealous of him?"

Ken laughed. "Darlin', Greta's not jealous of Guy. She's jealous of *you*. She looks at you, at your youth and beauty and talent—most of all at your talent—and she sees the future. And she doesn't like the future that she sees. She sees Demaris Hunter as the new star in Goliath's Galaxy, not Greta Gaynor. My God, did you listen to her dialogue? She was absolutely awful, all day. I've heard mules fart with more expression."

Demaris laughed. "I . . . I thought I was the only one who noticed."

"Are you kiddin'? Everyone on the set noticed it. Why do you think Guy stopped shootin'?"

"I wasn't sure. From what Greta said, I thought maybe I had done something wrong. Especially since no one would say anything to me."

"Darlin', that's because they're afraid of her. You see, this is a ball-bustin' business, and the last thing anyone wants to do is get on the bad side of someone who's on the top. If anyone had come over to say somethin' to you, that's just where they'd be."

"You aren't afraid. You're talking to me."

Ken looked over at her and smiled broadly. "Why, hell, honey, on this picture *I'm* king of the roost. I don't give a damn whether Greta's pissed off at me or not. You like Mexican?"

"Mexicans?"

"Mexican. Food. You know, tacos, tamales, chili, that sort of thing."

"Oh, uh, I don't know. Except for chili, I've never eaten any Mexican food."

"Well, get your taste buds ready," Ken said. "You're in for a treat."

He turned left in the face of traffic, paying no attention whatever to the angry honk of the driver of an oncoming Ford, then pulled the car under the portico of a red-tiled, tan-stucco building, where they were met by a mustached Mexican wearing a wide-brimmed sombrero and a colorful serape.

"Señor Allen! How it pleases me to see you again."

"Lopez, how're you doing? Still solicitin' for your sister?"

Lopez laughed. "Always you make the jokes." He opened the door for Demaris. "Ah, such a beautiful señorita. More beautiful, I think, than anyone you have ever brought."

"Shame on you, Lopez," Ken said. "Here I just about had the señorita convinced that I've never been out with another woman in my entire life, and you have to go and make a liar out of me."

Lopez laughed and wagged his finger. "Ah, Señor Allen, you are making the joke again. I think you are pulling the foot of Lopez."

"You're right, Lopez, I'm pullin' your foot," Ken said. "And one of these days if you don't watch it, I'm liable to just yank it right off. Take care of Clarence for me, will you?"

"*Sí*, señor. I will take good care of Clarence."

"Clarence?" Demaris asked, confused.

Ken patted the hood of his Cadillac. "This is Clarence," he said. "Some folks think you ought to name cars like boats, always give 'em a woman's name. Well, I tried that, but Clarence wouldn't hear of it. And by God, he's right. Look at him . . . he's a brute, don't you think? Look at those brown leather seat covers, the dark-blue paint job, the big motor, and that set of longhorns. And you know, I wouldn't be surprised if we found a pair of balls under all that if we looked. No sissy-assed name for my car, hell no. Clarence he wanted to be, and Clarence he is."

Inside the restaurant everyone came to greet Ken. At first Demaris assumed it was because he was a movie star, and this was the normal reaction of fans. Then she realized that these people weren't greeting him as a movie star, they were greeting him as a friend. Ken knew many of them by name, and he asked about their jobs and babies. Even those he didn't know by name received the same personable treatment from him.

"Your table is ready, señor," the waiter said.

"What are you tryin' to do, Jorge? Work me for a big tip? My table is *always* ready."

Jorge laughed. "Sí, señor. It is always ready," he said. "But tonight it is especially ready."

"Good, good. Lead the way."

The table was near the stage, where a mariachi band was playing. When they had finished their song, the band leader turned around and asked Ken something in Spanish. Ken answered in kind, and when the band leader made an announcement to the diners, also in Spanish, his words were enthusiastically applauded.

"What was all that about?" Demaris asked.

"I'm goin' to do a little song for them," Ken said. "But not to worry. I'll be finished by the time the food gets here."

One of the men on the stage gave the actor a guitar, and Demaris smiled. She knew that Ken was a singer, for she had heard some of his recordings. He had a deep, raspy voice that one critic had compared to "a railroad locomotive letting off steam." She assumed that was what she was going to hear now, but, to her surprise, Ken had no intention of singing.

After going through chord progressions a couple of times, adjusting the tuning, he hung his head for a few seconds of silence, then began to play. The music spilled out, a steady, never-wavering beat with two or three poignant minor chords at the ends of phrases and an overall simple melody, working in and out of the chords like a thread of gold woven through the finest cloth.

The sound was agony and ecstasy, joy and sorrow, pain and pleasure. It bored its way into Demaris's soul, and she found herself being carried along with the melody—now rising and now falling, steadily building, until finally the song ended with a crashing crescendo that brought a standing ovation from everyone in the restaurant.

With a self-conscious smile Ken returned the guitar to the man who had given it to him, then sat down across the table from Demaris. The food was delivered at almost the same time.

"I had no idea you could play the guitar so beautifully!" Demaris said.

"Didn't you listen to my introduction back at the studio, darlin'? I told you I could play the guitar," Ken replied.

"Next time I'll believe it," Demaris said.

She began to experiment with the strange-looking but good-smelling food that had been placed before her.

"She's going to quit the movie, you know," Ken said a few moments later, almost as an aside, keeping his attention focused on the enchilada in front of him.

"What?" Demaris had been only half listening, more involved with experiencing her first taste of guacamole.

"Greta Gaynor. There's no way she's goin' to complete this movie. If her fans heard that voice, she'd be laughed out of the industry."

Demaris lowered her fork and stared at Ken. "What is she going to do?"

"There are voice and drama coaches in town who

can work with her." Ken chuckled. "She's not the only one havin' trouble with talkies. Alphonso Delavente sounded like a banana peddler from Brooklyn. There are some who say that his dyin' may have been a blessin'. He'd never have made it in the talkies."

Demaris had also heard that idea expressed.

"The question is, what are *you* goin' to do?" Ken asked.

"What am I going to do? What do you mean? Do I need a coach? If you think I do, I'll get one."

"No, no, no," Ken said, putting his hand across the table to touch hers. "Darlin', most of the women in this town would give their left tit to sound like you . . . and their right tit to *look* like you." He laughed. "'Course, if they did that, then they wouldn't look like you at all, would they?"

"I guess not," Demaris said, laughing with him.

"No, I mean, what are you goin' to do when Guy comes to you and tells you he wants you to take Greta's role in this picture?"

"*What?*" Demaris asked, dropping her fork in surprise.

"Are you going to take it?"

"Mr. Allen . . ."

"Ken," Ken corrected. "Costars on the same picture usually call each other by their first name."

"You're getting a little ahead of things, aren't you, Ken? I haven't been asked, and there's been no indication that I'm going to be asked."

"You're goin' to be asked," Ken said. "Will you take it?"

"Well, yes! Yes, of course I will. If I am asked," she couldn't help but add.

Ken smiled. "Good! That means we'll have to go out and celebrate," he said.

"We *are* celebrating," Demaris replied, gesturing at their dinner.

"No, darlin', we're just eatin'," Ken said. "Wait till you see me when I'm celebratin'. I'm one hell-raisin', town-paintin' son of a bitch."

ST. LOUIS, MISSOURI

Even after Kendra Mills became Mrs. Tom Petzold she continued to write her newspaper articles under her maiden name, doing so because she believed her sources would talk to her more easily and be less intimidated by "Mills" than they would be by "Petzold." True to her declared intention, she began writing a series of articles exposing policemen and judges who had violated their trust.

With Paddy Egan and his East Siders effectively eliminated by gang warfare, the judges and police officers who had been in Egan's pocket were now scrambling to align themselves with Kerry O'Braugh, the new crime lord of St. Louis. Satirically noting, "You can't tell the players without a score card," Kendra, to the chagrin of the "players" involved, kept her readers up to date on the latest transactions.

One afternoon Kendra was sitting at her desk, writing her piece for the next day's issue, when she heard someone clear his throat. Startled, she looked up, surprised to find that a man was standing at her desk, for she had been so involved in her story that she had neither seen nor heard him approach.

"May I help you, sir?" she asked pleasantly.

The well-dressed man was in his midthirties, balding and wearing wire-rim glasses. "Are you Mrs. Petzold?"

"Yes," Kendra answered, smiling and putting down her pen.

"And you write as Kendra Mills?"

"Yes," Kendra said. "What's this about? Is there anything I can help you with?"

The man reached into his inside jacket pocket and pulled out a folded sheet of paper. He handed the paper to Kendra, announcing, "Mrs. Petzold, also known as Miss Mills, I am a court clerk, assigned to Judicial Circuit Four. And *this*, Miss Mills, is a subpoena, ordering you to appear tomorrow before His Honor, Circuit Judge Matthew G. Bailey."

"For what reason am I to appear?" Kendra asked, looking at the man in surprise.

"To show cause, Miss Mills, to show cause," the man replied cryptically. He smiled smugly. "You made your bed, and now you must sleep in it. You're being held in contempt of court."

The clacking typewriters in the newsroom began to fall silent, the circle of silence moving out concentrically from Kendra's desk like ripples in a pond. Reporters, columnists, and copyboys watched as the court clerk strode triumphantly from the large room. For a long moment there was dead silence; then everyone began talking at once as they rushed to Kendra's desk to see what was going on and to offer their support.

Thomas Petzold had been out of his office when the subpoena was served, but he heard of it as soon as he returned. After a few preliminary telephone calls to his lawyer and other advisors whom he respected, he summoned his entire editorial staff for a meeting. The staff was now much too large to meet in the conference room, so they assembled at one end of the newsroom. Even then they were crowded, filling to capacity the aisles between the dozens of desks that occupied the enormous room, and Petzold had to climb up on one of the desks in order for everyone to see and hear him. He was surprised at how many new, young faces there were. But he was also gratified at the number of faces of his old friends, people who had been with him from the day he had bought the paper more than twenty years before.

He took off his glasses and polished them vigorously before he began to speak—a habit he had developed years ago when English was still a new language to him and that gave him time to translate his German thoughts into English words. He still used it when he wished a moment or two to gather his thoughts.

"I am sure by now you've all heard what happened to Kendra," he finally said. "She has been summoned to appear in court tomorrow to show cause why she shouldn't be held in contempt for writing the truth. I made a few telephone calls and was told that Judge Bailey will withdraw the summons if we print a retraction of her stories and if, in print, Kendra offers an apology to those judges and police officers she has named. If this doesn't happen, Kendra will be subject to a jail sentence, and this newspaper will be assessed a heavy fine, said fine to be levied every day until such time as a retraction is printed."

There was an immediate reaction to this news, and among the restless and discordant objections, people shouted out such things as, "He can't do that," and "Who does that judge think he is?"

"What are you going to do, Mr. Petzold?" one of the reporters asked, his voice rising above the others.

The publisher held up his hand to call for quiet, and when he had everyone's attention again, he replied, "This is what I'm going to do." He looked at his managing editor and directed, "Mr. Dillard, whatever we had planned for the lead story today, move it. Redo the front-page budget. I want room for a box eight columns wide by twelve inches long."

"That's half of a page, Mr. Petzold," Jim Dillard replied.

"Yes, I know it is. But I want to get Judge Bailey's attention. And I want that box above the fold."

"You're the boss," Dillard said with a shrug.

"Say, did you hear that, Kendra?" Petzold said to his wife in a bantering voice. "They think I'm still the boss."

The others laughed.

"This is what will run in the box," Petzold continued. "And I want it set in twenty-four-point type. Bold," he added. He pulled a piece of paper from his pocket, cleared his throat, and began to read:

"*The Chronicle* will continue honestly and fairly and sincerely to criticize the courts and police department.

"*The Chronicle* will not be intimidated.

"*The Chronicle* will not be shackled.

"*The Chronicle* will not be gagged."

Thomas Petzold's announcement was met with loud

cheers and whistles from his entire staff, and when the meeting broke up they hurried back to work, galvanized for battle.

"Let the corrupt judges and policemen do their damnedest," Dillard shouted. "We are newspapermen, by God, and the freedom of the press is one of the most sacred rights in America!"

When Kendra showed up in court the next day to respond to the subpoena she had been issued, the courtroom was so full that Judge Bailey had to order the doors sealed so that no one else could come in. He sat at his bench and looked out over the packed gallery. If he was surprised at the number of people attending, he didn't show it. His face was totally impassive as he brought his hammer down and called Kendra's case.

"Is the defendant represented by counsel?" Bailey asked.

"She is, Your Honor," Kendra's lawyer, a tall, skinny man with thinning gray hair, said, rising from his seat at the defendant's table.

"For the record, please give your name."

"I am Daniel Fenton, Your Honor. I have been retained by the newspaper to represent Mrs. Petzold, also known as Miss Mills."

"Very well," the judge said. "Are you aware, Mr. Fenton, that the court has offered Mrs. Petzold a way to avoid being found in contempt?"

"Begging your indulgence, Your Honor, would you please reiterate the conditions whereby contempt of court may be avoided?" Fenton asked.

"I would be pleased to," Bailey replied. "In her newspaper columns, Mrs. Petzold has leveled some serious and unsubstantiated charges against the judiciary and law enforcement agencies of St. Louis and St. Louis County. I ask you now, as Mrs. Petzold's counsel, if your client is ready to retract any of those stories?"

Fenton leaned down to confer with Kendra. They

spoke in quick, quiet whispers for a moment, and then Fenton straightened.

"No, Your Honor," he said, "Mrs. Petzold is not prepared to retract any of her stories."

A murmur of astonishment rose from the courtroom, but Bailey stilled the onlookers with a stare. He cleared his throat, obviously surprised by Kendra's lack of cooperation, then said, "I see. Then may I ask if she is prepared to back those charges up with witnesses, or other evidence?"

"Your Honor, there seems to be a difference of opinion as to the use of the term 'charges,'" Fenton said.

"How can there be a difference of opinion?" Bailey retorted, clearly annoyed at the lawyer's tactics. "'Charges' seems to me to be a word that is easily understood."

"But our case depends upon—"

"*You have no case, Counselor,*" Judge Bailey interrupted sternly. "I think you should understand that we aren't determining guilt or innocence here. This is a case of contempt, and *I* am the sole arbitrator."

"But Your Honor, if it pleases the court, Miss Mills did not bring charges. She merely wrote a story, detailing the facts as she understood them. Any charges that may result from the information found in those stories would have to be filed by the courts themselves."

"Very well," Judge Bailey grumbled. "If you prefer, we'll refer to them as allegations. But that does not change the situation. If Mrs. Petzold does not wish to withdraw her allegations, then I ask if she is prepared to provide witnesses or evidence to support them."

"May I answer that myself?" Kendra asked.

"You may," Judge Bailey replied.

"Your Honor," Kendra said, standing, "if I were to expose the people who gave me this information, I would be placing them in a great deal of physical danger. I can't do that. It wouldn't be fair to them."

"You will not give me the information?"

"No, Your Honor, I will not."

"Judge Bailey," Fenton said quickly, "what my

client means to say is, is it possible we may explore another avenue of cooperation with the court?"

Bailey shook his head. "There are only two options available: Retract the allegations, or support them with eyewitnesses and evidence."

"Your Honor, it would seem you have my client caught upon the horns of a dilemma. She feels it would be unethical to do the former and dangerous folly to do the latter. Therefore, she can do neither."

"Then we are at an impasse, aren't we, Counselor?" The judge looked at Kendra. "Would the defendant approach the bench?"

With Daniel Fenton at her side, Kendra walked up to stand before Bailey. The expression on the young woman's face wasn't one of challenge or defiance, but neither was it one of submission. She held her head up proudly as Judge Bailey issued his decree.

"I have no recourse, Mrs. Petzold, but to sentence you to jail for twenty days and to fine the newspaper one thousand dollars per day, every day, until such time as you either retract your stories or prove by reliable witnesses and evidence that what you have printed is the truth."

"Your Honor, I request a delay of execution of this sentence, pending appeal," Fenton said.

"Your request is denied, Counselor. Mrs. Petzold is to begin serving her time immediately. Bailiff, escort the prisoner to the holding cell."

The bailiff came up to Kendra, took her by the arm, then led her away. Not until she was out of the courtroom did Judge Bailey bring his gavel down with a loud bang.

"Court is adjourned," he announced.

Immediately after adjournment, the courtroom erupted as the angry spectators gave voice to their concern and outrage over the sudden and unexpected turn of events.

"Judge, may I have a word with you?" Thomas Petzold called across the rail.

Bailey was halfway to the door that led to his

chambers, but he stopped and looked around. "It will do you no good, Mr. Petzold," he replied. "There is a matter of principle involved here. Nothing you can say, short of a printed retraction and apology, will make me change my mind."

Petzold stepped around the rail and approached the judge. "Perhaps if you discussed this matter with Leonard Cline?" he suggested, speaking just loudly enough for the judge to hear but so quietly that no one else could.

Bailey's eyes flashed fearfully, and when he reached up to brush back a shock of silver hair, his hand was shaking. "Leonard Cline?" he replied, his voice little more than a hoarse whisper. "I . . . I don't think I know the name. Why should I want to discuss this with him?"

"Of course you know the name, Judge," the publisher said. "I could remind you of how well you know him, but someone might overhear us, and I'm sure you don't want that."

"What . . . what do you know about Leonard Cline?"

"I'm a newspaperman. I know quite a bit about Mr. Cline. In fact, you might say that I know everything. Of course, what I do with this knowledge is a matter for me to decide. What do you think I should do with the knowledge, Judge? Do you think I should print it?"

"No! That . . . that would be most disastrous," Bailey added weakly.

"Yes, I thought you might feel that way. Perhaps we could come to an accommodation."

"What sort of an accommodation?"

"I think you know. I want you to let Kendra go. Now."

"This is . . . this is blackmail," the judge complained in a shaken voice.

"I suppose you might look at it that way, Judge," Petzold said. "But I would rather regard it as an exchange of favors. You do a favor for me and I'll do one for you. Anyway, from what I hear, you're an old hand at exchanging favors, aren't you?"

The judge glared at his adversary. "Are you proud of yourself, Mr. Petzold?"

"No, Your Honor," Petzold replied candidly and with a surprising amount of respect in his voice. "I am not at all proud of myself. But I cannot . . ." He sighed and pinched the bridge of his nose while he closed his eyes for a moment. Finally he continued, "I *will* not see my wife sent to jail on these charges."

"Very well," Bailey acquiesced. "You wait here. I'll have her released on her own recognizance."

"No, Your Honor," Petzold said. He shook his head sadly. "I'm afraid it has gone much too far for that, now. If I'm going to engage in this type of devilish activity, then I am going to go all the way. What you will do is drop all charges."

"I can't do that, Mr. Petzold. How would that look to everyone?"

"It will look exactly as I want it to look," Petzold replied. "After all, I am the press. Remember?"

"You go too far, sir."

"Drop all charges, Judge," Petzold said simply. "That's the only way we can deal."

Bailey rubbed his chin and stared at the publisher with ill-concealed hate. Finally, with a defeated sigh, he nodded.

"Very well, Mr. Petzold," he said. "I will drop all charges. But your newspaper—"

"Will continue to publish the truth as we see the truth," Petzold interrupted.

Glaring at him, Judge Bailey turned abruptly, then walked quickly out of the courtroom.

Thomas Petzold returned to the defendant's table, where Daniel Fenton was already busily drafting an appeal on his lined tablet. He looked up when Petzold arrived.

"Okay, Tom, listen to this," Fenton said eagerly. "I'm going to appeal this case on the grounds—"

"An appeal won't be necessary," Petzold said, waving off any further discussion.

"What do you mean, it won't be necessary? Of course it will be necessary. You don't think I'm going to let Kendra serve twenty days in jail, do you?"

"The charges have been dropped."

"I'll go to the Missouri Supreme Court today and—" Fenton stopped in midsentence. "What did you say? Did you say the charges have been dropped?"

"Yes."

"But . . . how? I don't understand."

"I had a talk with the Judge."

"Tom, what did you do? My God, you didn't give in, did you? We can beat this. We have very good grounds for a reversal."

"I didn't give in. I just asked him if he would reconsider his action, and he agreed to do so."

Fenton stared at Petzold incredulously. "No," he finally said. "No, there's more to it than that."

The publisher took off his glasses and polished them vigorously as he looked down at the floor, unable to meet Daniel Fenton's gaze. "Yes," he finally admitted. "There is more to it than that."

"What is it? What did you do?"

"I reminded Judge Bailey that as a newspaperman I am often privy to information that would best be kept secret. And I told him that what I know about Leonard Cline is just such an example."

"Leonard Cline?" Daniel was obviously puzzled. "Who the hell is Leonard Cline?"

"Leonard Cline is Judge Bailey's homosexual lover," Petzold explained.

Fenton gasped, staring at Petzold for a long, pregnant moment. When he finally did speak, his voice was barely above a whisper. "His homosexual lover?"

"His current one."

"My God. How on earth did you ever find out about such a thing?"

"I'm the editor of the largest newspaper in St. Louis," Petzold replied. "People are always coming to

me with information like that. I've known about Judge
Bailey and his homosexuality for nearly as long as he has
been on the bench. I never said anything about it before
because I consider a man's private life his own affair."

"But you're using it against him now. That's hardly
the action of a man who considers such things private."

"Yes, I'm using it against him now."

"You don't need to do this, Tom," Fenton said
heatedly. He pointed to his tablet. "We have at least
three excellent reasons for appeal here. I'm certain we'll
get a reversal."

"I appreciate your effort, Daniel, honestly I do. But
I can't take the chance that our appeal would be denied.
I won't let Kendra go to jail, and I'll use any means
necessary to prevent it."

"Do you think Kendra would approve of the means
you've selected?"

"Oh, if she knew about it, I'm quite certain she
wouldn't approve," Petzold admitted. "But she isn't
going to find out, is she?"

The lawyer started putting his material back into his
briefcase. "Are you asking me if I'm going to tell her?"

"I suppose I'm asking you not to tell her."

"Don't worry. She'll not hear of this from me."

"I want you to know that I'm not very proud of
myself," Petzold confessed. "But like Jabez Stone, I was
willing to make a deal with Mephistopheles himself."

"You were, were you? Well, just don't expect me to
win any arguments with your conscience, Tom. My
name is Daniel Fenton, not Daniel Webster."

"Tom! Tom, they let me out!" Kendra abruptly
shouted from the doorway on the other side of the
courtroom. Bubbling with happiness, she ran over to
kiss her husband. "I don't know how the two of you did
it, but you were wonderful!"

"Yes, weren't we?" Fenton said coolly as he buckled
the strap closed on his briefcase. "Well, I must be going.
I'll see you two later. I'm happy for you, Kendra," he
said. "I'm very happy."

"What's wrong with him?" Kendra asked as the lawyer walked away

"Nothing. Why do you ask?"

"I don't know. He seemed to be acting a little strangely," she said. Kendra gasped. "Tom, you didn't promise to stop the articles, did you?"

"No. I made no such promises. You just continue to write as you see fit."

Kendra smiled broadly and kissed Petzold on the cheek. "I knew you wouldn't make any compromises."

When the Petzolds returned to the newspaper office, they found that practically everyone on the staff—from editorial to mechanical to sales—had gathered in the newsroom for an impromptu celebration. There were cookies, cakes, and potato chips, and even a few bottles of bootleg liquor—though someone remarked that it seemed somewhat hypocritical to be drinking in celebration of a victory over the criminal element, since drinking made them a part of the criminal element themselves.

One of the reporters had gone down to the press room for a long piece of newsprint. Now, stretched like a banner all the way across the newsroom, it proclaimed in very large painted letters: JUSTICE TRIUMPHANT!

Many of those present had gone down to the courtroom, and now they were telling the others their version of what had happened. The mystery to everyone was how Kendra had been released, because, according to the last thing any of them had heard, she was to serve a minimum of twenty days in jail.

Regardless of how it happened, though, it had happened, for here she was, among them and celebrating with them. Everyone came around to congratulate her on her victory, and all swore to continue the crusade against crime and corruption.

But through it all Kendra couldn't help noticing that her husband seemed unusually quiet. She knew there was something he wasn't telling her, and it bothered her because it was obviously bothering him.

Less than an hour into the party, Kendra saw Jim Dillard whisper something in Petzold's ear. The publisher turned ashen, excused himself from the others, and left the newsroom.

"I think you ought to go after Judge Bailey now, Kendra," someone was saying to her. "He needs to be shown that he can't dictate to the press."

"Yeah," someone else added. "Let's make him squirm for a while."

"Excuse me," Kendra said. "I need to speak with Tom for a moment."

"Don't be gone long," someone called. "This party is just getting started."

Leaving the noisy, happy throng behind her, Kendra picked her way past the empty desks and through the shadows at the back of the big newsroom to her husband's office. The opaque glass showed a darkened room. She was sure Petzold was in there, because she had seen him enter, but for some reason he hadn't turned on the lights.

Worried, Kendra hurriedly opened the door and saw her husband sitting in the chair behind his desk, leaning forward slightly and resting his forehead on his hands. He didn't even look up when Kendra opened the door.

"Tom?"

"Yes?"

"Tom, darling, what is it? What's wrong? Why are you sitting here in the dark?"

Petzold sighed. "It's Judge Bailey," he said.

"Judge Bailey? What about him?" Kendra groaned and sat down, her spirits sinking. "He's changed his mind, hasn't he? I'm going back to jail." She reached over to touch Petzold. "Don't worry, darling, I'll be all right."

"No," he said. "No, it isn't that."

"It isn't? Then what is it? What about Bailey?"

"He's dead."

"Dead?"

"He just blew his brains out."

"Oh, my God! Oh, Tom, how awful!" She paused for a moment, then asked in a small voice, "You don't think we're the cause, do you?"

"No, my sweet, not we," Petzold answered. "*Me*. I am the cause."

CHAPTER EIGHTEEN

MAY 1927, HOLLYWOOD

As it turned out, Ken Allen had known what he was talking about when he told Demaris Hunter that Greta Gaynor was going to quit the picture. He was also correct when he said that the part would be offered to Demaris. Overnight, it seemed, Demaris had become a star . . . and her first picture wasn't even finished.

Her "stardom" came about as a result of a very active and imaginative publicity department. Pictures of her began appearing in all the local newspapers and in the movie magazines. Babs Benedict's *Hollywood Chatter* column, syndicated in over fifteen hundred newspapers, carried a three-part interview with her, though no such interview ever really took place.

"I never wanted to be a movie star," Babs quoted Demaris as saying. "All I ever really wanted was to become a nurse. But when I saw what enjoyment my poor dying sister got from the movies, I realized that I could provide comfort to millions more people this way than I ever could as a nurse. So, I came to Hollywood and set out to become a movie star, as much for my dead sister as for myself."

Needless to say, Demaris never had a sister, dead or otherwise, and she had never had the slightest intention of being a nurse. Even the smell of a hospital made her sick.

There was, however, some degree of accuracy in the reports that linked her with Ken Allen. At first she spent time with him because they were working in the same movie, and it seemed convenient to do so. But as she got to know him, she couldn't help but like Ken. He was basically a good and sensitive man, always concerned about his fellow workers and equally friendly to everyone from the director to the lowest-paid laborer on the set. He also had the most outrageous sense of humor she had ever encountered.

It was the last day of shooting for *Guns of the Mesa*. During their lunch break Ken asked Demaris if she would spend the weekend with him at his cabin, not too far up the coast from Los Angeles at a place called Point Montoya. She accepted the invitation without a second's thought.

A steady rain began before they reached the cabin, and Demaris thought they might not even make it up the narrow mountain road that led from the coastal highway to his cabin. Despite the hard rain, they got through with very little difficulty. However, Ken's normally spotless midnight-blue Cadillac was well covered with mud by the time they reached their destination.

"You go on in," Ken suggested when he stopped the car in front of the cabin. "I'll bring in our gear."

"Don't you want me to help?"

"No, no, go on in, darlin'," Ken said. "Hell, it's rainin' like pourin' piss out of a boot. No sense both of us gettin' drenched."

Demaris hurried inside, then waited as Ken stood out in the rain, working the latches on the trunk of his car. She felt guilty just standing and watching him get soaked while she was high and dry inside, so she turned away from the door and began exploring the place Ken called his "little retreat."

The small cabin, quite beautiful in a rustic sense, consisted of a bedroom, a large living/dining room, and a kitchen. It had no electricity, but, thanks to a hydraulic system Ken had built, it did have running water. And, as a result of that, there was a complete bathroom, including a bathtub.

Because the approach was by a road that meandered its way up the front side of the mountain, Demaris didn't realize until she was inside the cabin that the structure was clinging to the edge of a cliff, and the back half of the dwelling was actually cantilevered out over the mountain. The living/dining room was in this part of the cabin, and the view through the window was as breathtakingly beautiful as anything Demaris had ever seen.

Ken finally came in, managing somehow to carry all four suitcases in one trip. He kicked the door shut behind him, then, with a grunt, set the bags down on the floor.

"Ken, my poor dear!" Demaris murmured. "You're absolutely soaked!"

"Ah, no matter. I'm not made of sugar; I won't melt," Ken said. "So, what do you think?" he asked, grinning broadly and taking in the cabin with a sweep of his hand.

"Oh, I think this place is absolutely wonderful," Demaris said enthusiastically.

"Yeah, me, too. I thought you might like it."

For the next few minutes Ken showed her around the cabin, pointing out how to use the kerosene stove, how to light the kerosene lamps, and explaining the complicated system of valves and pipes to let the water into the kerosene hot water tank for heating before drawing a bath. When he had finished explaining it, Demaris suggested that she might give that particular feature a firsthand try, if he didn't mind.

"I don't mind at all," Ken said. "That's why I built the damn thing in the first place."

In short order Demaris had drawn heated water for a bath. Lying in the tub, she felt an added sense of luxury over the fact that she could do this in what was otherwise nearly the rugged outdoors.

When the temperature of the bathwater had gradually changed from warm to tepid and then from tepid to cool, Demaris stepped out of the tub, dried off, and put on the scandalously thin robe she had brought to wear. She opened the door and stepped out into the living room, then gasped once before she burst out laughing.

Ken, his back turned to her, was standing at the big window that looked out over the sea. He was wearing a cowboy hat, a pair of boots, and a monogrammed cartridge belt and holster, complete with a pearl-handled pistol.

He was wearing nothing else.

"What's the matter?" Ken asked innocently as he slowly turned to face her. "Why are you laughin'?"

"Oh, no particular reason," Demaris replied, trying to choke back the laughter that bubbled up from deep inside. "I was just wondering. Are you expecting trouble?" she asked, pointing at the pistol. She laughed again.

"What? Oh, you mean this?" Ken asked. He pulled the pistol out and spun the cylinder. "Ah, don't worry, it isn't loaded," he explained. "But you know, darlin', I've been wearin' this so much lately that, well, to tell the truth, I just feel plumb naked without it."

"Do you now?" Demaris giggled. "Have you ever stopped to think that maybe that's just the way I want you?" She walked over to him and began unbuckling his gun belt. "Naked, I mean."

"Is that a fact?" Ken asked.

"That's a fact."

Ken smiled. "Well, I was sorta hopin' we'd get around to that sometime durin' this weekend," he admitted. "I just didn't know we'd get there so quick." He started to take off his hat.

"No, no," Demaris said, reaching up to stop him. "You can keep your hat and your boots on."

"I can?"

"Yes, you can."

"Well, that's awful nice of you, darlin'. But if I do that, how am I goin' to take care of little Demaris?"

Demaris guided Ken to an overstuffed chair and sat him down.

"You don't worry about little Demaris," she said, smiling sweetly as she threw one leg over him and prepared to take him inside of her. "All you have to do is sit there and let little Demaris take care of herself. I'll do all the work for both of us."

ST. LOUIS, MISSOURI

"Let's see," the man in the white apron and hat said, leaning on the diner counter and studying the check in his hand, "you had coffee, a hamburger, and a piece of pie. All told, that's thirty-five cents."

"Thirty-five cents? Since when're you chargin' me to eat here?" Eddie Quick snapped. "For two, maybe three years, I been eatin' at this fuckin' joint, and I ain't never had to pay nothin'."

"Let's just say that the price of business has gone up," the counterman—who was also the owner—said. "Thirty-five cents, Eddie. Let me see your money."

With a growl, Eddie took a quarter and a dime from his pocket and slapped them down on the counter. "When I get the gang re-formed, don't think I ain't goin' to remember this little insult here," Eddie complained.

"Eddie, you get the gang re-formed so that you're the man I deal with instead of Kerry O'Braugh and I'll be glad to go back to the old way of doin' business," the diner owner said. "But until that time I got to go with the man in charge . . . and that ain't you."

"Ahh," Eddie grumbled, "you wait. Folks'll be hummin' my tune pretty soon. You just wait."

"Come see me on that day, Eddie," the diner owner

said. "Right now, you're just another customer." He pulled on the crank, and the cash register popped open. He dropped the quarter and dime inside the drawer and started to shut it when he caught Eddie looking covetously at the money in the drawer. The diner owner reached down to the shelf just below the cash register and came up with a sawed-off shotgun in his hand. He moved it around slowly, almost casually, so that both barrels were pointing at Eddie. To Eddie they looked like the barrels of a couple of Army cannons.

"Don't even think what you're thinkin'," the diner owner warned.

"What the fuck's wrong with you, pointin' that gun at me like that?" Eddie asked, doing his best to sound offended. "I ain't thinkin' nothin'! You're crazy, you know that? You're fuckin' crazy!"

"Next time you get hungry, Eddie, do me a favor, will you? Go someplace else. I don't need your goddamn business."

Eddie slammed out of the diner, then walked on down the street, passing by a dozen or more other businesses where the East Siders—and, by extension, he—once controlled numbers, protection, and a number of other illicit enterprises. He went by a bakery, a tobacco store, a shoe repair shop, and a newsstand, bristling over the fact that even in these small establishments things weren't as they once were. Always before, when the East Siders were in control, Eddie got respect from these people. Paddy Egan had told him once that it wasn't actually respect, it was fear, but as far as Eddie was concerned, one was as good as another.

Now there was neither respect nor fear. In fact, there was ill-concealed contempt, and the same people who used to go out of their way to please him—"Yes, sir, Mr. Quick. No, sir, Mr. Quick"—now turned their backs to him as he walked by.

Well, he'd show them. Damn right. Once he was running things around here, he'd show all of them.

As Eddie started to turn the corner onto his own street, he stopped short. Then he smiled at his lucky break. Through the corner display window of a candy store he glimpsed Kerry O'Braugh going up the front steps of Eddie's apartment building. Eddie didn't know what the gang leader was doing there, but he'd lay odds that it wasn't a friendly visit.

Eddie chuckled. This was the opportunity he'd been waiting for! If he could take out Kerry O'Braugh, he'd be in an ideal position to get back into power again. Hell, he thought, even better, for if he got rid of O'Braugh, that would leave O'Braugh's operation and the East Siders without a leader. Eddie could consolidate both groups.

Instead of turning down his street, Eddie backtracked, then veered into the alley that ran behind his apartment building. Reaching his building, he climbed up the back stairs to the third floor—his floor—then opened the rear door just a crack and peeked through.

It was just as he'd figured: Kerry O'Braugh was waiting out in the corridor for him, his back to Eddie, just standing there as plain as you please. No doubt Kerry had it in mind to start firing when Eddie came up the front stairs. Well, Kerry had some news coming. Eddie Quick was already up the stairs, and if there was any firing to be done, he'd be the one to do it.

He pulled out his pistol, then opened the door as quietly as he could. Slipping out of his shoes so he could move more quietly and keeping his back against the wall, Eddie inched his way down the hall, briefly flattening himself in the doorway of each apartment he passed.

Suddenly the entrance door downstairs opened and slammed. Kerry immediately halfturned and looked over the railing down through the stairwell, forcing Eddie to slip back into one of the door recesses to keep from being seen.

"Iceman," a voice floated up the stairs. "Anyone who doesn't have your cards out . . . Iceman!"

"Mr. Lewis, I'll have fifty pounds," Eddie heard a woman's voice call. That would be Mrs. Callahan. The dumb bitch never put out an ice card, and Eddie was sure it was just so she could flirt with the iceman.

"Yes, ma'am, Mrs. Callahan," the iceman replied.

Kerry, obviously satisfied that it wasn't Eddie arriving home, moved back to where he'd been standing, beside the fire extinguisher. He leaned back against the wall and began examining his nails, while Eddie resumed his slow advance.

It took Eddie about three minutes to work his way down the long corridor. All the while he could hear Lewis the iceman working the two floors below—his banter with the housewives, the opening and closing of doors, the squeak of stairs as he climbed them while carrying his heavy load. Eddie was grateful for the noises, which created the perfect distraction and also covered any slight sound his own stealthy progress made.

Now Eddie was just twenty-five feet from Kerry . . . then fifteen feet . . . then ten . . . then finally close enough to step out, his gun in his hand.

"Looking for me?" he asked, holding the automatic just inches away from Kerry's head.

Kerry O'Braugh whipped around, clearly startled by the sound of Eddie's voice behind him. His hand darted toward the inside of his jacket.

But Eddie cocked his gun and shook his head, warning menacingly, "I wouldn't if I was you. I sure can't miss from this close. What are you doin' up here, anyway?"

"I came to talk to you," Kerry said easily.

"Yeah, I'll just bet you did," Eddie scoffed. "What'd you want to talk about?"

"I want you to come work for me."

"Why should I work for you? Now that Egan's gone, I got my own organization."

"You've got nothin'."

"Wrong," Eddie said. He waved his automatic. "I've got this."

"Yeah, I see."

"You were pretty dumb to come here like this, you

know it?" Eddie said. "I mean, all I got to do is rub you out, then move in and take over . . . not only Egan's operation but yours, too."

"You think you can do that?" Kerry asked smoothly. "You think my boys'd work for you?"

"Some will," Eddie said. "The ones who don't, I'll take care of."

"Like you took care of Rana McClarity?"

"Rana?" Eddie paused for a moment and smiled at the memory. "Yeah," he finally said. "Like I took care of Rana." He laughed a short, mocking laugh. "Don't tell me you was stuck on her." He cocked his head and studied Kerry for a moment; then his mouth spread into a grotesque grin. "You was, wasn't you? You was stuck on her."

"She was a sweet kid," Kerry said. "She deserved better."

"Sweet? Oh, yeah, she was sweet all right. I'll tell you how sweet she was. She was so sweet that when I killed her, I come in my pants."

"You filthy bastard!"

"Does that get to you, O'Braugh?" Eddie taunted. "Well, think about this. When I was chokin' that whore, she started floppin' around like a fish outta water, so I pulled her up against my cock. That was probably the best piece of ass that bitch ever gave." With his free hand, Eddie reached down to grab himself. "Damn me, if I ain't gettin' a hard-on now, just thinkin' about it."

"I'm going to kill you, you son of a bitch," Kerry snarled.

Eddie laughed. "*You're* going to kill *me*? Well, now, that's goin' to be pretty hard for you to do, ain't it? I mean, seein' as how I got the drop on you." He made a motion toward the door of his own apartment. "Since you was wantin' in there so bad, suppose you go on in. Here, I'll give you the key."

Eddie tossed the key to Kerry, then indicated by a nod of his head that Kerry should open the door. Eddie moved in behind him and stuck the gun in his ribs, growling, "Just go on inside."

"Mr. Quick, will you be wanting ice today?" the iceman suddenly asked as he appeared at the top of the stairs with a large chunk of ice on each shoulder.

"No, get out of here, Lewis!" Eddie growled angrily, halfturning toward the intruder.

That brief distraction was all the opportunity Kerry needed. He whirled around, catching Eddie on the bridge of the nose with his elbow. The blow knocked Eddie halfway across the corridor, and he dropped his gun. Both men then dived for the weapon, but they only succeeded in knocking it farther, and it hit the top step, just beside the iceman, then clattered down the stairs one at a time.

The iceman wisely dropped both chunks of ice, then turned and ran, following the gun down the stairs.

Eddie managed to get to his feet first. Spotting the fire extinguisher on the wall, he reached for it to use as a club. In his haste and panic Eddie didn't remove the extinguisher from its clamp, but just wrenched it from the wall, clamp and all. The clamp had been secured to the wall by four long nails, long rusted in place, and when Eddie swung the fire extinguisher at Kerry, Kerry ducked, just missing being ripped open by the nails.

The fire extinguisher was so heavy that swinging it pulled Eddie off balance, his hands extended. That left him wide open for a counterpunch, and his opponent took advantage of the opening, hitting Eddie hard and catching him right on the point of the chin. Eddie's head snapped back, and he went out like a light.

When Eddie Quick opened his eyes several minutes later, he was aware of two things. He couldn't move, and he was cold. For just a moment or two he wondered where he was and what was going on. Then he remembered the fight.

Almost as soon as he remembered the fight, he also became cognizant of where he was, why he couldn't move, and why he was cold. He was lying on the floor of his apartment, he couldn't move because he was bound hand and foot—and he was cold because he was securely wedged between the two large chunks of ice that Lewis had been carrying.

"What the hell?" He heard the words in his brain, but they hadn't come out of his mouth, for he also discovered that he had been gagged. However, he could still see, so he moved his gaze around the room, trying to figure out what was going on.

"Ah, good, you're awake," Kerry O'Braugh said, almost conversationally, as he came to stand over Eddie and looked down with an expression of complete satisfaction on his face. "I wanted you awake," he continued. "I wanted you to know what was happening to you."

"Uhmm, uhmm, uhmmm," was all Eddie could mutter.

"Yes, I suppose you *are* curious," Kerry replied, as if he had understood. He was holding two long boards in his hand, and he lay them a foot apart across the chunks of ice so that they made a bridge over Eddie's chest. "These are slats from your bed," Kerry offered.

Eddie opened his eyes wide in fright and confusion.

"You do remember this, don't you?" Kerry asked, picking up the fire extinguisher. "You tried to brain me with it a few minutes ago." Kerry suspended the fire extinguisher between the two boards, positioning the four long nails directly over Eddie's heart.

"Uhmm, uhmmm, uhmmm!" Eddie squeaked in terror.

Smiling sardonically, Kerry said, "You're right, this damn thing *is* heavy. But I don't think it's quite heavy enough to do the job. Actually, I was kinda worried about that when I decided what I was goin' to do to you, but then I found this hundred-pound bag of sugar in your kitchen. Now, what are you doin' with so much sugar, Eddie? Are you plannin' on makin' your own wine or somethin'? Or do you have one helluva sweet tooth? You should watch it, Eddie. That much sugar isn't good for you."

Straining to lift the heavy bag of sugar, Kerry laid it on top of the fire extinguisher. "Ah, perfect!" he said. "It not only adds more weight, it also holds the fire extinguisher in place on the boards." He paused, then added, "It also helps keep the ice in place, which keeps *you* in place." Kerry got down on his hands and knees, lowering his head so that he could peer underneath the boards. "I'd say there's, oh, no more than half an inch clearance between the points of the nails and your heart," he remarked. "It shouldn't be too long."

He stood up again and smiled down at Eddie. "You understand what's going to happen, don't you?"

"*UHMMM, UHMMM, UHMMM!*" Eddie's muffled scream filled his own ears but barely went any farther. His heart was pounding so hard, he feared he'd impale himself.

"The ice will melt, you see," Kerry explained, though no explanation was needed, "and as it melts, the weight of the sugar on the fire extinguisher will drive the nails into your heart. But it's going to be slow, Eddie. Oh, it's going to be slow."

"*UHMM, UHMMM, UHMMM!*"

"But look at it this way," Kerry concluded. "It'll give you that much longer to remember what a fine old time you had when you killed the woman I loved."

Kerry then turned and walked toward the front door. He looked back and gave Eddie a small salute. "So long, Eddie," he said, smiling coldly. "Nice knowin' ya."

The door closed softly behind Kerry, and Eddie cast his eyes toward the blocks of ice. Despite the cold, he could feel sweat trickling from his armpits, mingling with the puddles of melted ice forming at the bottom of each block. He desperately tried to free himself from his weird prison, but the way his hands and feet had been tied together made any forward or backward movement virtually impossible, and the blocks of ice had him wedged too firmly in place to effect any sideways movement.

He lay there whimpering. Suddenly he felt the point of the longest nail beginning to make the first slight penetration of his skin. Eddie's scream of terror filled his brain like the wail of ten thousand banshees.

LINDBERGH IN DEATH-DEFYING DASH ACROSS ATLANTIC
FLYER MAKES AIR HISTORY
WORLD PAYS TRIBUTE
Paris Applauds St. Louis Pilot's Heroic Flight

(*Special by Cable to* THE CHRONICLE) PARIS, May 22—The French capital, and indeed all the world, viewed Captain Charles A. Lindbergh's arrival today as a modern miracle from the skies. A belief among many is that the young St. Louis man is an incarnation of all the heroes of myth and history.

"Lindbergh has accomplished what most experts believed could not be done," one of the Paris newspapers stated. "With no one to replace him at the wheel or to provide him with some relief from his exhaustion, he crossed the ocean, defeating death by his tenacity and daring. His greatest asset was his courage, and that courage prevailed."

NO NEW LEADS
IN BIZARRE LOCAL MURDER
Mysterious Death Still Unsolved

ST. LOUIS, May 23—According to police, there are no leads in the three-week-old unsolved murder of Edward W. Quick. The body was found bound and gagged on the floor between two puddles of water, with four nails from the bracket of a fire extinguisher, which was held in place by a hundred-pound bag of sugar, driven into his heart. The police have no theory as to why Mr. Quick was killed in such a bizarre way, though the presence of the sugar suggests that it may have been a falling-out among partners in a bathtub-gin scheme.

Unemployed at the time of his death, Mr. Quick had been an associate of Paddy Egan, the well-known racketeer who was himself recently killed in a gang war shoot-out.

FINANCIAL NOTES

STOCK MARKET REMAINS STRONG

NEW YORK, May 22—Summed up, last week's financial news was a medley of satisfactory and unsatisfactory developments. On the satisfactory side may be ranged a continuation of easy-money rates, the influx of gold, the advance in commodity prices, an increase in the purchasing of seasonal goods, and an improved outlook for the iron and steel industry. On the negative side of the picture might be listed the continued refusal of Canfield-Puritex to go public, the devastating floods in the South, the lateness of work on all crops, and ineffectual attempts to stop the tremendous outpourings of crude oil from newly discovered fields.

In the main, the stock market paid little attention to these developments. No one knows, of course, what the market will do in the future, but Wall Street as a whole has been obliged to reach the conclusion that at the present time trading is under strong and skillful professional and institutional control, in which the main thrust is to bid up stocks.

HOLLYWOOD CHATTER

WEDDING BELLS FOR KEN ALLEN AND DE-MARIS HUNTER

Syndicated Column by Babs Benedict

LOS ANGELES, MAY 22—All Hollywood is excited over the fairy-tale wedding of Ken Allen, King of the Range, and director Guy Colby's scintillating new find, Demaris Hunter. They were married in a special ceremony performed at the world premiere of Goliath Studios' first talkie (and Demaris's first starring role). The bridegroom arrived for the wedding ceremony astride his famous horse, Comet, while the bride was delivered to the theater in a limousine provided by the studio.

Guy Colby was best man, and Miss Evelyn Reynolds of Sacramento served as maid of honor. Miss Reynolds earned the honor by winning Goliath Studios' contest on "Why I would like to be Demaris Hunter's maid of honor in 25 words or less."

Advertising copy for Canfield-Puritex Corn Toasties

CORN TOASTIES began on the banks of the Mississippi, where barefoot boys who love to fish and pigtailed girls who love to dance start their days with a crunch. Why do we make them? For the Huckleberry Finn and Becky Thatcher in us all. So full of vitamins and nourishment and vigor is this wonderful treat that it's a shame to call it just a cereal.

CORN TOASTIES, THE BREAKFAST OF WINNERS, is available in grocery stores everywhere. Look for the familiar blue-and-white diagonal-stripe logo, and pick up a box for now and a box for spare. CANFIELD-PURITEX MILLS, ST. LOUIS, MO.

CHAPTER NINETEEN

ADVERTISING COPY FOR CUNARD LINES, 1927:

(In a causerie in the Louis XVI restaurant)

"... AS FOR US, WE ALWAYS TAKE THE AQUITANIA"

"We waited until the last minute . . . had to get a fast ship direct to France . . . Lucy will linger at Newport, with an engagement to see the Grand Prix at Longchamps . . . John has to report at the embassy in Paris in less than a week . . . Jim is down for polo at Ranelagh . . .

"And the new staterooms are so large and comfortable . . . actually room for our wardrobe trunks . . . I'm trying to duplicate their chintzes for the guest rooms we're putting into the new wing of

our Palm Beach house . . . their bathrooms outdo
my own latest extravagances . . .

"As for food, last night—for pure swank—Mildred
asked for caviar *au blinis;* replied imperturbable
Auguste, 'Certainly, Madame. And with your order
may I suggest a simple dessert: a pineapple royale
from St. Michael's in the Azores?' . . . John cried
for spring lamb and got it—straight from the South
Downs . . . Wonder if we could afford to buy
Auguste away from the Line.

"Our friends all go Cunard."

LATE SUMMER 1927, ABOARD THE AQUITANIA

"Oh, Eric, isn't it beautiful?" Tanner Twainbough
enthused as they dressed in their first-class stateroom on
the boat deck on what was their first night out on the
New York-bound Atlantic crossing. The passage had
been arranged and paid for by Pendarrow House, because the publisher wanted Eric to return to New York
for a launching party for his second book, *Stillness in the
Line*.

"I must confess that it's certainly different from the
accommodations on our last crossing," Eric remarked.
He was standing in front of a mirror, trying to tie his bow
tie but having little success. "Damn!" he swore. "Can't
we just send out for sandwiches? Why do we have to
dine with the captain, anyway?"

"Because it's an honor to be invited to the captain's
table," Tanner replied. "Besides, he's a fan of yours. I've
heard that he read *A Time For All Things* and thinks it a
wonderful book."

"If he's that big a fan, maybe he'll accept me without
a tie," Eric suggested.

"Here, let me do it," Tanner said, coming over to
perform the task. As she stood in front of him, Eric put
his arms around her waist and pulled her to him.

"I still like my idea of sending out for sandwiches.
We could get naked, eat them in bed, then afterward we

could . . ." He let the sentence hang, though he raised and lowered his eyebrows a few times in a comical expression of lechery.

"You're impossible," Tanner said with a laugh. "Anyway, who's to say we can't eat at the captain's table and *then* afterward we could . . ."

"Naked?"

"Afterward, yes. However, I think it would be a terrible breach of etiquette to be naked at the captain's table, don't you? Now, hold still and let me get this."

There was a discreet knock on the door.

"Come in," Eric called, and when the door opened, a pretty young woman, dressed in a Cunard Line uniform, stepped inside.

"Excuse me, your worship," the girl said with a slight curtsy. "Would you be the party in need of a nanny?" She spoke with a heavy Irish brogue.

"Yes, we are," Tanner replied. "What's your name?"

"Molly Magee, madam."

"It's good of you to come, Molly," Tanner said. "The baby is in the other room."

"And how old would the wee one be?"

Tanner laughed. "He's not exactly a wee one," she said over her shoulder while continuing her effort at getting Eric's tie done right. "He's five-and-a-half and quite a young man—though perhaps not quite old enough to dine at the captain's table. Ohh," she groaned disgustedly at her sloppy attempt at tie tying, undoing the little piece of cloth and starting over again. "I'm not doing any better tying this thing than you were," she told Eric.

"Would you be wantin' me to tie that for you?" Molly asked.

"Can you?"

"Aye. 'Tis one of my few accomplishments," the girl said, her eyes twinkling. She stepped up to Eric and with a few deft moves had the bow perfectly formed.

"Why, thank you, Molly," Eric said, checking out his reflection in the mirror.

"What's your young lad's name?"

"Hamilton," Tanner answered. "Ham Twainbough."

"Hamilton is it, now? Ah, 'tis a fine-soundin' name," Molly said. She started toward the other room to check on her charge. "Now, off with the two of you. Have a fine time at the captain's table. And don't you be frettin' none about young Hamilton. I'll look after him as if he were my own."

"Thank you, Molly," Tanner said, grabbing her beaded evening bag from the chair. "Come along, darling," she said to Eric, propelling her reluctant husband out of the cabin.

After meandering along several corridors, they reached the *grande salle à manger*, and Tanner smiled with pleasure at the sight. The walls of the dining room were made of etched-glass panels three stories high and illuminated from behind to cast a bright but nonglaring light. The great dining hall was alive with the rustle of silk and the buzz of conversation, and all the men were appropriately dressed in either tuxedos, tails, or dress uniforms, while the women wore butterfly-bright gowns and sparkling jewelry that glistened and glittered at their neck, wrists, and earlobes.

Eric and Tanner stepped to the chief steward's podium, although Eric's attention was focused on the room at large.

"May I have your name, sir?" the chief steward asked.

"Mr. and Mrs. Twainbough," Eric replied absently, still looking out over the room as he handed the steward a card that indicated they were to be seated at the captain's table.

"Eric? Eric, lad, is that you?" the chief steward asked in an astonished voice.

Eric immediately turned and looked at the elegantly dressed officer. Suddenly twenty years peeled away, and the author grinned broadly.

"Hello, Snuffy."

"My God, it *is* you!" the chief steward exclaimed. He glanced at the young steward standing beside him who was observing the conversation with curious interest, then told Eric, "Uh, nobody calls me Snuffy any-more. I use Jarvis."

Eric laughed. "Well, it's good to see you again, no matter what you're called nowadays. I remember when the *Lusitania* was sunk, I thought for a while you may have gone to the bottom with her."

Jarvis chuckled. "I did go into the water at that. But, then, you know what that's like, eh, Eric?"

"I do indeed. I do indeed."

"I read your book," Jarvis said. "I guess all that scribbling you used to do in the cabin finally paid off."

Eric nodded. "It took a while, but I finally came up with a few words someone was willing to read. But, now, look at you. You've come up in the world a bit yourself. You always said that one day you'd be a chief steward, and here you are."

"Aren't we a pair, though?" Jarvis mused. "Me here at the chief steward's roost, and you, with your lovely missus, dining at the captain's table as only the most important passengers do." He cleared his throat. "And here I am chatting with you like a bloody idiot, just as if you had nothing better to do."

"What better is there to do than talk with an old shipmate?" Eric asked.

"Did you say shipmate, sir?" the young steward asked, his curiosity obviously finally getting the better of him.

"Aye, shipmate," Jarvis answered. "Now, get on with it, Adams. Escort Mr. and Mrs. Twainbough to the captain's table."

"Aye, aye, sir," Adams replied, starting through the dining room with Eric and Tanner behind. When they were well out of earshot of his superior, Adams turned toward Eric. "What was that you called Mr. Jarvis, sir? Snuffy?"

"I called him that," Eric admitted. "But I wouldn't recommend that *you* do."

"No, sir," Adams replied, trying hard to cover his laugh. "I wouldn't think of it."

The captain greeted Eric effusively, then introduced him to the others at the table as "one of the finest writers" he had ever read. Eric was a little self-conscious over all the praise and felt somewhat out of place at a table occupied, in the main, by titled Englishmen and very wealthy Americans. One of the Americans, who was third-generation money from Louisville, didn't make it any easier for him. The man's name was Samuel Roberts, and apparently his money came from thoroughbred horses, for he had been talking about breeding when Eric and Tanner joined the table. He continued to monopolize the conversation, though changing his focus.

"Twainbough, Twainbough . . . now, what kind of name is that?" Roberts asked. "Is it English?" He looked at the man to his left. "Sir James, have you ever heard that name?"

"Not that I can recall," the man who had been introduced as Sir James Eddington replied.

"It's my name," Eric explained.

"Yes, to be sure. But what are the ethnic origins of the name? Where are you from?"

"Wyoming."

The others around the table laughed.

"Samuel, leave the man alone," someone said. "He isn't one of your horses, so there is no need to establish his lineage."

Again the others laughed.

"Yes, but, breeding will tell . . . in humans as well as horses. I mean nothing by it, you understand, Twainbough, but quite often people such as you, who come into wealth rather suddenly, as say a movie star or a very successful athlete or someone who writes a best-selling book, are quite unprepared to deal with the responsibilities of their position. And, of course, the poor young woman who marries such a man is even more ill-equipped to handle the situation."

"Are you talking about me, Mr. Roberts?" Tanner asked innocently.

"Yes, I am, actually. You'll pardon my bluntness, but truth is blunt. Now, here you are, my dear, mingling in a society that, in your youth, you could have only dreamed about. But I tell you now, it takes more than mere money to give one the background necessary to function in company with the better people. One must be born to it . . . the mere acquisition of an enormous amount of money means nothing. And in this case it is a much more difficult lesson for the wife to learn than for the husband. Suppose, for example, your husband's books quit selling. Suppose you had to return to, say, the same style of living you experienced before you were married. Could you do that?"

"Oh, I would never do that," Tanner said sweetly. "I am married to Eric for better or worse. So, no matter what happens, I will always be by his side."

"You don't understand what I'm saying," Roberts continued, shaking his head slightly.

"No, Sam, *you* don't understand," Sir James said. "You *are* an ass, aren't you? Excuse the language, ladies, but there is no other way to describe him. He *is* an ass. Don't you know who this lady is?"

"Why, she's Mrs. Twainbough."

"Yes, but she is also . . ."

"That's all right," Tanner said, holding up her hand. She smiled sweetly at Roberts. "I am perfectly content to be known as Mrs. Eric Twainbough."

Happily, the subject of the conversation moved on to other things, though, by the expression on Samuel Roberts's face, it was obvious that he was still trying to figure out who Tanner was and if he had committed an unpardonable faux pas by not recognizing her.

It turned out that the captain was not the only one at the table to have read Eric's book. Sir James and one of the ladies had also read it, and the conversation was enlivened by the fact that they could go to the source to ask about specific events.

"My favorite scene was on board the *Lusitania*," the captain said. "I was particularly struck with the authenticity of the scenes in the crew's quarters. How were you able to capture that so vividly?"

Eric chuckled. "I was a cabin steward on the *Lusitania*," he replied.

"Were you now? Well, so was my chief steward. Perhaps you knew him?"

"Oh, yes, I knew Mr. Jarvis quite well. In fact, we were cabin mates then. Do you recall the part in the book where one of the stewards is washed overboard during a storm, and another steward saves him by throwing him a line?"

"Yes, that was quite a vivid scene."

"I was the foolish steward who was washed overboard, and Donald Jarvis was the brave young man who risked his life to save me."

Later that night Eric stood at the open porthole of his cabin, looking out at the moon-silvered carpet spread on an otherwise black sea. He was naked, and on the bed behind him Tanner was in the same condition.

"Uhmm," Tanner said, stretching lazily. "Wouldn't it be nice if we made another baby that time?"

Eric chuckled. "You really think you could go though having a baby again?"

"I could, but I don't know about you. You're the one who fainted, remember?"

"You're never going to let me live that down, are you?"

Tanner snickered. "Never."

Eric returned to the bed and sat down beside her. A small night-light burned from a wall socket near the floor, and Tanner's breasts were clearly visible in the soft light. From there on down, however, she was in shadow. Eric put his hand into the shadow and caressed her, feeling the sharp edge of her pelvic bone, a smooth expanse of skin, and the damp, tangled bush of her pubic hair. Tanner shivered under his touch.

"Cold?"

"No," Tanner said. "Excited."

"Excited?" Eric laughed. "My God, woman, you are insatiable."

Tanner giggled. "Not *that* kind of excited," she said. She raised her arms and put them around his neck.

"Though I could get that way again real soon. Sooner than you, I bet."

Eric kissed the palms of her hands and the inside of her wrists. "Don't be so certain about that. Anyway, what are you excited about?"

"Going home again," she said. "I'm looking forward to finishing the business in New York so we can visit St. Louis, where I can show off."

"Show off?"

"Of course, show off," Tanner replied. "My beautiful son and my best-selling-author husband. It will be what you might call a triumphant return."

"I wish we weren't coming home like this, though," Eric said.

"Like what?"

"Oh, first class, on a ship full of pompous asses."

Tanner laughed. "Mr. Roberts was rather full of himself, wasn't he?"

"I can't travel like this, Tanner," Eric complained. "If I do, I'll lose connection with real people and with reality. I won't be able to write."

"Well, how do you want to travel?"

"I don't know," Eric said. "I'd like to look into it, though. Maybe we could come back on a freighter or something. You can book passage on them, you know. The accommodations are rather spartan, I understand, but I'd much prefer something like that to this pampered, perfumed, pretentious passage."

"Ooh, four p's," Tanner said. "That's quite the alliterative sentence." She laughed, then pulled Eric's face down closer to hers. "Any way you want to come back is fine with me, darling," she said. "You choose, Ham and I will follow. Now, about what you said a moment ago . . ."

"What?"

"When I said I could get excited sooner than you, you said, 'Don't be so certain about that.' Did you mean it?"

Eric smiled at her, then guided her hand through the dark. "You tell me."

She gasped in surprise. "Oh!" she said. "You were right! How long have you been that way?"

"Do you want to talk or make love?"

Tanner kissed him then, a deep, tongue-tangling kiss, and pulled him down on top of her, spreading her legs to facilitate his entry. Eric chuckled deep in his throat, for that was just the answer he wanted.

EXCERPTS FROM THE ST. LOUIS CHRONICLE, OCTOBER 1, 1927:

TORNADO STRIKES CITY

73 Dead, Hundreds Injured

ST. LOUIS—A deadly funnel cloud dipped out of the dark, threatening sky yesterday afternoon, ripping up several houses in the western part of the city. So far the death count is at 73, though it may go much higher as the debris is cleared. Six square miles were affected by the storm, which destroyed over 5,000 homes and buildings. Damages may exceed $75 million.

The chief of police for the city of St. Louis has issued an order that all looters are to be shot on sight.

From the sports page:

BABE RUTH HITS 60 HOME RUNS

NEW YORK—Thomas Zachary, a southpaw pitcher for the Boston Red Sox, delivered a fast ball, high and inside, to George Herman (Babe) Ruth yesterday. The bambino slapped the old pill into the right center-field bleacher seats of Yankee Stadium and established at 60 a new record for the number of home runs hit in one year.

As hats soared into the air and handkerchiefs were waved in celebration, Ruth very precisely put his foot on each bag as he rounded the bases, as if underscoring his feat.

All four Yankee runs were the result of Ruth's hits, and with that victory the Yankees were assured of the American League pennant, just edging out the St. Louis Grays.

SWAMPWATER PUCKETT WINS 27TH GAME

ST. LOUIS—"I'd rather have the pennant," Lenny "Swampwater" Puckett said when he was informed that he had been selected as the American League's best pitcher of the year. The young man from the swamps of southeast Missouri was modest and reserved as he was presented with the prestigious award by the Baseball Writers Association of America. He seemed more interested in the fact that the St. Louis Grays barely missed winning the pennant this year than in the honor he had just received.

Puckett didn't want to talk about himself and refused to set any personal goals for next year, preferring instead to discuss the goals of the team. He promised that in 1928 St. Louis baseball fans would see the Grays in the World Series. When asked if the Grays might play against the Cardinals, Swampwater said that it didn't matter to him whom they played, as long as they made it to the October classic.

Swampwater Puckett won 27 games while losing only 5 this season. An added distinction in this year of the long ball is the fact that Puckett gave up only 5 home runs all year and only one of those to Babe Ruth.

Book Review:

STILLNESS IN THE LINE. Eric Twainbough, Pendarrow House. $2.95.

In this riveting book of the Great War, Twainbough proves to one and all that his phenomenal success with *A Time for All Things* was well deserved.

Stillness in the Line follows one platoon of American soldiers and depicts how the war affects them, humanizing an event that all too often is portrayed in terms too gargantuan for the average person to comprehend. In the opinion of this reviewer, *Stillness in the Line* is the best book of the season—and perhaps the best book to come out of the war.

From the entertainment page:

HOLLYWOOD CHATTER

Syndicated column by Babs Benedict

Demaris Hunter visited Havana, Cuba, last week to "absorb the atmosphere" for her new picture, *Havana Holiday*. Though the movie will be filmed in Hollywood on back-lot sets and sound stages transformed by movie magic into Havana, Miss Hunter felt that her performance would be greatly improved if she actually visited the location before they started filming. Goliath Studios agreed and sent her on a "goodwill journey."

The trip had an added benefit, as far as Miss Hunter was concerned. The lovely young actress hails from St. Louis, Missouri, and on the way back to Hollywood she was able to visit family and friends during a stopover in the Gateway City. This was Demaris's first opportunity to return home since becoming one of Hollywood's brightest new stars.

Society News:

PUBLISHER'S WIFE GIVES BIRTH TO SON

At 7:37 P.M. on September 30, Mr. and Mrs. Thomas Petzold became the proud parents of a baby boy, named Thomas Amon. The baby, born at St. Luke's Hospital, weighed in at 6 pounds 12 ounces and measured 23 inches long.

Mother and baby are doing very well and are receiving friends until 4:00 P.M. on October 3, at which time Mr. Petzold plans to return his family to their home on Lindell Boulevard.

MR. AND MRS. ERIC TWAINBOUGH HONORED BY RECEPTION

A reception was held at the St. Louis Country Club last night in honor of the visit home of best-selling novelist Eric Twainbough, an adopted St. Louisian, his wife, Tanner, a St. Louis native, and their young son, Hamilton. Host for the reception was Ludwig Tannenhower (of Tannenhower Brewery), the father of Mrs. Twainbough.

At either end of the long buffet table were magnificent ice sculptures, one of the Eiffel Tower and the other the Statue of Liberty, signifying the fact that the Twainboughs live in France. As an added item of interest, a tiny model of Lindbergh's *Spirit of St. Louis* was suspended halfway between the two sculptured pieces, paying homage to the recent flight of another St. Louis celebrity.

CHAPTER TWENTY

Rocky Rockwell glanced over at Willie Canfield, who was looking out the right side window of the airplane. From their vantage point of five thousand feet up, they could clearly see the extent of the damage done by the tornado that had struck St. Louis two days before. It looked as if a giant bulldozer had cleaved an erratic path through the western part of the city.

Rocky shouted over the engine noise, "It's amazing to see just how much destruction that tornado caused, isn't it?" Rocky was sitting in the left seat, holding a three-quarter-round wheel in his hands.

"Yeah, it sure is," Willie answered. "Rocky, what would happen to an airplane caught in a tornado?"

"That's not something you ever want to think about," Rocky said.

"It'd be pretty bad, huh?"

"Oh, it depends on what you call bad," Rocky replied. "If you call ripping off the wings and tail assembly, then crushing the plane into a little ball bad . . . then, yes, it'd be pretty bad."

Willie laughed. "I get the point," he said. "Stay away from them."

"And thunderheads and ice," Rocky added.

"Okay," Willie agreed. "You're the instructor, I'm the student. I'll do whatever you say."

"Damn right you'll do whatever I say," Rocky remarked, "if you want to remain my student."

"Oh, I do, I do!"

Rocky smiled at the youth and thought again of how much Willie reminded him of his uncle, whom he had first met in a railroad depot in Paris, France, proudly come to join in fighting the Great War. He could recall that initial meeting as if it were yesterday.

A dozen trains sat inside the cavernous track shed of the train station on the day Rocky went down to pick up a fresh new recruit for the Lafayette Escadrille, or "Lafayette Squadron" as the Americans who flew for the French called themselves. The new man's name was William Canfield, and the word was that this Canfield was a very wealthy young man. Rocky thought about that as he waited to meet him, wondering if the new guy was nothing but a spoiled and pampered rich kid for whom the war was just a diversion. If that was all it meant to him, the moneyed young fellow was going to have a quick, and perhaps rude, awakening.

That awakening would immediately come if Canfield so much as looked over at the hospital train, where scores upon scores of litter patients lay four rows deep for the entire length of the train. Besides those patients on litters there were dozens of ambulatory wounded, still in their frontline uniforms and covered with the mud and sometimes the blood of the trenches. Some of the walking wounded were wearing arm slings, others

hobbled about on crutches, while still others had their
heads swathed in dirty bandages.

Neither the wounded soldiers nor the civilians
looked at each other, and Rocky knew why. The soldiers
were inhabitants of a world so alien to that of the civilians
that they had closed ranks about themselves, as if
refusing to recognize that anyone else existed. Rocky
was a part of that soldiers' world, and now he was going
to bring someone new into it . . . perhaps to die. He
hoped that the recruit would be worthy of the honor of
dying.

Taking a deep breath as if about to plunge into an
icy stream, Rocky stepped out onto the train platform
and began calling out in English. It was an effective way
of paging, for if Canfield was here, he'd easily be able to
hear English being spoken in the midst of all the French.

"I'm looking for Canfield! I'm looking for William
Canfield!" Rocky shouted. He repeated the call several
times, then declared, "If there is an American here by
that name, I wish you'd answer me. I feel foolish as all
hell standing here yelling like this!"

"I'm Billy Canfield," a young American finally answered, coming toward him.

Rocky met him halfway and stuck out his hand in
greeting, introducing himself. Then he asked for and got
Billy's baggage claim ticket as well as several francs.
Rocky handed the ticket and franc notes to a porter,
instructing the man in French as to the luggage's dispo-
sition. He then led the new recruit out of the station.

"I'm from St. Louis," a talkative—and obviously
excited—Billy told Rocky as they snaked their way along
the platform. "I attended Jefferson University there. Did
you go to school anywhere?"

"No," Rocky told him. "I could've, I suppose, but I
was too busy racing cars."

"Racing cars?" Billy snapped his fingers and stared
at his new acquaintance. "Rocky Rockwell! Yes, I thought
your name sounded familiar. You set the world's land-
speed record, didn't you?"

"Not just land, my friend. I did one hundred sixteen

miles per hour. No one has ever gone that fast in *anything*."

"I did."

"You? The hell you say! When? How?"

That was when Rocky learned about the airplane Bryan McPheeters had designed and built, how it handled, and how it had been clocked at over 150 miles per hour during a test flight for the U.S. Army. The speed was unofficial, Billy explained, because a collapsed wing had made it impossible for the aircraft to land safely, and so the terms of the test flight weren't met. He went on to say that he thought a strengthening of the wing spar would have prevented the wing failure, but it was too late; the Army wouldn't let the tests continue.

It was there in the first moments Rocky and Billy spent together that the dream of designing, building, and flying bigger, faster, and better airplanes was born. And during the next several months of the war, Billy brought that dream out over and over again, polishing it and refining it and honing it until by the sheer power of his own dedication he managed to pull Rocky into the dream with him.

But the dream ended for the young St. Louisian when he proved, beyond a shadow of a doubt, that he was worthy of the honor of dying with brave men. Billy Canfield was shot down and killed during an air raid conducted against a German airship field in the closing months of the war.

Rocky had lost many friends during the war, and the loss of each one of them had hurt him. But Billy Canfield was a special friend, so losing him had hit very hard. It was, therefore, particularly gratifying to Rocky to be able to be a mentor to Billy's nephew, young Willie Canfield. Not only was Willie named after his uncle, he shared the same love of flying, coupled with a lack of pretension over what was considerable wealth. In fact, Rocky thought as he looked over at the youth, Willie reminded him so much of his good friend that the two established a quick and abiding friendship unaffected by the difference in their ages.

"What?" Willie asked, realizing that Rocky was looking at him.

"Nothing," Rocky replied, shouting to be heard over the noise of the engines.

"I thought you were about to say something."

"If I say something, you'll know it," Rocky yelled.

Willie looked through the side window again. A mere six feet away, suspended from the high wing of the monoplane, was a 450-horsepower Wright-Whirlwind engine, dutifully spinning its large wooden prop. When Willie faced front again, he was looking through the whirling propeller of the nose engine at the Mississippi River just off to the left and running parallel with their course. Hanging from the left wing was a third engine. Willie and Rocky were riding in the Tri-Star, a new three-engined, all-metal monoplane that had been designed and built by Rockwell-McPheeters Aviation.

Willie looked down at the instrument panel. More than a dozen needles quivered in their respective dials, more than twice the number of instruments he'd ever seen on any other airplane panel.

"How do the instruments look?" Rocky shouted above the roar.

"Great!" Willie shouted back. "They're all showing just what they should."

"Glad to hear it. Well, it's about time to go back. You want to take us in?" Rocky offered.

"What? Do you mean I can have the landing?"

"Sure, you can have the landing," Rocky said. "After all, you're nineteen now—old enough to be responsible. Just stay out of tornadoes," he added jokingly.

"I'll stay out of them, I promise!" Willie said, placing his hands on the control wheel that protruded from the instrument panel in front of him.

"Okay, you've got it!" Rocky said, holding his hands up in the air to show Willie that the youth was now in control.

After relinquishing the wheel, Rocky turned and

looked back through the small door at the rear of the cockpit toward the rows of empty seats in the long cabin behind them. On the left side of the airplane were four rows of two seats. Across the narrow aisle a single file of seats ran down the right side of the cabin. The right side also had two additional seats across from the rear door, making a total of fourteen passenger seats. The plane also had a tiny galley and restroom.

"Ah, just look back there," Rocky mused proudly. "Can you picture it, Willie? Full of passengers, every one of them holding a ticket for our airline that they bought with cold hard cash?"

"And you and me up here," Willie added excitedly.

Rocky turned back around in his seat and patted the instrument panel in front of him. "This airplane is the baby that'll do it for me and Bryan, Willie," he said. "I know it is."

"What did Demaris Hunter think of it when you showed it to her?" Willie asked.

"Why would you ask that? What makes you think I showed it to Demaris Hunter?"

"She was here, wasn't she? I read in the paper that she was here."

"As a matter of fact, she was."

Willie looked over at Rocky and smiled. "And you *are* sweet on her, aren't you?"

"Sweet on her?" Rocky laughed. "Now what in Sam Hill makes you say a thing like that? She's married, for crying out loud."

"Yeah, to Ken Allen, the movie star. But you've got her picture on the inside of your locker in the hangar."

"Well, if I've got her picture on the *inside* of my locker, how did you see it?"

"I looked."

"So, you looked, did you?" Rocky said. He raised a knuckle on one of his fists, then reached over and began rubbing on top of Willie's scalp. "This is for young men who look into places where they have no business," he teased.

"Ow!" Willie cried, laughing. He twisted around in

his seat and when he did, the airplane fell off on one wing.

"Careful, you're going to break our airplane," Rocky quipped, but he quit applying what he called the "Dutch rub."

"Well, did you show it to her?"

"I thought you were going to take us home," Rocky said without answering the question.

"Oh, yeah," Willie replied, rolling the airplane to the right, beginning the 180-degree turn that would take them back to Lambert Field.

Willie Canfield was now a junior at Jefferson University, and, as had his older brother, John, before him, Willie was studying business. Unlike John, however, Willie's heart wasn't in it. Willie loved to fly, and he had pestered Rocky until the aviator had agreed to teach him. Now Willie used every spare moment he could find to build up his flying time, and when Rocky had offered him the opportunity to come along on the final shakedown flight of the Tri-Star, Willie jumped at the chance.

This was the Tri-Star's final flight before the expected Civil Aviation Authority certification. Rocky didn't expect any trouble. From the first flight until this one the Tri-Star had been the sweetest-flying airplane he had ever flown. It had performed exactly as it was supposed to.

Rockwell-McPheeters Aviation Company had built the Tri-Star to use as the flagship of its new airline, Mid-America Transport. Because the Tri-Star had not been certified, Mid-America was not yet flying passengers. But they did have their routes assigned to them and were due to start soon. Mid-America was given routes north to Chicago, south to Memphis, and west to Kansas City. In addition to Tri-Star 1, the plane they were currently flying, two other Tri-Stars were sitting on the ramp, waiting to begin service. Only one of them had to be certified by the CAA; the others of its type would automatically pass.

"For your information, she didn't even see the

airplane," Rocky said a moment later, finally answering Willie's question about Demaris Hunter.

"Why not?" Willie asked. He had shortly before entered the landing pattern, and now he lined up for his final approach. "I mean, you are sweet on her, aren't you?"

"She's a good kid," Rocky said, "but we're just friends, that's all. I told you, she's married, and so am I."

Willie looked at Rocky in surprise. "You aren't married."

"Sure I am," Rocky insisted. "I'm married to this," he said, patting the airplane. "Watch your sink rate. Better add a little more power."

Willie responded by moving the three throttles forward. The engines increased in power, and the rate of descent of the airplane flattened out enough to correct the error.

"Sorry. I've never flown anything this big or this heavy before," Willie apologized.

"Not many people have," Rocky replied. "Once we get this baby certified and flying, it'll be the biggest transport in America. She's eight hundred pounds heavier than the Ford Tri-Motor and twenty miles per hour faster."

Willie rounded out at the bottom of the descent, held the wheels off the runway for as long as the airplane would fly, then let it drop gently onto the ground.

"Beautiful, kid, beautiful! I may make a pilot out of you yet," Rocky joked.

Suddenly, from nowhere it seemed, another airplane landed just in front of them. Apparently the single-engine biplane had started its final approach above and slightly behind the Tri-Star at an angle that made each of them invisible to the other. The pilot of the biplane apparently had no idea he had come so close to disaster and was still unaware that a huge aircraft was bearing down on him.

Willie stood on the brakes of the Tri-Star, putting so much pressure on the system that the line to the left brake ruptured. That caused the right brake to grab, and the large airplane whipped sharply to the right in an extreme ground loop, then flipped over on its back.

The nose propeller was chewed up as it came in contact with the ground. That was immediately followed by the smashing of the windshield, and Willie threw his arms in front of his face to keep from being cut by flying glass. The plane slid upside down along the runway for the length of two football fields, screeching, snapping, and popping in an awful cacophony of sound before it finally came to rest in the grass about fifty feet to the right of the runway.

Stunned, Willie hung suspended from his seat belt, staring through the grotesquely twisted frame of what moments before had been the front of the plane. He could see nothing but misshapen sheet metal, splintered tubing, and dangling hoses and lines. With the sudden stillness of the three engines and the cessation of the screeching slide, Willie found himself wrapped in a blanket of eerie silence. However, that silence wasn't absolute, for the youth could distinctly hear something dripping.

"Kid, are you okay?" Rocky asked, also suspended upside down from his seat.

"Yeah, I think so. How about you?"

"I'm all right for now, but we'd better get the hell out of here," Rocky replied. "I smell fuel."

"Gasoline? Oh, shit!" Willie exclaimed. He fumbled wildly with his seat belt, feeling a hot rush of panic when he thought he couldn't get it open. Finally he succeeded, getting free at about the same time Rocky managed to get loose from his own restraint.

"Here!" Rocky directed. "Let's go out through here. I can see a little space under the wing."

Rocky was indicating the window just to the left of the pilot's seat, and because he was nearest the window, he went through first. Once outside he turned to help Willie, half lifting and half dragging him through the small opening. There was practically no room for maneuvering, so the two men had to crawl, or more accurately wriggle, on their bellies to squeeze out from under the wreckage.

After what seemed an eternity they were clear of the plane, and they started running. They had gotten about fifty yards away when the fuel tanks exploded. Willie could feel the sudden blast of heat at his back, but by now both had run far enough that neither of them were hurt.

"Oh, Rocky, I wrecked your plane," Willie groaned as they turned to look at the fiercely burning fire.

"No, you didn't kid," he said. "You saved our hides. If we had hit that guy who landed in front of us, we'd both be dead now. Him, too."

"What the hell did he land in front of us like that for?"

"Wasn't his fault either," Rocky said. "We were in each other's blind spot. It's just one of those freak things."

The air filled with the sirens of the airfield's fire truck and ambulance as the two vehicles rushed out to the scene of the accident. In addition to the emergency vehicles, the crash also managed to attract everyone else at the airfield so that a large crowd of people emptied out from all the hangars and buildings, then came running toward Willie and Rocky.

Byran McPheeters was the first person on the scene because he was riding on the running board of the fire truck. He jumped off before the truck had completely stopped and ran toward the plane.

"Rocky!" the Irishman shouted anxiously. "Rocky, are you and the lad all right?"

"We're fine," Rocky said. He nodded toward the burning, twisted wreckage. "But I can't say the same for the Tri-Star."

"To hell with the plane," Bryan said. "'Tis the two of you I was worried about."

The firemen began playing their hoses on the burning wreckage, but the gasoline-fed flames seemed impervious to their efforts. The fire continued to roar, and the smoke boiled high into the sky, shooting up a pillar of heavy black smoke that could be seen from all over St. Louis.

A few minutes later a black Ford Roadster came bouncing out across the field. When the car stopped, a thin, wiry little man got out and walked over to look at the burning wreckage. His eyes were quick and expressive, but there was a sadness in them, too—the sadness of a man who genuinely loved airplanes and was witnessing the death of one of the newest and finest models.

"Uh-oh," Rocky said.

"Who's that?" Willie asked.

"McKirk, the CAA Inspector."

Jack McKirk walked over to stand near Rocky and Willie. "What happened?" he asked.

"Didn't you see it?" Willie replied. "That Bellanca landed right in front of us."

"I wasn't watching the landing, I'm afraid," McKirk said. "I was so certain I was about to certify a new airplane that I spent the time getting the forms ready for the event."

"Yes, well, we sure don't want to cause you any problem," Rocky said. "If you want to, you can just certify one of the other two Tri-Stars we have. They're all identical."

"Uh-uh," McKirk said, shaking his head. "I can't certify either one of them until you get at least five hundred hours on the airframe of one of them."

"But our inaugural flight is next Monday," Rocky countered.

"Not in a Tri-Star it isn't," McKirk replied, matter-of-factly.

In another part of St. Louis, in the investment offices of Hunter, Klein, Trevathan, and Gunn, Bob Canfield stood in Charles Hunter's tenth-floor office, looking through the window at the column of black smoke rising high into the sky from the northwest part of the city. The smoke was very black and very intense, though there didn't seem to be enough of it to indicate a burning building. Bob decided that it was probably a pile of automobile tires being burned in some junkyard.

"Ah, here it is," Hunter said, coming back in and carrying a file with him. "I have your portfolio here as well as those of your sons."

Charles Hunter, the president of the investment firm, was also Bob's personal broker. He picked up a small cedar box of cigars and held them out to Bob.

"Cigar?"

"Thanks," Bob replied, taking one.

"What did you find so interesting through my window?"

"That smoke," Bob said, pointing toward the towering column. "I was just wondering what it was."

"That's out by the airport. They're always burning something out there." Hunter held a match to his client's cigar, and Bob puffed until it was well lit and a generous cloud of blue smoke had gathered around his head.

"Good cigar," he said.

"Genuine Havana," Hunter said proudly. "My daughter got them for me when she was down there."

"Ah, yes, I read in the paper that she was there looking the place over because she was going to make that movie . . . What's the name of it again?"

"*Havana Holiday*," Hunter supplied.

"Yes, that's it. Well, I'm sure she'll be very good in it. But then, she was very good in *Guns of the Mesa*, too."

"She *was* good wasn't she?" Hunter asked, almost as if he were surprised. "You know, I tried to talk her out of it."

"Making that movie?"

"Not just *that* movie. *All* movies," the broker admitted. He laughed sheepishly. "The truth is, I didn't think she had a chance of ever getting into pictures, and I didn't want her to stay out there and have her heart broken. I guess I just didn't have enough faith in her talent . . . or her determination. I must confess that this isn't the life I would have chosen for her, but it is her life, and I suppose all I can do is let her lead it and hope for the best."

"Then I would say your hopes are well-founded. Things seem to be going very nicely for her now," Bob said.

"Yes, they are," Hunter agreed. "And how about your two sons? How are they doing?"

"Willie has one more year at Jefferson, but John has already graduated and is working in the family business. He's taking a very practical approach to matters—he realizes that he has more things to learn than could be taught in a business course, regardless of how good the school is. So, he plans to spend several months on the job, learning the operation of each department: production, shipping, acquisition, and so forth. Right now he's in production." Bob chuckled. "As a matter of fact, when I left him, one of the extruders had broken down, and John was down on the floor with the mechanics, his hands covered in grease as he helped them—or called it helping them—make the repairs."

"Good for him," Hunter said, laughing. "He'll make a fine chief executive officer some day. In fact, he'll be just the kind of man investors will have faith in. Which brings up the same old question."

"I know the question," Bob responded in a please-not-again voice.

"I'll ask it anyway. When are you going to go public with Canfield-Puritex?"

"We've talked about this before, Charles. I don't have any plans to do that."

"But you can't mean that. You're missing out on a golden opportunity," Hunter insisted. "Bob, don't you realize that if you were to go public with your company, I could double its value almost overnight?"

"Yes, so you've said—even though I don't understand just how you'd do that."

"It's quite simple, really," Hunter explained. "The first thing we'd do would be to capitalize the company at double the assessed value of your operation. You would then reserve fifty-one percent of the stock for yourself, while placing forty-nine percent of the stock on the market at full par value. When all forty-nine percent of the issue has sold, you will have money equivalent to the present value of the entire company—yet, as you have retained fifty-one percent, you'll still own controlling interest."

"What you are saying is I can sell my company yet hang on to it. Sort of like having my cake and eating it too."

"Yes," Hunter said, nodding his head and smiling broadly, "that's exactly what I'm saying."

Bob flicked an ash from the end of his cigar. "Then you aren't actually doubling its value, are you? You're just doubling the price."

"It amounts to the same thing."

"No, it doesn't. A thing's price isn't necessarily its value."

"All right, perhaps it isn't the same thing," Hunter conceded. "The important thing is, it will generate more capital."

"Is that legal?"

"Of course it's legal. It's done all the time. In fact, I'd say that eighty to ninety percent of all the companies listed on the New York Stock Exchange are handled in that same way."

Bob took another deep drag on his cigar, then exhaled audibly and studied Hunter through the resulting blue cloud of smoke. "I hope that isn't true, Charles," he finally said, "because if it is, we are creating an economy that's little more than a house of cards. What if one of the major corporations—say, General Motors— suddenly had to liquidate all its assets? What you are telling me is that General Motors is actually worth half its stock value."

"Wrong. General Motors is worth what the public *thinks* it's worth. That's the beauty of it, don't you see?"

"And if suddenly the public thought it was worth nothing? Does that mean General Motors then becomes worthless?"

"Don't be absurd. Why would the public ever think that about a company like General Motors?"

"Why would they think it about *any* company? Why did they think it about the Knickerbocker Trust back in 1907?"

"1907?" Hunter laughed nervously. "Good heavens, that was twenty years ago. As I recall, some chicanery with financing caused a bit of a panic in New York. It had very little effect on the rest of the market—or the country, for that matter."

"That's only because J.P. Morgan intervened," Bob said. "I was there, Charles, watching it happen. I can tell you that we came within a whisker of having the economy of our entire nation ruined."

"But it *didn't* happen," Hunter said.

"No, it didn't happen. And the reason it didn't happen is because Morgan, almost single-handedly, kept it from happening. He raised millions and millions of dollars to shore up some of what had been until the panic the most fundamentally sound banks in New York. By extension, Morgan also saved the New York Stock Exchange. Therefore, you're right when you say the value of our nation's economy is exactly what the people think it is. Only, for a short time back in 1907, the people thought it was worth nothing."

"Well, perhaps so. But nothing like that could ever happen today. This is 1927, not 1907. Confidence in the stock exchange system has never been stronger. Why, did you know that over half the money invested in the stock market today has been invested by the working class? Schoolteachers, taxi drivers, mill workers, policemen, grocery clerks, farmers—yes, even newsboys— invest in stocks. People quote stock values the way they quote batting averages. It's no longer a rich man's game, Bob. It's the lifeblood of America."

"All the more reason the money should be protected by assets that are equal to, or at least nearly equal to, the amount of their declared worth," Bob insisted.

"You know, Bob, to hear you talk, one would think that you have no stocks at all. And yet you have as much money invested as any client I have. If you feel this way about it, how is it that you continue to support the stock market?"

"Oh, I don't mind investing in the market with my own money. It helps provide a source of financing that I feel is very important to maintaining a healthy economy. And if something goes wrong, it's my money, so I'll be the only one hurt. On the other hand, if I involve my company, I put at risk the well-being of the several thousand people who depend on Canfield-Puritex for their livelihood."

"I think you're making a huge mistake," Hunter said. "If you went public with Canfield-Puritex, you'd have a powerful leverage position, what with a great increase in cash available plus the par market value of your stock. However, I'll not be greedy. I am very grateful for the business you are already giving me, and I hope to continue serving you."

"Oh, I think you can count on that," Bob said, smiling. "I may not want to go public with Canfield-Puritex, but that doesn't mean I'll pull back from any of my own investments. And, of course, I have my sons' portfolios."

"Yes," Hunter said, separating the boys' folders from Bob's. He opened Willie's file and began looking through it. "They are both fine portfolios." He chuckled. "I notice your younger son seems especially interested in aviation stock."

"Yes. For the most part I'm letting them choose the stock to invest in." Bob peered at the broker. "Let me ask you, Charles, do you think Willie's enthusiasm for aviation is misplaced?"

"No, not at all. Ever since Lindbergh's flight, aviation stock has become what we call a 'high stepper.' Aviation and airline stocks have skyrocketed in popularity, and people are buying anything that appears to be remotely connected to aviation." Hunter laughed. "In fact, there's a railroad on the Atlantic coast named Seaboard Airlines that has nothing to do with aviation at all, though its stock is climbing out of sight just because people don't know any better."

"I wish I could get Willie less interested in aviation and more interested in business," Bob said with a sigh. "But I know it's useless to even try. He's just like my brother was. He has his head literally up in the clouds, and nothing will make him come down."

Hunter smiled. "Far be it from me to give you any advice, but take it from a father who watched his child go her own way: It's best just to let the cards fall where they may. They have their own lives to lead—and who's to say that what they have in mind is wrong?"

"Who is to say, indeed," Bob agreed. "I remember when I told my father I wanted to give up on the lumbering business and drain the swamps to make farmland." He chuckled. "I'm sure he thought I was crazy, but he told me it was my shot to call, and he backed me one hundred precent. If Willie thinks aviation has a future, far be it from me to step on his dream."

OCTOBER 17, 1927

"I've got it all figured out," Rocky said, coming into Bryan's office to deliver the log report of the morning's flight. "It came to me while I was flying this morning."

"Well, I'm happy that you've got it all figured out," Bryan said, looking up from a drawing he was working on. "But would you be tellin' me just what 'it' might be?"

"Why, I've figured out the best way to get the hours we need for certification."

Bryan shrugged. "By the saints, what's there to figure? We fly them, is all."

Rocky walked over to the window and looked out on the ramp at the two remaining Tri-Stars sitting side by side, their corrugated sheet-metal skins gleaming bright silver in the morning sun. The tails of the two airplanes were yellow, with the letters *MAT* painted in green and flowing back from a stylized bird's wing forming the logo of the as yet unlaunched airline.

Two employees of Rockwell-McPheeters Aviation were crawling over the airplane Rocky had just landed. One man was sitting up on the high wing, putting in fuel, and the other was up on the bright-yellow maintenance stand, adding oil to the port engine. The size of the two mechanics relative to the Tri-Star gave some indication as to just how big the three-engined plane really was.

"Number two has how many hours now, Bryan? Three hundred seventy, three hundred eighty?"

Bryan referred to a chart he kept on his desk. "As of your flight this mornin' we have three hundred eighty-two hours and twenty-seven minutes," he said.

Rocky turned away from the window and faced Bryan with a big smile on his face. "How would you like to put the last hundred hours on that plane in such a way that it would guarantee that everyone in America—hell, everyone in the *world*—would know about Mid-America Transport?"

"Just what do you have in mind?"

"I'm going to fly it to Europe."

"It's been done, laddie," Bryan pointed out. "A lot of times now. And besides, you'd not be thinkin' you can top Lindbergh, would you? None of the others have. Charles Lindbergh is still the only name anyone remembers."

"Yeah, but what was his airplane? A single-engine monoplane, that's what. It was all tank and engine and wing," Rocky said. "Bryan, Lindbergh's flight was a stunt and nothing more. Oh, he'll be famous enough for now, but there's nothing practical can come of such an adventure."

"Are you sayin' Lindbergh's flight across the Atlantic was a waste of time?"

"No, I'm not saying that at all. I think what he did—and the others since him have done, too, for that matter—has to be good for aviation. And, in the long run, anything that's good for aviation is good for us. I'm just saying it wasn't very practical."

"So what is it that you have in mind?"

Rocky smiled. "Suppose we crossed the Atlantic in the Tri-Star? And suppose that Tri-Star was carrying passengers? Can you see the benefit we'd get from such a thing? By the time we got back, we'd have enough hours for certification that we could start our airline right away. And we'll advertise MAT by telling people that the airplane they'll be flying in will be the same plane that made a successful Atlantic crossing. Bryan, we'll have so many people wanting to fly with us that we'll have to stand at the door and beat away the passengers."

"Would you mind tellin' me just how it is you plan to carry these passengers from New York to Paris without certification?"

"Easy," Rocky answered. "All we have to do is find several people who have a taste for adventure. We can carry passengers without certification as long as we don't charge them a fare. And by the way, I didn't say anything about New York to Paris . . . I said from here to Europe. Specifically, Vienna."

"From here? You mean from St. Louis to Vienna?"

"Sure! Consider the beauty of it, Bryan! We could bill the flight as one made from middle America to middle Europe. And can you think of any city in America with closer ties to Vienna than St. Louis?"

"But the airplane won't fly that far, not even if you took everything out and filled it with fuel."

"I don't intend to try it in one hop," Rocky was quick to explain. "And though I'll lighten the airplane somewhat, I wouldn't strip it all the way down, for if we did, we'd have no room left for our passengers. And don't you see? By keeping the airplane substantially the same, we wouldn't be performing a mere stunt, but rather an actual service to the field of aviation. It would be a demonstration of the practicality of using airplanes as long-distance carriers."

"Oh, what a fine thing that would be!" Bryan agreed, now beginning to catch some of Rocky's enthusiasm. "But do you actually think it can be done?"

"Do I think it can be done? Hell, I *know* it can be done. I told you, I figured it all out this morning. At full RPMs, the Tri-Star consumes ten gallons per hour, per

engine," Rocky said. "That works out to about one
hundred miles for every thirty gallons of fuel burned.
The designed fuel load is three hundred gallons, which
would give us a range of a thousand miles. If we take out
eight of the fourteen passenger seats, we could add
another three hundred gallons of fuel and, by so doing,
double our range. And by scheduling our stops at no
more than fifteen hundred miles apart, we'd be able to
make each stop with a reserve of five hundred miles."

"Yes, but it's *more* than fifteen hundred miles across
the ocean," Bryan reminded him.

"No, it isn't. Not the way we're going to go," Rocky
replied. He walked over to the globe and put his finger
on St. Louis. "It's about a thousand miles from here to
New York. From there it's another seven or eight
hundred miles to Gander, Newfoundland. Eleven hundred more to Reykjavik, Iceland, then seven hundred on
to Dublin. Not one leg would push us beyond the limit."

"Dublin?" Bryan looked up, his eyes shining brightly.
"You'd be goin' through Dublin?"

Rocky smiled. "Well, now, you don't really think I'd
take you with me and not give you a chance to visit
Dublin, do you?" he asked. "What kind of friend would
I be? That is, if you want to go," he added.

"Oh, yes, I'll be wantin' to go, you can count on
that, laddie," Bryan said. Then he added pensively,
"'T'would be the fulfillment of all my boyhood dreams if
I could touch down on the old sod in a craft I designed
myself."

"Then come with me you shall," Rocky said. "Now,
it's only a thousand miles more from Dublin to Vienna
and then, my friend, we'll have made a mid-America to
mid-Europe flight."

"How long would such a flight take?"

"In actual flying time, about forty-six hours. Say, no
more than an hour on the ground at each stop, and we'd
be adding another four or five hours. I think we should
be able to do the whole trip in about fifty hours."

"Make it forty-eight hours," Bryan said.

"Forty-eight?" Rocky asked. "Well, we'd have to

shave several minutes off the time it takes us to refuel and try to gain a few miles per hour in the air, but I guess it could be done. Why is forty-eight hours so important?"

"Seventy-two hours is the time it takes someone to go coast to coast on the fastest train in America," Bryan explained. "If we could show them that a person could fly from St. Louis to Vienna in only forty-eight hours on one of our planes, one full day faster than he could go from coast to coast within the United States, I would think it would be a good sellin' point."

"Good idea," Rocky agreed. "Okay, forty-eight hours it'll be."

"We'll be needin' a few modifications, I'm thinkin'," Bryan said. He walked over to pull out the original drawings for the ship and began studying them. "We'll have to consider the placement of the new tanks carefully so as not to affect the weight and balance. And that also means a new cross-feed fuel system."

Rocky started to say something else but he saw that Bryan was already immersed in the technical problems that needed to be solved before the flight could be made. The pilot smiled. That was just the way things should be. Let his partner figure out the technical angles; all he had to do was plan the flight, locate the passengers, and get a copilot. And he already knew whom he wanted as his copilot.

"Me?" Willie Canfield said in response to the question Rocky put to him later that same day. "You're asking me if I'd be your copilot on a flight from St. Louis to Vienna?"

"Yes."

"But are you sure? I mean, there must be hundreds of people, thousands even, with more experience."

"Not in the Tri-Star," Rocky said. He smiled broadly. "And anyway, experience isn't the only thing that's important here. What's also important is heart. You've got to have heart for a flight like this . . . and you've got as much of that commodity as anyone I've known since your hard-headed uncle. Now, what do you say? Do you want the job or what?"

"Do I want the job? Are you crazy? Why do you even ask? *Of course* I want the job!"

Nodding, Rocky said, "Now comes the big question: What will your papa say about it?"

"It doesn't make any difference *what* Pop says," Willie replied. "I'm going."

"Oh, but it does make a difference," Rocky retorted. "Your papa has a financial interest in our company. It wouldn't be right, or smart, to make him angry. And besides, I have too much respect for him to do something like that to him. No, Willie, if you're going to be sitting in the right-hand seat when the Tri-Star lifts off the runway, it's going to be with Bob Canfield's blessing."

"All right," Willie said, his voice determined. "I'll have his blessing."

"How are you going to get it?"

"Mom can get anything out of Pop she wants," Willie replied. He grinned. "And I can get anything I want out of Mom."

After dinner that same evening, Connie Canfield settled into her favorite chair in the library and began to read. Earlier in the day, when she had been downtown, she had passed a bookstore, and in the store's window was a poster advertising:

STILLNESS IN THE LINE
ST. LOUIS
AUTHOR'S NEWEST NOVEL!

Excerpted on the poster were glowing reviews from various newspapers and journals.

Connie had remembered the young man who had been a protégé (almost an adopted son, really) of Bob's old mentor, Loomis Booker. Eric had always talked about wanting to be a writer, and now, all the critics agreed, he was not only a writer, he was a very good writer.

Connie had read and loved Eric's first novel, and now she was settling in and very much looking forward to reading his new one.

"Hi, Mom."

Connie looked up from her book to see her younger son standing just inside the door of the library.

"Why, hello, Willie," Connie said. "Come on in."

"Is that a new book you're reading?"

"Yes," Connie said, holding it up for him to see the cover. "It's Eric Twainbough's new one. You've heard us speak of him, I'm sure."

"Yes, I have. Is it good?" Willie placed a cup of coffee on the table beside Connie's chair, turning the handle toward her for her convenience.

"Well, I don't know. I haven't gotten into it yet," Connie answered. "I'm sure it is, though. His other book was quite good." She picked up the coffee and took a sip, examining her son over the rim of the cup. "Thank you for the coffee," she said. "It's just right."

"Nothing's too good for my mom," Willie replied with a broad, easy grin.

"Oh, I'm sure nothing is too good for your mom," Connie said with amusement, "especially when there's something you want."

"What makes you think I want something?"

Connie chuckled. "Really, dear, we didn't find you under a cabbage leaf yesterday, you know. You've been around long enough for me to learn a few things about you. Now, what is it you want?"

"I need you to talk to Pop," Willie admitted.

"I thought so. What is it this time?"

"I want to take a flight with Rocky."

"Take a flight with Rocky? Well, good heavens, Willie, you already do that, don't you? I mean you were nearly killed when the two of you crashed a couple of weeks ago."

"I wasn't nearly killed," Willie said quickly. "I wasn't

even hurt. And we didn't really crash, we were *avoiding* one."

"Well, nonetheless, you could have been killed." Connie shuddered. "It frightens me to even think of that. Anyway, we didn't forbid you from flying after that, so what's the problem now? What do you mean, you want to take a flight with Rocky?"

Willie pulled the footstool up close to Connie's chair and sat on it. He put his hands on his mother's forearms and his eyes shone brightly as he looked at her. "Mom, it will be the most wonderful experience of my life! It's something that I'll remember forever. You and Pop have *got* to let me do it. You've got to talk him into it."

"Well, for crying out loud, Willie, how am I going to talk him into anything if you don't tell me what it is I am to talk him into!"

"Rocky is going to make a flight in one of the Tri-Stars," Willie said. "The most magnificent flight in the history of aviation. He's going to fly from St. Louis to Vienna . . . with passengers . . . and he wants me to be his copilot!"

"Vienna? As in Austria? Look here, do you mean to tell me that he intends to try to fly that infernal machine from St. Louis all the way to Europe?"

"Yes!" Willie answered. "Isn't it wonderful?"

"It's insane."

"No, Mom, it's not," Willie said. "We have it all worked out and—"

"*We* have it all worked out?"

"Well, Rocky and Bryan have it worked out," Willie said. "We'll have plenty of gas to make it to every stop they have planned . . . and there are three motors on the plane so that even if one of them should stop running, the airplane would continue to fly."

"Why would he want to do such a wild stunt anyway? Since Lindbergh's flight a half-dozen others have made the trip, and who can even remember their names? Any glory you might get from it is *not* worth the risk involved."

"It isn't for glory, Mom," Willie insisted. "It's a very

practical way to show people that the Tri-Star is a safe airplane. That way when Rocky and Bryan start their airline, people won't be afraid to fly with us."

"With *us*?"

"Yes. I'm going to be one of the pilots."

"Willie, I can understand your interest in flying. Your Uncle Billy had that same interest. But you should keep it in perspective. If you want to fly as a hobby, I think that's fine. But flying is not something one considers as a vocation—especially someone with a college degree from a fine university like Jefferson. Why, if you became a common aviator, it would mean that all your fine education was going to waste."

"There is nothing 'common' about being an aviator. But I agree with you that it's a waste of time to continue my education. I don't plan to finish school. I'm going to drop out."

"You *are* going to finish college!" Connie declared heatedly. "It would break your father's heart for you to drop out of school now. Why, you only have one year remaining."

"Mom, I'm not like John. He has a head for business. Ever since we were kids, all he's ever thought about was the day he could start working at the company. And all this time I've been dreading the prospect. Well, now I believe I've found my calling. Flying is something that I love, and it's what I want to spend the rest of my life doing."

Connie studied Willie's face for a long moment, measuring its intensity. She knew that he had inherited her passion for commitment to a goal, and she knew that if she didn't grant him permission, he would do it anyway.

"Will you compromise with me, Willie?" she finally asked.

"What's the compromise?"

"I'll speak with your father about letting you make the flight. In return, you must promise that you'll finish school."

"But, Mom, I've already told you, I don't plan to go into the business, so—"

Connie held up her hand. "It doesn't matter. Realistically, there's no way we can force you to go into the family business. After all, you must lead your own life. However, it can't hurt your career plans, whatever they may be, for you to have a degree. As you know, Jefferson University is very important to your father and to me. Believe me, we would both be very hurt if you chose to drop out now, this close to finishing."

"If I stay in school, you'll convince Pop to let me make the flight?"

"I'll try."

Willie laughed and kissed Connie on the cheek. "What do you mean 'try'?" he asked. "If you ask him, Mom, he'll let me do it. You can make him do *anything*."

"Will you finish school?"

"I'll finish school," Willie promised.

"All right," Connie said. "I'll talk to your father."

"Thanks, Mom!" Willie said, hugging his mother so tightly that she let out a little squeal of protest. "You're the greatest mother in the whole world!"

OCTOBER 25, 1927

The Tannenhower home, built on the banks of the Mississippi River, was on one of the several short, privately maintained residental streets with no names other than "private places." These pink-pebbled roads, guarded by ornate entrance gates, featured the largest and most palatial homes in St. Louis. Though deed restrictions maintained forever the private, one-family ownership character of the neighborhood, there were no restrictions on architectural design, and a Frank Lloyd Wright home might stand next to an Italianate palace or a Cotswold cottage or a Georgian mansion—or one of the extremely large and ornate homes St. Louisians called "Brewer's Baronial."

The Tannenhower home was just such a place,

situated on five rolling acres and complete with a stable and formal garden. Inside the house, in one of its fourteen bedrooms, Tanner Twainbough sat in front of a dressing table, brushing her hair. Eric stood watching her for a moment from the doorway, then closed the door behind him and walked over to her. He kissed her on the cheek, then sat on the bed behind her so that though her back was to him, they could see each other in the mirror as they talked.

"Ham is a big hit," Eric said. "He's downstairs right now, entertaining your folks." He chuckled, adding, "We sure named him right. He's hamming it up for Grandpa and Grandma."

"Did you see the little St. Louis Grays baseball uniform Papa got for him? He's really proud of his grandson."

"I know. It makes me feel almost guilty about taking him back to Paris with us."

"Papa is really after me to get you to come back to St. Louis," she said. "Or, at least, come back to the States."

"Yes, he was talking to me about the idea of starting my own publishing house here in St. Louis. He offered to put up all the money I'd need."

Tanner laughed. "At least he's finally accepted the idea that you're a writer. When we were first married, you know, he wanted you to give up the idea of writing altogether and come to work in the family business."

"Well, I couldn't have represented a very good risk for his daughter at the time," Eric remarked. "I was a 'novelist' who had yet to publish a novel."

"What did you tell Papa when he offered to help you start a publishing house?"

"I thanked him for the offer. Then I tried to explain how publishing is only half of it—how you also need a national distributor and how that could only be arranged in New York."

"If I know Papa, that didn't even slow him down," Tanner said dryly. "He probably offered to set you up in New York."

Eric studied her face in the mirror, then asked, "Tanner, he told me that he was sure you would be much happier in the States. Is he right?"

Tanner put down the brush and turned to face her husband. "Darling, do you even have to ask? Don't you know by now that I am happiest when I am with you, no matter where you are? If you choose to live in Paris, then Paris is where I want to be. If it's New York, then that's fine, too. The place means nothing to me."

"You're sure?"

"I'm positive."

Eric smiled, then walked over to hold her. "Good. Because I *do* want to go back to Paris for a while longer. It may change soon, but right now, with the collection of writers and artists who've gathered there, Paris is the most creatively vital city in the world. I'm doing good work there, and I don't want to walk away from it. It would be a little like leaving a card game while you're holding the winning hand."

"Then of course we'll go back," Tanner said. "Only let's do go soon. The longer we stay here, the more determined my father is going to be to keep us."

"Is Friday soon enough?" Eric asked.

"Friday? Have you booked passage for Friday?"

"Not yet," Eric said. "But I'm about to."

"How are we going?"

"I'm not sure. I have to try to make some arrangements . . . that is, if you're game."

"Darling, I told you. However you want to go is fine with me."

"You haven't heard what I have in mind."

"It doesn't matter. Go ahead and make whatever arrangements are necessary. I'll be there."

"You're sure?"

"I'm sure."

CHAPTER
TWENTY-ONE

It was raining hard, a late-fall rain that stripped the last brown leaves off the trees and left them piled and sodden on the sidewalks and in the gutters. Though it was only six o'clock in the evening, the shortened autumn days and the heavy cloud cover made it dark enough to require all the lights to be turned on in the Rockwell-McPheeters hangar.

On one side of the hangar Tri-Star 2, or—as it was now being called—the *Twentieth-Century Voyager*, sat surrounded by tall maintenance stands and crowded worktables. The freshly repainted yellow-and-green tail of the airplane shone under the overhead lights, and the corrugated aluminum skin glistened brightly.

The cowlings had been removed from all three engines, thus exposing the cylinders, magnetos, carburetors, fuel pumps, and other vital components of the

407

power plants for the fine tuning and adjustments Bryan McPheeters demanded. The inspection plates on the fuselage and wings had also been opened so that the airplane's network of cables, fairleads, pulleys, bell cranks, and pushrods could be properly examined and adjusted. The doors were off, the seats were out, and the cabin floor was pulled up to give the mechanics room to work as they fitted the craft with the long-range tanks necessary to extend its range. Hoses hung loose, wires dangled freely, and disconnected controls flapped unbound. Yet even in its denuded, exposed condition, the *Twentieth-Century Voyager* looked as if it were being held to the ground only by the strength of its tethers, as if it might of its own volition suddenly take wing and fly.

On the opposite side of the hangar from the airplane, Rocky Rockwell had covered an entire wall with maps and U.S. Navy navigational charts, piecing them together so that he had a continuous plot from St. Louis to Vienna. He had marked the intended route with a long piece of red yarn, while the scheduled stops were designated with yellow thumbtacks.

The seasoned pilot was standing in front of the map, examining it carefully and making notes on one of the smaller maps he would be carrying with him, when a tall, broad-shouldered man stepped into the hangar. The visitor took off his hat, then shook the water from it.

Rocky turned to the man and smiled. "Good evening. Can I help you?"

"Yes, I hope so. My name is Eric Twainbough," he said, extending his hand. "We've never met, though we do have some mutual friends," he added.

"Yes, I've heard of you. You're the writer," Rocky said, taking Eric's hand. "As a matter of fact, I just read *Stillness in the Line* and liked it very much." The wartime flying ace smiled, then said, "I'm no critic, but to me it's a damn good book. It talks in a language a soldier can understand."

"Thank you."

"I saw in the paper where you were in St. Louis."

"Yes, my wife and I brought our son here to meet

his grandparents," Eric explained. "We're about ready to
return home."

"You live overseas somewhere, don't you?"

"Paris."

"Paris," Rocky repeated. He smiled. "I have very
fond memories of Paris. Is it still . . .? Ah, but you
wouldn't know. You're married."

Eric chuckled. "I'm married, but I'm not blind," he
said. "Yes, it is still . . ." Eric let the sentence hang, for
no other words were needed.

"I plan to go back there one day. I don't know
when," Rocky said.

"How about now?" Eric pointed to the airplane that
was being readied for the trip. "There's your ticket."

"You're talking about flying to Paris?"

"Sure, why not? Several people already have, of
course. In fact, even before Lindbergh, Byrd and Cham-
berlin did it."

"I know. As a matter of fact, I'm getting ready to
cross the Atlantic, too. But I am going on to Vienna."

"Well, make Paris one of your stops."

"I can't," Rocky said, shaking his head. "I've got the
flight all planned."

"Change your plans."

Rocky studied Eric for a moment, then smiled.
"You're not saying all this just so I can get to Paris, are
you?" he asked.

"No. I'm saying it so *I* can get to Paris. To be more
specific, I'm doing it so my wife, my child, and I can all
get to Paris. I understand that you're looking for passengers for the trip. I'd like for you to take us."

"How did you know I was looking for passengers? It
hasn't been in the paper."

"As I said, we have mutual friends," Eric replied.

"Look here, did you say you, your wife, and your
child?"

"Yes."

Rocky shook his head. "Absolutely not. Out of the
question."

"It was your plan to take passengers, wasn't it?" Eric asked.

"Well, yes. But I don't plan to risk the lives of a woman and a small child."

Eric smiled mischievously. "Maybe I've misunderstood the concept here. I thought the whole idea of this flight was to show that flying *wasn't* a risk. When you establish your airline service to Chicago, Kansas City, and Memphis, do you plan to carry adult males only?"

"Well, no, but . . ."

"But what? Surely you can see the benefit that could be derived from having safely delivered a family from St. Louis to Paris."

"Yes. But if something goes wrong, it could really backfire on us."

"What could go wrong?"

"Well, for starters, we could crash in the ocean and be killed," Rocky suggested.

Eric laughed. "If we're all killed, what difference would it make? None of us would be here to worry about it."

Rocky laughed as well. "You do have a point there."

"Here's something else for you to consider," Eric proposed. "I'm a writer. I will write about the flight. Now, that has to be beneficial to your plans for building an airline, doesn't it? Think of it as free advertising."

"Why do you want to do this?" Rocky asked.

"As I said, I'm a writer," Eric replied. "Experiences are a writer's stock-in-trade. I've traveled by horse and wagon, dogsled, train, ship, and automobile, but I have never traveled by airplane. I feel this is something I should do."

"What about your wife?" Rocky asked. "What does she think about it?"

"Tanner is a good sport with a taste for adventure. She'll find the idea most appealing. What do you say, Mr. Rockwell? Are you serious about starting an airline? Because if you are, I'm offering you the perfect opportunity to do so."

Rocky stroked his chin for a moment or two as he

studied Eric; then, without saying another word, he walked over to the map and picked up a yellow thumbtack. He pushed the thumbtack into the map at Paris. "Mr. Twainbough, you just bought a ticket," he announced.

Eric smiled broadly. "Good."

"But we're going to see just how good a sport your wife really is," Rocky added. "Tell her the only things she can bring are the clothes on her back."

"At least it'll make packing easy," Eric quipped.

"Be here at the hangar at two-thirty, Friday morning," Rocky said. "We take off at three."

"Two-thirty, Friday morning," Eric repeated. He stuck out his hand again. "We'll see you then."

FRIDAY, OCTOBER 28, 1927

The Chrysler "60" bounced along the long dirt road that led from the airport highway out to the Rockwell-McPheeters hangar at Lambert Field. Eric, Tanner, and Hamilton Twainbough were in the back seat of the car. Ham, dressed in the miniature St. Louis Grays baseball uniform that he had insisted on wearing, was asleep across Tanner's lap.

Loomis Booker, who had driven to St. Louis from Jefferson City the day before, was driving the car. When Eric had told him during a good-bye phone call how Ludwig Tannenhower couldn't face up to seeing his daughter, son-in-law, and grandson off—especially in an airplane—Loomis had made the offer to bring them to the airport. Sitting in the front seat beside Loomis was his new wife, Della.

"Eric, are you sure this is where we're supposed to be?" Loomis asked. "I don't see any lights or anything."

"This is Friday morning, isn't it?"

"It had better be," Tanner joked. "I'd hate to think I got out of bed in the middle of the night on the wrong day."

"Then this is where we're supposed to be. Rocky

said be at the hangar at two-thirty this morning," Eric insisted.

Loomis downshifted the car. "Well, it's just about that now," he said, "and there's nothing there."

Della turned around to face Tanner. "I have to tell you that you have a lot more courage than I do. Honey, you couldn't get me up in that thing for love or money."

"Oh, I'm looking forward to it," Tanner said. "I think it'll be great fun."

"What did your papa say about it?" Della asked.

"Well, frankly, neither he nor my mother was too keen on the idea. But I talked him into it. I thought he would put up more of a fight about us taking Ham with us, but he said a baby belongs with his parents."

"I want to thank you for bringing us out here, Loomis," Eric said, leaning forward and putting a hand on Loomis's shoulder.

"I brought you, but I want you to know I don't approve of this any more than Tanner's father does," Loomis replied. He chuckled. "But what else could I expect from you? From the very first time I ever saw you, more dead than alive, lying alongside the railroad track, you've always been off on one adventure or another."

"I've never heard that story," Della said. "What happened?"

"I was riding the rails," Eric explained. "Hopping freights from Wyoming to St. Louis, coming to see the wonders of the great World's Fair in 1904. A railroad bull found me and—"

"Who found you?" Della interrupted.

"A railroad detective," Eric explained. "He worked me over a little—"

"A little? Huh! He half killed you," Loomis put in.

Eric chuckled. "Okay, he worked me over more than a little, and then he tossed me off the train. Loomis found me, nursed me back to health, fed me, clothed me, gave me a place to stay, and eventually educated me."

"I was just obeying the Biblical command to feed

the hungry, clothe the naked, and educate the ignorant," Loomis quipped.

"That's not in the Bible," Della insisted.

"It's not? Well, it should be. Oh, look, someone *is* here, after all. They just turned on the lights."

The sudden flood of light came from a battery of large, outdoor electric lamps that illuminated the front of the hangar. As the car approached, the *Twentieth-Century Voyager* became visible, poised and ready to go.

"Is that it?" Della asked in a hushed voice. "Is that what you're going to ride in?"

"That's it," Eric replied. Beside him he felt Tanner shudder. "Are you okay?" he asked, taking her hand in his.

"Oh, yes," she said. "I'm just excited, that's all."

"That's young Willie Canfield there, looking at one of the motors," Loomis pointed out.

"He's one of the pilots?" Della asked. "My goodness, you're going to trust your lives to that *boy*? Why, look at him, Loomis! He's no older than your Andrew."

"I'm sure he's quite capable, or he wouldn't be doing this," Loomis replied. "Anyway, what if people say that about Andrew after he becomes a doctor?"

"Andrew isn't a doctor yet . . . but that boy is already a pilot," Della said. "And I still say he looks awfully young."

"His age doesn't bother me," Eric explained. "I knew several aviators during the war who were no older than he is now."

The car reached the concrete ramp. Loomis stopped, switched off the engine, and set the parking brake. Eric opened the back door and got out, then took Ham while Tanner stepped out. Loomis and Della also got out of the car and came around to stand beside Eric and Tanner.

"My, my," Della said. "Look at all those folks working on that plane."

In addition to Willie Canfield, who was examining something on one of the engines, there were a number of mechanics crawling around on, under, and alongside the big airplane, examining every inch of it with extreme care.

"Let me have a screwdriver!" one of the mechanics called. "Here's a loose fastener on this inspection plate."

"Jerry! Jerry! We need about two more pounds of pressure in the right tire," another called.

"At least they're checking it out right down to the wire," Loomis said.

"Yes, but if they're just now finding all that stuff, doesn't it make you wonder whether there might not be something they're forgetting? Like, maybe they didn't screw down one of the motors or something?" Della suggested.

Eric grinned. "Della, you are just full of pleasant things to think about," he said dryly.

"Don't mind me," Della said. "I'm just nervous, that's all."

"Twainbough!" Rocky called, coming from the hangar then, carrying his flying helmet. "If you're ready, go ahead and get your family settled on board. We're going to try to get away a few minutes early."

"We'll be right there," Eric promised. He reached out and clasped Loomis's hands. "It was great seeing you again, Loomis," he said. Turning to Della, he gave her a quick hug and told her, "And it was a joy meeting you, Della. By the way, I do approve of the marriage."

"You approve, do you?" Della asked. "And what if you didn't approve? What was Loomis supposed to do, toss me aside like so much dirty laundry?"

"Well, now, how do you know I wouldn't have done just that?" Loomis asked.

"And how do you know I won't just fly off with them and leave you here?" Della retorted. Then she looked at the airplane. "Fly off in that thing? My God, what am I saying?" she asked, and the others laughed.

"You take good care of this man, Della," Eric said. "He's the closest thing to a father I've got."

Della put her hands on Loomis's arm and smiled broadly at Eric. "You don't worry any about that. Now that I've got him, I aim to hang on to him."

"Okay, get all the maintenance stands pulled away!" Rocky shouted. "Everyone into the plane!"

Spontaneously, Eric embraced Loomis, and Tanner did the same with Della; then they hurried across the concrete ramp toward the open door of the plane.

Eric held Ham, who was managing to sleep through it all, while Tanner climbed up into the plane, helped aboard by Willie and Bryan McPheeters, who reached down to offer their hands. Once Tanner was on board, Eric handed Ham up to her, and then he, too, boarded the plane.

He stopped short and grinned. Just across the aisle from the door sat a small makeshift bed with extra-high sides, complete with a mattress, pillow, and straps for securing.

"We fixed this for the boy," Willie said proudly. "Go ahead, put him in."

"Oh, how thoughtful of you," Tanner said, laying her son down in the bed.

"He's almost too big for it, isn't he?" Willie said. "I guess I didn't know how big he was."

"Well, he's six years old," Tanner said. "And he's big for his age. But don't worry. This will work fine."

"Here's your seat, Mrs. Twainbough, right in front of the bed," Willie said. "Mr. Twainbough, you're going to have to sit here, on the other side of the plane. And a word of caution: Only one of you at a time can be behind this line. That's for weight and balance."

"Okay," Eric said, settling into the wicker seat Willie pointed out to him.

"Now, the, uh, privy," Willie said, as if embarrassed to say the word, "is just forward of that big bump you see in the floor. You'll have to climb over that bump, while at the same time ducking your head under that protrusion hanging from the top."

"What are those things?" Tanner asked. "Why are they in the way like that?"

"Those are the extra fuel tanks," Willie explained. "They had to go there, right under the wing, so they wouldn't affect the overall balance of the plane."

"I see two more seats up there," Tanner said. "Who are they for?"

"One is for Mr. McPheeters here. He's the fella who designed the plane. He's also going on this trip," Willie answered. "The other chair folds down into a cot. It's the only one we have on board, so we'll have to take turns using it."

"Why, I think everything is quite cozy," Tanner said. "I'm sure we'll have a delightful trip."

"Here," Willie said, handing over a package. "You'll need these."

"What are they?" Eric asked, taking it.

"Cotton wads," Willie explained. "Stuff them in your ears. It'll help keep down some of the noise."

Rocky climbed aboard then. "Everyone in your seats," he called as he started toward the front of the plane, stepping over the lower fuel tank and bending under the upper bulge. "We're about to take off."

Eric settled down into his seat and began fastening the belt as he heard Willie close the cabin door behind him. Willie latched the door shut; then he, too, moved toward the front of the airplane to take his place to the right of Rocky. From Eric's position, he could see the pilot and copilot at their stations, their hands moving quickly and expertly about the various knobs and levers, readying the airplane for starting.

"Ready to start number one!" someone shouted from outside the plane.

"Starting number one!" Willie shouted back.

The Tri-Star had self-starting engines, and Eric heard the ascending hum of the inertia starter, then the mew and cough of engine number one as it caught.

With engine number one running, the noise became deafening, and it awakened Ham. He began crying, and Tanner quickly reached around for him. She gathered him onto her lap and held him close, kissing him reassuringly as engine number two caught. Ham's cries diminished, and by the time engine number three was running, he was looking out the window excitedly.

Eric remembered the cotton then, and he pulled a

couple of wads out of the sack and stuffed them in his ears. It did help, and he passed the package over to Tanner, reminding her, by sign language, what to do. Nodding that she understood, Tanner stopped up her son's ears, then did her own.

The big plane began bouncing and trundling out across the field, but it was so dark outside his window that Eric couldn't see anything. Suddenly the lights inside the cabin went off, and for a moment Eric thought there was some problem with the electrical system. Then he realized that either Willie or Rocky had turned the cabin lights off so they could see outside. Eric looked out the window himself, and he could see in the distance the early-morning lights of the city of St. Louis. Little by little his eyes adjusted, and he could make out other features in the still-darkened landscape—including certain details of the plane itself.

The plane stopped, turned, and sat still for a moment. One by one the engines roared, but since the aircraft wasn't moving, Eric assumed that the pilots were testing the engines in some way. Then all three engines began roaring together, and the plane started taxiing again. This time the movement was completely different from what it had been. This time it was swift and urgent.

The plane started going faster and faster, until Eric felt the tail rise from the ground. A moment later he saw the big left front wheel lift up from the runway. The tire continued to roll for a few revolutions, then stopped. The airplane started its long, slow climb, and Eric could see the lighted hangar they had just left. He also saw Loomis's car parked under one of the lights, with Loomis and Della standing just in front. They were waving up at him and he waved back a bit self-consciously, for he knew there was no way they could see him.

But it didn't matter that they couldn't see him. Eric's act of waving was a connection with other human beings and with the earth itself, for at that precise moment he felt, for himself and the five other souls on board this airplane, a sense of detachment that was as strong as if they were on another planet.

A sudden tugging on his sleeve made Eric open his eyes. Ham was standing beside his seat, asking to sit with him. Eric shifted in his seat to make room for his son, and Ham scrambled up beside his father. Sunlight was now streaming into the plane, and when Eric looked out the window, he saw farmland far below. He had been asleep, though he wasn't even aware of when—or even that—he had drifted off.

"Well, what do you think, big fella?" Eric asked Ham. "This is quite something, isn't it?"

The boy had his face pressed to the window. He turned to look at Eric with a big grin on his face.

"Wow, this is fun! I'll bet you can see the whole world from up here!"

"Yep, I'll bet you can," Eric agreed, and father and son watched steadily out the window at the wondrous sight.

NOVEMBER 2, 1927, SOLOVETSKY ISLANDS, U.S.S.R.

Ten years of confinement in a forced-labor camp had extracted its toll on Katya Lvovna. Once a very beautiful young woman, she was now old beyond her years, with a badly misshapen nose as a result of a beating she had received during the early days of "adjusting to the new order." Poor diet had caused the loss of several teeth, which then had the effect of reshaping her face. Her hair was lusterless and prematurely gray, and her skin had taken on a permanent yellow tinge.

Though still a prisoner, she did not labor as hard as she once did. She was now assigned to the prison hospital where she kept records of admissions, discharges, and deaths. It was she who had chosen the three designated categories on the patients' charts: *Admitted, Survived,* and *Died.* The distinction in the choice of the term "survived" rather than "cured" was subtle to be sure, but it was one of the few ways that Katya had managed to fight back.

"Comrade Lvovna," Major Pilnyak called from his office. "Have you today's figures?"

"Yes, Comrade Major," Katya said, taking her tally sheet into his office. She no longer feared going into the major's office, for she was no longer pretty enough to be desired by him or by any of the guards.

That hadn't always been the case. She had been raped a number of times in the early days, sometimes taken by physical violence and sometimes taken by intimidation. *"If you value the life of your daughter, you will try your best to please me,"* she could recall the major saying.

Katya Lvovna was a third cousin of the Czar. She was a princess—a minor princess and far down the ranks of succession—but a princess, nevertheless. That relationship to the Czar, distant though it was, was the cause of her current predicament. At the time of the Revolution she had been living in Petrograd with the man she loved, an American journalist, and pregnant with his child. They had wanted very much to get married and tried several times to do so, but civil law had broken down, and the American embassy had had no authority to marry them. Worse, Princess Katya Lvovna's name had been on a list issued by the American government of people who were specifically forbidden to emigrate to the United States. Despite the all-too-obvious danger that any of the Czar's relatives faced, U.S. politicians had not been anxious to make waves with the new regime.

Before Katya's baby was born, Katya had been arrested by the new "people's police" of the Revolutionary Council. Her daughter had been born in prison and had spent all ten years of her life with no idea of what it was like to be free.

"Here is the list, Comrade Major," Katya said, handing it over. Turning to leave, Katya noticed a newspaper on Major Pilnyak's desk and had to stifle a gasp as she looked at the photograph on the front page. AMERICAN JOURNALIST CROSSES ATLANTIC BY AEROPLANE, the headline read.

Wordlessly, Major Pilnyak held out his glass as he

studied the figures on Katya's chart. Obediently, she walked over to the teapot, then carried it back to pour some into the proferred glass. As she did so, she spilled some on the paper.

"Watch what you're doing, you clumsy cow!" Pilnyak barked angrily.

"I am very sorry, Comrade Major," Katya said, picking up the newspaper. "I will clean the mess up."

"It's lucky for you I've read the paper," Pilnyak growled.

Katya wiped the rest of the tea up from Pilnyak's desk, then threw the paper into the trash can and hurried out of the office.

For the rest of the day Katya could barely restrain herself from recovering the newspaper. Newspapers were officially forbidden to the prisoners, though occasionally one would work its way through the camp without too much being made of it by the guards. But if Pilnyak knew that Katya had a specific interest in this particular newspaper, he'd make certain that she didn't see it.

Finally at the end of the day Katya went through the normal, daily process of cleaning up Pilnyak's office. She washed his glass, cleaned out his ashtrays, swept and mopped the floor, and emptied the trash. As she was attending to this last task, she managed to hide the tea-stained newspaper under her dress and was thus able to sneak it back into the room she shared with Valentina, her ten-year-old daughter.

There in her tiny room, by the light of a single candle and oblivious to the cold wind howling outside, Katya avidly read the story of Eric Twainbough. The article was full of references to the fact that the American author was a friend of the Soviets, having been a correspondent in Russia during the Revolution and writing many stories reporting the heroism of the brave men and women who had taken part in the struggle to overthrow the Czar.

Primarily, though, the article was about how Eric Twainbough, his wife, and his child had flown across the

Atlantic as passengers on an airplane. It was, the story pointed out, an even more significant journey than Charles Lindbergh's flight because it proved that ordinary men and women would soon be using the airplane as a means of transportation to any point on the globe.

"*That is all the more reason,*" the article concluded, "*that the people's revolution that unchained the citizens of Russia must be continued, to bring that same opportunity to all the peace- and freedom-loving peoples of the world.*"

As Katya studied the picture of Eric, she drifted back in time. She closed her eyes and could see again the colorful uniforms and beautiful ball gowns of a Christmas Eve party they had attended when first falling in love. Again she could hear the music and the jangle of bells and the laughter of the celebrants. Again she could smell the greenery and the perfume of votive candles, smell the fur lap robes dampened by snowflakes as she rode, invigorated, in a horse-drawn sleigh. And again she could feel Eric's arms around her in the warmth of their bed as they made love.

"Mama? Mama? Mama, are you all right?"

Katya opened her eyes and saw that Valentina was standing in front of her, looking at her anxiously. Only then was Katya aware that her daughter had been calling to her.

"Why are you crying, Mama?" Valentina asked.

Katya wiped her eyes, then smiled. "I am crying because I am happy," she said.

"Why are you happy?"

Katya turned the newspaper around so that Valentina could see Eric Twainbough's picture and explained, "Because I never knew if he was alive or dead. Now I know that he has gone on to have a good life. And that makes me very happy."

"Who is he, Mama?" Valentina asked, looking at the picture curiously.

"He is your father," Katya explained.

Valentina's eyes widened, and she studied the

picture with such intensity that it was as if she were fusing the image into her soul.

"Will I ever see him?" she finally asked softly.

"Someday, my darling," Katya said. "God willing, someday."

ABOUT THE AUTHOR

Writing under his own name and 25 pen names, ROBERT VAUGHAN has authored over 200 books in every genre but Science Fiction. He won the 1977 Porgie Award (Best Paperback Original) for *The Power and the Pride*. In 1973 *The Valkyrie Mandate* was nominated by its publisher, Simon & Schuster, for the Pulitzer Prize.

Vaughan is a frequent speaker at seminars and at high schools and colleges. He has also hosted three television talks hows: *Eyewitness Magazine*, on WAVY TV in Portsmouth, Virginia, *Tidewater A.M.*, on WHBQ TV in Hampton, Virginia, and *This Week in Books* on the TEMPO Cable Television Network. In addition, he hosted a cooking show at *Phoenix at Mid-day* on KHPO TV in Phoenix, Arizona.

Vaughan is a retired Army Warrant Officer (CW-3) with three tours in Vietnam where he was awarded the Distinguished Flying Cross, the Air Medal with the V for valor, the Bronze Star, the Distinguished Service Medal, and the Purple Heart. He was a helicopter pilot and a maintenance and supply officer. He was also an instructor and Chief of the Aviation Maintenance Officers' Course at Fort Eustis, Virginia. During his military career, Vaughan was a participant in many of the 20th century's most significant events. For example, he served in Korea immediately after the armistice, he was involved in the Nevada Atomic Bomb tests, he was part of the operation which ensured that James Meredith could attend the University of Mississippi, he was alerted for the Cuban Missile Crisis, he served three years in Europe, and of course, the above-mentioned three tours in Vietnam.

The saga continues with

THE AMERICAN CHRONICLES

VOLUME FOUR

HARD

TIMES

ROBERT

VAUGHAN

Turn the page for an exciting preview of HARD TIMES, on sale in March 1993 wherever Bantam Domain Books are sold.

CHAPTER
ONE

The rain which was falling on Washington D.C. on the night of July 28th, 1932 was not a hard, cleansing rain. It was a soft spray, which carried trapped within its fine mist some of the ash from the burned buildings along Pennsylvania Avenue.

John Canfield rode through the rain in a taxicab, enroute to the Willard Hotel where the National Democratic Committee kept a suite of rooms for visiting members from Franklin Roosevelt's Presidential Campaign Staff. John was in Washington at Roosevelt's request so that he might render a first-hand report on the unrest being caused by the Bonus Marchers.

Twenty-five and handsome, John was on everybody's list as "most eligible bachelor." He was the son of Robert Canfield, majority owner and Chief Executive Officer of Canfield-Puritex, a cereal and food processing company headquartered in St. Louis, and one of the wealthiest and most powerful corporations in America.

John Canfield was bright, energetic, and ambitious. He was a member of the Board of Directors for Canfield-Puritex and an active officer in the company. But he was also a young man of great personal convictions so he had asked his father for an extended leave-of-absence from the family business in order to do what he could to alleviate the suffering of those who had been caught up in the great depression.

Like many other wealthy and compassionate young men, John's earliest efforts were well-intended, but ineffectual. He had toured the country making large donations of food, clothing, and money to the various relief agencies. He had provided food to the sharecroppers in Arkansas and renovated buildings for the homeless in Detroit. He had distributed clothes in Cleveland and helped stock the soup kitchens in New York.

But John had seen all that as nothing more than "patch-work." What he really wanted to do was get involved in some movement, some "great crusade" which would find the cause of the depression, eliminate it, and restore America to economic greatness. When he stated those aspirations to Champ Dawson, the senior senator from John's home state of Missouri, Senator Dawson convinced him that the best way to accomplish his goal would be to get Franklin D. Roosevelt elected President. John met the Governor, listened to what he had to say, then undertook the task of getting Roosevelt elected with all the unbridled zeal a 25-year-old could muster.

John leaned forward to talk to the taxi-driver.

"Did you see any of the riot today?"

"Yeah, I seen it."

"What happened?"

"The veterans and the police fought it out."

"What I mean is, what caused the trouble? I thought their stay here had been peaceful."

"Used to be. Ain't no more," the driver replied. "'Course, them that's camped down on the Anacosta Mud Flats swill ain't causin' nobody no trouble. But there was bunches of 'em in those abandoned buildings down on Pennsylvania Avenue and they was gettin' pretty bad. The police tried to move 'em out, make 'em get back across the river to join the others, but they didn't want to go. So they started fightin'. The veterans used bottles and bricks, the cops used bullets and tear gas."

"How did the fires start?"

"Don't nobody really know. Some say the police did it, some say the veterans did it themselves. Could of been from the tear gas and smoke grenades, too."

"Yes, I suppose so," John said. "Tell me, what do you think of them?"

"You mean the veterans?"

"Yes."

"They got no business here."

"I see."

"Don't get me wrong, I'm all for the veterans. I mean, my oldest brother was killed in France. But when you got this many people just hanging around the city like this all the time . . . well, most folks here aren't too happy about it. Why don't they just all go home?"

"Many of them don't have a home to go to."

"Well, they came from somewhere, didn't they?"

"I suppose they did."

"Then they should go back to where they come from. They should go back and go to work. You can't tell me there aren't jobs out there to be had. Maybe a fella can't get the kind of job he feels he should have, but there's work to be had. Hell, I know there is."

"If there are jobs out there, I can't find them," John said. "And I've been all over the country looking for them."

The cab driver looked at John in his mirror. "You'll excuse me for sayin' so, mister, but it sure don't look to me like you're hurtin' none. That's a nice suit you're wearin', that's a good haircut you got, and you ain't hungry in your eyes. I've seen enough hungry people to know what it looks like to be hungry in the eyes."

"I'm sorry," John said. "You misunderstood me. I mean I have been looking for work for others."

"Oh. You're one of them do-gooders, are you?"

John chuckled. "You might say that."

"Yeah, well, I still say there's work out there. A

well-dressed, well-fed man like you just don't know where to look, that's all."

"Perhaps you're right," John said, not wanting to argue any longer. "Oh, let me out here, will you?"

"What you want out here, for? You still got four or five blocks to go to the hotel."

"I know, but I'd like to walk."

"Okay, it's your shoe leather," the taxi-driver replied, pulling over to the curb.

John paid the fare, then began to walk. Despite the rain, some of the buildings continued to burn and he could see flames licking at the night sky and underlighting the low-hanging clouds with a diffused, orange glow. From far off he could hear the echoing wail of sirens, the sporadic rattle of gunfire, and the occasional muffled thump of a tear-gas bomb.

The crimson light of the city's night glow disclosed a pile of rubble and the charred, smoking timbers from a building which had burned earlier in the day. As John walked by the fire it was still smoldering, and the falling rain hissed and popped like the sputtering fuse of a live grenade. Scattered pockets of tear gas hung in visible clouds, and here and there John could see people scurrying about with a handkerchief clutched against their nose and mouth.

For several weeks the city of Washington had been under siege by an army of 20,000. Though the invading army wasn't foreign, tensions among the residents were as high as if it had been. When 20,000 hungry men gathered together in one spot and for one common purpose it tended to make those around the gathering place, very nervous.

The Bonus March Roosevelt had sent John to observe consisted of an army of veterans from the World War. John had done his background work and he knew the history of the Bonus Army. The veterans, like many others in the country, had suffered great deprivations as a result of the depression which held the nation in its grips. Congress voted a war bonus to be paid to everyone who fought in World War One, but the bonus wasn't to be paid until 1945. To the veterans, that was like giving someone a can of food without a can opener.

Finally the frustration came to a head and a small group of veterans from Portland, Oregon decided to go to Washington to pressure Congress into paying them now. As that little group travelled across the country, news of what they were doing spread to other desperate veterans and by freight-train, car, truck, and on foot, new marchers found their way to the advancing column. The little group began to grow exponentially, gathering followers in platoon strength from Montana, swelling by a company in Nebraska, a battalion in Missouri, adding a regiment in Ohio, picking up a division in Pennsylvania, until they reached Washington with the strength of an entire army.

They stayed in Washington for several weeks, standing out on street corners and milling around by the thousands on the Capitol grounds. They lobbied for their cause with emaciated bodies, gaunt faces and soul-scarred eyes. When the House passed the bill the veterans thought they had won and they congratulated each other and talked about the "tough campaign they had just come through," as if it had been one of the battles they fought in France. They began to wave and smile at the passing motorists, some of them smiling for the first time in over a year.

Then word came that the Senate had voted the bill down. The veterans were stunned! It seemed to them that they had just seen victory snatched from their grasp. Their smiles and congratulations turned to ashes in their mouths and for several days they milled about without direction, resorting on the old military axiom of waiting until someone told them what to do.

The leaders of the Bonus Army, some self-appointed, others elected, finally decided upon a "death march" in front of the Capitol. This was a slow, shuffling march in an oval, right in front of the Capitol steps. Working in relays, the veterans kept the march going 24 hours per day for several days, each marcher keeping his dead eyes fastened on the back of the neck of the man in front of them. It made quite an unnerving sight to the solons and federal employees as they arrived for work each morning and left each evening. Most of those who worked in the Capitol began coming in through side doors so they wouldn't have to see this group of haggard, physically and emotionally exhausted men, shuffling around in a slow, mind-numbing circle.

Then Congress adjourned without bringing the bill up for reconsideration. After that, they sneaked out through underground tunnels to avoid seeing the veterans. The battle was lost. When the veterans learned what happened, the peaceful lobbying turned ugly. The Washington police ordered the veterans to disperse and when the veterans didn't move quickly enough, the police began to move in on them.

It was like dipping sand out of a bucket. As soon as one group of veterans was moved another group would flow in to take its place. The police accomplished nothing and finally, today, there was rioting in the streets. One veteran was killed, several were wounded, and hundreds of veterans and Washingtonians had to suffer through the effects of tear gas.

Fear and tension gripped the entire city and those who were responsible for President Hoover's safety ordered the White House to be guarded at all times. Now, everywhere John looked, he could see soldiers on horseback and soldiers on the back of big trucks, fully armed and staring out over the smoldering city. Great banks of spotlights lit up the ellipse, washing out all color and painting a stark scene of harsh white and featureless black.

Then John saw something that made his blood run cold. He saw an army on the move . . . not the rag-tag "army" of World War veterans, but well-disciplined, uniformed, regular-army soldiers. Some were riding in the back of trucks, others, with drawn sabers, were mounted on horses. In addition, he saw a dozen or more light tanks.

John saw a taxi standing empty along the curb and he hurried over to it.

"Follow them," he said, pointing to the moving army.

"Are you crazy, mister?" the driver replied. "Those boys look like they're about ready to hand out some trouble and I don't want to be any part of it."

"You can stay a safe distance behind them," John

said. "When they stop, you stop. I'll go the rest of the way on foot."

"That's not a very good idea," the driver demurred.

"I'll pay double what's on the meter," John offered.

The driver smiled broadly, then reached back to open the door of his cab. "Get in, Mister. You just hired yourself a hack."

When the army stopped, the cab stopped, and John paid the driver double as he agreed, then got out and walked up to see what was going on. Soldiers poured out of the trucks and deployed, along with the tanks, around the bridge that crossed the Anacosta River. Officers and noncommissioned officers issued orders and bayonets were fixed to the ends of rifles and bolts were worked, slamming cartridges home with metallic clicks. Huge, truck-mounted spotlights, were turned on and the light beams swept back and forth across the little ramshackle village that had grown up across the river on the mud flats.

John knew of the great "Hooverville" as such villages were called, but this was the first time he had seen this one. It was huge, consisting of thousands of shelters made from cardboard, tin, scrap-lumber, and even bits of paper and cloth. Most were so meager that they looked as if they would come down with a good sneeze but a few had been well constructed and elaborately decorated. John even saw one that looked like a perfect little bungalow. It was white, with green shutters, and a little picket fence.

There were nearly as many signs as there were shelters.

BONUS NOW! MOST OF US WILL BE DEAD BY 1945!
WE WILL NOT STARVE TO DEATH IN THE LAND OF PLENTY!
WE FOUGHT FOR THIS COUNTRY. DON'T DESERT US NOW!
HOOVER! WHERE IS YOUR COMPASSION!
GIVE US OUR BONUS! GIVE US WORK!

More dramatic than the signs and shelters however, were the people. They were frozen into immobility by the sweeping beams of light, like an animal on the road will sometimes freeze when caught in the lights of a car.

There were many, many women in the little village, and an even greater number of children. The women were holding in their arms the children who were small enough to be held. The rest of the children were clustered around the women's legs, hanging on to their skirts and peering around from behind.

What impressed John most was their faces. They were wan and drawn, with their eyes gleaming in the artificial light as if the people were actually trapped *inside* their bodies and were merely looking out. The villagers weren't frightened, despite the fact than an army was assembling just across the river. They weren't defiant either. They were just looking on with an almost detached curiosity.

John recognized General MacArthur, impeccably dressed in a be-ribboned, dark-brown blouse, khaki riding breeches, and highly polished boots. He strolled around behind his soldiers, slapping a riding quirt against his leg as he watched his army move into position. Then, responding to a slight motion of his riding quirt, the army began to sweep forward.

There were a couple of hundred veterans on the city side of the river and they stood defiantly at the bridge as the army swept forward.

"You don't want to come after us, do you now, lads?" one of the veterans cried out. "We were soldiers, just like you!"

"We fought in the war," another shouted.

Most of the young, uniformed soldiers were too young to have fought in the war and they were impervious to the cries for pity from the old veterans. The young army moved inexorably forward, bowling over the old, hungry, emaciated veterans with the weight of their horses, slashing at them with their sabers and knocking them down with wicked butt strokes from their rifles.

"My ear! My ear!" one veteran shouted, slapping his hand up to the side of his head after a cavalryman made a slash with his saber. Bright, red blood spilled through the veteran's fingers.

Several shots were fired into the air then and the veterans, realizing they were beaten, turned and ran back across the bridge to the safety of their makeshift village.

"That's it, the soldiers won't go any further," John heard someone say. That was when John realized that there were several civilian bystanders observing the scene. Most of the civilians were newspaper and radio reporters. There were also newsreel cameras present, grinding away as they recorded the scene.

"What makes you think they won't?" one of the other newsmen asked.

"Because I heard it from the top. MacArthur has orders not to go across the bridge."

John relaxed a little. He didn't want to see the army cross the bridge because he didn't want to see them terrorize the women and children as they had the men. Then, to John's surprise, and the voiced surprise of the other observers, General MacArthur did order his men across the bridge.

The horses galloped across first, their clattering hooves raising a thunder from the bridge planking. The horses were followed by the tanks, then by the infantrymen. The Bonus Marchers, surprised that they had been chased all the way into their sanctuary shouted out in anger and frustration. The women screamed in fear, the children began crying in terror. Here and there one of the veterans would try and defend his pitiful little shelter, and he would rush forward with a rock or bottle or brick, only to be beaten back with grim efficacy.

Fires began breaking out throughout the entire little village and John was puzzled as to their origin. Then he saw soldiers running from structure to structure, setting them alight. Fires licked at the night sky and, silhouetted against the orange flames, soldiers could be seen shoving, herding, crushing the final, futile efforts of resistance.

Soon flames covered the entire flat, creating a huge glowing circle of light in the black of night. Just beyond the wavering flames the bloodied veterans and their terrified families gathered in large crowds, weeping silently as they stood in the protective cloak of darkness.

"General, the village is secure," an officer said, reporting to General MacArthur with a crisp salute.

"We'll keep our people here overnight," General MacArthur replied. "Tomorrow, we will bring in the bulldozers and knock down anything that might still be standing. I don't want two sticks left together."

"Yes, sir," the officer replied, again saluting crisply.

It took John thirty minutes to describe, over the phone, what he had seen.

"Yes," Roosevelt said from the other end of the line. "We listened to a report over the radio and it pretty much matches what you said. Though, I must say, your own insight adds a great deal to it."

"It was awful, Governor," John said, quietly. "I never thought I would live to see the day when American soldiers turned against their own people."

"You know what this means, don't you, John?" Roosevelt asked.

"What's that, sir?"

"It means President Hoover has just handed me the election on a silver platter."

MARCH 4, 1933
WASHINGTON, D.C.

When the car bearing Champ Dawson, the senior senator from Missouri, drove alongside the Anacosta River, Faith Dawson, the senator's beautiful 21-year-old daughter shivered in revulsion.

"Oh," she said. "What a horrible sight."

"What is it, dear?" Mrs. Dawson asked.

"There were rats out there, crawling around on that rubble. Did you see them?"

"No, dear," Mrs. Dawson answered. "I try and not look at such things."

"What is all that stuff out there, anyway? Why don't they get it cleaned up?"

"That is all that is left from the village the Bonus Marchers built here, last summer," John Canfield explained. "You remember reading my report about how

President Hoover ordered General MacArthur to destroy it."

"So, that's where it was," Faith said. "Yes, I remember reading your report. And I know that Governor Roosevelt believes that did as much as anything to get the governor elected."

Senator Dawson chuckled. "We'll have to remember that it isn't Governor Roosevelt anymore," he said. "It's President Roosevelt now."

"*President* Roosevelt. I like the sound of that, don't you?" John asked.

"Yes, it does have a certain ring to it," Senator Dawson replied.

Three blocks away from Anacosta Flats the senator's car passed a long line of defeated men and downtrodden women. They were shuffling slowly along the street as they waited for the handout of a loaf of bread and a small amount of cheese. Washington was a city which depended upon the Federal Government for employment and as such, the life-long residents barely experienced the depression. But the city had drawn hundreds, even thousands of out-of-work, starving people from around the country, some as a part of the Bonus March, others in a futile effort to go somewhere and do something . . . anything . . . to improve their lot.

"Oh, look at those poor people," Faith said, sadly. "My heart just goes out to them. I wish I could do something to help."

"That's what we're trying to do," John said.

"Did any of you see the article in the paper this morning?" Senator Dawson asked.

"Which article is that, Senator?" John replied.

"The one which called upon the Capitol police to close down all the bread and soup lines for the day. The writer of the article said it created a bad image for the city of Washington to have visitors see so many hungry and destitute people."

"I didn't see the article," John replied. "But I'm glad the police didn't pay any attention to it. It sounds like a pretty heartless idea, to me."

"That's what I thought," Senator Dawson said. "I called the newspaper and reminded them that Washington certainly isn't the only city in the country which is undergoing such turmoil. This same thing is happening in hundreds of cities and towns all across America. In many cases the bread lines and soup lines are all that stands between these poor people and starvation."

John knew the senator was right. Whenever a soup kitchen or bread line would be set up, no matter where it was, the people would find out about it through their own grapevine and gather quickly until the line stretched out for several blocks.

John knew that there had always been soup kitchens and bread lines, most of the time operated by some religious group hoping to exchange a slice of bread for someone's soul. In those cases the customers were almost always men, and a few women, who had known a lifetime of destitution. They were the alcoholics and mental-deficient to be found in all societies. They were the pathetically struggling people whose lot could never be improved.

Now, however, the bread and soup lines were different. The lines of 1933 were filled with men who had been bankers, electricians, stockbrokers, welders, business-managers and mechanics. There were women in the lines as well; former store-clerks and school teachers and housewives, many of whom carried one baby and clutched the hand of another.

Forty million Americans were either unemployed, or the member of a family in which the principle bread-winner was unemployed. And it wasn't just the town and city people who were suffering. More and more farmers who had grown up on the land their fathers and grandfathers and great-grandfathers had worked before them, were finding sheriffs' foreclosure documents plastered on the doors of their homes and barns, and on the fences around their fields. The notices were to inform the public that the buildings, land, equipment, heritage and dreams of these farmers were to be sold at public auction.

But the depression didn't affect only those who were unlucky enough to face unemployment. In hundreds of cases wealthy families who were already enjoying the third generation of affluence were thrust into instant bankruptcy with the total collapse of the financial institutions in which they kept all their money. These men and women who had once been millionaires, now found themselves standing in line with the same men and women who had once been their servants.